THE SECRETS OF THE ROSE

NICOLA CORNICK

Boldwood

First published in Great Britain in 2025 by Boldwood Books Ltd.

Copyright © Nicola Cornick, 2025

Cover Design by Alice Moore Design

Cover Images: Shutterstock and Rachel Fraser / Arcangel

The moral right of Nicola Cornick to be identified as the author of this work has been asserted in accordance with the Copyright, Designs and Patents Act 1988.

Every effort has been made to obtain the necessary permissions with reference to copyright material, both illustrative and quoted. We apologise for any omissions in this respect and will be pleased to make the appropriate acknowledgements in any future edition.

A CIP catalogue record for this book is available from the British Library.

Paperback ISBN 978-1-78513-730-3

Large Print ISBN 978-1-78513-731-0

Hardback ISBN 978-1-78513-729-7

Ebook ISBN 978-1-78513-732-7

Kindle ISBN 978-1-78513-733-4

Audio CD ISBN 978-1-78513-724-2

MP3 CD ISBN 978-1-78513-725-9

Digital audio download ISBN 978-1-78513-727-3

This book is printed on certified sustainable paper. Boldwood Books is dedicated to putting sustainability at the heart of our business. For more information please visit https://www.boldwoodbooks.com/about-us/sustainability/

Boldwood Books Ltd, 23 Bowerdean Street, London, SW6 3TN

www.boldwoodbooks.com

For Julie.

Time holds all the secrets.

— ANON.

PROLOGUE
DOROTHY – BAMBURGH, MIDSUMMER EVE 1709

The midsummer bonfire burned high and hot; the flames were silhouetted against the midnight blue of the sky. It was the perfect night, with barely any wind and the sea lying calm and silver under the half-moon, its ceaseless waves hushed. The wide stretch of sand was thronged with people; there were booths on the beach selling spiced wine and gingerbread and sweetmeats. There were travelling players, musicians leading the dance with the high notes of the fiddle and the deep echo of the horn, and there were very many drunks in the crowd who had been indulging in the ale and the sport all day and were now a great deal the worse for wear.

Dorothy picked her way between the weaving dancers, stepping over the legs of those who were sprawled on the sand sleeping off their excesses, keeping to the shadows, although there was little chance that she would be recognised in the darkness and the crowd. She had borrowed the kitchen maid's second-best cotton gown, plaiting her fair hair and pushing it beneath a plain white cap. A faded spencer jacket completed the outfit, along with a pair of sturdy boots. Anyone who did notice her would merely see another servant given a night off to enjoy the annual Bamburgh midsummer fair.

Back at the Hall, her father would be sitting up late, engrossed in the copy of *Discourse on the Plants of the Sandy Soils of the North-East* which had arrived by carrier from London earlier that day. It was unusual these days to see Sir William Forster excited – the loss of his wife had turned him into a shell of a man and the apoplexy that followed had weakened him even further – but botany was one of the few topics that could still rouse his interest and Dorothy had been happy to see him animated for a change.

Her chaperone, meanwhile, would be sleeping the deep sleep of ignorance in the belief that her charge was safely tucked up in bed. As for her uncle, Lord Crewe, who now owned the best part of the Bamburgh estate, he considered the midsummer revels to be ungodly and had taken himself off to his bishop's palace at Durham, deploring the pagan antics on his estate under the shadow of the mighty Bamburgh Castle.

'Dot. Dorothy...'

The call of her name slid into her mind like a whisper on the wind, as it had done for as long as she could remember. He – and she was sure by some deep instinct that it was a he – had always called her Dot, especially if he were teasing or being affectionate; Dorothy when he was serious. It was never Doll, like her aunt, Lady Crewe, who had been universally praised in her youth as 'pretty Doll Forster'. Doll was too light and airy a name for Dorothy who was both too substantial and too practical ever to resemble a child's toy.

'Are you here tonight?' She sent back a cautious message and was immediately rewarded with the warmth of his amusement.

'Of course. The whole world is here tonight...'

'*Shall we dance?*' She had taken none of the ale or wine, but knowing he was close to her made her reckless. She had known him all her life and yet they had never met. This night might be the moment when imagination and reality came together at last.

But he was fading, withdrawing from her.

'*Perhaps...*' There was more regret than promise in the word.

She did not want to let him go. '*Ross...*' In the absence of knowing his real name, she had once asked him what she should call him and that was what he had chosen. Whether there was a clue there to his real identity, she did not know. She knew nothing of him, other than that they had known each other since childhood, stepping into each other's thoughts and dreams as though it was the most natural thing in the world.

There was no reply. He had shut her out, as he had done on each occasion when she had pressed him to meet. Now she was annoyed. Standing here on the beach, with the noise and scent of the fair swirling around her, the mingled smells of woodsmoke and horse manure and the sweetness of spiced wine, she was not prepared to let the matter go.

'*You were the one who called out to me...*' Cross, contradictory, like children squabbling. She started to search the crowds for a glimpse of him, certain her intuition would be able to pick him out from the hundreds who swarmed the sands. But all she received in return was the faintest of fading signals, regret, apology even. All she saw was blank faces, revellers wrapped up in themselves or each other, but no one looking for her.

She stood on the edge of the firelight feeling frustrated and lonely. She saw John Armstrong, the village blacksmith, with his widowed sister-in-law and her son Eli at his side; Doria Eyre, the village seamstress; Nat Pether, the cordwainer. Did they recognise her as Sir Thomas Forster's daughter and Lord Crewe's niece? Did it matter? No one stood on ceremony on a night like this. It was one of the few occasions when rank and ceremony were forgotten.

'Would my lady care to dance?'

She turned. A gentleman was bowing to her in courtly fashion, holding out his hand. And he *was* a gentleman, no question about it, young and handsome, his fair hair drawn back in a queue and tied with a ribbon, white lace at his throat, his jacket dark velvet. She took his hand and it was warm, for he wore no gloves, and a thrill of pleasure and excitement ran through her.

'*Ross, is this you?*'

His smile was warm too as his gaze rested on her, but there was no answer to her question. It did not matter to her now, though.

As the fiddle struck up for a lively jig, they spun into the fray accompanied by the clapping and shouts of the crowd. Dorothy had never enjoyed dancing so much as she did that evening, with the moon on the sea and the crackle of the bonfire, the sparks dancing alongside them. The fiddler played an encore and then a courante and another jig and by the end she was out of breath and eagerly accepted the flagon of ale pressed into her hands. The stars were still whirling over her head and the excitement was fizzing in her blood. It felt as though the world was new, as though she was at the start of a grand adventure at the equally grand age of eighteen years old. But then it was over. After three dances, the gentleman bowed and thanked her, turning away, already swallowed up in the crowd by the time she had lowered the bottle of ale.

'Who was that?' She turned to the nearest bystander, John Armstrong, who, like everyone else, was staring after the tall stranger.

Armstrong's dark face was shadowed and thoughtful. At only twenty-seven, he was already a widower, a man whose forge was at the centre of the community, not only a blacksmith and farrier but a wheelwright, carpenter, even a doctor at times, for those who could not afford the physician's fees. Everyone listened to and respected John Armstrong.

'That was Lord Derwentwater,' he said. 'He has returned from France to take up his inheritance.'

The Earl of Derwentwater... The word ran through the crowd like quicksilver, men and women staring in the direction the Earl had gone, like Dorothy seeking another look in vain.

Everyone knew about the Earl. He had grown up at the French court in exile of James Francis Edward Stuart, son of the late King James II of England. Derwentwater and the young prince had been inseparable as boys and now the Earl supported the Stuart claim to the throne with a fervour that few could match. His return to Northumberland from France had been one of the chief topics of conversation for months. No one could understand why the government had allowed such a prominent supporter of the Pretender, as James Stuart was known, to take up his inheritance.

There was a moment of quiet, then the fiddler started a mournful lament that hung on the night air, a tune that promised love and heartbreak and seemed to cut right through to Dorothy's soul.

'Enough of that dirge!' The crowd started to grumble, albeit good-naturedly, and the fiddler gave in to their pleadings and struck up another country dance.

John Armstrong turned towards her. 'Would you like to dance, Mistress Forster?'

Dorothy was taken aback. 'You know who I am!'

'It wasn't difficult to tell.' He was smiling, nodding towards her mob cap, which lay discarded on the sand. She had not realised. Nor that her hair had come loose from her plait and was curling about her flushed face. It was so fair, spun silver in the moonlight, that it would always give her away. 'Have no fear, though,' Armstrong continued, 'there is not a soul here tonight would give you away to that dour-faced dragon who chaperones you. Your secrets are safe with us, Mistress Forster.'

'I thank you for that,' Dorothy murmured. 'But I think I shall not dance again. It is time for me to go home.' Her head and her heart were both still too full of the Earl of Derwentwater to even consider dancing with another man. She could still hear the music in her ears and feel the touch of his hand.

'As you will.' Armstrong bowed. There was none of Derwentwater's elegance there. His was the unpolished and abrupt bow of a working man who, Dorothy suspected, nevertheless believed himself the equal of the gentry. 'Goodnight, Mistress Forster.'

One of the village girls caught his hand to claim his attention, drawing him into the dance, and Dorothy walked away, cutting through the dunes towards home, the firelight fading behind her and the grains of sand running beneath her boots. The magic notes of the dance were still in her blood, but the sound was fading now and her excitement with it. Cautiously, she sent out a call.

'Ross... Was that you?'

There was no reply, nothing but the whisper of the breeze through the marram grass and the distant notes of the violin. It was odd; it felt as though he had left her for good and there was only emptiness where he had been. She did not like it. It was lonely without his presence, but she was sure he would return. Through all her eighteen years, he had been a constant in her life, his thoughts and feelings sliding into her mind as though it was the most natural thing in the world. Tonight, she had met him for the first time. She felt sure it was him. Now he was even more real to her.

Back at Bamburgh Hall, she lay in her bed and hugged close the memory of the excitement and the moonlight, the leaping shadows, the music, the dance. She was not to know that this night had not been a new start at all, but the beginning of the end.

1

HANNAH – THE PRESENT, MAY

Hannah was early. It was the habit of a lifetime.

She parked neatly in the cobbled courtyard, between a battered quad bike and a mud-spattered estate car, turned off the engine and sat quietly for a moment. Bamburgh Hall.

Home.

It still felt like home, a place she was rooted in, even though she had left twelve years before. She visited as often as she could. Her present home was a flat on Bristol's harbourside, some three hundred and fifty miles to the south-west. And yet something about Bamburgh had always called to her, as though it was entwined in the very essence of her, drawing her back like the pull of the tide.

On the back seat, Tarka's whining gave way to a sharp, short bark. She wanted out. It had been a long drive. Hannah opened the door. The air was fresh after six hours in the fug of the car. It carried a clear, sharp edge that was instantly familiar. Her legs felt stiff as she scrambled out and released Tarka from her harness. The retriever leapt out into the courtyard with enviable energy, feathery tail swishing with excitement. She could smell the sea.

Hannah left her bags in the car, pulled on her jacket and walked back up the drive and around the front of the house. A former farmhouse, it was an elegant four-square building set back from the road to Budle Bay. To the west stood the church of St Aidan, its ancient gold and pink stone glowing softly in the low afternoon sunshine. Behind it, the fields stretched away to where the ridge of the Spindlestone Hill was silhouetted against the blue of the sky. It was a beautiful late-spring day.

A black wrought-iron gate opened onto a lawn as flat and well-kept as a bowling green, surrounded by shrubs and gnarled fruit trees that were showing the fresh green of spring growth. Over the front door was a sign: 'Bamburgh Hall, Bed & Breakfast. No vacancies.' Below that, stuck on one of the windowpanes, was a handwritten note in Diana's flowery script: 'Back at 4 p.m.' A moment later, Hannah heard the church clock strike the hour of three.

'It looks as though you're going to the beach,' she told Tarka, who skipped with glee, her tail now going at double speed.

They retraced their steps into the courtyard, Tarka not bothering to hide her impatience as Hannah collected her lead from the back of the car and zipped up her fleece jacket. When Hannah sat down on the mounting block to put on her walking boots, Tarka squeaked encouragement. It was an odd noise for a big dog to make but she had done it ever since she was a tiny puppy when there was something she wanted and now, as always, it made Hannah laugh.

'Give me a moment.' She grabbed the lead and patted her pockets to check for poo bags and treats.

Another wrought-iron gate led out of the courtyard into the fields at the back of the house, where a farm track cut diagonally north-east, towards the sand dunes. There were no sheep grazing there today, so Tarka bounded along through the dewy grass, every so often stopping to wait politely for Hannah to catch up with her.

Crossing the narrow road called The Wynding, they skirted the children's play park and the castle green, Tarka on her lead now that there were cars and people about. Not everyone appreciated twenty-five kilos of excited retriever racing up to them and although Tarka was very friendly and had excellent manners, Hannah never wanted other people to be uncomfortable around her.

The sheer walls of Bamburgh Castle soared above them as they passed the sally port high on the crag. A rough flight of steps scrambled up the rock face to an iron gate. It was very *Game of Thrones*, Hannah thought. The sheer scale of Bamburgh Castle was very impressive, even though she had grown up seeing it every day, but Hannah had always found it ominous as well, towering over the village, as much a threat as a protection.

Once they had passed the northern end of the castle with its odd, truncated windmill, Hannah let Tarka off her lead again and the dog joyfully scampered off down the path towards the dunes. Out of the lee of the towering crag, the wind off the sea cut like a sharp knife, almost taking Hannah's breath away. The last time she had visited Bamburgh it had been late summer of the previous year, a hot, dry time when the sea had glittered as hard and blue as the Mediterranean and the beach was crowded. She had almost forgotten how wild and isolated this coastline could sometimes feel. The south had turned her soft.

The sun popped out from behind a cloud and she immediately felt its warmth on her face. At this time of year, it really was a different season in the sun and the shade.

Tarka reappeared at the top of the dune a few metres ahead of her, then turned and made a headlong rush down the other side to the beach. Hannah followed, smiling a little as she absorbed the sense of familiarity and belonging. She travelled a lot with her work these days and it made more sense for her to be based in the south of England but there was not the same sense of affinity.

'There's no doubt Dorothy was right, Tarka,' she said to the dog, who had also been born and bred in Northumberland. 'There's no place like home.'

Ironically, it was work that had actually brought her back to Bamburgh this time. She had been commissioned to write a biography of the Victorian heroine Grace Darling, the daughter of a local lighthouse keeper who had shot to unexpected fame when she had helped her father rescue the survivors of a shipwreck in 1838. Grace had never been one of Hannah's favourite historical characters and she had always thought her heroism over-exaggerated, but both the money and the prestige on offer for the book had been very generous. The publisher had wanted someone with local background and knowledge, so Hannah had been the ideal candidate. She hoped she might warm to Grace as the project went on.

The tide was halfway out and the beach looked almost empty, a huge swathe of flat sand curving along the seaward side of the castle and the dunes, pale golden white in the sun. Hannah could pick out a few people, wrapped up against the edge of the easterly wind. A number of dogs were running over the sand or splashing in the shallows. Further out, where the waves curved in beautiful rollers before coming crashing down, she could also see a tiny black dot, a lone surfer taking advantage of the conditions that made Bamburgh one of the best places to practise the sport in Northumberland.

Tarka gave a happy bark and raced across the sand to greet a couple of Jack Russells and their owner. Hannah followed more slowly, calling Tarka back and giving the other dog owner a friendly wave before turning left along the beach, away from the castle. Here, a small stream flowed down from the hills to the west, fanning out across the beach before it met the sea. A number of Second World War anti-tank blocks, now painted like dominoes and Rubik's Cubes, stood at the foot of the dunes. Hannah stopped and looked out to sea, where the outline of Lindisfarne Castle was etched clearly against the skyline, another castle, on another crag, guarding this coast and the Scottish border.

The sand gave way to stone as they approached the Black Rock lighthouse at the northern end of the beach. This was not Grace's lighthouse but a much more modern one. There was the rock with the white-painted stag that had fascinated Hannah from the very first moment she had seen it as a child. No one seemed to know when or why it had first appeared on the promontory, although there was a local legend that centuries ago a stag had jumped into the sea at the point to avoid hunters. Now Hannah stood and gazed at it again as the sea washed against the rocks beneath it. It was such a rustic drawing to possess such magic. There was none of the stylised beauty of something like the iconic White Horse of Uffington, for example, and yet it still captured the attention.

Tarka was sniffing around the rock pools whilst Hannah searched for sea glass in the nooks and crannies. When the cold water started to numb her fingers, she called Tarka over and turned back towards the castle. It was almost a quarter to four; by the time they got back to the Hall, Diana should have returned.

The tide was coming in now, eating up the footprints both she and Tarka had made only a half-hour earlier, wiping them out as though they had never existed. As she got closer to the stream,

Hannah saw that the surfer was also heading back to land. He emerged, a sleek figure dressed in black from head to foot, with the water streaming off him in a shining trail. As he splashed through the shallows, board tucked under one arm, he pulled off his surf hood with his free hand and she recognised him at once. *Aaron Salter.*

She felt an odd shift of emotion, a shiver of memory. How strange that the first person she should see on her return to Bamburgh was Aaron. His sister Alice had been Hannah's best friend at school and they had kept in touch ever since. Aaron had been two years above them and had been one of her brother Brandon's closest friends. Somewhat predictably he had also been Hannah's first serious crush. Just the memory of how tongue-tied and lovestruck she had been around him made her feel an echo of embarrassment even after all this time. Aaron had also saved her when she had broken her leg on the rocky outcrop beyond the lighthouse. That had been another mortifying experience.

Tarka gave another excited woof and galloped over to greet Aaron as though he was an old friend. Hannah cursed under her breath, wanting a little more time to prepare for the unexpected meeting. Aaron had gone off to college and to take on a boat-building apprenticeship when she had been sixteen and she hadn't seen him much since then. He'd married young and set up his own business further down the coast, so although he was around sometimes when she'd visited Alice, they hadn't really reconnected.

'You're almost as wet as I am!' Aaron was laughing as he bent to stroke Tarka's smooth golden head. He looked up and saw Hannah, and his polite smile faded into a look of surprise before warming again in a way that made her feel slightly breathless.

'Hannah?' he said. ' Wow. Haven't seen you in a while. How are you?'

'Hi, Aaron.' Hannah aimed for breezy and was proud that she hit the tone exactly right. 'I'm good, thanks. How are you? You look well.'

It was an understatement. Aaron looked hot, his teenage lankiness having developed into a tall, loose-limbed body that looked perfect for the surf. His brown eyes, such a striking contrast to his fair hair, were as dark as she remembered, although the wary expression shadowing his face was definitely new.

'Fine, thanks...' Aaron ran a hand across his face as though to scrub the expression away, though not before Hannah had wondered what was prompting his sudden reticence. Fortunately, Tarka nudged his hand, begging for more attention, and the moment passed. 'She's yours?' Aaron gestured to Tarka and his smile was even broader now. 'She's adorable.'

'Thank you.' Hannah had often found that Tarka was a great asset in smoothing over awkward situations. 'She's called Tarka and she's very friendly. She loves the beach.'

Aaron nodded. 'Tarka's a good name for a dog who likes the water.' He nodded to the path up through the dunes. 'Are you heading back? My van's in the car park up here.' He fell into step beside her as Tarka scampered away to half-heartedly chase some seagulls. 'Does Alice know you're back?' he asked. 'She didn't mention it.'

Hannah shook her head. 'It was all rather last minute. I'm actually here to work. I'm writing a biography of Grace Darling, so I'm staying at the Hall whilst I do some research at the museum and the county archives. It's easier than trying to do everything online from Bristol.'

Aaron raised his brows. 'That's an interesting commission. I seem to recall you weren't keen on Grace Darling at school, though.'

'You've got a good memory.' Hannah was astonished. The entire school had had to do a project on Grace since she was their local heroine, but she had grumbled, wanting to write about Dorothy Forster instead. Dorothy was the *other* Bamburgh heroine, a woman who had never been as famous as Grace Darling but whom Hannah found far more interesting, the darling of the Jacobite 1715 rebellion in support of the Stuarts. However, Hannah's plea had been ignored and Dorothy was consigned to oblivion once more; they had all contributed to a mural about Grace's life that was displayed in the school hall and they had put on a play about the shipwreck and rescue. Aaron, Hannah remembered, had taken the role of the heroic lighthouse keeper, Grace's father.

'Grace has never been my favourite historical figure,' she admitted, 'but she's an interesting person to write about, especially as she had her life transformed by celebrity at a time when that didn't happen often, particularly not to a woman. I was lucky to get the job really. The publisher wanted someone who could add a personal perspective on the environment and natural history around here, as well as the more conventional historical stuff.' She paused to look back over the dunes and out to where the Farne Islands seemed to float against the horizon, Prior Castell's Tower a hazy landmark against the sky. 'I suppose I'll need to take a boat tour out to the islands,' she said with a sigh and Aaron laughed at her tone.

'So you're still no keener on sailing, then?' he asked, and Hannah shook her head with a rueful smile. It had been acutely embarrassing when she was younger that she was the only person in the whole village who seemed to suffer seasickness simply by stepping onto a jetty, let alone a boat. In a place where so many people had traditionally made a living on the water and now turned out for the sport, she had felt an outsider.

She glanced at Aaron who had shortened his stride to match hers as they followed the well-worn path through the dunes. The dark golden sand looked like demerara sugar here and slid beneath the soles of her boots. It was a good workout. 'Alice told me that you're based in Seahouses now,' she said. It was only a few miles south along the coast. 'She said you have a traditional boat-building business there?'

Aaron nodded. 'Yeah. We make small boats, up to about twenty feet, and offer repairs and conversion for yachts and fishing boats. It's hard work, but it's what I always wanted to do.'

'I remember,' Hannah said. 'It was always your passion. I'm glad that worked out for you. Do you still volunteer with the RNLI as well?' She could recall a teenage Aaron helping out with fundraising at the lifeboat station, hanging about the boats and doing odd jobs, and putting his name down for crew training. Hannah, who had never felt that she had a vocation in the same way at that age, had been envious of his confidence and his certainty of where his life was going. Aaron had seemed to be one of those people who was very sure and settled in his course from early on. He'd married a local girl and had a son, but a few years ago he and Daisy had divorced. Hannah had been shocked when Alice had told her, as though nothing should have gone wrong in Aaron's charmed life.

'I'm on the crew at Seahouses,' Aaron replied, 'and I help maintain the boats and do some other stuff too.' He tilted his head to look down at her. 'I suppose Alice told you I got married – and divorced – and that I have a son called Leo?' He smiled crookedly. 'That's an update of my personal history in about twenty seconds. Oh, plus I now live back in Bamburgh – your stepmother rents me Forge Cottage. I moved in a couple of weeks ago.'

Hannah smiled sympathetically at his dry tone. 'I'm very sorry things didn't work out with you and Daisy,' she said. 'That must have been very hard for you all, especially for Leo.' Her parents had also divorced when she was young and she could still remember the fear and confusion she had felt as a child who had no control over the situation. Later, her father had married Diana, the wicked step-mother, as she had been wont to describe herself drolly, which had been another upheaval, although one that had worked out very well.

'It's been very tough,' Aaron acknowledged. His gaze was fixed on the horizon and something about the tight lines around his mouth told Hannah just how difficult the subject was for him. 'It still is,' he added, surprising her with his candour. 'Daisy's new partner has taken a job in New Zealand for a couple of years, so I won't be seeing Leo so much—' He stopped. 'Daisy's happy, which is great,' he added. 'And Rob's a good bloke, so I felt I had to give my consent, but...'

Hannah did not consider herself the most demonstrative of people, but there was a rawness in Aaron's tone that made her want to reach out to him. The strength of the instinct startled her.

'That's an incredibly generous thing to do,' she said, 'when the price of it will be not seeing your son as much as you'd want. That aspect is utter crap.'

Aaron was surprised into a laugh. His expression eased a little. 'Nicely put. Yes, it is.' He moved his shoulders back as though shaking off a weight. 'Life never quite works out how you anticipate, does it? I tried everything I could to make things work with Daisy but...' He shrugged. 'It wasn't to be.'

Tarka pressed herself against his leg as though to offer comfort and he smiled and ruffled her head.

'Thanks, bud,' he said.

They'd almost reached the car park and Hannah put Tarka on her lead. Aaron rested his board against the side of a battered blue van, unlocking the back door to reveal an interior littered with surfing kit.

'Alice will be pleased to see you,' he said, over his shoulder. 'So will Diana. I know she wouldn't dream of telling you, but she's missed you. And now, especially—' He broke off, the sudden wariness back in his tone.

'I have been back to see her a lot over the years, you know.' Hannah knew she sounded defensive because she *felt* it. The last time she had been in Bamburgh, it had only been for one night en route to Scotland with Mike, her partner at the time. Mike and Diana hadn't really got on, although both of them had tried to hide it for her sake, their deliberate politeness only seeming to emphasise the distance between them. It had made the trip painfully awkward, unlike her usual visits, and she felt she had some lost ground to make up now.

'Sorry,' Aaron said now. 'I know you do. I didn't mean it to sound like criticism.'

'Brandon drops in to see Diana whenever he's passing, as well.' Hannah realised that Aaron hadn't mentioned her brother at all, had not even asked how he was. She knew they had had a spectacular falling out at the end of their final year at school, but that had been years ago, surely long enough to have moved on. Yet now a chill had come over the air with the mention of Brandon's name.

'Of course,' Aaron said with scrupulous politeness. 'If you'll excuse me...' His broad back was turned towards her and it didn't encourage further conversation.

'Right,' Hannah said, feeling confused and annoyed. 'Well, it was good to catch up with you, Aaron. Perhaps I'll see you around whilst I'm here.'

'Perhaps.' He spared her a brief smile before hefting his surf-board into the van. 'I hope the work goes well. Bye, Hannah.'

'That was a brush-off if ever there was one,' Hannah said ruefully to Tarka as they crossed the car park and went out onto the sea road. 'I'm not sure if it's me or Brandon or both of us Aaron's not keen on, but...' She shrugged. 'I doubt we'll be seeing much of him.'

Away from the beach, it was sheltered and felt much warmer. Hannah and Tarka walked back along The Wynding, beside an old wall that sprouted valerian and maidenhair ferns and yellow stonecrop. Sheep and lambs drowsed in a field on the left. The gardens of the houses that lined the street were full of tulips and scented wallflowers, whilst clematis draped over fences. When they reached the junction with Front Street, they turned right. The little wood in the centre of the village was thick with new leaves and also with the black shapes of the rooks that roosted there. Their mournful cawing filled the air. A steady stream of cars passed by as they headed down towards the castle and the sea.

Hannah was still thinking about Aaron's falling out with Brandon and how strange and sudden it had been. One moment they had been hanging out together, surfing, partying on the beach, inseparable friends, then they had not been on speaking terms. When she'd asked Brandon what had happened, he'd refused to talk to her. Alice had got nothing out of Aaron either. It had been very odd. It was all old history now, of course. Except it seemed Aaron still remembered.

Despite her irritation with him, it had been nice to see Aaron again. More than nice, Hannah acknowledged, with a stirring of some emotion that felt like an echo of the old crush she'd had on him. It was strange how strongly teenage emotions could endure, even years later. Or the memory of them. Perhaps it was all part of the nostalgia of being home. Or perhaps it was simply that she had felt things so sharply when she was young and those feelings still had resonance. Whatever the reason, she had no intention of going there again. Fifteen years had passed and Aaron was recently divorced and facing the grim prospect of seeing far less of his young son, which would be devastating for both of them. She was here for a fortnight maximum and researching a book, not looking to become a holiday romance cliché. Besides, Aaron had never given the slightest indication that he had any romantic interest in her.

Tarka was giving her the side eye. 'I know *you* like him,' Hannah said, 'and you're a good judge of character. But that's all in the past, Tarka. We don't look back, we look forward.'

Tarka, with a wag of agreement, headed towards the Hall and her next meal.

Aaron finished stowing his gear in the back of the van and slammed the door shut. He'd rubbed down his board but would need to give it a good wash when he got home. Fortunately, the cottage, and a hot shower, were only five minutes away. He did a few stretches – he hadn't wanted to do them whilst Hannah was in sight in case he looked like a pretentious idiot, which was ridiculous since she knew as well as anyone that it was important to stretch after as well as before surfing. His left shoulder was a bit stiff; there had been a moment when a wave had caught him out and given him a buffeting, but it was nothing serious. Similarly, there was a small crack on his board, but that could be fixed easily with the ding kit. All in all, it had been a good day.

He slid into the van and reached for his bottle of water and sandwich box. Even if it was only five minutes to home, he was glad he'd made himself a cheese roll before he'd come out. The thought of going back to the dark, empty cottage and forcing himself to cook a proper meal suddenly left a sour taste in his mouth. The hours out on his board had given him a pleasant sense of physical exhaustion, but he could feel his mood plummeting.

Thinking back to his meeting with Hannah didn't help. Why had he been such an ungracious idiot with her? He'd frozen her out when she'd mentioned Brandon and then he'd blown her off when she'd made an innocuous comment about seeing him again. He groaned and ran a hand through his hair. He knew why. He'd always known why. Sharp as glass, a memory slid into his mind of a row he had had with Daisy when things had started to go badly between them.

'You know what's really wrong with us?' she'd yelled at him, literally throwing Leo's toys out of the pram and onto the living-room floor. 'It's that I'm not Hannah Armstrong! You've never got over her!'

He'd denied it so vehemently at the time that he'd probably made the point for her. After all, he and Hannah had never been together as a couple. Sure, he had noticed her when they had been teenagers. He had liked her – more than liked her. Hannah had always been bright and sunny and generous, an optimist despite the crap that life had thrown at her. She'd lost both her parents in different ways whilst she was still young, yet she had pushed on through with resilience and determination. He realised suddenly that her example had actually been an unacknowledged inspiration to him over the past couple of years when things had gone so badly wrong in his personal life. Yes, there had always been something about Hannah...

His phone rang.

'Hi!' It was his sister, Alice, sounding unnaturally cheerful, as she always did when she was worried and checking on him. 'Where are you? Have you had a good day?'

Aaron grunted. 'Remember I told you never to ask me more than one question at a time?' He swallowed half the sandwich. 'I'm at the beach, and yeah, it was pretty good.'

'See, I knew you could concentrate on more than one thing at once,' his sister said triumphantly. There was a slight pause. 'You haven't forgotten Sunday lunch with the family tomorrow?' Her tone had changed to super-casual, which did not fool him. He'd known Alice all of their lives. They were the youngest of four siblings. She knew he would have remembered the lunch date, but this was her excuse for calling him.

'No,' Aaron said wearily. 'I haven't forgotten.' He took a breath. 'You don't have to keep an eye on me, Al. You know I won't do anything stupid.'

'Gosh, of course not!' Alice almost sounded convincing. 'But anyone can have an accident, Aaron, and if you're out surfing, it's only common sense to check in with someone to let them know you're safe.'

She was right, of course. Since Daisy and Leo had left, Aaron had taken to going out at all hours of the day and he seldom bothered to tell anyone. It was irresponsible of him. He certainly didn't want his washed-up surfboard to be the first his family knew that he had had an accident, but on the other hand, he wasn't feeling very sociable. Scratch that, he was feeling low a lot of the time. It was understandable, but it annoyed him.

He sighed. 'Fair enough,' he said. Then, 'By the way, Hannah Armstrong is back. I saw her just now on the beach, walking her dog.'

'She's just texted me.' Alice sounded pleased. 'I can't believe she's home! She didn't mention she'd seen you, though.' She hesitated. 'Did you tell her about Diana?'

Aaron was still absorbing the fact that Hannah hadn't mentioned him, which seemed to grate on him far more than it should have done. 'No,' he said, after a moment. 'She didn't seem to know anything was wrong and I didn't think it was my place to break the bad news. Did *you* tell her?'

'No,' Alice said. 'I had the same thought.' Her tone changed. 'Do you think Brandon will come back too, once Hannah knows the truth and tells him Diana is ill?'

Aaron's mood turned grimmer. That was all they needed. Brandon Armstrong, arrogant, entitled and, as it had turned out, downright dangerous, was not welcome back in Bamburgh. He thought of the innocent way that Hannah had referred to Brandon and wondered if she had the first idea of how destructive and disliked her brother was. It felt as though there were a lot of secrets that Hannah did not know...

'Are you still there?' Alice said sharply, and Aaron jumped. He'd been completely lost in his thoughts for a moment.

'I hope he stays away,' he said. 'But if Diana wants to see him, that's up to her. Look, I need to get home and warm up. I'll see you tomorrow, okay? And thanks for calling, Al. You know I appreciate it.'

He cut the call and started the van, turning the heater to max to get rid of the chills he could feel down his spine, even though he knew they had nothing to do with the cold.

He could still remember the night he'd finally called Brandon out for his behaviour. He'd known his former friend had been going off the rails for some time, but he'd chosen to ignore it until matters became so bad he couldn't pretend any longer. They'd had a terrible fight, one he had been emotionally, if not physically, unprepared for at the age of only seventeen. He had never forgotten it.

The van had warmed up. Aaron turned the headlights on, as it was too old to do so automatically, and crunched it into gear. A sea fret was coming in, cloaking the castle in mist so that it looked even more like something from a fantasy.

The sandwich had taken the edge off his hunger, but he decided to drive down to Seahouses to get some fish and chips. It was good comfort food and would help things feel less bleak when he got back to the empty cottage.

As he drove along the coast road, he admitted to himself that he wanted to see Hannah again. Three years of going through the emotional wringer over Daisy had given him an unavoidably good insight into his own character and feelings, and he wasn't going to try to fool himself. When Hannah had reflected ruefully that she would need to visit Longstone for her Grace Darling research, he had been ready to offer to take her out in his boat. Fortunately, he'd managed to keep his mouth shut. He knew it would be as pointless as it was self-destructive to get involved. There was no space in his life for more complications. In a week or two, Hannah would be gone.

He ate the fish and chips in the van on the harbour at Seahouses so that he could enjoy them piping hot. As the smell of fat filled the air and the warmth of the food heated his hands through the paper, he looked out beyond the flashing navigation lights on the harbour wall and reflected that he had always wanted to stay near his roots and to do the things his ancestors had been doing for centuries: making boats, working to save lives at sea, being a part of the community. Because Daisy had come from the same background, he had assumed she had wanted the same things. But she hadn't; like Hannah, she had wanted broader horizons.

His phone pinged with a text and he squinted at it.

> Can I swap my Tuesday shift at the museum with your Saturday one at Seahouses? Something's come up. Thanks, Em.

Emma was one of his colleagues at the RNLI, currently dealing with a pile of family issues. Given the amount of support they had all offered him when he went through his divorce, Aaron knew it would be churlish to refuse. But the museum... He swore under his breath.

Once a month, the members of the crew did a shift at the Grace Darling Museum in Bamburgh, talking to the public about their work, answering questions, generally being available for recruitment, fundraising and PR. All the money they raised locally went directly to their lifeboat station rather than to the central coffers, which made it an invaluable contribution to the community. Aaron had done his monthly shift there only the previous week. Plus, it wasn't his favourite task because he wasn't in the mood to make nice with people at the moment. Not at any time. He sighed.

He wiped his hands on the napkin thoughtfully provided by the chip shop, picked up the phone and wrote:

> Sure, no problem. Let me know if I can do anything else to help.

He pressed send before he could change his mind.

Back came the message 'Thanks, pet. You are the best!' and a string of emojis emphasising the point.

Aaron threw his phone back down on the seat and swore again. Hannah would probably be at the museum next week doing her research. Well, hell. That was all he needed.

* * *

Hannah and Tarka passed the Victoria Hotel, its lights warm in the dusk, and the walled garden that had once been a kitchen garden for the castle and was now being transformed into a visitor centre. Bamburgh Hall appeared on the right, set back from the road, this time with Diana's red sports car in the drive. Tarka did a little skip and speeded up towards the door, and for a moment it felt to Hannah as though the past fifteen years had fallen away and she was running back from the school bus, brown plait flying, heavy black shoes clumping.

The door opened before she reached it and Diana was silhouetted in the space, crouching down to greet Tarka, who had arrived first and was making a huge, delighted fuss of her.

'Darling!' Diana, achingly stylish in a way that had always made Hannah feel slightly dowdy, straightened up and opened her arms wide. Hannah knew this was not an invitation to hug but to approach close enough for a double air kiss.

Diana smelled of expensive face powder and classic perfume, Chanel or Dior. Again, Hannah was hit by a wave of nostalgia and perhaps it was this that made her transgress and draw her stepmother in for a proper hug instead. Diana's body felt frighteningly thin and for a moment she froze, brittle in Hannah's clasp, before she hugged her back fiercely.

'It's so lovely to see you,' Diana said, and a tear slipped down her cheek, surprising them both. 'Now you have *destroyed* my mascara,' she added, drawing back and gathering her composure like a cloak. 'How *could* you?'

Hannah laughed, recognising her stepmother's retreat from intimacy. Diana had, from the first, been quite a reserved person, which was perhaps why it had taken Hannah so long to bond with her as a child. After their mother had run off and left her and Brandon behind, Hannah had withdrawn into herself, not wanting to trust the new woman in her father's life, no matter how warmly he had spoken of her. It was only gradually that the two of them had grown close and Hannah had seen the kindness and generosity beneath Diana's facade.

Tarka, however, did not recognise boundaries and was all over Diana, which she, a true dog-lover, bore stoically. 'I have a treat for you in the kitchen,' Hannah heard her whisper in Tarka's furry ear.

'I'll go and fetch my bags,' Hannah said, laughing, 'while you two have a love-in.'

Crossing the wide hall to the back door, she took a moment to absorb the familiar surroundings; the faded elegance of the antique Persian rugs, mixed with some starkly modern art, the Georgian longcase clock with its sonorous tick and the combination of Edwardian and Art Deco furniture that somehow all worked together because Diana had such an intuitive eye for style. As she passed the walnut table by the door, she noticed a new painting hanging in the space where previously there had been a still life. It was a woman in eighteenth-century dress; the dark corner cast the picture into shadows, concealing the colour of the gown – was it blue or green? – yet somehow making the face more vivid, with bright, intelligent eyes and a half-smile on her lips.

I know a secret, the portrait seemed to say, drawing the viewer in to share it with her.

Hannah smiled back at the sitter, feeling a rush of warmth. No matter the centuries between them, here was someone she instinctively felt she wanted as a friend.

'I like the new portrait,' she commented to Diana when she came back in, laden with Tarka's bed under one arm, the retriever's travelling bag and her own suitcase. 'I've got a few more bits and pieces in the car,' she added, 'but that's most of the luggage.' She put Tarka's bed down by the Aga and the dog hopped straight in. 'Totally at home,' Hannah said. 'There I was, thinking you'd want to be upstairs with me.'

Diana came with her out into the hall. 'It is a lovely picture, isn't it,' she agreed, pausing to look at it. 'One of the bed and breakfast guests gave it to me a few years ago. She said it felt as though it belonged here.'

'Wow, that's a generous gift,' Hannah was taken aback. 'And I know what she means – it does feel as though she fits in here, somehow. Who is she?'

'Don't you recognise her?' Diana gave her a quizzical look. 'It's your favourite Bamburgh heroine – Dorothy Forster.'

'Really?' Hannah stared. 'I've only seen pictures of Dorothy painted when she was younger. I wouldn't have recognised her. Her hair is darker for a start, but perhaps that's just the light in here.' She put down her case so that she could look more closely. 'I was thinking about Dorothy earlier,' she added, 'and wishing I was writing about her rather than Grace.'

'You always said that Dorothy was far more interesting.' Diana was smiling at her. 'But I think that's because you prefer the courageous Jacobites to the worthy Victorians, isn't it?'

'The historian in me sees the Jacobites' attempts to return the Stuarts to the throne in the eighteenth century as a terrible waste of life and effort,' Hannah admitted, 'but I suppose that's only because we know with the benefit of hindsight that all their rebellions against the Crown ended in failure. The romantic in me admires their loyalty to the cause.'

Diana was looking at the picture with her head tilted to one side. She reached out and touched the frame lightly. 'It's easy to forget, isn't it, that Jacobitism wasn't only a Scottish phenomenon. The English elements of it often get ignored, but there was such strong support for it here in the North East and in plenty of other parts of the country too.'

'The divide wasn't entirely religious either,' Hannah said. 'Dorothy Forster's family weren't Catholic but Protestants, albeit of the High Church, Tory persuasion. They were involved in the 1715 rebellion, which, arguably, the Jacobites could have won if they had had better military leaders and had pressed their advantages.'

'So often history can turn on the smallest action or decision,' Diana sighed.

'There's a lot of Jacobite symbolism in the picture,' Hannah remarked, leaning in so that the light fell more clearly on the details. 'Roses, the butterfly, the sunflower... I'm not an expert on art history, but I can spot a motif when I see one.' She took in the white rose whose stem Dorothy Forster was twirling between her fingers. There were more roses in the background of the picture, interspersed with the tall golden sunflowers. The setting was a walled garden with a seat in the shade of an oak tree. The butterfly was poised on one of the roses, its wings pointing downwards towards a sundial in the shape of a woman holding what looked like a pair of scissors.

With a start, Hannah drew back. Her Greek mythology was rusty, but she was certain that the small stone figure on the sundial was Atropos, the eldest of the three Fates, who ended the life of mortals by cutting the thread. She gave a little shiver. The picture, which on the face of it looked so bright and summery, was actually full of rather more sinister images.

A curl of blonde hair lay in the hollow of Dorothy Forster's neck and now that the sun had crept round and was illuminating this corner of the hall, Hannah could see that her velvet gown was dark green, with little golden brown oak leaves painted on the hem.

'She has something of a look of you about her, I think,' Diana said unexpectedly. 'I didn't spot it until I saw you and the picture side by side because it's not an obvious likeness, but...' She turned to consider Hannah judiciously. 'It's in the shape of your face and your eyes...' She smiled. 'Or perhaps I'm imagining it.'

Hannah took a moment to see if she could spot the resemblance. Dorothy's hair was golden, where hers was brown, and Dorothy's eyes were brown too, whereas Hannah's were blue, but beyond those superficial differences, she could see that Diana was right; they both had the same oval face, straight nose and finely arched brows.

'Pictures could be very stylised in the seventeenth and eighteenth centuries, couldn't they?' Hannah observed. 'I wonder if Dorothy Forster really looked like that? As far as I know, we're not descended from the Forsters; not that I have ever looked into the family genealogy much. That's Uncle Peter's hobby.' Her father's sister Clara and her husband lived in Sussex and though Hannah kept in touch with her cousins she didn't see them very much and when she had, the family tree hadn't been a topic of conversation.

'You could ask him,' Diana said, 'if you really want to find out more. It might be interesting – although I know that's not what you're here to research.'

'It isn't,' Hannah agreed, 'but I'm feeling completely fascinated by Dorothy Forster now. I'll email him. And perhaps I could ask Brandon about the painting as it's his area of expertise.'

'Mmm...' Diana sounded less than keen and, once again, as with Aaron, Hannah had the sense that she had somehow put her foot in it. She opened her mouth to ask what it was she didn't know, but Diana had turned away and already started up the stairs, so Hannah hoisted her backpack over her shoulder and picked up her suitcase, following her.

'I take it you don't have any guests staying at the moment?'

she said. One of the ways Diana had made the Hall pay its way after her husband's death was to offer luxurious bed and breakfast stays to very carefully chosen visitors. She also owned the Airbnb in the village that Aaron had mentioned he was renting.

Diana shook her head. 'I've been even more selective in who I accept this year, because...' She stopped and Hannah waited for her to finish the sentence, but Diana was staring off into space and let the words trail away. 'I've a small group coming in ten days,' she resumed. 'Two couples. They've been before. They're quite delightful. In fact, one of them is Lizzie, the person who gave me the portrait.'

'How nice,' Hannah said. 'Well, if I'm still around, I promise not to get in your way. Am I in my usual room?' she added.

The last time she'd stayed at the hall, she and Mike had had one of the guest rooms but back in the old days, she'd had a bedroom on the second floor that she suspected had been a maid's chamber when the house was first built. It was plain and small, but she had made it her own and she'd loved being up there with a view above the rooftops and over to the sea. It had felt like her own little kingdom, especially as Brandon had chosen a room on the first floor at the front of the house that was more in keeping with his grandiose ideas as the son and heir.

Diana shook her head. 'I'm afraid there was a leak whilst I was away over Christmas and your room was flooded,' she said. 'It's dried out but it needs redecorating. Plus, I thought that as you would be working, you might need a bit more space, so I've given you the blue room at the back of the house.'

Hannah couldn't quite repress a shiver, but Diana hadn't noticed. Still talking, she led the way up the second flight of stairs and turned left. Lamplight glowed along the dark corridor, lighting the way to the big room at the end.

'I asked Bill to move one of the desks from the study in here in case you wanted to lock yourself away to concentrate. Although you're welcome to work wherever you like. I thought this would be nice for you. It's the room with the best view, but you know that...'

Diana was chattering, Hannah noticed, which was very unlike her, and hadn't her voice caught for a second when she said Bill's name? He was the farmer who rented the land that came with the hall and had been around for as long as Hannah could remember, a dour but practical man who had been a great support to Diana when Hannah's father had died.

Hannah felt another trickle of unease down her spine. Something was out of kilter and it wasn't simply that she was channelling her childhood ambivalence towards the blue room. The grandest room in the house, it had always been out of bounds when she and Brandon were children, the place where guests stayed and where Diana kept her most precious antiques and collector's items. Naturally, the very fact that it was forbidden to them had made it a place of special excitement; Brandon had boasted that he often sneaked in to sleep in the four-poster bed and that he had seen the ghost of a chambermaid on several occasions as she drifted across the room and disappeared through a blocked-up doorway in the wall. That alone had been enough to make Hannah fearful of ever being in the room, her nerves on edge to the slightest sound or movement glimpsed out of the corner of her eye.

And now she was going to sleep there. She straightened her shoulders. She wasn't eleven now and scared by Brandon's boasting about the supernatural. She was a grown-up. Even so, she hoped that the moth box, as she had called it, had gone. A large square box, lacquered black, with a vivid design of a huge moth or butterfly on the top, which was displayed in the middle of the oak bookcase, it had seemed to dominate the room and

Hannah had been irrationally terrified of it, particularly as on more than one occasion she had been sure she could hear the sound of wings beating against the box's lid as though a live moth was desperately trying to escape. Brandon had jeered at her and told her the moth was a death's-head hawkmoth and would haunt her... She shuddered, quickly smothering the movement so that Diana wouldn't notice.

She followed her stepmother along the landing and into the room at the back of the house. The room faced north-west and the had a view of Spindlestone Hill, all lush green and golden gorse. Now that the sea mist was moving in, there was an other-worldly quality about the view. An early barn owl, hunting over the fields between, caught the sunlight on its wings, a white wraith that melted into the mist even as she watched.

Diana was staring at the barn owl too. 'The harbinger of death.' She shook herself. 'Sorry. They are so beautiful but so sinister.'

Hannah was surprised that Diana, usually the antithesis of superstitious, gave the old folklore any credence. 'I love them,' she said. 'Fragile but such fierce predators.'

'Birds of prey are fascinating,' Diana agreed. She turned to Hannah with a smile. 'Do you remember when I had a stuffed buzzard in here?'

'I could hardly forget,' Hannah said drily. 'It added to the general scariness when I was a child.'

'I hadn't realised,' Diana replied, with a hint of vulnerability that Hannah found endearing. 'You can have Brandon's room if you prefer, but I thought that you might like to have the extra space.'

'This is lovely,' Hannah said truthfully, because it was, with its elegant furnishings and cosy blue and cream tartan rugs. 'It's a treat to be in here.' She took a quick glance around and was relieved to note that the moth box was nowhere to be seen. 'Won't you need it in a few weeks, though, if you've got guests arriving?' she added. 'I mean, it's still the best guest room...'

Diana waved that away. 'There's plenty of other space. The Green Room has an en suite now and I've done up Brandon's bedchamber, as we used to call it.'

Hannah giggled. 'I remember. He was always so full of his own importance that it felt appropriate.' She dropped her suitcase with relief and put the backpack down on the bed. 'I'll get myself sorted out and join you downstairs in a bit. Thank you so much, Diana.'

* * *

'I can't tell you how lovely it is to have you staying for more than just a few days,' Diana said later, over dinner of shepherd's pie accompanied by some of the expensive red wine Hannah had brought with her. Diana had served the meal on the 'good' china, with some antique crystal glasses she had bought in an antiques shop in Alnwick.

'As soon as I saw them, I *knew* I had to have them,' Diana had told her when Hannah had commented on them. 'They came from a house clearance over at Adderstone. You remember the old manor house there? It's been derelict for years, but apparently its being turned into holiday flats now. The antiques dealer said these were quite a find.'

'They're beautiful,' Hannah had said truthfully, but in fact they were so fragile that she felt nervous to touch them. Hers was engraved with a circle of entwined oak leaves and Diana's had a rose on it. In the cupboard on the wall, Hannah could see the rest of the set sparkling in the light, each with a different motif – a butterfly, sunflower, crown and rosebuds. The symbols were the same as the ones in the portrait of Dorothy Forster in the hall.

She realised that she had been momentarily distracted from Diana's conversation and quickly turned back to her.

'Having a couple of weeks will give us a proper chance to catch up,' Diana was saying. 'Maybe we could go shopping together in Alnwick, like we used to do? And I can look after Tarka if you need to go to places that aren't dog-friendly, such as the records office.'

Tarka raised her head at the mention of her name and yawned loudly before burrowing back into her bed.

'That would be such a help, thank you,' Hannah said and, for a moment, Diana's thin, beringed hand rested over hers and it felt cold despite the warmth of the kitchen. It was unusual of Diana to be so unguarded, Hannah thought. Normally, she was brisk, not demonstrative. Even as a mother, she had been comforting but never indulgent.

'Here's a plaster and a hug. Now run along…'

'So,' Diana said, her gaze speculative. 'Your new book. Grace Darling? Never one of your favourites.'

'I know,' Hannah said ruefully. Like many people, she had her historical idols – Anne Boleyn, Robin Hood, Richard III and many more. Grace hadn't even made the longlist. 'It's my job,' she added, 'and I feel that as a professional biographer I should be able to give it a good shot, even if Grace wouldn't be my first choice of subject.'

Diana still looked quizzical. 'Surely after two bestselling biographies and highly successful film adaptations you can pick and choose now? Your book on Mary Shelley went to number one, didn't it?'

Hannah smiled at the pride evident in her stepmother's voice. 'It did,' she admitted, 'and the Horatio Nelson book was even more fun to write as it upset all those old male naval historians! The success has been amazing, of course, and I never imagined it, but I'm not in a position to be too fussy yet. There's a lot of competition out there.'

Diana nodded. 'I understand.' A twinkle came into her eye. 'I expect you have your career plan all worked out on a spreadsheet.'

'Of course,' Hannah said with dignity. When she had decided to try to make a living as a writer ten years before, she had been under no illusions as to how difficult that would be without the safety net of another form of income or support. She'd researched it as thoroughly as she did everything else in her life, checking the statistics on author earnings, analysing the best agents and publishers for her subject, talking to experienced authors about their careers. She still backed up her income from the biographies by writing obituaries for newspapers.

It wasn't that she was without creative dreams; it was simply how she felt most comfortable. She'd always been a planner. Even at the age of eleven, when her father had remarried, she had given Diana a questionnaire to see whether the 'wicked step-mother' was someone they could live with. Her father had been appalled, but Diana had simply laughed and answered with her trademark honesty and no-nonsense approach.

Brandon, Hannah's polar opposite, disorganised, insecure but also very acquisitive, shuddered at her pragmatism and called her lifestyle boring, but Hannah didn't care about his opinion any more. It was because she was so organised that she could manage her life in the way she did. Her Bristol flat was small compared to Brandon's palatial London townhouse, but she didn't need a huge place and she was simply grateful she had earned enough money to buy it when the cost of property was so high. Brandon might drive a Porsche because he thought it fitted his image as a high-end art dealer, but she needed something more comfortable for Tarka, so had settled on a small SUV which suited them both. She had a tidy approach to her life and that was fine.

'I planned to start at the Grace Darling Museum straight away,' Hannah said, taking some more green beans from the bowl Diana proffered, 'but then I discovered that it isn't open until Tuesday.' She saw Diana's lips twitch. 'What?' she asked, smiling in return. 'You know I like to crack straight on with a project.'

'Of course you do, darling,' Diana said. 'You've always been quite driven.'

Hannah watched the way that Diana picked at her shepherd's pie, unlike the way she was digging into her own portion. The meal had always been one of her favourites.

'But this is supposed to be a little holiday for you as well as a work trip,' Diana continued. 'Why don't you take a few days to settle in? Go for a walk on the beach, see what's changed in the village, get a feel of things? You always say that setting and atmosphere are as important in a book as the person who inhabits it, whether that's fiction or non-fiction.'

'I do, don't I,' Hannah said, smiling. Diana was right; there was no reason why she couldn't relax and spend more time here if she wanted. A friend of a friend was renting her Bristol flat for a few weeks whilst they found somewhere more permanent to stay. They would probably be delighted if she decided to extend her trip. In fact, she'd call Harry later and let him know he could have the flat for a month. She could do most of her research and writing at Bamburgh as easily as she could at home.

Diana was watching her with her shrewd, dark eyes and Hannah wondered what she was thinking. She recalled Diana's unexpectedly emotional greeting and the fragility she had already seen in her, and although she knew that her stepmother generally shrugged off more personal questions, suddenly she was determined to ask.

'How are you, Di?' she said. 'I mean how are you *really*? You look a bit tired and this is a big house for you to keep up and be rattling around in...' She saw a spark of humour in Diana's eyes and stopped. Hell, she sounded like Brandon, wanting to 'realise the asset' of the house, as he had put it when he'd tried to persuade Diana to move out after their father had died. 'Sorry,' she said helplessly. 'I didn't mean to imply you were incapable, or nag you about moving, or anything like that. I'm just worried about you.' She stopped again, feeling inept. But there was something else in Diana's gaze now, a regret, a poignancy that made her heart thump with fear.

Then Diana smiled and said quite simply: 'I'm the one who's sorry, darling. I should have told you much sooner, but you know me, so bad at confiding. I'm afraid I'm not very well. I'm having treatment for lymphoma and, well... the prognosis isn't very good at all.'

2

DOROTHY – BAMBURGH, JULY 1715

'Mr Railton, I am very conscious of the honour you do me...' Dorothy repeated the well-worn words with as much sincerity as she could muster given that this was the fifth proposal of marriage that she had refused that year and it was still only July.

'I am glad that you realise the honour that is entailed in marrying a clergyman.' Mr Railton, puffed up with his own importance, let her get no further. 'It *is* a privilege to be my help-meet and to serve the Lord and my congregation, as well as serve a husband.' He stopped to draw breath and Dorothy took her chance.

'However,' she added sweetly, 'you do me too *much* honour. I am in no way suited to be the wife of a clergyman, especially one as devoted as you. I regret that I must decline your very generous offer.'

Mr Railton smiled the smug smile of a man who was utterly convinced of his own superiority and of the fact that she was only refusing him out of convention. 'You do yourself a disservice, Miss Forster! Why, are you not the niece of a most prominent churchman, one indeed, who supports my suit?'

He paused to let the veiled threat of her uncle's displeasure sink in.

'There could be no more appropriate partner in my life's journey than you, my very dear Miss Forster.' Mr Railton accompanied this encomium with a hearty pat of her hand, which Dorothy quickly withdrew. She understood all too well that the rector saw her as the perfect spouse for an ambitious churchman, for she was well-bred and well-connected. She had been brought up in the traditions of the Anglican church, her father was a former Member of Parliament and knight of the shire, and she was the niece of a rich and influential man, Nathaniel, 3rd Baron Crewe, the Bishop of Durham. She was also well-educated, which was probably a drawback in most men's eyes, but Mr Railton would overlook that to have her uncle's patronage in his career and to get his hands on Lord Crewe's money in due course.

The Forsters were an ancient Northumbrian family, but Dorothy was acutely aware that they were a poor one these days. It had been her uncle who had rescued their estates from penury a half-dozen years before, restoring her brother, Thomas, as a Northumbrian landowner and enabling them to reside here at Bamburgh Hall. She was suitably grateful to Lord Crewe for lots of reasons, but the gratitude did not extend to marrying his protégé – or indeed anyone. It was time to put an end to Mr Railton's pretensions. She stood up.

'You misunderstand me, sir,' she said. 'Whilst I am conscious that you pay me a great compliment in asking me to be your wife, I fear I must decline. My father needs me here in Bamburgh to care for him, and as you are aware, I also oversee my brother's business interests and estates whilst he is away at the parliament in London. Everything would be thrown into disarray were I to desert either of them.'

A hint of angry colour touched Mr Railton's cheeks. 'Your

brother takes advantage,' he said sharply. 'It is not appropriate for a woman to manage his business affairs; he should employ an agent. As for your father...' He paused and Dorothy realised he was trying to work out how to criticise Sir William Forster without appearing to do so. 'His situation is very sad,' Mr Railton remarked, sounding more cross than sympathetic, 'but you have any number of female relatives who could care for him, should you choose to follow the natural path of a woman of your age and class and make a good match.'

Dorothy gave a gentle sigh. 'Does not the Bible say that caring for the needs of a parent who is sick and in grief is the highest calling? Whatever I may do for any member of my family is surely my greatest duty.'

Mr Railton looked chagrined to be outmanoeuvred. 'Your loyalty is admirable,' he ground out, 'but misplaced, I fear, in putting family requirements ahead of mine and your uncle's.'

Dorothy repressed a smile. The sentiments were identical to those she had heard from every single man in her family, with the exception of her father; for some curious reason, they all seemed to think that *their* wishes should prevail over whatever she wished to do with her life. Even her aunt, Lady Crewe, had told her that she should have been married before now. But it suited Dorothy to remain at home to care for her father and to keep an eye on her brother's business affairs. She had a degree of independence that could never be achieved otherwise. Sir William Forster made no demands upon her and was simply grateful for her company and Thomas was a man who was easily led both in his political and his personal life. She had been able to impress upon him how much money he would save with her managing his estates rather than a man of business and he had enthusiastically embraced the extra cash to spend on his extravagant lifestyle in the capital.

'I merely seek to do my duty as I perceive it,' she said meekly.

'I will bid you good day, Mr Railton. Do take care on the ride back to Chillingham. They say that a highwayman haunts the road, but you should be safe as it is well before dusk.'

The rector glowered. 'I am eminently capable of protecting myself, Mistress Forster. Let the villain challenge me if he dares! Your servant, ma'am.' He gave her a curt bow and stamped out of the parlour, calling peremptorily for his hat and cloak.

Dorothy paused in the hall to check her appearance in the pier glass and tuck a strand of blonde hair back beneath her cap. Her hair mirrored her personality, in that it was wayward and, given its freedom, would curl outrageously. In the evening sunshine that spilled in through the high windows, it glowed a bright gold. Her aunt, so statuesque and classically beautiful with her brown hair and blue eyes, frequently sighed over Dorothy's less fashionable looks and small stature.

'If only Derwentwater had chosen to wed *you* instead of the Webb girl,' Lady Crewe was wont to sigh. 'But she is so tall and dark; a true beauty. They make such a handsome couple.'

'He's fickle, that one,' was the opinion of Mrs Selden, the cook and housekeeper, when the Earl of Derwentwater, having spent months informally calling on Dorothy at Bamburgh Hall, upped and married the daughter of a staunch Catholic nobleman. 'Spoiled. He didn't deserve you, Miss Dorothy. Better off without, as my mother always said.'

Three years after his marriage and six years after she had first met him on midsummer eve, Dorothy found it irritating in the extreme still to be thinking about the Earl of Derwentwater. At the time, it had made perfect sense to her that Ross, her constant companion from childhood, had vanished from her life and her thoughts at the moment when Derwentwater had entered it in person. Now, with the Earl married and already the father of a son and daughter, she had lost the man she had imagined to be her destiny and never regained the companion of her thoughts and dreams. Feeling suddenly lonely, she hurried down the corridor to the kitchen, seeking company.

She found Mrs Selden and Susan, the kitchen maid, struggling to heft a huge brass pot off the fire and onto the table. A delicious smell of stewed beef and vegetables made Dorothy's nose twitch and hunger rumble in her stomach. The combined heat of the fire and the fading warmth of the summer day made the room shimmer and she opened the back door to allow some fresh air inside.

'Was that another disappointed suitor?' Mrs Selden rubbed the sweat from her forehead with her sleeve. 'He won't be joining us for supper, I take it, Miss Dorothy?'

'Mr Railton has left,' Dorothy confirmed. 'I fear he did not take his rejection well.'

'Not good enough for you, eh?' Mrs Selden spoke with a hint of disapproval and the familiarity of a very old retainer.

'Really, Mrs Selden.' Dorothy gave her an admonishing look. 'Would *you* wed Mr Railton? What possible qualities does he have to recommend him?'

'You do have a point there,' the cook allowed, pointing her wooden spoon at her. 'Although marrying him would gain your uncle's favour and with it very likely his fortune.'

'Which would go directly to my husband,' Dorothy said tartly. 'Such is the way that our world works.'

Mrs Selden sighed heavily. 'Aye, that's the rub. It's a hard business being a woman, and no mistake. But what will you tell Lord Crewe? What shall we do when he no longer chooses to pay our bills?'

'I do not know.' Dorothy felt despondent. It seemed extraordinarily unfair that the financial profligacy of her male relatives had left her as the one who had to sacrifice herself in marriage to a rich man. She knew Mrs Selden was right; sooner or later, Lord Crewe would insist she make a match or he would refuse to support them any longer. Her father's remaining estate brought in next to no income, for the house at Adderstone was closed and the land dreadfully neglected. Her brother had business interests in Newcastle as well as London, but he was deep in debt and seemed to feel no obligation to marry an heiress to put matters to rights. Not that any self-respecting heiress would have him, Dorothy thought. As it was, he lived off the paltry sums she was able to scrape together from the accounts, plus the expectation of being his uncle's heir, since Lord and Lady Crewe were childless.

Dorothy reached for the herbs, took up a knife and started to chop them for the stew, whilst Susan went back to the fire to boil the potatoes and Mrs Selden covered the pot with a big metal lid to keep the heat in.

'No need to murder the parsley.' The housekeeper's tone had softened. 'I spoke out of turn and am sorry for it. It is none of your fault that your menfolk are as useless as a psalm is to a dead horse.' She sighed. 'I understand that Sir William is to take his supper in his chamber tonight?'

'Yes.' Dorothy paused her chopping for a moment. Her father's health was erratic since the apoplexy that had robbed him of most of his movement and his fluency of speech. Some days he was able to walk with a stick; on other occasions he complained of pains in his joints and sank into morose silence. 'Papa is not so well at present and needs to rest,' she said. 'I will take the food up to him.'

'At least his illness saves him from the attentions of *that woman*,' Mrs Selden said sharply. 'Preying on a sick man – it fair turns my stomach.'

'You refer to Mrs Danson, I assume.' Dorothy pursed her lips together to prevent her from smiling at the housekeeper's disgusted words. Maria Danson, a distant cousin of Dorothy's mother, had been left a penniless widow at a relatively young age and had arrived uninvited on the doorstep one day looking for a home – like a lost cat, Mrs Selden had said at the time. Out of respect for his dead wife, Sir William had agreed, and though the arrangement was supposed to be temporary, Maria Danson had simply never left. Mrs Selden was soon predicting that the young widow would set her cap at Sir William, and indeed she had done, whilst encouraging all of Lord Crewe's plans to marry Dorothy off.

'I can care for Sir William,' she had cooed on one occasion when Dorothy had turned down another prospective suitor, citing her need to stay with her father as a reason. 'His health should not stand in the way of your future happiness, dear Dorothy.'

It was one of the few benefits of Sir William's deteriorating condition, Dorothy thought, that he was impervious to Maria Danson's machinations. And, indeed, the widow had lately found a new target for her attentions.

'Mrs Danson is dining at the Castle tonight,' she said. 'My aunt is ailing again, and apparently she finds comfort in her presence.'

'Well, she's the only one who does.' Mrs Selden stirred the herbs into the stew.

'At least it leaves all the more food for the rest of us,' the kitchen maid said, then flushed when the cook gave her a sharp glance. 'Sorry, Mrs Selden.'

'You already eat us out of house and home, Susan,' the cook grumbled, but she spoke with rough affection. The maid was her niece and it was on her recommendation that Dorothy had given her the job. 'I'm sorry to hear that Lady Crewe is sick, God preserve her,' Mrs Selden continued. 'There's a weakness in the

Forster blood, it seems. Your dearest mama, and her husband, and now her sister... Too much inbreeding, I suppose. It leads to madness and death.'

Dorothy spluttered with laughter. She could not help herself. Mrs Selden was given to gloomy pronouncements on a variety of topics such as this. 'Oh really, Mrs S!' she said. 'You make us sound very backward. In truth, there is nothing out of the ordinary in our family circumstances, I am sorry to say. And look at me.' She smiled. 'I am as healthy as a horse.'

It was true that she seldom caught a chill or any sort of ailment and even as a child had not succumbed to the illnesses that had carried off more than one of her siblings.

'Aye, you're the best of the bunch in so many ways.' Mrs Selden gave her a hug. 'Now, will you want to take your papa's dinner up and eat with him, or take yours first?'

Dorothy's stomach rumbled again. 'I think I shall eat first and then go and sit with Papa for the rest of the evening,' she decided. 'He has been much agitated by the news sheets he received today from Newcastle and Carlisle and I will try to soothe his worries.'

'Let us hope so,' Mrs Selden said. 'Poor man, what a burden to have understanding and yet limited means by which to express oneself. It is no wonder he falls into a melancholy at times.'

'I had better tell him about the latest rejected suitor as well,' Dorothy said, sighing. 'In case my uncle calls to express his displeasure.'

'I for one am most grateful that you did not throw yourself away on that jackanapes Railton.' A masculine voice joined the conversation, speaking from the shadows of the garden doorway. 'He has neither the wit nor the address you deserve, Mistress Forster.'

Mrs Selden jumped visibly and Susan let out a shrill scream, letting go of the potato pan so that boiling water spilled across the floor and lapped at the boots of the newcomer. Vegetables scattered across the kitchen flagstones. Dorothy leapt up and grabbed some cloths from near the sink to try to staunch the tide.

'Forgive me for startling you,' the man said in the same lazy drawl, strolling forward into the kitchen in defiance of the flood. 'I did knock, but no one answered, so I invited myself in. You should lock the door, Mistress Forster—' he gave Dorothy a bow '—to deter importunate gentlemen from proposing to you.'

'We will bear that in mind for the future, my lord,' Dorothy said coldly as Susan grabbed the towels and frantically mopped at the floor. 'Perhaps it will also give us some protection against noblemen who cause havoc to our potatoes.'

Lord Derwentwater smiled in amusement.

'What may we do for your lordship?' Mrs Selden was blunt. She had not forgiven him for what she saw as jilting Dorothy, even though there had been no understanding between them. Dorothy found it endearing, if unnecessary, but she acknowledged that it was unlikely she would ever be able to look at Derwentwater with complete indifference. He was too handsome, for one thing. His fair good looks would always draw the eye. In their country kitchen, he looked as out of place as a peacock in a henhouse – slim, tall and elegant. But it was part of Derwentwater's charm that he had no sense of his own importance and was as comfortable chatting to his tenants and servants in a barn as he was mingling with high society.

'How are you, Dot?' he asked now, and the nickname made her smile despite her desire to resist his careless affection.

'I am very well, I thank you, my lord,' she replied. 'And you? I thought you were in London, with the new parliament being in session.'

A shadow touched Derwentwater's face. 'I have no desire to take my seat in the Lords and they have even less desire to have me there, knowing my sympathies are with the lawful King over the water...'

There was a clatter as Susan dropped one of the serving pans on the stone floor. Her mouth was hanging open as she stared at the Earl, and Dorothy was not sure whether it was because she was dazzled by him or terrified by his unapologetically treasonable words. Perhaps it was both.

Even here on the far north-eastern coast of the English kingdom, everyone was aware of the turbulence caused by the recent accession of King George I and the ruthless way in which he had purged his government of any who might have loyalties to the previous Stuart regime. The country seethed with rumour and discontent, with Jacobite mobs rioting in the cities and conspiracies suspected in every town and village, especially in Northumberland, where prominent members of the gentry and aristocracy were known to support the restoration of the Catholic prince James Stuart.

Mrs Selden snapped at Susan, who bent clumsily to retrieve the pan, almost sending another flying in the process.

Dorothy gave the Earl a warning glance. She was certain that the maid, like all the rest of the servants, was loyal, for the Selden family had been in service to the Forsters forever. But Derwentwater's parading of his beliefs was foolish. It was all a part of his character, however. He had been brought up at the exiled court at Saint-Germain with Prince James and passionately believed that James should be King of England in the place of King George. It was a shame, Dorothy thought, that the King was so thoroughly dislikeable. He spoke no English and made no bones about the fact he would rather be in Hanover than England. He was dull and charmless, bad-tempered and unmannerly. Had he possessed the common touch of the Stuarts, he might have won over more people, for the populace generally was disinclined towards rebellion. Most people had enough to do simply to survive. They did not want war and strife. It was only the firebrands like the Earl who stirred up trouble.

She might as well save her breath to cool her porridge, however, as Mrs Selden was frequently wont to say. Men of great estate – and it was generally men – went their own way, with little regard for the trouble it caused to others.

'I am glad that Tom's preoccupations are less dangerous,' Dorothy said smoothly. 'His main concerns are with trade and how it may benefit our northern cities.'

The Earl's blue eyes twinkled with mirth. 'That is indeed a worthy way for an MP to represent his constituency. However, I believe Thomas does not exert himself too much in the House of Commons.'

Dorothy's lips closed in a tight line. She was well aware that her brother, whilst nominally representing his voters, spent most of his time and money whilst in London in coffee houses, gambling hells and drinking dens.

'The purpose of my visit, however,' Derwentwater continued, 'was to bring you a gift. I met with him in Northampton and we travelled the rest of our journey together.' He thrust the door wider to reveal the figure who had been waiting in the corridor outside and who now burst into the kitchen, laughing, and swept Dorothy up and spun her around. Her bad temper vanished in an instant.

'Nick! What are you doing here?'

Nicholas, her younger brother, set her back on her feet and grinned boyishly at her. He was barely nineteen, had just completed his first year at Oxford University and Dorothy had thought that he had been spending the summer visiting with friends in the south of England. This trip home was unplanned but very welcome. 'Let me look at you,' she said in her best older sisterly voice.

She held him at arm's length, noting how he was already growing out of the expensive jacket he must have spent all his last term's allowance on, for his bony wrists were sticking out of the sleeves and his long, lanky figure still looked as though it needed to fill out. He would be taller than Thomas soon, she thought, and was dark whilst their older brother was fair. There was an irrepressible air of laughing gaiety about Nicholas that was so appealing, and she drew him in for another hug.

'You must go at once and greet Father,' she said. 'It will lift his spirits so much to have you at home. He has been ailing, but seeing you will cheer him.'

She saw the bright light in her brother's eyes dim a little. She knew it hurt Nicholas to see the father they adored sinking into sickness and misery.

'And you are just in time for supper,' she added. 'Though—' she looked at his dusty boots '—you will want to wash and change after the journey, I daresay.'

'Of course.' Nick gave her a smacking kiss on the cheek. 'It is delightful to have you fussing over me again, Dot. I have missed you. And Mrs Selden.' He turned to the cook and sketched a cheeky bow. 'Your servant, ma'am.'

'Go along with you.' Mrs Selden waved her wooden spoon at him even as she tried to suppress a smile. 'Putting on those gentleman's airs with me when I knew you in short trousers!'

Laughing, Nicholas went out of the kitchen and they heard him taking the stairs two at a time and calling, 'Papa! I am home!'

Dorothy turned to see Derwentwater looking at her with a faint smile on his lips and she felt herself blushing.

'Thank you, my lord,' she said. 'This is indeed a wonderful surprise.'

'I'll put the water on for the lad to bathe. Susan, fetch a bucket and fill it from the pump.' Mrs Selden shooed the maid towards the door and went over to stoke the fire. Her broad back was turned to Dorothy and the Earl in what seemed a rather knowing way.

Derwentwater, having glanced once in her direction, leaned closer to Dorothy. 'Thomas will also be home soon,' he said quietly. 'He has called to see Lord Widdrington at Stella Hall and will doubtless stay overnight, but he plans to be here by tomorrow night. I believe he has the intention of opening up Adderstone Manor again.'

A cool breeze swept into the room and raised the hairs on the back of Dorothy's neck. The pleasure she had felt on seeing Nick again melted away, to be replaced by suspicion. Why would Thomas be returning from London when parliament was in session? And why would he be calling on Baron Widdrington, whom she knew to be a staunch supporter of James Stuart, the Pretender?

She chose to ignore those questions for a moment. 'Surely Tom can stay here at the Hall whilst he visits,' she said. 'There is no need for him to use Adderstone, and no money to run it,' she added pointedly.

Derwentwater took her elbow and drew her out of the kitchen and into the corridor. Dorothy could hear the pump clanking in the yard as Susan laboriously filled the bucket with water for Nicholas's bath. The air was full of the scent of roses – sweet damask roses of pink and white that she had cut from the walled garden earlier and arranged in the hall. Yet despite the beautiful scent, she felt ill at ease, and even more so when Derwentwater began to speak softly.

'Dorothy, I know that you share our conviction that the rightful royal line should be restored to the throne,' he said.

'James Stuart is our true monarch, not his lumpen cousin George who sits on the throne.' Derwentwater swept on before she could speak. 'Your family has always been sworn to support the Stuart cause and now...' He took a deep breath. 'King James is preparing to invade. He has written to the Pope for his blessing on the venture. With God on our side, we shall win the victory.'

Dorothy's first thought was that God had not been on the side of King James's father in 1688 when he had been overthrown. She swallowed the flippant words, aware that her response was triggered by shock as much as anything else. It was true that the Forsters and their allies had been staunch in their service to the Stuart monarchs in the past, but rebellion against the anointed monarch was different; it was treasonous, placing anyone involved in deadly peril. And whilst there had been many rumours and much speculation about an uprising against the new Hanoverian King, to hear it confirmed so plainly was terrifying.

Her mind spun, even as Derwentwater carried on speaking: 'Your brother Thomas is committed to supporting us. We will be using the harbour here at Bamburgh to bring in some supplies to aid King James's return and build up an arsenal to equip our troops. Adderstone Hall is the ideal place to store our munitions, a house that has long been empty and is sufficiently isolated to be secret.' He saw Dorothy's frozen expression and added quickly, 'Thomas... *We* are at pains to ensure that you and your father will not be implicated in any way. We wish to do nothing to hurt you or put either of you in danger.'

'That is rather like saying that we will burn your house down but have no intention of leaving you homeless.' Dorothy was shocked at how angry she felt. 'My lord, you cannot expect to start an insurrection and yet do no harm. Such a belief is completely naïve.'

Derwentwater's eyes widened with a surprise that Dorothy might have found comical under other circumstances. She guessed that very few people ever challenged him. 'I thought that you would be on our side,' he murmured. 'Surely you cannot believe that George of Hanover is anything other than a usurper?'

'My political beliefs are not the most important factor,' Dorothy said sharply. 'I am on the side of all those whose lives and livelihoods depend upon preserving our peace and prosperity, my lord. I am thinking of the children who must be clothed and fed, those who will be left fatherless if there is fighting, the old, the sick and the poor. Rebellion can never do anything other than make their lot even worse than it already is.'

Derwentwater nodded, understanding in his eyes. 'You are a woman,' he said. 'Of course your concerns will be focused on the domestic sphere and that is quite as it should be. But we men must follow higher aims, Dorothy. Idealism, loyalty and true valour are our guiding principles—'

Dorothy had stopped listening. A new fear had gripped her, a thought that sprang into her mind and could not be dislodged. 'Nick,' she whispered. 'This is why Nick has come home. He means to join you and Thomas in rebellion, doesn't he? *Doesn't he!*' she repeated as Derwentwater shifted, discomfort shadowing his face.

'He is a young man who is ardent for adventure,' he said, keeping his voice low. 'I could not dissuade him.'

'I am sure you did not even try!' Dorothy squeezed her hands into tight fists. 'I am sure you applauded his idealism and his loyalty.' She swallowed hard. 'My lord, you speak of rebellion as though it were a game, but this is not an adventure, it is *treason!*' Her voice shook with suppressed emotion. 'How many people will suffer if you proceed with this uprising? How many homes will be plundered, villages pillaged, women raped, men murdered, businesses and families destroyed? All because you put principles above humanity?'

Derwentwater's face had turned blank with shock at her presumption. He took a step back from her. 'Some causes are worth any sacrifice,' he said, speaking more coldly than she had ever heard him.

'I have no objection if you wish to sacrifice yourself – and even Thomas – for your principles,' Dorothy said, 'for you are both of an age to make your own foolish decisions. But I will *not* permit you to take Nicholas with you. He is no more than a boy! Father will surely forbid it. At least spare a thought for those who will suffer because they have no power over their fate. And if you are beaten – what then? Have you even considered the consequences of failure?'

The silence in the house felt absolute. Dorothy could hear the rush of blood in her own ears and, much further away, the faint call of the birds in the garden and the approaching slap of Susan's footsteps on the cobbles and the slopping of water. Her gaze was locked with Derwentwater's and she felt utter despair because she could see the determination in him, the refusal to even hear her, let alone debate with her. How could he not understand that genuine compassion for one's fellow man should be manifest in protecting them, not throwing them in the way of danger? She made one last appeal.

'Less than a century ago, we suffered a Civil War,' she said softly. 'Are you to bring such horrors on us once again?'

'This is different.' He looked stubborn, flushed now with anger. He looked like a *boy*, she thought, and one who did not care to have his games challenged. 'This is a just cause,' he said. 'People will recognise that and rise for the true King. There was barely any dissent when his father was overthrown and it will be the same when his son returns to take up his rightful inheritance.'

Dorothy shrugged, turning away, suddenly tired. What a day. First there had been Mr Railton and his unwanted proposal and now this. The ridiculousness of her life struck her and made her want to laugh bitterly at the absurdity. Men. Always causing problems.

'Dorothy.' Derwentwater placed a hand on her arm and despite her exasperation she could not help but turn to him. 'I need the Rose. It is the one talisman that will unite the men to our cause and make them believe that we can win. And if they believe it, then it will surely come to pass. Will you give it to me?'

His words made no sense to Dorothy. 'The Rose?' she said. 'I do not understand. What is it?'

Derwentwater's gaze searched her face as though he was trying to assess whether she was telling the truth. Whatever he saw there must have convinced him, for she saw disappointment come into his eyes and something else... Was it doubt, for the first time, or fear?

'You do not have it.' He sounded disappointed and weary. 'Men have said it was lost centuries ago, but I still believed in it. It was a talisman of great power that could bring victory to all who followed it. Sir Bartholomew Forster was the keeper in the time of the Crusades, and I thought he had passed it down to his descendants, but perhaps not.' He ran a hand over his hair. 'No matter.' His tone strengthened again. 'We shall still triumph without it. We do not need luck, for our spirit is strong and our cause just.'

'Then I wish you good fortune in your ventures, my lord,' Dorothy knew there was no point in arguing against such conviction. 'Pray remember me to Anna, and send your children my love.' It was an unsubtle reminder of all he had to lose and he nodded, uncertainty flickering in his eyes.

'I trust you to keep our secrets,' he said, and Dorothy's temper flared again that he dared to doubt her discretion.

'Of course, I shall speak of this to no one,' she said coldly. 'And I shall pray for a just and right outcome without bloodshed.'

'Then I will bid you good day, Mistress Forster.' Derwentwater was very formal. He bowed and went out, closing the front door with a polite but very final click behind him.

'Well,' Mrs Selden said from the kitchen doorway, 'here's a to-do.' She had her hands on her hips and was looking at Dorothy with exasperation mingled with concern.

Dorothy sighed. 'You heard, then.'

'Everyone did,' Mrs Selden said. 'You were as good as shouting at one another at one point.' Then, as the maid's frightened face appeared at the end of the corridor, she added, 'Hurry up with that water, Susan. No need to tarry now, or Master Nicholas will not get his bath before the morrow and supper will be spoiled!'

'Someone had to speak truth to the Earl,' Dorothy said, as Susan trudged past them into the kitchen, the water still slopping over the edge of the bucket and splashing on the flagstones. 'It may do no good, but at least I have tried.' She realised she was shaking and wrapped her arms about herself for comfort.

'Come into the kitchen and take some wine,' Mrs Selden suggested. 'I'll wager you need it, what with two gentlemen leaving in high dudgeon in a single afternoon.'

Dorothy laughed. 'Two men who are too dazzled by their own importance to see beyond their noses.'

Mrs Selden poured her a glass of red wine from the cupboard beside the dresser. She passed the glass to Dorothy, who took an unladylike gulp. The wine was strong and she appreciated that, needed it.

When Susan had traipsed off to refill the bucket, Mrs Selden gestured Dorothy to sit at the table, sliding into the seat opposite.

'Are you still sweet on the Earl?' she asked bluntly. 'I only wonder because such passion is usually driven by strong feelings.'

Dorothy took another gulp of wine and took her time over answering. It was true that she had been completely bowled over by the Earl of Derwentwater when she had first met him, but then so had everyone. He was the grandson of King Charles II through his mother and had that monarch's legendary charm.

'No,' she said, knowing that she spoke the truth. 'I admit that I was dazzled at first, but I saw soon enough that he was too...' She paused. What was the word to describe the Earl of Derwentwater? Too idealistic, perhaps. He was certainly not on the same plane as most mortals. The matter had been blurred for her when she had thought he was Ross, the friend with whom she had shared all her hopes and dreams, but those follies were long gone too, banished by six years of silence. 'He is too impractical a man to suit me,' she said with feeling. 'He is full of high-flown but he has so little common sense! I would wish for a man who will solve problems rather than cause them, but sadly I have never met a single one of those.'

Mrs Selden gave a snort of laughter. 'Aye, well in the upper classes they are as rare as hen's teeth.' She patted Dorothy's hand. 'Never fret, my love. There have been plans and plots for as long as there have been kings and queens. I doubt it will come to anything.'

Dorothy was not so sure. She could feel the shadow of rebellion and danger creeping closer. Ever since King James II had been deposed, there had been attempts to restore him and his line to the throne. Every last one of them had failed, but at a cost each time in men's lives. And now Thomas, foolish, easily led

Tom, was mired in treason and looked set to drag Nicholas down with him as well. Derwentwater also had a younger brother, she remembered, a lad of a similar age to Nicholas, their lives barely begun. She wondered despairingly how she could stop this madness.

'You could betray them...' her thoughts whispered to her, and her fingers trembled so much that she almost dropped her wine-glass. 'You could stop this before it starts, save them from their own folly...'

It was a shocking idea. She could scarcely believe that she was contemplating it. It would be a desperate solution to a desperate problem. Yet even as she thought about it, she knew she could never do it. She could not betray her own flesh and blood.

Loud voices in the corridor distracted her. Nicholas was very gallantly carrying the bucket for Susan, who was blushing and almost tripping over her own feet, made clumsy by awkwardness and admiration for him. He hauled the water into the cauldron and set the bucket down, turning to Mrs Selden with a cajoling smile on his face.

'May we eat now, Mrs S, even if I am still all over dust and dirt? The stew smells wonderful and I am sharp set from travelling.' He turned to Dorothy. 'I swear I will bathe afterwards, Dot! And my hands are clean.'

He looked so like the little boy she remembered that Dorothy wanted to ruffle his hair with affection. She got up with a smile.

'Come and eat then, Nick. I shall take my supper and then go up to be with Papa. We have much to discuss, he and I.'

'He seemed well.' Nicholas had already helped himself to an apple from the bowl on the dresser and was crunching through it like a starving man. 'He was pleased to see me. It made him glad, I think.'

'Of course it did!' Dorothy said. 'We all are glad to have you back home, Nick.' She saw the shadow of guilt in his eyes and knew he was thinking of his pledge to Derwentwater and the Jacobite cause. Now, she thought, was not the moment to raise that. But tomorrow, when Thomas arrived, she would make it plain to him that he could not embroil his younger brother in his treasonous plans. In the meantime, it was more than enough to ignore the threat of rebellion, and chat over supper about inconsequential matters.

Nicholas kept them all entertained with his tales of his time at college, the pomposity of his tutors, the terrible food and the fights between the students and the townsfolk of Oxford. It was clear he was enjoying every moment of it – and equally clear that he could not see how fragile his world had become and how it might all come tumbling down.

Sir William was already in bed when Dorothy went up with his supper. Harris, his gentleman's gentleman who had been with Sir William since he had served his own time as Member of Parliament for Northumberland, took the tray from Dorothy and placed it on her father's lap, where he sat propped up on his pillows. Sir William's tired brown eyes lit up at the sight of the stew and Dorothy smiled. Mrs Selden's cooking could revive anyone.

'That's good,' Sir William said appreciatively after his first mouthful. 'Very good indeed.'

'We were both very glad to see Master Nicholas,' Harris said, drawing Dorothy a little aside, 'but the surprise has tired Sir William and he will need to sleep soon. He has, however, something most particular he wished me to show you.'

He walked across to the desk in the window that faced across to Spindlestone Hill. A letter lay on the top; he picked it up and presented it to Dorothy with a little bow.

'If you will excuse me, Miss Dorothy,' he said. 'I shall go and partake of my own supper.'

'Of course, Harris, and thank you.' Dorothy smiled at him as she took the armchair beside her father's bed.

Whilst Sir William tucked into the stew with surprising heartiness, she unfolded the parchment and scanned the contents. She recognised the writing immediately – it was from her father's cousin, Sir Guy Forster of Becote in Berkshire. The Forster family was huge and sprawled across the country, though since his illness Sir William could not travel to visit his cousins as he had previously and was in touch with only a few of them: Sir George Forster nearby, at Warkworth, and Sir Guy, who continued to write from London and the south. Dorothy always wrote back on her father's behalf as his hands shook too much to hold a pen these days.

Cousin, the letter began, without preamble, *I write to warn you of trouble. Town is alive with rumour of the latest challenge to the authority of His Majesty. They say there will be another uprising and I have heard mention of Thomas's name in connection with it, and from more than one source. I pray you, keep your sons at home and forbid them to join the cause. It cannot succeed. I trust you, as ever, to hold the Rose safe. The rebels will want its power for themselves, but it is not theirs to use. Your affectionate cousin, G Forster.*

Dorothy smiled a little at the letter's peremptory tone. She had never met Sir Guy, but she knew he was a former soldier, high sheriff and magistrate. He was old – older than her father – but his words still rang with authority. Her smile faded, though, as she took in the implications of the letter, for it was clear that Thomas's name was already being bandied about in London in connection with the uprising, and she knew that the government would have no truck with that. He was fortunate that he had not already been arrested and if he came to Northumberland, surely there would be troops hot on his heels.

'Insurrection.' Sir William had finished his stew and now his hands were plucking restlessly at the newspapers on his bedside table. Dorothy removed the tray from his lap and he spread out the broadsheets in front of her, some of them couched in fervent anti-Jacobite rhetoric, thundering that any Stuart sympathisers should be locked up immediately, others more moderate but still condemnatory. None of the official press would support any whiff of rebellion, of course, but Dorothy knew that there would be other pamphlets, printed in secret, that promoted the Jacobite cause equally fiercely. 'It's a bad business.' Sir William's voice was raspy and dry. He took the glass of water Dorothy offered and drank gratefully. 'We must pray it comes to naught.'

He pointed to the letter where Sir Guy had underlined Thomas's name.

'Stupid young man.' Sir William sounded gruff, but Dorothy thought that this time it was probably with emotion. 'I'll tell him —' He coughed. 'Not to be such a fool.'

Dorothy bit her lip, hoping it was not too late. Thomas tended to be swayed by the most recent person he had spoken to, so there was a chance that his father might be able to persuade him to change his mind. However, she knew how influenced he was by Lord Derwentwater and how flattered he would be that the great Jacobite lords wanted him to be party to their schemes.

'Tom must not involve Nicholas,' she warned and saw Sir William's gaze flash with alarm. Evidently, her father had not thought of that. To him, Nicholas was still a child and Thomas barely more than a boy himself.

Sir William's hand closed about her wrist. His expression was anguished now. 'You must stop him,' was all he said, but Dorothy understood.

'Have no fear,' she said softly. 'I will lock Nick in his room if I must, in order to keep him from the fight.' Anxious to distract him, she picked up Sir Guy's letter once more. 'What is the Rose?' she asked. 'Lord Derwentwater asked me to give it to him to aid the Jacobite cause and Sir Guy speaks of it as though it were a weapon, or some sort of lucky charm, but I have never heard of it before.'

Sir William's gaze grew cloudy and distant. 'It is a talisman,' he said. 'It gives protection to those who protect it in return. Your mother was the keeper of the Rose.' He wetted his lips with the water once more. 'The Bamburgh Forsters – your mother's family – have always been the keepers.'

Dorothy nodded. Her mother Frances had been the daughter of Claudius Forster of Bamburgh Castle and had married a distant cousin when she wed Sir William Forster of Adderstone. It was by this maternal route, rather than through their father, that Thomas had become co-heir to the bankrupt Bamburgh estate alongside his aunt, Lady Crewe. The Rose, she surmised, must be some sort of old family treasure, no doubt freighted with the sort of legends that always seemed to attach themselves to ancient objects. Mrs Selden claimed that in her grandfather's day there had been a mirror at the Castle that was reputed to be enchanted. Lord Crewe, who detested superstition, had had it destroyed. 'Where is the Rose now?' she asked. 'Did Aunt Dorothy inherit it when Mama died?' If so, she wondered whether Lord Crewe had taken that too.

Sir William's gaze was very sharp despite the lines of tiredness etched deep into his face. 'It belongs to the next female heir,' he said. He coughed again. Dorothy could hear the rattle in his chest. 'Your mother gave it to you, Dorothy.'

'But I...' Dorothy was at a loss. She had inherited her mother's jewellery on Frances Forster's death but had never seen nor heard anything about a talisman. She wondered whether her father was confused; it happened sometimes when Sir William was very tired and would mix up times, dates, places and people. But then she saw him nod towards the chain about her neck, with its little golden pendant, and she gave a gasp, her hand going to her throat. '*This*? But it... It's tiny!'

Her fingers shook a little as she undid the clasp and took the golden pendant in her hand. It was a rectangle, less than two inches long, smooth and warm from her body. Peering at the design of it in the candlelight, she could discern a faint pattern on the surface, the outline of a rose. She realised that she had never looked at it very closely, thinking that it had been a cross, but now she saw the spiky lines were petals and leaves. She had several finer and more expensive items of jewellery but had always been drawn to the simplicity of this one. As soon as she had slipped it about her neck, it had felt as though it belonged there.

'Oh...' she said, and there was revelation and delight in the word. Her fingers closed over it, holding it tightly. 'I have always loved it. Now I will treasure it even more.'

Sir William was smiling gently. 'Guard it with your life and it will guard you too. There are those who have tried to take the Rose for their own ends, but it will not be used. It makes its own choices.'

As she refastened the chain, Dorothy wondered about the legend; wondered as well about the power of the Rose. Magic and superstition could be very influential. Did it matter whether or not the Rose possessed the ability to guard and guide? If people believed that it did, that would make it true. No wonder Derwentwater had wanted it. It combined the Jacobite Rose symbol with Christian imagery and ancient mystical power. She paused, touching the Rose lightly, wondering whether she should give it to him, but her instinct told her that was not the right course.

Sir William's eyes were closing as he drifted into sleep. Dorothy pressed a kiss to his thin cheek, picked up the tray and left the room, closing the door softly.

* * *

Dorothy slept badly, tossing and turning, beset with broken shreds of nightmares in which she ran after Nicholas down endless blank corridors. She was calling to him, begging him to stop, but he never slowed and never turned around. Sometimes she was close enough to touch the edge of his sleeve, yet he always slipped away from her.

She woke abruptly when the full moon slipped through a gap in the curtains to shine directly on her face. She threw off the thin bed cover and sat up. The room felt oppressively hot, as though the ceiling were pressing down on her. She hurried to open the window and breathe some fresh air.

The sky was clear and the moon was riding high over the fields and silvering the sea. As she flung open the window, Dorothy caught the scent of roses from the garden below, mingled with the heavy night-time perfume of the honeysuckle. On impulse, she grabbed a shawl from the chair beside her bed, pushed her feet into her slippers and went out.

The house was not quiet – from Sir William's bedroom came the sound of loud snoring that mingled with the creaking of the beams and floorboards of the old house. Candlelight showed beneath the door of Nicholas's room. Dorothy hoped he had not fallen asleep and left the candle burning, but she caught faint sounds of movement and the rustle of pages turning.

She went downstairs and opened the front door, slipping out

into the garden. Bamburgh Hall was set back from Front Street, the village's main thoroughfare, but close enough that during the day you could hear the sound of the carts passing and the bustle of trade in the shops. Now, the alehouse was shuttered and quiet and the grocers turned blank windows out onto the street.

Dorothy paused on the doorstep, breathing in the cool night air. Gradually, the sense of oppression and panic that had made her feel trapped inside the house started to fade away; she still felt troubled, thoughts of rebellion and worries for her family lurking at the back of her mind, but the peaceful night and the distant rumble of the waves onshore lulled her senses.

She was about to turn and go back inside when she heard the sound of hoofbeats on the road and hurried over to the rose arbour by the gate, wondering whether Thomas had decided to ride back from Stella Hall that night rather than staying until the morning.

The shadows moved and the moonlight fell on a lone horseman riding up from the direction of the castle. The horse was black, and the rider no more than a tall, cloaked shadow. There was something almost supernatural in the way they moved, something that held Dorothy frozen with fear for a minute whilst her gaze took in the gleam of a sword at his side, the tricorne hat and the mask over the lower part of his face. She gasped in a lungful of air, on the edge of a scream.

And then he pulled down the mask and touched his hat in a gesture of respect. The sword vanished beneath a fold of his cloak.

'Good evening to you, Mistress Forster. You are out late.'

'As are you, Mr Armstrong.' Dorothy was pleased by how steady her voice sounded, even as she was wondering what on earth the village blacksmith was doing riding out at midnight, and carrying a sword. But perhaps he had been called out late to one of the farms; he often tended to sick animals along with his other duties, and travelling at night was a dangerous business requiring the protection of weapons, if one knew how to use them.

Armstrong's dark gaze swept over her with a certain speculation that she found surprisingly familiar – until she remembered that she was in her nightgown. She gasped in dismay, drawing the shawl closer about her.

'If you move a few inches to your right,' Armstrong said, his voice laced with amusement, 'you will be in the shade of the arbour and the moonlight will no longer shine through your gown.'

Dorothy made an exasperated huff. 'I am not out here to meet a lover, if that is what you were thinking, Mr Armstrong!'

'The thought never even crossed my mind,' Armstrong said solemnly. His voice had the rich Northumbrian burr of the locals, very different from Dorothy's speech. She had been educated by governesses from the south of England, as befitted her social status, but she had always liked the warmth of the local brogue.

'I assumed you might be waiting for your brother to arrive from Stella Hall,' Armstrong said. 'I heard that he was on his way home.'

Fear tickled the back of Dorothy's neck. Was everyone already aware that Thomas Forster and the Earl of Derwentwater were involved in a Jacobite conspiracy? In small communities like theirs, news spread like wildfire, and if the villagers knew, the government spies would not be far behind.

'Where did you hear that?' she asked cautiously.

'In the Black Swan in North Sunderland,' Armstrong said. Then, confirming her worst fears, 'There was some talk of rebellion and of recruiting men to fight, Mistress Forster.' He sighed. 'Your brother's tenants and workers seem disinclined to follow him into an insurrection, I fear. We have our own livelihoods to consider.'

'That is good news.' Dorothy felt a rush of hope. If this were true, then the ill-conceived rebellion might simply peter out for lack of support. 'I am of the same mind. I fear for all of us if this mad plan takes flight.'

Armstrong rubbed his chin thoughtfully. 'A plot to overthrow the government is seldom a good idea,' he agreed, 'and a plot to replace the King with another king, no doubt equally as bad, is also a fool's errand.'

Despite the dread heavy in her stomach, Dorothy laughed at the description. 'I fear that Tom has been seduced to the idea by Lord Derwentwater,' she said. 'You know his devotion to the Stuart cause. They plan to join with the Scots and the loyalists in the south and raise the country for the Pretender.'

The horse stamped sharply and she realised that Armstrong must have tightened the reins involuntarily. 'You cannot stop Derwentwater before it is too late, Miss Forster?' He leaned down to smooth a gentle hand over the horse's neck to steady him. 'Persuade him otherwise? They will never win.'

'You vastly overestimate my influence with the Earl.' Dorothy was rueful. 'I am sorry, Mr Armstrong. I know it for the dangerous folly it is, but how to prevent it?' She spread her hands in a gesture of resignation. 'If men do not rise in support, as you are suggesting, perhaps the threat will fade away.'

Armstrong was so quiet she wondered if he had heard her. Her words felt hollow of hope even to her own ears. After a moment, she thought she saw him shake his head.

'If I have heard the rumours,' he said, 'the King's spies will have done too. Very likely they were sitting at the same table, drinking the same ale as me. The authorities have long had

Derwentwater under suspicion, for he makes no secret of his allegiance.'

'Then they are doomed.' Dorothy tried not to despair. 'I shall do my utmost to persuade Tom to change his mind even if I cannot influence Derwentwater.' She hesitated. 'Was there any other useful intelligence from the Black Swan tonight?'

'Only that another consignment of contraband tea will be delivered shortly,' Armstrong said, 'at next dark of the moon.'

Dorothy nodded. 'And brandy for those who prefer something stronger, I expect.' With endless bays and landing places, and only three customs houses along the entire coast, Northumberland was ideal for the smuggling trade. Government taxes were punitively high and some said this justified the crime, making free trading no more than prudent economising. She wondered whether Derwentwater would also be looking to import more than contraband on the next French ship.

'Your uncle will be pleased, I imagine,' Armstrong said drily. It was well known that Lord Crewe turned a blind eye to the contraband entering Bamburgh in return for a bottle or two of the finest French brandy. Dorothy had often reflected how flexible her uncle's morals could be for a churchman.

'I am sure he will,' she agreed.

'I also heard that the rector of Chillingham lost a very fine silver snuff box tonight,' Armstrong finished. He took it from his pocket and tossed it in the air, and for a moment its bright silver sparkled in the moonlight before he caught it again in his gloved hand. 'I won it from a gentleman of the road in a game of cribbage.'

'Poor Mr Railton,' Dorothy said. 'I did warn him to be home before dark.'

Armstrong grinned, his teeth showing white in the darkness. 'He should have taken your advice, Mistress Forster. Instead, I hear he was clandestinely calling upon a widowed lady by the name of Nutford over at Beadnell, and on his way home he was robbed of all he stood up in.'

Dorothy's sympathy for her jilted suitor quickly vanished. 'In that case, he deserves it,' she said. 'What a hypocritical toad. He proposed to me this afternoon and visited his mistress the same evening!'

Armstrong looked amused at her outburst. 'I understood that you had refused him,' he said. 'Perhaps he was simply looking for solace.'

Dorothy snorted. 'He is a man of the Church. He should seek solace in prayer!'

Armstrong gave a crack of laughter, quickly smothered. 'Well put, Mistress Forster.'

'No wonder you carry a sword when you ride out, Mr Armstrong,' Dorothy remarked, 'if you take loot from highwaymen. I had no idea a blacksmith's life was so eventful. Did you take his horse as well?' She reached out a hand to stroke the glossy black neck of the stallion who was now standing quietly at the gate. 'He is most handsome.'

'He is mine,' Armstrong replied. 'I bred him. I stable him out at Lucker with family and should return there before my aunt becomes anxious at the lateness of the hour. She believes that only felons and miscreants are out after dark.'

Dorothy became aware somewhat belatedly that she should have terminated the conversation a great deal sooner. She was surprised that it felt so easy to talk to John Armstrong, to confide in him her thoughts and her fears and to ask his advice, for she did not know him well. Perhaps it was because the entire community trusted John – not only with their livestock, but with so many other tasks that kept the village running smoothly and safely. No doubt everyone told him their secrets; he was calm and thoughtful and gave the impression of discretion, and he had lived amongst them forever.

John had married young but lost his wife in childbirth almost a decade ago now; although she had only been young at the time, Dorothy remembered clearly the anguish that he had suffered on losing both mother and baby, his tightly drawn, pale face at the funeral, and how she had wanted to comfort him but had not known how or where to begin. More than one of the village girls had set her cap at John in the intervening years, but he seemed utterly uninterested in remarrying. He was skilled at his work and the forge was very successful and he was training up his nephew Eli to work with him now.

'I must bid you goodnight, Mr Armstrong,' she said. 'Thomas will not be here tonight and I should return to the house. I can only hope and pray that our worst fears are not realised.'

'Goodnight, Mistress Forster.' Armstrong touched his hat again. 'Take good care.'

As she ducked under the archway and trod softly along the path to the door, Dorothy thought that John Armstrong was exactly the sort of man the Earl of Derwentwater would wish to attract to his cause: young, strong and a good fighter. But it seemed that the men of the North East were not keen to rise up to support a Stuart king. They did not have an appetite for more war. It was true that King George was not popular with the people of England, but they had suffered much worse. She would pray that common sense prevailed.

The wind was rising, a summer storm coming in from the east. Clouds, driven on its edge, now obscured the moon. As Dorothy raised her hand to the latch, a gust of wind blew out the lantern burning in the porch. In the sudden darkness, she thought she saw a movement beyond the gate, someone else out on the road at night, someone moving covertly from shadow to shadow. Were the government spies already watching the house? Did they know that Derwentwater had come to Bamburgh that day? Were they all already under surveillance? A shudder racked her.

Above her, the light had also gone from Nicholas's window. She hurried through the door, locking it behind her, seeking the solid comfort of the house to ward off thoughts of disaster. Once up in her room, she burrowed into the bed, no longer finding the heat of the room oppressive but needing it to warm up her cold limbs. As sleep started to cloud her mind, she thought she heard the slightest whisper of her name, accompanied by a sense of peace and contentment that felt like someone holding her close. It was an echo of the long-lost friendship she had had with Ross. She was smiling as she fell asleep.

3

HANNAH – THE PRESENT

'I don't understand why she didn't tell me before.' Hannah was having hot chocolate with her old school friend Alice Salter in the Copper Kettle tea shop on the High Street. Normally, she was a cappuccino person, but the news about Diana had left her craving comfort and now she was stirring the mug so fiercely that some of the mini-marshmallows spilled over the top and swam around in the saucer. Even though she'd had a day to absorb Diana's bombshell, to talk to her and to start to adjust to the shock, it still felt raw and so painful. 'She's only sixty-four,' she added. 'It's no age, is it? It's so bloody unfair.'

'Cancer is like that.' Alice's brown eyes were sympathetic, fixed on Hannah's face. 'Vicious and indiscriminate. But Diana is a fighter. She's getting good treatment. It may go into remission, Han.'

'I hope so,' Hannah said sombrely, remembering with a sharp stab of pain the loss of her father fifteen years before. She'd been fourteen. He had been ill for a long time and so it hadn't been a shock; she had grieved for him before she lost him and then a second time after he had died. She had clung to Diana then and it had brought the two of them closer. But, somehow, she had imagined that Diana, strong as tempered steel, would live forever. It wasn't to be so. 'I suppose everyone in the village knows Diana is ill?' she asked, and Alice nodded.

'She kept it quiet for as long as she could,' she said, 'but you know how word gets out.'

'Typical Diana,' Hannah remarked. 'I realise now that what I always thought of as reserve is as much a desire not to cause anyone any trouble.'

'She's always been self-reliant,' Alice agreed, 'but, as you say, there is a reserve there as well, isn't there. Once you get past that, though, she is the kindest, most generous person...' She stopped as Hannah's eyes filled with tears and covered her hand comfortingly with her own.

For a moment, they sat in silence whilst Hannah composed herself.

'She kept apologising.' Hannah felt bruised and numb. 'Poor Diana, she said she wanted to tell me before anyone else got the chance to say anything to me first. I just wish she'd confided in me earlier, when she was having the tests. I could have supported her through them! We chat on the phone every week, but I didn't realise anything was wrong, and now I feel as though I've let her down.'

'She's told you now,' Alice pointed out. 'That's the important thing.' She sighed. 'Perhaps she wasn't ready to talk about it sooner, Han. It's so big and so devastating. Sometimes the people who are the most important to us are the last people we want to tell.'

Hannah squeezed her friend's hand. 'You're very wise, Al, and very comforting.' She rubbed her forehead. 'Well, I know now and I'm here for her. She apologised for distracting me when I have work to do, but that doesn't matter! I can reorganise everything, get an extension on my deadline so that I can stay here whilst she has her treatment—' She stopped as Alice put a gentle hand on her arm. 'Sorry, Al,' she said. 'This is the first time we've chatted in ages and I dump all this on you! What a nightmare.'

'It's fine,' Alice said with the same comfortable practicality that Hannah recognised so well from over the years of their friendship. 'If I can help, I will. We're all here for Diana – and you. That's how it works in Bamburgh.'

'It's funny how things have changed since Diana first arrived,' Hannah reflected. 'People are very protective of her now, but I remember when she first turned up a few of the locals seemed to think Dad had married a fortune-hunter and gave her the cold shoulder.'

Alice spluttered into her coffee. 'I remember! It was mostly Ellen Moxon at the post office, wasn't it? She spread all those rumours because she had her eye on your father for herself!'

Hannah nodded. 'It was one of the things that prompted me to leave Bamburgh when the time came. Not what Ellen said about Diana, particularly, but the small-mindedness. It made me think villages were too claustrophobic and insular.'

'Small communities don't suit everyone,' Alice agreed. 'But we do tend to rally round in a crisis.' Her eyes twinkled. 'As soon as Diana joined the WI, she was one of us as far as people were concerned, and we've all come to value her very highly.' She drew Hannah's cup surreptitiously towards her. 'Are you actually going to drink that or just play with it? Because it's too good to waste.'

Hannah grabbed the cup back and took a soothing mouthful of hot chocolate. 'Ah yes, you're right, that's very good.' She met Alice's gaze. 'I'm not sure what to do now,' she confessed. 'I'd only intended to be here for a week or so, two weeks max. But now I'm wondering if I should move back permanently, or—' She stopped as Alice put a hand on her arm again.

'Hannah,' Alice said gently. 'There's no need to decide now, is there? You're in shock and still processing the news. Give yourself a bit of time and find out what Diana wants as well.'

Hannah nodded. 'You're right, of course. You know me—' she gave Alice a wan smile '—always needing a plan, especially when I'm stressed.'

'Which is quite natural,' Alice said, 'but just be kind to yourself, okay?'

'Poor Aaron.' Hannah wasn't really listening, instead busily reinterpreting her meeting with Alice's brother the previous day. 'It must have been awkward for him when we met on the beach, knowing about Diana being seriously ill but not wanting to tell me before she had the chance to do it herself.'

'Aaron knew it wasn't his place to tell you,' Alice confirmed. 'He's not a gossip and he'd never break a confidence. I felt the same when you messaged me.'

'Yes, of course,' Hannah said. 'You're both very thoughtful like that.'

'What did you make of Aaron?' Alice asked casually. 'Do you think he's changed?'

Hannah grimaced. 'We've all changed in the last ten years.'

'Isn't that the truth.' Alice squinted unfavourably at her reflection in the mirror behind the cafe counter, twitched a strand of brown hair back into her messy bun and gave a sigh. 'I only ask because it feels to me that Aaron's become a lot less open lately. It's the divorce, I suppose. He went into his shell and doesn't really talk any more. Plus, there are countless women hitting on him now that he's single again, because he's the epitome of the hot lifeboatman hero. Not that there's a lot of competition at the Seahouses station. But he hates being in the spotlight. It makes him cringe.'

Hannah was surprised into a snort of laughter. 'Actually, I can

imagine that.' She took another sip of the chocolate. 'I do know
what you mean, though. There was a sort of...' She hesitated,
looking for the right word. 'Wariness about him – although I
hope he wasn't anticipating I'd hit on him too. Not that he isn't
hot, but I got over my crush on him about fifteen years ago, thank
goodness.' She could feel herself blushing at the lie. It was annoying, because Alice knew her so well that she might guess. 'He
seemed more comfortable with Tarka than me,' she finished
hurriedly.

'Oh well, everyone adores Tarka,' Alice laughed. 'You can't
compete with her.'

'Aaron was a bit offhand when I mentioned Brandon,'
Hannah said. 'Did you ever find out what it was they fell out
about...' She broke off as Alice looked away rather shiftily. 'What
is it?' she asked, feeling a flicker of concern. 'What don't I know?'

'I just wondered whether Diana had spoken to Brandon yet
about her illness,' Alice said, fiddling with the handle of her cup.
'I mean, does she want him to come home? He's barely been back
in the last five years and when he did...' She stopped, flushing
slightly.

'When he did – what?' Hannah asked. Her concern was
growing.

'I think there was some sort of quarrel,' Alice replied
evasively. 'I thought Brandon might have told you.'

'No,' Hannah said, feeling a bit taken aback. 'He never
mentioned it.' Although there was only two years between her
and her brother, they had never been very close, coming together
and then drifting apart as siblings sometimes did. They were too
different to be drawn much to each other's company as adults, but
Hannah was surprised that she hadn't known of a rift between
Brandon and Diana. It sounded serious and whilst she could
imagine Diana keeping quiet about it in order not to drive a

wedge between the siblings, Brandon was so prone to drama, she would have expected him to grumble to her. 'I'll speak to Diana,' she said. 'I was in shock yesterday and I never thought to ask if Brandon knew about her diagnosis. I certainly don't want to put my foot in it by talking to him about her illness if she doesn't want me to.' Disquiet stirred in her as she wondered what else she might have missed. She had always assumed that Brandon was, like her, fond of his stepmother, visiting her occasionally, a bit distant but basically there for her. The knowledge that her assumptions could have been totally wrong had rocked her.

Seeing her expression, Alice shook her head. 'Sorry,' she said. 'I hope you don't think I'm out of line, especially after what I just said about not being a gossip, but from what I heard, the argument was pretty bad and they haven't spoken since. That was about three years ago, I think.' She raised her hands slightly defensively. 'People only knew about it because Bill Hennessy was down the pub the night after, sounding off about Brandon, and for Bill to lose his temper about anything is pretty unusual, so it must have been bad.'

Hannah pulled a face. 'I had no idea. Diana said nothing, of course, and Brandon and I...' She shrugged. 'Well, we do talk, but not very often.'

'It could all be water under the bridge now, of course,' Alice said, 'but best to be aware, I suppose.'

Hannah sighed, thinking how much trouble her brother had caused down the years. There was something malicious about him, yet he had so much charm and was so good-looking that he was always forgiven. It sounded as though he hadn't changed.

She scooped the last of the cream and marshmallows from her cup. 'That was great. Just what I needed. I suspect I may develop something of a marshmallow habit before this visit is over.'

Alice laughed. 'Next time, let's make it a glass of wine or two in the Lord Crewe Arms. I'll invite Sarah along as well. She's teaching in Alnwick now and we meet up sometimes.'

'That would be great,' Hannah said. 'I haven't spoken to Sarah in ages.' The three of them had been inseparable at school, but when Sarah had gone travelling in her gap year, the ties had loosened.

'I'm sorry I've got to go,' Alice said regretfully, checking her watch. 'We've got Sunday lunch with all the family. Aaron's bringing Leo. I'm not sure how many more times we'll all see him before Daisy and Sam move to New Zealand.'

'I imagine it's going to be a huge wrench for you all,' Hannah empathised. She wondered how poignant it would feel for Aaron to see his son in the middle of a big family gathering for possibly the last time in a long time. Her heart ached for them both.

'There's FaceTime,' Alice replied, 'and WhatsApp and a million more ways to keep in touch these days, but yes, it's going to be terribly sad. He's a cute kid and Aaron adores him.' She stacked the plates and mugs neatly together. 'Are you having lunch with Diana? She always did a great Sunday roast.'

Hannah shook her head. 'Diana already had lunch arranged with friends for today, so I'm taking a picnic to the beach, just Tarka and me. It'll be good, just what I need. We'll have a long walk and it will give me time to think.'

Alice reached across the table to give her a hug. 'Have a lovely time. There's choir tomorrow night in the village hall if you'd like to join us?'

'I'm not sure. I'll see how I feel, thanks.' Hannah loved singing and she and Alice had been in the school choir together, but just for now it felt like too much of a commitment when everything was so uncertain. She hugged Alice back. 'Please give my love to your parents. I hope I'll see them before

I go home. And Alice...' She smiled at her friend. 'Thanks for everything.'

Alice grabbed her bag, waved her thanks to Mags behind the counter and went out while Hannah sat quietly for a few moments watching the street. She saw Aaron's battered van pull up opposite and Alice hop into the passenger seat. Aaron turned to glance in her direction as though responding to some comment Alice had made. He looked straight towards her and Hannah wondered whether he could see her, even though she was tucked away in a corner of the cafe. Then the van pulled away and they were gone.

Hannah's phone beeped with a text, making her jump.

> I hear you're in Bamburgh. Thought I might drop by for a catch-up in the next few days on my way back from Scotland. Brandon xx.

Hannah's finger hovered over the delete icon. There was something so irritating about Brandon's mode of communication, ignoring her for months and then breezily announcing that he might grace them with his presence. Who had told him she was in Bamburgh? She hadn't mentioned it to him. From what Alice had said, it was unlikely to have been Diana. And did he need to be so mysterious anyway?

She shoved the phone back in her pocket and stood up, stretching. The high street was filling up with people heading for Sunday lunch in the pubs and restaurants, families strolling along the pavement, curious children and friendly dogs. The overnight rain had gone, leaving a bright but breezy day. Hannah remembered how the wind had rattled her windows last night as she lay in the four-poster in the blue room, feeling a sense of familiarity being back in her old home and simultaneously an edgy unsettledness at Diana's news. The creaks of the house and the fitful flicker of the moonlight behind the thick curtains had kept her awake for several hours before she had finally fallen asleep, worn out by emotion and the long drive. She'd dreamed of the day fourteen years before when Aaron had rescued her from the sea cave. So many details had come back to her in the dream: the misery she had felt sitting on her like a big grey cloud because of her father's recent death, Brandon's infuriating way of deliberately winding her up when she felt most vulnerable...

She'd only gone out that Sunday afternoon because Brandon had been provoking her and she'd wanted to get away from him. She remembered the icy slipperiness of the rocks beneath her feet, the freezing edge of the wind stinging her face, tangling her hair and cutting straight through her lightweight coat. Some part of her, numb with grief and unhappiness, simply hadn't cared what happened. She'd walked past the painting of the stag on the rock, beyond the lighthouse where the sand gave way to rocky cliffs sprinkled with clumps of grass and sea thrift. Normally, she didn't walk there because Diana had impressed upon her how dangerous it was, with the hidden crevasses in the cliff, but Brandon had called her a baby for being scared of the path, scared of everything...

When she'd felt her feet slip from beneath her and the scatter of stones under her soles, she'd made a grab for one of the tufts of greenery, but it had come away in her hands, soil and leaves shredding as she fell. She had no phone – Diana considered fifteen to be too young in those days to have a mobile, although Hannah knew that Brandon had got hold of one somehow. So, when she'd found herself lying on a hard bank of sand within a sea cave, the sound of the incoming tide loud in her ears and a small patch of sky visible a long way above, she had known she was in trouble. Her leg was bent at an awkward angle, although, curiously, it did not seem to hurt.

She had lay there for a little while, feeling drowsy, thinking of her father, the sound of the sea strangely soothing until it had splashed on her face and she'd realised suddenly that she was going to drown here if she did not do something. It was then she had thought of Aaron; the image of him had burst into her mind like a shout in the dark. She had struggled onto her elbows and heaved herself up the bank of sand as far as she could go until she came up against the rock at the back of the cave. It was smooth and sheer, and she knew she couldn't climb any further, but she had felt calm, it was almost as though Aaron was beside her, talking to her: *'Hold on, Hannah, I'm coming...'*

She had not known how long she had waited, but then he was there, and she had wrapped her arms around him and said, 'I knew you would come for me...' and, probably fortunately at that point, fainted. It was a useful faint all round as it saved her the pain of being winched out of the cave and stowed in the air ambulance, and it meant that when Aaron came to visit her in hospital, she could pretend that she didn't remember what had happened and could just be grateful that he had apparently been passing and heard her shouting for help...

Hannah gave herself a little shake, picking up her jacket and taking the dirty crockery across to the counter for a grateful Mags. It had been an odd episode and even though it had been so long ago now, she remembered it so clearly and it was probably one of the old memories that was confusing her in the present; it made her feel closer to Aaron than she should, closer than was either real or sensible.

* * *

Hannah followed a trickle of other visitors up the wide tarmacked path to Bamburgh Castle. Although it was a Monday morning, there was a steady flow of cars into the village, some turning off towards the beach car parks, others making their way towards the shops and tea rooms. The approach to the castle twisted around the southern side of the crag, rising steeply as it turned to seaward, where a stiff breeze caught at Hannah's scarf and set the ends dancing. She tucked them back into her jacket, turning up her collar against the wind. It was embarrassing to admit that living in the south had made her soft, but there was something so keen and clear about the air here. It seemed to cut through all her summer clothes, making her shiver. And at the moment she was walking beneath the enormous bulk of the castle that reared so high overhead that it cast a deep shadow, adding to the chill.

She'd seen plenty of people who were out in T-shirts and shorts, people much hardier than she was. On the beach the previous day, she'd worn a fleece and felt warm enough, whilst she and Tarka were walking, but when they'd sat down in the dunes for the picnic, she'd pressed close to Tarka, whose solid, furry body was both cosy and comforting.

As it was Monday, the Grace Darling Museum was closed, and Hannah decided to use her day off to revisit the castle, which she hadn't been to since she was a teenager. Partly this was because she had been reading about Dorothy Forster and knew that Dorothy was descended, via her mother, from a branch of the family that had owned the castle for a time. She was fairly sure that there was something about Dorothy in the exhibition there and that had whetted her appetite. She had invited Diana to join her, but her stepmother, curled up like Tarka beside the Aga, had said she was too tired.

'Maybe I'll pop up later for a cup of tea with you in the cafe,' Diana had said. 'I'll text you.'

Hannah hadn't yet raised the issue of Brandon with her step-

mother as Diana seemed so frail. She was hesitant to mention the
row Alice had told her about, or the fact that Brandon had said he
might drop in. She would save that for later.

As she followed a couple in hiking gear through the gateway
and into the ticket office, Hannah reflected that when she had
been young, it had been the habit for the villagers to deride the
tourists who flocked there during the holiday season and
swarmed all over the castle in their droves. Now, that attitude
seemed rather superior and churlish. The visitors who came to
see Bamburgh Castle, to visit the ancient church and walk on the
beach, contributed to the livelihood of the coastal communities.
Besides, she was pretty much a stranger there herself these days.

The young woman behind the ticket desk wasn't someone
Hannah recognised and she handed over her money, took a free
map and strode up to the battlements. There was a magnificent
view of the beach far below, the tiny stick people walking with
their dogs, and the Farne Islands floating in a faint sea haze, grey
and insubstantial, further out. The huge stone keep now dominated the inner ward of the castle with its uncompromising four-
square stance. Most people stopped, voluntarily or involuntarily,
to take in the sheer immensity and scale of it. It was hard not to
stare and impossible not to be impressed even when it was so
familiar.

Ducking under the lintel of the entrance to the state rooms,
she found herself in a space styled to show a Victorian classroom.
This part of the castle, Hannah remembered, had been restored
in the eighteenth century under the auspices of the charity set up
by Nathaniel Lord Crewe. He had been a very generous bene-
factor to the village. Two ante-rooms displaying various items,
maps and pictures from the eighteenth century led into the Great
Hall, which Hannah was amused to see was dominated by an
exhibition of costumes and props from a TV series that had been

set at Bamburgh a few years before. Life-sized, sword-wielding Saxons snarled down at her. 'Explore Bamburgh's epic past as the capital of Northumbria,' excited signs exclaimed, whilst the air echoed with the soundtrack of the crash of battle, waves pounding the shore and screaming seabirds.

On the wall above the dais was a replica of the Winchester Round Table, twenty-four segments in green and white with a red rose encircling a white one in the centre and King Arthur at the top. The wall plaque stated that Bamburgh was believed to be the castle Dolorous Gard in the Arthurian legends. Sir Lancelot had claimed it from the Copper Knight and renamed it Joyous Gard. Matters had not been so joyous when Lancelot had betrayed Arthur through his affair with Guinevere, Hannah thought.

There was layer upon layer of myth, legend and history at Bamburgh. She'd seldom been anywhere else where there were so many entwined stories, from the Dark Ages tale of the princess who had been turned into a dragon known as the Laidley Worm by her wicked stepmother, to the Bebbanburg that was a Saxon stronghold. The castle on the rock was a huge symbol of power and might. It gave Hannah shivers to imagine that she was standing in a place that had had so much significance for so many centuries.

An arrow showed the way for visitors to progress into a hallway and staircase linking the great hall with the billiards room. It was quite dark, with faintly coloured light falling on the wide stone steps via the stained-glass windows. A few small portraits hung on the walls – there was a man whom Hannah identified as Nathaniel, Lord Crewe, Dorothy Forster's uncle, who had bought the Bamburgh estate from her brother to save it from ruin. Hannah recognised his face from the pub sign on the Lord Crewe Arms, but she had also read up about him the previous night when she should have been researching Grace Darling.

Lord Crewe had been Bishop of Durham, but he did not look very clerical in this portrait, which portrayed him as dark and dashing, a cavalier in style and manner – a throwback, Hannah thought, to the days of the earlier Stuart monarchs. Hannah's online research had told her that Lord Crewe had paid off the Forster family debts and had partially restored the dilapidated castle.

Next to his was a matching portrait of his second wife, according to the label beneath it. Dorothy Forster, known to her contemporaries as 'pretty Doll Forster', was a classic beauty of the early eighteenth century, with an oval face, straight nose, light brown hair and an elegance that was enhanced by the dark blue satin gown she wore and her air of sober dignity.

Hannah studied her with interest. This was not the same woman who was in the portrait at Bamburgh Hall. *Their* Dorothy Forster, as she was inclined to think of her, was the niece of Lady Crewe. She had been named for her aunt in the rather confusing way that so many families had of calling everyone by the same few first names.

Dorothy junior had had a number of siblings, but the only one that Hannah remembered much about was her elder brother Thomas. Thomas Forster had been a Jacobite general in the uprising of 1715 against the Crown – a fact the online article on Lord and Lady Crewe had referred to, adding, rather piously, that his disgraceful behaviour had nearly killed his aunt.

Thomas's portrait was also on display in the small hallway. He looked like a typical bewigged early-Georgian gentleman: fat, florid and self-satisfied. There was no intelligence behind the eyes, Hannah thought, only blandness and misplaced confidence. The plaque on the painting referred to him as General Thomas Forster, but Hannah felt this was rather overstating his abilities since she knew that when he was appointed commander of the English Jacobite forces he had had no military experience at all.

The final portrait was tucked away in the darkest corner of the stair. It was so dark that Hannah needed to turn on the torch on her phone to see the picture properly and when she did, she felt a shiver raise the hairs on her neck.

This was *her* Dorothy Forster, the same woman who was in Diana's portrait at Bamburgh Hall. She felt a jolt of recognition. The same sense of familiarity possessed her as before. Here was someone she felt she knew.

The girl in the frame looked much younger than the woman in the portrait at the Hall. In fact, she looked barely more than a child. Blonde ringlets framed an oval face, her eyebrows were arched as though in surprise and her eyes were an indeterminate brown colour. She wore a silk dress of a rich, deep blue embroidered with copious pearls. Pearls circled her neck as well and hung from her ears. The style was too sophisticated for her and made her look like a child who had dressed up in her mother's clothes. And yet there was something there, some spark of the woman she was going to be, a gleam in the eyes that reminded Hannah of the mischief she had glimpsed in the woman in her stepmother's painting.

Dorothy and her brother Thomas were born in Adderstone but resided for a time at Bamburgh Hall, the gold plaque below the portrait read and Hannah felt another little shiver of recognition. She hadn't known that detail of Dorothy Forster's life. Was that why she felt a kinship with her? Because they shared the same space but at a different time?

Hannah's phone pinged, breaking into her thoughts. It was a message from Diana.

Bill's giving me a lift up to the castle. See you in
the cafe when you're ready. Dx

Hannah sent a smiley face emoji and stood back as a group of
schoolchildren in hi-vis jackets came clattering past, heading
towards the billiard room, chattering like magpies and
marshalled by slightly harassed-looking teachers who counted
them in and out. She waited until their voices had died away and
looked at Dorothy's portrait again.

As well as the pearl jewellery, she had a bracelet around one
wrist that looked as though it was made of precious stones and
fastened with a heart-shaped lock. In her other hand were two
red roses. Hannah took some more pictures as best she could in
the dim light, focusing in on the details in the painting.

The schoolchildren had moved through the billiard room
now, so she followed and found herself in her favourite room in
the castle. The Faire Chamber, as it was called, was a beautiful,
light and airy room with delicate pink, blue and gold painted
decoration and plaster moulding. It was a room that always made
Hannah want to sit down on the window seat to look at the view,
or relax in an armchair with a good book. This morning, though,
her attention was drawn to a display which focused on various
women from history connected to Bamburgh. One was Queen
Bebba, after whom the castle was said to have been named in the
seventh century. There was also Philippa of Hainault, wife of King
Edward III, who, in the fourteenth century, had defended
Bamburgh during a military siege. Alongside them was a picture
of Dorothy Forster, described as a 'heroine of the Jacobite cause'.

The details on the interpretation panel provided little more
information than Hannah already knew, but reminded her of the
story that Dorothy had allegedly ridden from Northumberland to

London to rescue her brother after he was captured in the first Jacobite rebellion and imprisoned. Hannah wondered whether this was accurate or if it was an example of another legend weaving itself around a historical figure. She decided to try to find out. She also tried to reconcile the idea of a fearless Dorothy galloping the length of England with the picture of the young girl with the childish face, wearing the too-grown-up blue dress. That child must have grown into a formidable woman for even a small part of the story to be true.

At the bottom of the panel, Hannah saw a note: *Look for Dorothy's satin dress displayed in this room.*

The gown was in a case over by one of the windows. It had gold and pink stripes with a square, low-cut embroidered bodice and sleeves lined in navy. There was a matching pair of navy and gold slippers. Hannah's first thought was that they looked uncomfortable and her second that Dorothy must have been tiny. Both dress and shoes were very small indeed.

Dorothy's subsequent life was unrecorded, other than to state she was buried beside her brother in the crypt of St Aidan's Church. Hannah, who had absolutely no intention of being buried anywhere near Brandon, shuddered inwardly. Dorothy must have loved her brother very much to go to so much trouble to save him. It was the bare bones of a story that surely had to be a great deal more complex and had probably been embroidered over time as well. She wanted to know much more about Dorothy Forster.

A centuries-old passageway led from the Faire Chamber into the Keep, the oldest part of the castle. The temperature seemed to drop as Hannah walked along it; one of the signboards referred to the ghost of the 'pink lady' who had been seen haunting the stairs, a Northumbrian princess who was pining for her lost love. There was certainly a melancholy chill to the air, but it vanished as Hannah entered the Court Room, decorated with more family portraits.

There, high on the wall, was another picture she recognised immediately to be Dorothy, with her golden ringlets and sweet, round face. She was dressed as a shepherdess, or what the aristocracy of the time fondly thought a shepherdess would look like, in pristine blue and white silk with a pink silk shawl; a very clean sheep sat beside her and Dorothy was, rather oddly, placing a coronet of flowers on its head. Hannah stared at it for a long time. Both Dorothy and the sheep had similar expressions of bovine contentment. 'By a follower of Peter Lely' the attribution plate said and Hannah had to repress a smile at the simple bucolic charm of it all. It felt a far cry from Dorothy embarking on a dangerous expedition to London to spring her brother from gaol. Her story was certainly very intriguing.

Pausing only to buy a copy of the Forster family tree in the gift shop, Hannah bypassed the dungeons, where the schoolchildren were excitedly embracing Bamburgh's bloody history of warfare, and emerged onto the grassy square in front of the tower in time to see Bill's old Land Rover heading down the hill towards the cafe. The staff on the gate, presumably knowing about Diana's illness, must have waved them through, which Hannah thought was very considerate. She suspected, though, that Diana would hate the fuss, and as she caught up with them outside the cafe, she was proved correct.

Diana was emerging from the passenger seat, a frail but always-elegant figure in black jodhpurs, boots and a fitted jacket over a silk shirt. She folded up the tartan rug that had evidently been covering her knees and handed it to Bill, who was hovering by the door. 'Here you are, you old fusspot! There was never any need for all this mollycoddling – I'm not dead yet!'

'I wouldn't bother wrapping you in a rug if you were,' came

Bill's testy response, but his gentle touch on her arm as she stepped down contradicted his tone. Hannah was smiling as Diana turned to greet her.

'Hello, sweetie! Did you enjoy your tour? Did you find out anything interesting about Grace?'

Grace who? Hannah wondered for a moment before realising with a slight pang of guilt that she hadn't even noticed whether there was any information about Grace Darling in the castle because she was too wrapped up in Dorothy Forster's story.

'Nothing new,' she said evasively, 'but I did enjoy looking round. It's been years since I visited and Uhtred has moved in since then. Hello, Bill,' she added, smiling at the stocky farmer who stood four-square in his wellingtons and work clothes. 'It's good to see you again.'

Bill's smile was broad and sincere. 'You too, pet.'

'Are you joining us for coffee?' Hannah asked. 'It would be lovely to catch up.'

The look Bill exchanged with Diana told her all she needed to know about their relationship, even if she hadn't already guessed they were in one.

'Please do, Bill,' Diana said formally, and his smile widened still further.

* * *

'So, you two are an item,' Hannah said once they were seated on the terrace – the tartan rug had come in useful again for Diana – looking out across the battlements to the sea. Bill almost snorted his mug of tea, but Diana simply smiled.

'Of *course*.' She put her hand over Bill's gnarled one as it rested on the table. 'We have been for a number of years, darling – not when your father was alive; perish the thought – but afterwards, on and off. Bill is...' She paused and took a dramatic breath whilst Hannah noted the slight hint of trepidation in Bill's eyes, 'My constant support and stay. My love.' Diana's eyes were a little misty with tears. 'I've asked him to marry me a number of times, but he always refuses. He says everyone will think he is on the make, seducing a rich widow. So foolish to care about what other people think, especially as I have *no* money at all!'

'I can still look after you without the blessing of the Church.' Bill seemed unperturbed by Diana's comments, which Hannah suspected he had heard a hundred times before. 'Besides, we're both set in our ways.' He picked up his mug again. 'We're good as we are.'

'I'm very happy for you both.' Hannah got up to go round the table and give Diana a hug, surprising Bill with a kiss on his leathery cheek. 'But do let me know if you change your mind. I've never been a bridesmaid.'

'Really?' Diana's eyes opened wide. 'How surprising.' She gave Bill a nudge. 'There you are then! You could make both Hannah and me happy in one fell swoop, but do get a move on if you decide to do it. I'm not sure how long I have – six months maybe, or a bit more, and it takes *ages* to arrange a wedding.'

'Nonsense,' Bill said comfortably. 'Down the registry office with Hannah here and another witness, then back for a fish and chip supper.'

'You old romantic!' Diana cut off a sliver of her rainbow cake.

'You don't sound completely averse to the idea, Bill,' Hannah said mildly, and he smiled.

'Mebbe not,' he said.

'I wanted to tell you about us...' Diana toyed with her forkful of cake, 'in case you felt obliged to come back to Bamburgh to care for me. Not that that wouldn't be lovely, of course, darling, but there's no need at all. You have a busy life and I wouldn't dream of imposing on you. Bill will keep an eye on me and he will stay in touch with you.' She glanced up from moving crumbs around her plate, met Hannah's eyes and looked imploring. 'That came out quite the wrong way,' she complained. 'My brain cells must be dying off faster than I imagined.'

Bill gave a snort. 'What Di means, Hannah, is that she would love for you to stay in Bamburgh but doesn't want you to feel obliged. We both know you have commitments elsewhere and I'm happy to care for Di and let you know how she's getting on.'

Diana turned her gaze on him gratefully. 'Thank you, Bill darling. You put it so succinctly.'

Hannah realised that this was just another example of her stepmother not wanting to ask for help. Previously, Diana's independence had been absolute, worn like armour. Now, though, she seemed so vulnerable.

Hannah smiled and covered Diana's hand with her own. 'I planned on hanging around for a while, if that isn't inconvenient,' she confirmed. 'I had a good think about it yesterday when Tarka and I were on the beach.' She flashed Bill a smile. 'I can work from Bamburgh as easily as I can from Bristol and then I can also be Bill's backup.'

Diana's eyes filled with tears and she reached out to Bill with her other hand. 'I'm very lucky to have you both,' she said. 'And it means I get more dog time with the lovely Tarka as well.'

Bill cleared his throat loudly, evidently uncomfortable with the show of emotion. 'Reet then,' he said. 'That's agreed.'

'There's just one thing,' Hannah added. She squeezed Diana's hand, then let her go. 'Have you spoken to Brandon lately? Does he know you're ill?'

Diana and Bill exchanged another meaningful look. Bill's mouth had tightened to a thin line and Hannah saw him clench his fists before he deliberately loosened them and raised his mug, which was already empty. He avoided Hannah's eye and said nothing. Tension wrapped around the table like an invisible shroud.

'I haven't spoken to Brandon for several years,' Diana said carefully. 'I'm sorry if it upsets you, Hannah darling, but I don't really want to see him. You see, the last time we met we quarrelled quite badly—'

Bill made a growling sound that was unintelligible to Hannah, though Diana seemed to understand what he had said.

'Yes,' she agreed, 'he is a "wee shite", Bill, but he's also Hannah's brother.'

This time, Bill muttered some comment about chalk and cheese.

'Look,' Hannah said quickly, 'I know about the quarrel with Brandon. Alice told me. And I heard that Bill was angry about it, but I don't know more than that.' She looked between them. 'But you should know that Brandon's planning on stopping by. I had a text from him last night saying he'd drop in sometime soon on the way back from Scotland. So...' She spread her hands. 'At least you're forewarned. And of course you don't have to see him, or even tell me what all this is about, but I do wish I knew what was going on.'

'Yes,' Diana said, subdued. 'Yes, of course. That's only natural. But I don't want to criticise your brother to you, Hannah, or for you to feel you have to take sides. That isn't fair.'

Hannah gave a sharp sigh. 'Years ago, just after Dad died, Brandon and Aaron fell out over something as well. I don't know what that was about either, but I know it was so serious they never spoke again. It's obvious Brandon is a troublemaker. I've known that for almost thirty years.'

Diana and Bill seemed to have been holding another wordless conversation. They had either got something telepathic going on or they knew each other so well that they could follow each other's thought processes, which was as good as the same thing. After a moment, Diana gave a little nod.

'Very well,' she said. 'I didn't know about Aaron, but it doesn't surprise me.' She looked over her shoulder at the crowded cafe. 'We can't talk here and I've got an appointment at the hospital this afternoon; let's have a chat about it over dinner.'

'Aye,' Bill added grimly, 'and in the meantime I'll get the key for the gates in case that wee shite turns up.'

'The key won't work after all these years, Bill,' Diana said. 'The lock is full of rust.' She smiled fondly at him. 'There's no need to be so theatrical about this. It's only Brandon.'

Bill stood up. 'I'm taking no chances.' He shoved his hands in his pockets. 'I'll see you out at the car.'

'That's Bill's subtle way of giving us a moment,' Diana remarked, fondly watching his retreating back. 'Isn't he marvellous? So rugged.'

'I'm glad he's around,' Hannah said truthfully. 'But, Diana, at least give me a hint about Brandon. I realise we can't talk properly now, but I'm imagining all sorts of awful things. Surely he isn't dangerous?'

Diana sighed. 'Of course not. Bill's just being melodramatic. No, Brandon may be a troublemaker, but he's not a threat. It's just that he... he's taken things from the house sometimes. Jewellery, and pictures and ornaments – things he can sell. He's a bit of a magpie, that's all.'

'You mean he's been stealing from you?' Hannah was horrified. 'Oh my God, Diana, that's terrible!'

Diana started to collect up her bag and her scarf. 'I don't think Brandon sees it like that,' she said. 'I think he believes it all belongs to him since your father died.'

'Huh.' Hannah knew what Diana meant as Brandon had

always viewed Bamburgh Hall as his inheritance and made a big fuss about selling the house and capitalising on its value. As far as she remembered, their father's will had stipulated that everything should be left to Diana in the first instance, then split between the two of them after she had died. She wondered what part of that Brandon didn't understand. The part that meant he didn't get everything, she supposed. Brandon always had been greedy.

She helped her stepmother up and steered her out to where Bill was waiting with the Land Rover.

'I'll see you later, darling.' Diana kissed her cheek, then slid into the passenger seat. 'Bill's taking me over to the Royal Victoria in Newcastle. It's just a check-up. Hopefully I'll be fine for a bit of supper later. We can talk more then.'

Hannah waved them off, then walked slowly down to the West Ward of the castle where the ruins of the windmill stood. There was a compass disc on the top of the wall, a circle with spokes radiating from the centre that pointed to all the places of interest nearby: Lindisfarne, Spindlestone Hill, St Aidan's Church, the Dovecote, Longstone Lighthouse and the other Farne Islands. It was charming, with engraved faces of the four winds blowing – West, North, South and East. Down in the Outer Ward, she could see an archaeological dig in progress; a research project had been taking place at the castle for decades.

Hannah could also see Bamburgh Hall from here, its roof nestling amongst the jumble of tile and slate of the village; the merchants' houses and the fishing lofts now converted into elegant holiday homes and flats. The Hall was rooted in the history of Bamburgh as much as the castle was and now that she knew that Dorothy and Thomas Forster had resided there, she was even keener to research Dorothy's story. Dorothy was definitely a kindred spirit, she thought. If they'd met, they would have bonded over the trials of having a trouble-making brother.

Hannah rested her elbows on the battlements and thought about Brandon. Diana had made light of his behaviour, perhaps in an attempt not to upset her, but Bill clearly didn't think Brandon was as harmless as his stepmother made out. Theft was theft regardless of who you were stealing from and it was typical of Brandon's conceit and entitlement that he thought he could just help himself to the contents of the Hall. It also put the incident with Aaron in a different light. Perhaps Brandon had stolen from his best friend as well as his family. Hannah felt hot with mortification to think of it. She knew she couldn't let it pass. She was going to have to ask Aaron what had happened.

4

DOROTHY – SEPTEMBER 1715

Dorothy lay flat on her stomach, hidden in the long grass, nettles and cow parsley that flourished within the old walls of what had been the gardens at Adderstone Hall. The day was hot and drowsy for early autumn, the sky heavy with dark grey clouds that threatened thunder. The buzz of insects filled her ears and she could feel something crawling up her neck. She slapped it away with an impatient hand, but quietly, for she had no desire to give away her position deep in the shrubbery.

It was a bittersweet experience to revisit her childhood home. The shuttered windows of the house stared out blankly at her and the whole place looked lost and uncared-for, yet in Dorothy's memory it was a place full of life and laughter, until her mother Frances had died and a pall of silence had fallen over the place. Then, her father had withdrawn into his grief and she had assumed responsibility for Nicholas, still barely more than a chubby baby. Eventually, Sir William had shut the house up for good. The roses and honeysuckle had run wild, ivy shrouded the crumbling walls and there was an air of unloved neglect that made Dorothy's heart ache for what had been.

Yet the silence and emptiness were also illusory. She knew Thomas was hiding out at Adderstone; she had glimpsed him earlier when she had followed Nicholas from Bamburgh. Spying on her younger brother was not something that she was proud of, but she had been determined to find out what he was up to. She had suspected that, whilst blamelessly sitting at home pretending to be studying his Greek, he had been planning something completely different. Nicholas had never been a scholar. And her suspicions had proved correct. He had ridden directly to Adderstone, and he had brought a second horse with him from the stables at Bamburgh Hall, along with a selection of antiquated pistols from Sir William's gun room. Dorothy almost found it touching that he thought a spare horse and a few old flintlocks would aid the Jacobite cause, but she was too angry with him to be amused. Since Thomas had arrived from London three weeks earlier, the matter of the rebellion had been all that Nicholas had thought and spoken about; hero-worshipping his elder brother for his role as one of the leaders of the English Jacobites and elevating the Earl of Derwentwater to such godly status that Dorothy was surprised he did not actually kneel down before him.

Her discussion with Thomas had gone badly. As soon as he had arrived at Bamburgh Hall, she had dragged him off to the drawing room to try to impress on him the danger he was in and ask him to reconsider his support for the rebellion. Predictably, though, he was in no mood to listen. He had no time for her doubts and caution, for he was as carried away by his own heroism as Nicholas was, playing the part of the loyal and courageous soldier.

'This is a matter of conscience and sovereignty,' he had said loftily to Dorothy. 'I beg you not to meddle in political affairs of which you have no understanding.'

'I have a very clear understanding that you and Derwentwater and Nicholas and a thousand other men may well lose your lives over this folly,' Dorothy had snapped, 'and bring the rest of us down with you. This is treason, Thomas! Even if it does not get as far as all-out warfare, you could lose your head over it.'

'It is not treason to support the rightful King!' Thomas had turned puce with fury. 'Prince James's father was anointed by God! No man can put that divine right aside and all men – and women – have a duty to overturn his usurpation.' He had brought his face very close to hers; Dorothy could see how bloodshot were his eyes and the tracery of broken veins beneath his skin that she suspected were a sign of his excessive drinking. He smelled of spirits, even though it was barely past noon. 'You should have a care, sister,' he had spat out. 'Derwentwater told me that you had no allegiance to our cause. Perhaps I should take you with me and lock you up at Adderstone until King James is safely on the throne? We cannot afford to leave spies and turncoats on the loose.'

Dorothy had itched to slap his face, but for her father's sake she knew she had to remain calm. 'I told Derwentwater that I would never betray you,' she had said, her voice shaking with suppressed anger, 'and it ill becomes you to threaten me, Thomas. All that concerns me is your safety and that of our family.' She had straightened. 'I know father feels the same. He has told me so.'

Thomas had laughed harshly. 'Father! He is old and weak and counts for nothing. He tried to forbid me to fight, as though he has the authority to censure my actions!' He had turned on his heel, heading for the door. 'Well, you may both rot, for all I care. When King James is on the throne, then we shall have a reckoning.' He had left, shouting angrily for the groom to bring his horse around, and although Dorothy knew Nicholas had heard and had been shaken by the argument, she also suspected it would not influence him against his brother.

'I am surprised that horse can bear the weight of Master Thomas and his self-importance,' Mrs Selden had said sourly as Thomas had ridden off. She shook her head. ''Tis fortunate that at least one member of the family possesses the common sense he lacks.' She gave Nicholas a hard stare. 'You listen to your sister, young man, instead of letting your head be filled with all that nonsense about fighting for noble causes. And remember there would be no porridge for breakfast on campaign, only maggoty biscuits, and only those if you are lucky.'

Nicholas's face had crumpled in disgust, but neither the threat of starvation nor the pleas of his father and sister had proved strong enough to change his mind. He had bided his time, but that morning he had disappeared. Dorothy had tracked him easily enough to Adderstone Manor as Nicholas had no idea how to be covert, but now he was inside and the house was silent and still again.

Dorothy felt her stomach churn at the thought of the dangerous games her brothers were playing. She knew Thomas would scarcely be delighted to see her on his doorstep – he would probably accuse her of spying – and she was at a loss to know how to compel Nicholas to come home if he had decided to throw in his lot with the rebels. Still, she knew she had to try. She had promised their father.

Creeping forward through the grass, Dorothy edged towards the steps that led down to the basement. The wood store, the wine cellar and the gun room had all been there amidst a maze of servants' corridors and passages. This had been the ideal place for the games of hide-and-seek they had played as children. But these were not games.

She peered into the barred and cobwebbed windows but

could see nothing. The place looked deserted. She wondered whether the government spies were also aware that this was Thomas's hiding place. Despite the heat of the day, an icy trickle of fear crept down her spine.

'And who might you be, pretty maid?' The muzzle of a pistol pressed against the side of her neck and she felt a man's arms go about her, pulling her back hard against his body. He was short and fat, but there was strength in his grip. She could smell the sweat on him mingling with the scent of leather and glue; it stuck in her throat and made her want to retch. It also identified him to her as Nat Pether, the village cordwainer. Was he a Jacobite, guarding the house, or was he a government spy? How could she get away? The thoughts tumbled over themselves in her mind as she felt his grip tighten and the pistol press deeper.

Ever since her father had told her about the Rose, she had been far more aware of the pendant and its supposed powers, and today, before she had set off for Adderstone, she had taken it off and put it in her jewellery case, reasoning that she did not want to risk losing it. Damnation, she thought. She could really have done with its protection now.

She took a breath and spoke in her most regal tones. 'If that is the pistol my brother took from Bamburgh Hall this morning, Mr Pether, you will find that it will not work. The mechanism is broken.'

She felt Nat Pether recoil with surprise, biting off a curse. He let her go.

'Mistress Forster!' He was stammering as she turned to face him, his round face redder than the evening sun. 'I apologise, ma'am. I had no notion—'

'That I would be making one of my visits to the old manor garden to cut flowers for my father,' Dorothy finished smoothly for him. 'Of course not. Just as I was not aware that you would be here, Mr Pether.'

The cordwainer looked so at a loss and Dorothy felt a little sorry for him.

'However,' she added, 'it will be as forgotten as soon as I walk back through the gate. Good day to you, Mr Pether.' And she made her escape before the cordwainer could notice that she had cut no flowers at all.

A distant rumble of thunder and the fall of the first fat drops of rain reminded her that a storm was on the way. She hurried to the ruined gate in the garden wall, pushing her way through the entwined stems of rose, honeysuckle and bramble, feeling her skirts rip and cursing beneath her breath.

By the time she reached the path that led back to the road, she could feel the sweat running between her shoulder blades and her gown sticking to her, along with various grass seeds that had worked their way between material and skin and were very itchy. They only served to add to her bad humour, which, combined with the relief of escaping from Nat Pether, made her feel strangely shaky and light-headed.

Approaching the barn where she had left Garnet, her mare, tied up with a pile of hay and a bucket of water, she heard the horse whinnying, the sound she made when she recognised someone she knew.

Dorothy froze. Out here, with the open fields around her, she felt suddenly conspicuous and her panic returned. It had been foolish of her to imagine Pether had been on his own. There could be any number of men – rebels or soldiers – all around her.

She pressed herself against the rough, sun-warmed stone of the barn and peered cautiously around the door. All she could see was Garnet's tail swishing contentedly as the mare nuzzled up to someone whose voice was a low rumble and whose long shadow lay across the stone floor.

'Where's your mistress, then, girl? What is she doing leaving a beautiful mare like you all alone?'

Dorothy's panic melted away. 'She is not alone,' she said, stepping through the doorway. 'Good afternoon, Mr Armstrong. What are *you* doing here?'

If John Armstrong was surprised by her sudden appearance, he gave no sign of it. He continued to stroke the white star on Garnet's forehead and the mare, whickering a greeting to Dorothy, continued to nudge his pocket for another treat. Dorothy felt slightly de trop.

'You need not fear that I had any plans for horse-stealing,' Armstrong said with a smile. 'My ancestors gave that up a century ago.' He straightened, giving Garnet a final pat. 'Not that she is not worthy of it, for she is a beautiful horse. But I was heading back from Bellshill, having taken Farmer Edward's cob back for him, when I heard her calling to me.'

'She recognised you,' Dorothy said.

'Aye, they all do,' Armstrong agreed. He looked thoughtfully at her. 'And you, Mistress Forster – where have you been?'

It was perhaps an impertinent question, but Dorothy thought she would appear even more suspicious if she stood on her dignity and refused to answer. 'I've been visiting Adderstone Manor,' she said.

'I see.' Armstrong's tone was completely expressionless.

'I like to return every so often,' Dorothy hurried on. 'The place holds many memories for me.'

'Of course.' Armstrong's gaze was sweeping over her, taking in the dishevelled hair, the torn gown, the grass stains and the seeds clinging to her skirts. 'It seems you particularly enjoy the gardens,' he said. He reached out and plucked some rose petals from her hair, allowing them to float from his fingers down onto the floor.

For some reason, the gesture disturbed Dorothy, who felt even hotter than she had in the full sun.

'What's that?' Armstrong's voice sharpened suddenly. He was staring at her neck, where Pether had dug the muzzle of the pistol into the soft skin. Dorothy touched the spot. It felt sore and she wondered if there was a bruise forming.

'I tripped...' She started to say, but the words withered under Armstrong's glare.

'Onto the muzzle of a pistol?' he enquired silkily. 'That would require some acrobatic skill.'

'I might have known you would be sarcastic,' Dorothy complained. She put her hands on her hips. 'Very well, if you must have the truth, I suspect that Thomas is using the manor to store arms and as a secret Jacobite meeting place. I followed Nick here and was trying to ascertain if was in the house when I—' She stopped. Armstrong's expression had hardened into something akin to murderous rage.

'You fell foul of the rebels and someone assaulted you,' he said, the very softness of his tone more dangerous than any full-blown anger. 'Tell me the name of him and I shall ensure he understands his mistake.'

'No.' Dorothy met his furious gaze directly. 'It was a misunderstanding. I took no hurt other than a slight bruise.'

Armstrong searched her face and she felt herself holding her breath and the anger and tension she could feel within him.

Garnet also sensed the atmosphere and shifted, her hooves clattering on the earthen floor. Immediately, Armstrong reached out to soothe her and the moment was broken.

'As you wish,' he said.

'Thank you.' Dorothy felt shaken, though she was not entirely sure why. She busied herself unhooking Garnet's reins from the manger and fastening the buckles on her saddle. 'I need to get home,' she said over her shoulder. 'We are dining at the castle this evening.'

'I'll walk with you,' Armstrong said. 'Unless you plan to gallop back to Bamburgh to avoid the rain?'

'Garnet would like that,' Dorothy admitted, leading the horse out onto the track, 'but I suppose I should be more decorous.' She felt better out of the close confines of the barn with its shadows and strong emotions. It felt as though something had shifted between them, but she was not sure what.

The hint of a smile touched the corner of Armstrong's mouth. 'Miss Forster, you may well not have seen a mirror for a while, so I feel I should tell you that you already look most *in*decorous.'

Dorothy scrubbed the grass self-consciously from her skirts and only succeeded in smearing the mud on her hem.

'You will need a brush for that,' Armstrong said. 'And the attentions of a maid for your hair.' He offered her a leg up into the saddle. 'Forgive my familiarity,' he added, 'but I felt it better to warn you in case someone sees you on the way back.'

Dorothy's mind flashed back to their last meeting when, once again, she had been very indecorously clad in only her nightgown and a shawl. Why was she always at a disadvantage with this man? It was annoying. She crammed her bonnet down to cover the worst of her unkempt curls and keep off the rain as best she could.

'Thank you for your concern, Mr Armstrong,' she said crisply.

'And, on reflection,' Armstrong added, 'it would be better were we not to return to Bamburgh together. People might draw inappropriate conclusions.'

The colour flamed into Dorothy's face at the implication of his words. Meeting in a barn in the middle of nowhere, riding home in a state of disarray... Oh yes, people might well suppose all manner of scandalous things about them, things that she found she did not object to as much as she ought...

'I will bid you good day then, Mr Armstrong,' she said, and kicked Garnet to a canter and then a gallop across the field, the rain in her face and the bonnet flying off after only a few paces. She looked back once and saw that Armstrong was standing where she had left him, his figure growing smaller with every stride Garnet took away from him.

The gallop was exhilarating and she arrived back at Bamburgh Hall in a far better mood than she had set out, even if it took over a half-hour to remove the tangles from her hair once she was home.

Later that day, the carriage from Bamburgh Hall laboured up the track to the castle, passed beneath the ruined gatehouse and drew up outside the entrance to the Keep. Dorothy would have been quite happy to have walked from home, for it took no more than ten minutes and the thunderstorm earlier that afternoon had blown over, leaving a fresher evening. However, her cousin, Mrs Danson, would not hear of it. A formal dinner invitation required a formal response and that meant the carriage had to be readied and brought round. Mrs Danson boarded it with a great deal of ceremony, and they drove for five minutes so that she could descend with equal fuss and fanfare.

Now, as a uniformed footman opened the door and waited to hand the ladies down, Dorothy sat back to allow Mrs Danson to descend first. Strictly speaking, she should have taken precedence as Lord Crewe's niece, but such small courtesies mattered to Maria Danson much more than they did to her.

Mrs Danson alighted in a fluster of skirts and scurried towards the lighted doorway as though the fresh air on the top of the crag might kill her. 'Come in, Dorothy, come in,' she called, 'before the wind perishes your lungs.'

Dorothy, however, took a moment to look around before she followed Mrs Danson inside. As usual, she was aware of the unease she always had on visiting the castle. There was a familiarity about it, but it was tinged with a dislike she could never quite explain. Perhaps it was that the building itself was simply too overpowering. It felt both primitive and dominant. Even now, when Lord Crewe had undertaken such modern repairs to much of the structure, it was still a grim monument rather than a home. However, she could understand why her uncle liked it – there had seldom been a more obvious statement of power and authority than Bamburgh Castle, and Lord Crewe was a man who relished demonstrating his importance.

It was the beginning of September and the evenings were shortening, summer almost gone. Lord and Lady Crewe always kept town hours, even though they were in the depths of the country, so dinner was later than Dorothy was accustomed to and she was hungry. It would not do to show any unladylike eagerness to get to the food, however. Lord Crewe would want to hold forth first over a glass of wine, treating them all to his views on everything from the price of corn to the state of the roads. Dorothy pressed a hand against her stomach and hoped it would not rumble too loudly.

Lord and Lady Crewe were awaiting them in the drawing room, Lord Crewe standing by the fireplace, hands behind his back, and his wife ensconced in an armchair, a rug over her lap. In the lamplit chambers inside the castle, it felt warm and cosy, in contrast to the Great Hall, where they would eat later.

Dorothy followed Mrs Danson into the room, almost tripping

over her cousin when she stopped just inside the doorway to curtsy fulsomely to Lord Crewe. The baron greeted her warmly, but his hearty tone cooled immediately as he turned to Dorothy.

'How do you do, niece?' he asked. 'I trust that you are well?' His tone suggested that it would please him more if she admitted to some sort of ailment. Dorothy suspected he would view it as a righteous judgement on her for refusing Mr Railton's marriage proposal, for which he had still not forgiven her.

'I am very well, thank you, Uncle,' she said. 'In fact, I am in very fine fettle.' She saw the lines around Lord Crewe's eyes tighten with irritation and Lady Crewe, sensitive to her husband's mood, fluttered her hands a little as though in distress.

'Are you sure, Dorothy dear?' she said. 'You are looking a little flushed, as though you have a touch of fever.'

Dorothy had indeed caught the sun during her afternoon lying in the grass at Adderstone Manor, but she was hardly going to admit to it. In fact, she had already resolved not to mention her elder brother at all that evening. Nothing that Thomas did could ever incur Lord Crewe's approval, particularly not now there were so many rumours swirling about his part in a potential rebellion. Their uncle, who had in his younger days been rather too close an advisor to King James II, the Pretender's father, was extremely sensitive to any suggestion of disloyalty. He had worked hard to regain royal favour and patronage, and anything that threatened that would likely make him apoplectic with rage. It was most certainly not a topic for a dinner conversation.

Fortunately, Mrs Danson unwittingly came to Dorothy's aid by hurrying over to kiss Lady Crewe and exclaim loudly over her russet silk gown.

'It is *so* becoming on you, my lady, and so *very* stylish!'

Lady Crewe, easily distracted, fell to talking about the

comparative merits of silk and damask, and the latest order she had placed with her London dressmaker.

'I am very hopeful that the package will arrive before the autumn is too far advanced,' she was saying, 'for then I shall surely need more new clothes!'

Dorothy, who had been covertly studying her aunt, was shocked by her appearance. It was little over a week since she had last seen her, yet she appeared to have declined in only that short time. The russet gown hung on Lady Crewe's frame and she looked pale and tired, all colour and life drained from her. Although over twenty years younger than her husband, she was a shadow beside his robust presence.

'How are you, dear Aunt Doll?' Dorothy whispered to her as she bent to kiss her aunt's papery-thin cheek.

Lady Crewe grasped Dorothy's hands tightly, her blue eyes intent on her face. 'I am very ill indeed,' she said pitifully. 'I was hoping that your father would be here this evening so that we might compare symptoms.'

This, Dorothy knew, would have entailed Lady Crewe rehearsing her own ailments in great detail whilst Sir William merely nodded in acknowledgement.

'Papa sends his apologies,' she said. 'I am sure he would have enjoyed that, but alas, he has taken something of an ague in the last couple of days. If you have any ginger jelly you could spare for him, he would be most grateful, for, as you know, it is sovereign against a chill.'

'Of course!' Lady Crewe's face lit up at the news of Sir William's illness. 'I shall send for some directly.'

'And your brothers?' Lord Crewe's voice was still loaded with disapproval. 'I note that neither of them has graced us with their presence this evening, nor has Thomas called to pay his respects since his return to Northumberland.'

Dorothy's heart sank. She had hoped her uncle would let that topic lie.

'Nicholas is studying,' she lied. 'He works very hard and seldom leaves his chamber, which I know you must approve of, sir, being so great a scholar yourself.'

Lord Crewe was not immune to such outrageous flattery and softened a little, although not enough to forgive. 'He should not allow his scholarly diligence to override good manners,' he opined. 'We would have been glad to have seen him tonight. As for Thomas—'

'I have not seen him for the past three weeks,' Dorothy said hastily. 'I believe he may be attending to business matters in Newcastle.'

'I heard otherwise,' Lord Crewe stated ominously. 'There are disturbing rumours of his involvement in quite a different matter, a *Scottish* affair. Why else would he leave London when the parliament was sitting?'

'I am afraid that I do not know.' Dorothy gratefully accepted the glass of wine proffered by the butler and took a fortifying gulp. 'You know how unconscionably bad Thomas is at keeping in touch with his family, sir. None of us have the slightest idea as to where he is.' She was glad that despite his suspicions, Lord Crewe had not come out and accused Thomas directly of treason, whether out of discretion or a lack of certainty. Thomas did not deserve her to lie for him, but blood was thicker than water and she still hoped that somehow the disaster of rebellion might be averted.

'I do indeed know what your brother is like.' Lord Crewe was rocking back and forth on his heels, his face set in grim lines. 'Tell him to cease his actions immediately. Tell him I am most displeased with him.'

'I cannot tell him anything, my lord,' Dorothy said staunchly.

'We are not in communication.' She took another mouthful of wine and realised she had already almost emptied her glass. At this rate, she would have drunk an entire bottle before dinner commenced.

'I should warn you that we have guests tonight.' Her uncle evidently was torn between suspecting and believing her and was annoyed that he did not know which way to jump. 'It is important for me to show that I am loyal to His Majesty King George,' he continued, 'so I have invited the son of an old college friend of mine to dine here, along with some of his colleagues. He is a colonel in the Duke of Argyll's forces and I wish there to be no suggestion of any family discord.'

'I hear you perfectly, Uncle.' Dorothy met his gaze directly. 'There is no conflict. All I care about is protecting my father's health and Nicholas' future.'

'Good.' Lord Crewe looked satisfied. 'Then I foresee no difficulty.'

The faint ring of the bell echoed through the castle, followed by the sonorous footsteps of the butler.

'Colonel Lestrange, my lord,' he announced, 'Major Henley and Major Lang.'

Mrs Danson gave a squeak of intense excitement at the sight of so many soldiers in the drawing room. 'Redcoats!' She clasped her hands together in ecstasy. 'What a treat!'

'Lestrange, may I present my wife Lady Crewe, my niece Mistress Forster and our dear cousin, Mrs Danson?' Suddenly, Lord Crewe was the genial host, his ill temper swept away.

There was a flurry of bows, curtsies and greetings. Colonel Lestrange, a man of about five and forty, with dark hair greying at his temples and a rugged, high-coloured complexion, was bowing over Lady Crewe's hand: 'Pray do not get up, ma'am... We have no wish to incommode you and are only grateful for your kindness in inviting us this evening. Ladies...' He bowed to Mrs Danson and then to Dorothy. 'We have been quite starved of polite company at Berwick and are delighted to make your acquaintance.'

Whilst Mrs Danson preened and smiled, Dorothy watched the effect that Bamburgh Castle was having on the colonel and his younger officers. Seeing through their eyes, Dorothy noticed again the rich opulence of their surroundings, the highly polished furniture, the sparkling silver, the tapestries and bright carpets that all attested to Lord Crewe's wealth, taste and desire to be seen as an influential man.

Major Henley, whose dark and watchful gaze gave very little away, was smoothing his uniform with a slight nervous gesture as though he was over-awed. Major Lang, in contrast, looked as openly delighted as the colonel had proclaimed they all were. A dashing young man with windswept brown hair and bright blue eyes, he took the chair beside Dorothy and crossed his legs with an elegant flourish. Major Henley obeyed the order implied in the infinitesimal tilt of his colonel's head and moved over to engage Mrs Danson in conversation. It was all very smoothly done.

A shiver tiptoed down Dorothy's spine. There was more to this evening than a social visit. She was certain of it. Lord Crewe had implied that he had invited the men to dine, but perhaps Colonel Lestrange, aware of her uncle's previous Stuart sympathies, had also been despatched by the authorities to sound out the situation at Bamburgh and ensure that he remained loyal. She had not missed the flicker of awareness in Lestrange's eyes when her name had been mentioned either. He must know that Thomas was involved with the rebels. They were all walking on eggshells.

Major Lang claimed her attention. 'I say, ma'am, what

extraordinary good luck to find myself escorting you. I thought this dinner might prove more a dull duty than a pleasure, but I am richly rewarded for my attendance.'

His admiring gaze was fixed on her face, but there was something in his eyes that made her feel cold, something both calculating and acquisitive. She did not trust him an inch, although she tried to keep a friendly smile on her face.

'I would wait a little while before you make any judgements, Major,' she said drily. 'The dinner may be inedible or the company more tedious than you imagine.'

'Impossible!' Major Lang declared. 'I am enchanted already. Those who say that the North is a barbarous place have no notion of what they are missing.'

The butler announced dinner, sparing Dorothy the need to reply. Clearly, Major Lang intended to flirt with her and imagined she would be receptive, but she had met many charming men in her time and was no more susceptible to this one than to any of the others. Nevertheless, she took his proffered arm and they followed the others into the great hall, the colonel escorting Lady Crewe, and Mrs Danson hanging off Major Henley's arm, apparently already on excellent terms with him. This was not too difficult, Dorothy observed, for Henley said little and listened attentively, and that was all Mrs Danson needed as she chattered away about the dismal weather and the lack of polite company in so out-of-the-way place as Bamburgh.

'When my dear husband was alive, we spent a great deal of time in London and at Windsor,' she was saying. 'Alas, that the towns and cities of the North cannot in any way compare.'

'York and Durham are very fine,' Lord Crewe corrected her. 'Almost as elegant as the capital.'

'Oh, of course,' Mrs Danson agreed readily, 'easily as fine, especially your own See of Durham, my lord.'

Lord Crewe preened himself and Dorothy hid a smile. It was very difficult to imagine her uncle as a man of the Church sometimes. There was something very worldly about him. But perhaps it was naïve of her to imagine that bishops would be any less ambitious than other men.

Sometimes when it was only family, they ate in the small dining room – another of the chambers that Lord Crewe had had restored within the shell of the old medieval castle. Tonight, however, he was intent on showing off Bamburgh's grandeur and so the huge old hall had been lit with a hundred or more candles, the long oak table polished and a fire set in the grate. It made no difference to the chill. Dorothy could see the brightly coloured tapestries that lined the walls rippling in the draughts that scoured the room. She wished she had worn a warmer gown and a thicker shawl, although the high neck she had chosen to hide her bruises was at least some compensation.

'Here is barbarism for you, Major Lang,' she said, as he held her chair for her. 'A huge barn of a place, unfit for modern habitation.'

Lang laughed heartily. 'It is most imposing. A splendid tribute to your ancestors, Mistress Forster.'

'Oh, the Forsters have only held Bamburgh for a hundred years,' Dorothy said lightly. 'It was granted to my ancestor Claudius Forster in 1610. The castle is too grim and bare to suit a modern way of life, I feel, although I concede that my uncle and aunt have repaired it as elegantly as is possible.'

'You are sparing in your praise.' Lang took the seat beside her. 'For my part, I think it quite beautiful, and a splendid fortress into the bargain.'

'I doubt that the castle would be much use as a fortress any more,' Dorothy said. 'Arriving in the dark as you did, sir, you would miss the ruined walls and tumbledown turrets. It is no more than a shell, a monument to past glories which...' She paused. 'I'll allow were very glorious indeed.'

'It certainly has a grand air to it.' Major Lang was admiring the polished glasses and shining silver. 'Your uncle must be a rich man indeed – or adept at giving that impression.' He smiled at her. 'Lord and Lady Crewe have no children, I believe?'

'Sadly not,' Dorothy said. 'It is a great pity.' It was easy enough to follow the train of the major's thoughts, since almost every man she had ever met had seen her as a potential heiress.

He smiled at her. 'And now I see you are thinking me either tactlessly outspoken or a fortune hunter.'

'Or both,' Dorothy said sweetly, and he gave a crack of laughter.

'I doubt any fortune hunter would get the better of you, Miss Forster.'

'I hope not.' Dorothy smiled at the footman as he placed her potted lobster before her. 'Thank you.'

There was a short silence as everyone settled down to eat. The length of the table made conversation between members of the party difficult since there were acres of oak between them all, but Dorothy could see that Colonel Lestrange was as deep in conversation with Lord Crewe as one could be at such a distance, whilst Major Henley appeared engrossed in whatever Mrs Danson was saying. Only Lady Crewe, at the far end of the table, seemed dispirited and quiet, eating little and saying less.

'I have been making a new cambric nightshirt for Papa to wear this autumn,' Dorothy said to her, more to draw her aunt into the conversation than out of a desire to talk about men's undergarments. 'I wonder if you could advise me on the ribbons for the sleeves and the pattern for the embroidery? I thought lace would be too fine, but some bands for the collar, perhaps?'

'A half-shirt would be better,' Lady Crewe said, nodding to the footmen to remove the dishes, 'for that allows the air to circulate more. A long shirt will be too restrictive and may lead to bad humours.' She lapsed into silence, staring at the hash of lamb that had replaced the potted lobster but showing no sign of wishing to eat it.

'Have you seen Lady Belford recently?' Dorothy ventured. Usually, it was Mrs Danson's role to keep Lady Crewe's spirits up – a task at which she was eminently more skilled than Dorothy knew herself to be. Mrs Danson, though, was having far too entertaining a time with Major Henley to spare a thought for Lady Crewe. Dorothy could see her talking animatedly and waving her fork around in emphasis.

'She has the consumption,' Lady Crewe said. 'It may be contagious, so I have stayed away from her.'

The conversation lapsed. A salmagundi followed the lamb, and then a huge, stuffed fowl accompanied by artichokes. The butler had evidently been told to be liberal with the wine and Lord Crewe's face became flushed and his voice louder as he held forth about the fecklessness of the younger generation.

'Where were you stationed before you came to Berwick, Major Lang?' Dorothy asked.

'I was in Ireland, ma'am,' the major replied. He gave her an easy smile as he speared a piece of beetroot. 'I have made something of a career of hunting Jacobites.'

Dorothy managed to keep her expression bland and her voice equally steady. 'I see,' she said. She was not going to pretend that she was stupid or ill-informed. 'I presume that is why you are now in this area? Because of the threat from the Scots?'

'You presume correctly.' For the first time, there was a note of grimness in Lang's voice. 'Although, sadly, the threat is not from the Scots alone. Plenty of the English – and Irish – support the Stuart pretender. That was one reason why I was most curious to see Bamburgh.' He looked around the hall again. 'There are strong rumours of an uprising here in the north of England and a place like this might be a useful base for rebels to provision.'

'Then you will have been reassured to know that it is largely in ruins,' Dorothy said. 'But you also overlook the most important point, Major Lang.' Her voice strengthened as she glanced down the table towards Lord Crewe at the head. 'My uncle would never permit any treason here. His allegiance is, and always has been, to King George.'

Lang took a breath. 'That is what we have been told,' he said. He leaned closer and lowered his voice. 'Yet some loyalties are older than others and there was a time when Lord Crewe was high in King James's favour.'

Dorothy put her glass down with a quiet snap. 'That was over twenty years ago! My uncle was also held in high esteem by the late Queen Anne and has always shown loyalty to King George.' She moderated her voice. She did not wish her uncle to overhear the conversation or, even worse, Lady Crewe. She would likely have the hysterics at any confirmation that her husband was under suspicion. 'It seems uncharitable to take a gentleman's hospitality and speak ill of him at his table,' she said sharply.

Major Lang did not look particularly abashed. 'Forgive me,' he said, 'but I was only trying to sound a note of caution. We have heard that there are other Jacobite sympathisers in your family, ma'am – it is little surprise, then, that the authorities are suspicious.'

Dorothy knew he was referring to Thomas. It was precisely as Lord Crewe had feared; the entire family was under surveillance as a result of her brother's ill-advised adherence to the Pretender's cause.

'I seem to have silenced you, ma'am.' Lang sounded slightly mocking. 'Surely you are aware that Oxford has for many years been a centre of Jacobite activity? Your brother Nicholas has in the past year been implicated in plenty of the disorder in the town stemming from the misplaced Jacobite sympathies of some college men and citizens.'

Dorothy was still thinking about Thomas and it took her a moment for Lang's words to register. Then she realised he had referred to Nicholas, not to Thomas, and the shock hit her in the chest, stealing her breath. It had never once occurred to her that Nicholas might already have been embroiled in Jacobite plotting whilst he was at college. Yet she had known that Oxford had always been staunchly for the Stuarts because her uncle had been Bishop of Oxford before he was Bishop of Durham, and the city was firmly against King George.

She felt cold with fear. Why had she not paid more attention to the other, more political lessons Nicholas had been learning alongside his studies of the Classics? Yet even had she done so, what action could she have taken? Their father was the only one who might have had the authority to make both his sons see sense, but now it was too late and there was nothing Sir William could do.

The roasted fowl had lost its appeal. Dorothy pressed her napkin to her lips and laid it down carefully. 'Young men always seem drawn to such matters if it provides an opportunity for them to get drunk and have a fight,' she said as casually as she could. 'I shall speak to my father. He will surely forbid Nicholas any further involvement. But I thank you for the warning, Major Lang. I did not know.'

Lang was watching her, eyes narrowed intently. 'I can see that you care deeply for your younger brother, Mistress Forster. I pray he may be brought to see sense.' He made no mention of Thomas, which to Dorothy seemed more sinister than if he had.

And even as she thought about Thomas, she heard Maria Danson speaking animatedly to Major Henley.

'Mr Forster is a very talented man, of course, a dedicated member of the parliament and with so many business interests in these parts as well. We see him so rarely, Major, for he is far too occupied with great matters of state to spare any time for his womenfolk!'

Dorothy did not hear the major's response, but the chill in her blood seemed to intensify. It could be no coincidence that Henley was quizzing Mrs Danson about Thomas whilst his colleague Lang was speaking to her about Nicholas. Lang had heard the exchange too and there was a spark of amusement in his eyes at Dorothy's discomfort. The only saving grace, Dorothy thought, was that Maria Danson knew nothing of either Thomas's or Nicholas's exploits, for she had spent the greatest part of the previous three weeks at the castle with Lady Crewe.

'May I offer you some of the rose custard?' Major Lang gestured to the desserts that the footmen had brought to the table: tarts, bread and butter pudding and marchpane. Normally, Dorothy would have enjoyed any and all of them, but now the thought of eating sweetmeats curdled her stomach.

'No, I thank you,' she said curtly, and the conversation waned until Lady Crewe stood up to indicate that it was time to withdraw to leave the gentlemen to their wine and tobacco.

Dorothy leapt to her feet with relief, only to stop, frozen in her place, as a thundering knock at the castle door echoed through the depths of the hall. All conversation ceased in that moment and, to Dorothy, they looked like a tableau preserved in time: Lady Crewe a mannequin with a hand to her throat, her expression one of fear; Mrs Danson, with curiosity writ large on her face and her mouth in its habitual 'O' of excitement; Lord Crewe and the colonel cut off mid-sentence; and the other two military men suddenly wary and alert. Major Henley's hand was on his sword and he had already half-risen from the table.

Neverson, the butler, was not a man to be either hurried or thrown into confusion. His steady tread could be heard a moment before he opened the door to the hall and announced, 'A messenger for Colonel Lestrange, my lord.'

The poor horseman, who, Dorothy thought, looked as though he could do with a moment to draw breath, was thrust into the candlelight. Mud mired his boots and cloak and he was sweating profusely. He pulled off his gloves.

'Your pardon, my lord...' He gave Lord Crewe a jerky bow. 'But I have news of the utmost urgency for the colonel.'

He took a letter from inside his jacket and handed it to the colonel, who ripped it open, scattering the wax of the seal across the highly polished oak dining table. He read the contents swiftly.

'Your pardon, my lord.' He echoed the words of the messenger. 'I fear our delightful evening must come to a premature end. The Duke of Argyll sends to inform me that the Earl of Mar has raised the Jacobite standard at Braemar and his army is marching on Inverness. Ladies—' he sketched a bow to Lady Crewe '—you must excuse us.'

Lady Crewe's knuckles were white as she held her shawl tightly about her neck. She swayed and Dorothy hurried over to her, slipping an arm about her waist to support her.

Mrs Danson, in contrast, seemed quite overexcited to be part of such a dramatic moment. 'Of course you must march to save our country from these blackguards!' She pressed her hands together theatrically as the officers' cloaks were brought and the order sent for the horses to be readied. 'Godspeed you, gentlemen!'

Major Lang turned to Dorothy. 'I shall hope to see you again in better times, Mistress Forster.'

Dorothy was hoping never to see him again, but she gave him a short nod. 'Take care, Major Lang.' She could tell that the prospect of action was stimulating to him. The Jacobite hunter had work to do and he relished it.

In the ensuing silence, Lady Crewe collapsed into her chair like a melted candle. 'Oh, my dear—' she looked at her husband '—what will happen now?'

'Mar is no soldier,' Lord Crewe opined. 'The Highlands may rise with him, but the government will soon crush his foolish plans.'

'But if the Pretender invades with foreign troops, there could be war.' Lady Crewe was fretting, her hands visibly shaking. Dorothy could see the shudders that racked her frail body. 'The rebels may advance over the Scottish border and we will all be murdered in our beds! We must abandon Bamburgh and move south, where it is safer. Oh, I cannot bear to be turned from my home like this...' She looked close to fainting.

'Now, Doll, there is no need for such dramatics. None of that will happen.' Lord Crewe took his wife's hand and patted it awkwardly, whilst Mrs Danson hurried forward with hartshorn.

'I will stay here with Lady Crewe tonight,' she said to Dorothy. 'You should return to the Hall and tell your father the news.'

'I shall not trouble him with this,' Dorothy said firmly. 'You know he has no interest nor involvement in politics these days and it would only serve to disturb him. Besides, as my uncle says, nothing may come of it.'

Lord Crewe looked smug, but Mrs Danson's gaze snapped with sudden, startling venom. 'Then perhaps your time is best spent in warning your brother?' she said with poisonous sweetness. 'I am sure you know where to find him. I hope you are grateful that I dissembled when Major Henley was questioning me just now. We all know about Thomas's suspect loyalties.' She pointed her fan at Dorothy. 'Nor should I be required to cover up for you!'

'Cover up for *me*?' Dorothy took a step back. 'I assure you, Mrs Danson, you have nothing to protect me from.'

'We shall see,' Maria Danson said. 'Consorting with known Jacobites like the Earl of Derwentwater—'

'I have *consorted* with no one!' Dorothy was incensed now. 'What are you suggesting, ma'am?'

'Indeed, you are mistaken, Maria.' Lady Crewe unexpectedly came to Dorothy's support. 'We all know that Lord Derwentwater jilted Dorothy, and that is very fortunate, as it turns out. We all felt sorry for you at the time, Dorothy—' she turned to her niece '—but look now how you are saved the ignominy of marriage to a renegade!'

'Yes, aren't I fortunate,' Dorothy said sarcastically. She gave Maria Danson a sharp look. 'You are correct, ma'am, you will do much better here with Lady Crewe than at Bamburgh Hall.' She dropped a curtsey. 'I shall call tomorrow to see how you fare, Aunt Doll.'

'I expect I shall be very ill indeed.' Lady Crewe leaned heavily on Maria Danson's arm.

'I shall pray you will feel better than you are anticipating,' Dorothy said. 'Sir.' She curtsied again, formally, to Lord Crewe. 'I am sorry our evening has ended this way. Thank you for your hospitality.'

Lord Crewe and Maria Danson were talking softly together, heads bent close, and her uncle barely broke off to wish to Dorothy goodnight. She accepted her cloak from Neverson with a word of thanks and went out onto the carriage sweep. The coach was waiting, lanterns alight, but Dorothy walked over to the battlements for a moment, drawing in a deep breath of the cold sea air. It was full dark and she could see little of the shore below, but she could hear the waves breaking on the beach and catch a faint glimmer of sea foam. Out to sea, on Inner Farne, there was the flare of the beacon on Castell's Tower to warn ships of the dangerous shoals.

The hair on the back of Dorothy's neck prickled suddenly. She had the strongest sensation that she was being watched. She turned to look back at the castle, but the door was closed now and all the windows shuttered. There was no one in sight.

With a shiver, she wrapped the cloak more closely about her and hurried to the security of the carriage. Once the door was closed tightly and the vehicle in motion, she released the breath she had been holding. Soon she would be home. Yet the comfort that gave was illusory. They were all being watched now and the worst of it was, she did not know whom she could trust and whom she could not.

Back at the Hall, she went up to Nicholas's chamber and knocked softly on the door. There was no reply. She had not expected one, but her heart still sank all the same. She pushed open the door and peered inside, just to be sure. The bed was rumpled, papers scattered across the desk, a quill pen leaving a smattering of ink drops on a parchment. Some of Nicholas's clothes were carelessly discarded on a chair and the room smelled of dust and the faint scent of the pomade her brother had recently taken to wearing in another attempt to emulate Thomas. Her heart contracted at the thought; Nicholas, so young, growing up with Thomas as his hero. No doubt what she saw as her elder brother's foolhardiness, Nicholas saw as admirable passion and loyalty to a cause. She shook her head sadly and closed the door, praying that despite everything, by the morning Nicholas would have returned.

5

HANNAH – THE PRESENT

After Diana and Bill had gone off to the hospital, Hannah made herself a sandwich, took Tarka for a walk and tried to settle down to do some work. She felt edgy and unhappy, though whether that was because of Diana's illness or the revelations about Brandon, she wasn't sure. Perhaps it was both. But she had a deadline and she was a professional writer, so she took her laptop and all her books and files to the study and sat down to work. There were authors who could escape into their writing when things were difficult in their personal life. Unfortunately, she was not one of them and the shadow of Diana's diagnosis hung about at the edge of her mind even as she tried resolutely to ignore it.

She'd chosen the study because there was no view to distract her, as there was in the blue bedroom upstairs; here, instead of the golden green lines of Spindlestone Hill and the beach disappearing into shimmering infinity, there was a high wall outside the window. It was a very nice old wall, with pink and golden stone pitted into all sorts of shapes and patterns by the weather and the sun was shining on it and reflecting back into the room, warming the rather austere white walls. Hannah could understand why this was Diana's least favourite room in the house. Somehow it had resisted her attempts to make it either stylish or welcoming and instead was simply functional. That was all Hannah needed, though, and Tarka curled up on the rag rug, giving the place a homely feel.

Hannah was at the point in Grace Darling's life where, following the shipwreck of the *Forfarshire* and her rescue of the survivors, her whole existence had been turned upside down by the unexpected celebrity. The Duke of Northumberland had taken on the role of her self-appointed guardian and founder of a trust fund for Grace and her family, taking care of all the donations and gifts that had rolled in. Hannah was writing, a little wryly, about the irony of the duke making these decisions unilaterally, and giving Grace a watch and silver teapot into the bargain to add to the mountain of gifts she did not know what to do with.

Hannah paused. Having sketched out the rest of the book and written some of the early chapters, she had deliberately skipped to the end of Grace's story because it was the bit that interested her the most, but tomorrow, when she went to the museum, she would focus on the rescue itself and Grace's early life on the Farne Islands. One of a family of nine children, Grace had been educated by her parents on Brownsman Island, and later on the neighbouring Longstone Island, where her father was the lighthouse keeper. Longstone was an inhospitable island, bare and rocky, and Hannah wondered how the children had found it after the relative freedom of growing vegetables and keeping animals on Brownsman. The family had lived mainly in one room and William Darling had been known to disapprove of reading novels or of anything he considered frivolous, although he would sometimes play folk songs on his violin.

Hannah sighed, knowing that if she was to do the job properly, she would need to take a trip out to see Brownsman and

Longstone islands, like she'd told Aaron. Her stomach dipped with nausea simply at the idea of stepping on a boat. Evidently, Grace had had no such problems, since at the age of only eighteen, she had helped her father rescue the passengers of the *Forfarshire*. Grace had held the rowing boat steady in the storm whilst her father had assisted the victims, a truly remarkable feat.

Hannah sighed again, feeling more than a little inadequate in comparison. Her train of thought broken, she gave into temptation and checked her emails. There was a message from Alice with a few suggested dates for the get-together with Sarah at the Lord Crewe Arms. Harry, who was renting her Bristol flat, had confirmed enthusiastically that he was happy to caretake it for as long as she needed and had sent lots of messages from her friends, commiserating over Diana's news and sending love. Hannah smiled a little mistily at all the hug emojis.

She'd sent a message to her Uncle Peter the day before, asking if there was any connection between the Armstrong and Forster families and he had already replied; he and her aunt were on holiday, but as far as he remembered, there had been a Forster/Armstrong marriage in the eighteenth century that could be the link she was looking for. He promised to check the details when he got home. He sent his best wishes to Diana but he didn't mention Brandon.

With mounting excitement, Hannah reached for the Forster family tree that she had bought in the gift shop at the castle. She'd already had a quick look at it, but it was so detailed and complex that she hadn't been able to locate Dorothy Forster immediately. Now she was looking for the Armstrong connection as well. Unrolling the poster from the tube, she spread it across the desk and weighted the corners down. There was a magnifying glass in the top drawer which proved ideal for peering at the spidery handwritten names.

After a couple of moments, she found Dorothy, born in 1686, the daughter of Sir William and Frances, Lady Forster. A sister also called Frances and three brothers, Thomas, Nicholas and John, were listed, although there were no dates next to anyone other than Thomas, suggesting that the other children might have died in infancy. Hannah's heart leapt though as she saw the tiny letter m. next to Dorothy's name, indicating that she had married. The spouse's name, however, was blank.

More in hope than expectation, Hannah typed 'Dorothy Forster marriage' into the search bar on her laptop. The story of Lord and Lady Crewe came up in the results, along with various other Dorothys from genealogy sites, none with the correct dates. Hannah added in the words 'Jacobite heroine' and this time a book appeared: *Dorothy Forster* by Walter Besant, a Victorian historical novel. She downloaded a copy – and forbade herself from starting to read it immediately. She needed to get back to work.

However, one line of the online summary had caught her eye: 'The Forsters were the keepers of the Rose, a legendary golden talisman said to have been forged in the fires of the castle of Joyous Gard itself...'

Hannah raised her eyebrows. This was another Bamburgh myth and one she had not come across before. She remembered all the roses in the paintings of Dorothy both at the castle and Diana's portrait, along with all the other Jacobite symbolism. It was intriguing.

She could not help herself. She put in another search, this time on Jacobite imagery. As she had suspected, all the motifs in Dorothy's portrait were Jacobite emblems. The oak leaf and acorn represented the oak tree that had protected King Charles II from the parliament troops who had been searching for him in 1650.

The sunflower was also a nod to royalty. The butterfly was more sinister, representing the resurrected human soul.

Thoroughly distracted now, Hannah went into the kitchen to make herself a cup of tea. Tarka padded after her, sensing an opportunity to go outside. When Hannah opened the back door, she bounded out and down the steps into the walled garden with a woof of pleasure. Against the sheltered south-facing wall, the pink climbing rose was already starting to flower. A yellow butterfly opened its wings to the sunshine. Roses and butterflies and sunlight sparkling off the old glasses in the cupboard with their engravings of sunflowers and oak leaves... Suddenly Hannah felt as though she was surrounded by Jacobite secrets in a house that she had thought she knew well. Had Dorothy stood here, looking out at this familiar view, or had the design of the house been different in the eighteenth century? She wondered if there were any old drawings of the house in the library. Her father had been an architect so might well have collected some.

Tarka barked twice, sharply, and Hannah looked outside to see that someone was walking along the far side of the wall that separated the gardens from the graveyard of St Aidan's Church. She could only see his neck and the back of his head, and only for a few seconds, but she was certain it was Brandon. She hurried out of the house and over to the iron gate that led through to the graveyard. Tarka was at her heels. Her hand slipped on the latch and then she was through, standing amongst the gravestones, searching left and right for any sight of him.

There was no one there. The breeze blew through the long grass and seagulls called overhead and Hannah could hear the muted hum of traffic from the road fifty yards away. A couple came along the path towards the church door, talking quietly together. They glanced across at Hannah and smiled. She waited, breathing hard as though she had been running. No one else was visible, either in the churchyard or the field to the north-west.

With a sigh, Hannah released her breath and leaned against the stone gateway. She was certain it was Brandon she had seen. You didn't grow up with someone for sixteen years and then not recognise them. Yet where could he have gone? She could see some flattened stalks in the grass, as though someone had passed close to the wall, but a person couldn't simply disappear. Besides, why would Brandon be skulking around the graveyard? Even if he knew Diana wouldn't be rolling out the red carpet for him, he still had no real reason to hide.

Hannah shook her head in frustration. She was getting edgy and seeing things that weren't there. It was only the previous day that Brandon had texted her; it wasn't likely he would have rushed down from Scotland straight away. She was feeling so unsettled at the moment, it would have been easy to mistake a random stranger for her brother.

She called Tarka, who had been snuffling eagerly around in the compost heap, and went back into the walled garden. The incident had left her feeling even more troubled and she hurried inside, shutting the door after them with rather unnecessary firmness. The house was quiet and nothing seemed any different, yet Hannah felt as though the air around her had been disturbed and was humming with an odd energy.

Telling herself that she was imagining things, she went through to the hall. The door of the library was open; she was sure she had left it closed. Something was wrong. The back of her neck prickled with uncomfortable awareness. An instinct she could not ignore told her that something had changed and she needed to be very careful.

She stood on the faded red and blue rug in the centre of the hall and listened. Tarka, beside her, stood still like a sentinel, her head cocked. There was no sound from inside the house and Hannah was fairly certain that if there was an intruder, Tarka would already have sniffed them out, even if she then licked them in enthusiastic welcome. Everything was in place – with the exception of the open door.

Hannah strode across to the study and looked inside. All her papers and books were lying as she had left them, her laptop lid closed. She closed the door and went back out into the hall. Everything was in its appointed place, the Georgian table with its shiny brass handles and white vase full of tulips; the old wooden chair that Diana had reupholstered in a bright red and green William Morris print; the painted chest. On the wall, the huge modern print of Bamburgh Castle in moody grey and green, and above the little side table, the portrait of Dorothy Forster with her sunflowers and butterflies and... Hannah felt her breath catch as though she had missed a step in the dark. There was a picture on the wall above the side table, but it wasn't Dorothy Forster.

She almost tripped over the rug in her rush to cross the room and turn on the lamp so that she could see clearly. She pressed the switch but nothing happened and, looking more closely, Hannah saw that the bulb had been removed.

Using her phone torch, Hannah raised it to the painting. She could see why, under other circumstances, they might not have noticed the substitution immediately. Superficially the paintings were similar, being roughly the same size and shape, both in a gold frame and both featuring a female sitter. But this woman was an indeterminate figure in a dark blue gown with dark hair and a pale blur of a face. There was none of Dorothy's vibrancy or mischief here.

Hannah stared in complete confusion. She tried to remember when she had last looked at Dorothy's portrait, looked properly, rather than glancing over in the direction of it. Had it been that morning before she had gone to the castle, or later, when she had come back for lunch? She could not be sure. She only knew that the previous night, it had been Dorothy's portrait hanging in this corner, not this all together duller picture. And why was the light bulb gone from its socket? That was odd, to say the least.

Hannah turned off her phone torch and stepped back. Perhaps Diana was having the picture cleaned and had swapped it for another one that morning before she had gone out. Or maybe she had simply decided it was time for a change and moved a few items around. It wouldn't be the first time; Hannah vividly remembered the day she had come home from school and thought that she had gone into the wrong house when confronted by a huge sculpture of a mermaid in the hall. Then there was Diana's china dog phase, when at least twelve of the life-sized ornaments had appeared in different rooms...

Oh yes, Diana liked to design and redesign all the time. She said it kept her mind buzzing and her ideas fresh. It was the most likely explanation, and yet, it didn't feel right to Hannah. Diana would surely have told her if there was something planned for Dorothy's picture when she knew that Hannah had been so taken with it and was doing some unofficial research into Dorothy's life.

She ran upstairs, Tarka trotting alongside, to check all the bedrooms, but it wasn't there. Then she came back down and looked in the drawing room, the parlour, and ended in the library where she had started. There was no sign of the painting; whatever the reason, Dorothy Forster had vanished.

* * *

Diana and Bill arrived home an hour and a half after Hannah had noticed the disappearance of the portrait. She had finally forced herself to go back into the study and focus on Grace's biography and so missed the moment when the Land Rover swung into the courtyard and pulled up at the door. Tarka, however, got up to greet them both with anticipatedly wagging tail, and soon Hannah heard Diana's key in the lock and the echo of voices through the hall. She shut her laptop and went through into the kitchen and put the kettle on.

'How did you get on?' she asked.

'Oh, you know...' Diana sounded deliberately vague, she thought. 'They're suggesting another course of radiotherapy soon, but I'm not sure if I want to go through it again. I'll think about it.'

Hannah caught Bill's eye and saw how much this hurt him. He pressed his lips together and shook his head slightly but didn't say anything. Looking at Diana, Hannah could see how utterly exhausted she was, translucently pale and thin. She went over to give her stepmother a gentle hug and resolved not to nag her, no matter how much she wanted Diana to take whatever treatment was on offer.

Diana subsided into her rocking chair with a sigh of relief and slipped off her shoes, accepting the mug of tea gratefully. 'Thank you, darling. The people at the hospital are marvellous, but the tea is truly awful.' Her gaze rested on Hannah. 'How have you got on this afternoon?'

'I've managed to get some words down about Grace,' Hannah said. 'I also noticed that Dorothy Forster's portrait had been moved? Have you sent it for cleaning or something?'

'Dorothy?' Diana looked bewildered for a moment and then her face cleared. 'Oh, the portrait in the hall! Yes, of course. I... Um... Yes, I sent it to Alnwick this morning to the restorer I use. When we were looking at it yesterday, I noticed some damage to the paintwork and I thought I'd better get it repaired before Lizzie comes next week. I don't want her thinking that I'm not taking care of her present.'

'Ah, I wondered,' Hannah said. 'The new picture doesn't have Dorothy's charm, somehow.'

'No, a very ordinary sitter,' Diana agreed. 'But it fills the space.'

'I almost didn't notice,' Hannah added, watching her step-mother covertly as she filled Bill's mug, 'but I was doing a bit of research into Dorothy and wanted to check the details of her gown and the other Jacobite symbols in the picture—'

'Shouldn't you be concentrating on Grace Darling?' Diana cut her off, sounding snappy. She raised a perfect eyebrow, moderating her tone. 'You said yourself that she's the focus of your work here.'

'I... Yes, she is.' Hannah was taken aback. Diana was so seldom sharp with her that it came as a shock, and though it was true that she was there to research Grace, she was old enough to manage her own workload. It also seemed odd that Diana, having encouraged her to find out more about Dorothy's story previously, now seemed reluctant to discuss it. But perhaps it wasn't strange at all. Her stepmother must be exhausted after a stressful and upsetting hospital trip. She certainly wasn't going to snap back at her or tell her that she'd make her own decisions on who to research, thank you. That would be childish and unkind when Diana was so sick.

'Well,' Bill spoke into the slightly awkward silence. 'I need to go out and see to the sheep.' He put his mug down on the table half-full. 'I'll pop by later, Di. You take care now. And make sure you lock the door after me,' he added. 'I know you leave it unlocked half the time and Brandon might turn up at any moment.'

'Oh really, Bill.' Diana now sounded as cross with him as she had with Hannah. 'How you do fuss! I really do think that you believe if the cancer doesn't kill me, Brandon will.'

'Aye, well don't underestimate that wee shite,' Bill said. Unlike Hannah, he wasn't going to hold back. 'Ellen Moxon at the post office told me this morning she'd seen him in the village last night. Like as not she saw nothing of the sort, but you never know.'

'Ellen's a troublemaker—' Diana started to say, but Hannah interrupted her.

'Mrs Moxon saw Brandon?' she demanded. 'Then I might have been right when I thought I saw him this afternoon.'

Both Bill and Diana looked shocked.

Hannah gave them a brief summary of what had happened earlier. 'I could be wrong,' she concluded, 'because there was no sign of him when I went out to check. I wasn't even going to mention it until you—' she looked at Bill '—said he might have been seen.'

'Reet.' Bill was looking furious. 'The wee shite is still playing his silly games then.' The last few words were said with particular venom. 'When I've put the sheep to bed, I'll go and ask around in the village. We'll soon find him.'

'Bill, darling, you can't ban him from the village,' Diana protested, but Bill had gone out, slamming the door behind him. 'I really don't think Brandon is dangerous,' Diana said after a moment. 'Bill exaggerates. But it's true that he was a difficult and disruptive teenager, and we did have a spectacular falling out a few years ago, so I can see why people think he's a bad lot.' She sighed. 'This is probably as good a time as any for me to tell you about the other stuff that went on. Are there any Florentines in that tin on the dresser, darling? I need some chocolate if I'm to tackle this.'

Hannah fetched the box and sat down opposite her. 'Are you

sure you want to talk about this now?' she asked. 'It's been a long day for you and, frankly, you look worn out. Maybe you should have a rest?'

Diana shook her head. 'I'll rest presently, but I need to tell you about Brandon to get it off my mind.'

Hannah nodded. She felt tension coiling in her stomach. She reached for Tarka, relishing the softness of the fur under her fingers and taking comfort from her warmth as the dog leaned into her.

'It started the summer after your father died,' Diana began. She was sitting very upright now, as though she was giving a witness statement in court, Hannah thought. She understood why her stepmother was being so formal; talking about Brandon like this was painful for her and she wanted Hannah to understand it wasn't gossip or idle chat. 'Brandon was never an easy child, at least not for me to deal with.' Diana had knitted her fingers together tightly. 'He was so charming on the surface, but there was – is – a disruptive element to him. He enjoys causing trouble.' She reached out to Hannah and touched her lightly on the arm. 'I'm sorry, darling.'

'It's all right,' Hannah said numbly. 'I know better than anyone what Brandon can be like.' She was remembering the times without number when her brother had hidden her PE kit or stolen her pocket money, little things that could be passed off as jokes or mistakes but that felt like spite. Occasionally, he had gone further, such as the time he had locked her in the cellar and swore that he hadn't realised she was down there. Or when he had put a laxative in her birthday cake. As Hannah had grown older, she had become more capable of challenging Brandon, but she'd known deep down that he would never change. He seemed to thrive on discord.

Diana nodded. 'Yes, you do.' She smiled sadly. 'Your father

knew too, but he was very indulgent of Brandon. Of both of you, really.'

Hannah's memories of her father were of a gentle man who had been a bit absent-minded and otherworldly. He had been very wrapped up in his work but affectionate and generous to his children. It had been Diana who had created order out of the chaos that had followed their mother's desertion and who had ensured that everyone's lives had run smoothly. She had clearly loved Richard Armstrong very much and had taken on two children fearlessly, or so it had seemed to Hannah, with very little experience and even less thanks. Hannah suddenly wanted to hold her tight and never let her go. Instead, she took the cosy off the teapot and topped up their mugs.

'You know that I had my own interior design business,' Diana continued. 'It was how I met your father when I won the contract to redesign his offices.' She smiled. 'For a firm of architects, they had appalling taste. Anyway, I digress.' She added a spoonful of sugar to her tea, stirring thoughtfully. 'As you know, I always was something of a collector – paintings, objects, whatever caught my eye, any era or style that I felt *worked*.'

'You always had the most amazing eye for design,' Hannah agreed, wrapping her hands around her mug. 'Things I wouldn't have put together in a million years, but they looked brilliant. I used to wonder how you knew, because you did, instinctively.'

'It's like any creative talent, I think,' Diana said. 'Your creativity comes out in your writing, Hannah. Mine is more visual.'

'And Brandon's creative talent is for making life difficult for other people,' Hannah remarked. 'What did he do?'

Diana sighed. 'Soon after Richard died, small pieces of my jewellery started to go missing. At first, I thought I had misplaced them, but after the third or fourth piece disappeared, I knew they had been taken, not lost. I knew it was Brandon – I saw him taking a necklace from my jewel box one day – but I hesitated to challenge him because he was so angry and moody about losing his father, which was completely natural. He was hurting. I tried to talk to him, but he always pushed me away. So I waited, hoping the problem might pass. It didn't. It got worse.'

Diana paused, taking a sip of tea. She grimaced. 'I forget that my medication can make tea taste very bitter. I need more sugar.' She stirred in another spoonful. 'Ah, that's better.' She put her mug down with a precise click. 'After the jewellery, he started to take some of the paintings,' she said, 'small ones, including a miniature of my mother and an eighteenth-century portrait that used to hang in the study.' Diana looked up and met Hannah's eyes. 'Everything Brandon chose was something that mattered to me, usually for sentimental reasons. The thefts felt very personal, and calculated to hurt.'

Now it was Hannah's turn to reach out to her. 'I'm so sorry, Diana,' she said. 'That must have been horrible for you.'

'In the end, I caught Brandon trying to take one of the big landscape paintings from the dining room. He was going down to the cellar to hide it, wrapped up in a sack. I challenged him and he was completely brazen about it. He said it would all be his one day and that he was just capitalising on his inheritance ahead of time because he needed it to finance his future. He was very cocky.'

'What did you do?' Hannah felt horrified that she had been unaware of all of this happening at the time, and equally horrified that Brandon had been such an arrogant idiot. They had all been mourning in their different ways, including Diana, whose grief he had clearly not given a toss about.

'I took advice,' Diana said wearily. 'I spoke to the school and, off the record, to the police. I can't be certain, but I think that some other people had had problems with Brandon as well – a few cases of property damage and graffiti...' She shrugged. 'Everyone was kind and tried to shield me because Richard had been dead less than a year. No one wanted to make more trouble. We all attributed it to Brandon reacting to his father's death. The school tried to persuade him to have some counselling, but Brandon wasn't keen. And then things went quiet, and I hoped it was all over.'

'I'm guessing that it wasn't,' Hannah said. Tarka, responding to the tension in her voice, rested her head on Hannah's lap, staring at her sympathetically with her big brown eyes. Hannah smiled and stroked her ears.

'No,' Diana agreed. 'It wasn't over. Brandon went off to study art history and then to work in London, and for a while he would pop in to see me a couple of times a year, and it was...' Her voice caught. She fell silent.

Hannah wondered what she had been going to say. Had everything that had happened before been swept under the carpet and ignored, as though the stealing and the criminal damage had never happened? It would have been the easiest thing to do and she could imagine Diana taking the practical view that since everything was now on an even keel, why rake up the past?

'I last saw Brandon about two years ago,' Diana resumed. 'We had an argument because he tried to persuade me to sell the house and contents and pass the money to the two of you. To avoid inheritance tax, he said.' She met Hannah's eyes. 'He claimed you agreed with him that I should move out, and I told him I didn't believe him. There was an undignified tussle over possession of a china vase and I fell.'

'Oh my God, Diana!' Hannah found she was on her feet. This

was so much worse than she had ever imagined. 'Were you hurt? Did you call the police?'

'Bill said that I should have done,' Diana admitted. 'He found me nursing a badly bruised arm and was absolutely livid. But it was just a row that went too far.' She spread her hands in a gesture of appeal. 'I don't think Brandon meant to hurt me. He was only interested in the Meissen.'

Hannah felt horribly shaken. 'Bloody Brandon,' she said vehemently. 'I'll kill him myself for this. Bill will have to get in line.'

Diana laughed, but it sounded forced. 'Brandon clearly has a problem, whether it's impulsivity or kleptomania. I'm no expert, I can't diagnose, but there has to be a psychological or emotional reason. He needs help.'

'Well, that's a very generous interpretation,' Hannah said. 'It seems to me that he's always been greedy. Or jealous, or both.'

'Don't forget that I raised the two of you from a young age,' Diana pointed out with a sigh. 'I've seen you both grow and change. Brandon was a genuinely sweet child when he was young, but something happened that warped that. Your father's death made it more acute, but by then Brandon was already causing problems.' She yawned widely. 'Sorry. I'm absolutely exhausted.'

'Go and take a nap,' Hannah advised, pushing all her thoughts about her brother to the back of her mind. 'I'll bring supper up for you in a few hours.'

She was rewarded with Diana's warm smile. 'Thank you, darling,' her stepmother said.

Hannah pottered about the kitchen for a while, stacking the used crockery in the dishwasher, tidying the dresser, doing all the things she had done for years and years in the familiarity and comfort of her old home. Her hands moved automatically, whilst her mind struggled with everything that Diana had told her. She itched to call Brandon straight away and confront him, but she realised that her thoughts were in far too much confusion to tackle him at the moment. Maybe later, when Bill had come back with news of whether anyone knew if Brandon really was back in Bamburgh.

But, in a sense, that didn't matter. She simply wanted to talk to her brother, tell him that Diana had told her everything and give him a strongly worded piece of her mind about his behaviour. She also wondered whether Brandon still had a key to Bamburgh Hall. She had given hers back to Diana years before, feeling that it wasn't appropriate to keep it when she had moved out, but knowing Brandon, he would not necessarily have done the same.

'Come on, Tarka,' she said, aware of an ache gripping the back of her neck. 'We both need some fresh air. Let's go to the beach.'

She texted Bill to let him know that Diana was resting and she was going out, and to invite him over for supper later, which he replied to with a thumbs up.

The beach was almost deserted. A few family groups were packing up their deckchairs and buckets and spades. There were the usual dog walkers crossing the windswept sands. Hannah and Tarka walked through the sand dunes at the foot of the castle, heading south towards Seahouses. The marram grass was sharp and whipped at Hannah's legs, but she had always loved the dunes, with their hollows, pools and wild flowers. Tarka, entranced by the different scents, scampered about, with her tail waving enthusiastically. Gradually, the sound of the sea, the fresh breeze and Tarka's unbounded happiness helped Hannah to relax.

They went down onto the beach, where Tarka ran through the shallows chasing her ball and Hannah took out her phone to call Brandon. She was shaking and felt a bit panicky, but she knew that if she didn't talk to him, it would only eat away at her until she did. She had rehearsed what she was going to say to him in her head, something simple to start with, her tone bright and breezy: *'Hi, Brandon. I thought I saw you earlier. Are you in Bamburgh?'* That was probably a better approach that to call him a deranged narcissist who needed to be locked up.

The number rang and rang, whilst Hannah waited, feeling the racing of her heart. It was odd that there was no voicemail option. After counting thirty-two rings, she cancelled the call, feeling a mixture of relief and frustration. She was about to slide the phone into her pocket and head for home when it pinged with a text.

It was from Bill, short and to the point.

> No one else has seen B in the village today.

Hannah sighed, once again feeling a sense of relief. It looked as though both she and Elaine Moxon had been mistaken. With all the talk about Brandon's dramatics over the years, it would be easy to get things out of proportion. What she needed to do now was focus on looking after Diana, get her research done, and if Brandon did turn up, she'd tackle the situation then.

But something else was niggling at her mind, something that she didn't want to think about but knew that she must. She was almost certain that Diana had been lying to her. Not about her fight with Brandon, or even about what he had done as a teenager, but about what had happened since then. There had been more than one occasion when Diana had caught herself and changed what she had been about to say. And her initial reaction when Hannah had asked her about the missing portrait had been odd. It had taken her a moment before she had explained about the restoration, as though she was thinking it through.

Hannah shook her head in exasperation. She didn't want to hassle Diana when she was so ill, and she knew her stepmother well enough to be sure Diana was acting as she was for the best of reasons. But she was not telling Hannah the whole truth, and Hannah was not sure what to do about it. Sleeping on it was probably the best option.

She called Tarka over and they started the walk back to the Hall. It was just after six o'clock and the evening was turning grey, with clouds piling up to the west. The seaward side of the castle was in deep shadow and the air felt chill. Hannah quickened her pace. As they reached the tarmac path that led up past the postern gate, she looked up at the ruined battlements, which sprouted valerian and speedwell and scented wallflowers tumbling over the stones.

A figure was standing beside St Oswald's Gate, the cutting through the rock that had been one of the medieval entrances to the castle but which was now out of bounds behind safety barriers. Hannah assumed it must be one of the castle staff or perhaps an archaeologist, as there was a dig taking place that was exploring the medieval history of the site. As she craned her neck to see, the person raised his arm and waved, a jaunty wave to go with the smile he wore, which even at this distance felt as though it was full of malicious amusement.

'Brandon!' Hannah's voice echoed off the castle walls and bounced back to her, but there was no reply from above, nothing at all, and when she looked again, Brandon's figure had disappeared.

6

DOROTHY – OCTOBER 1715

The interior of the forge was roasting, the air thick and hot. Dorothy stood close to the door, allowing the chill breeze of autumn to take the edge off the searing heat. How John Armstrong was able to work in such a place, especially during the summer months, she had no idea.

She watched him as he worked because there was a fascination in seeing someone do their job so well. His sleeves were rolled up to the elbow and his collar was open. He was fashioning a candlestick with an intricate pattern, a project that was very different from the farriery and agricultural metalwork that made up the main part of his livelihood. She wondered whether the candlestick was a gift for someone. John could and did turn his hand to crafting all manner of items, from the household cutlery that the villagers needed, to parts for carriages. Dorothy realised, with a little shiver of fear, that he would also be good at making armour and weaponry. Soon, he would be much in demand.

She drew her gaze away from him and focused on the neatly swept cobbles of the smithy. She was standing behind the counter where the customers waited, an area that was kept clear of all the dirt and cinders of the forge. And then John was laying aside the candlestick and coming forward, wiping his hands on a cloth. Smears of soot blotted the material.

'Mistress Forster.' He was, as always, formal with her in public. 'Do you have some work for me?'

She had brought a necklace. It had been left to her by her mother and the gold clasp had been damaged a few years past when it had caught on the lace of one of her gowns. Dorothy had never liked it so she hadn't bothered to have it mended, but it served as a pretext for coming to the smithy. Nicholas had been missing for five days now, his room empty, a sheen of dust already lying over his books and papers. The space felt abandoned. Dorothy knew now that he did not intend to come back. He was with Thomas and the Earl of Derwentwater, preparing for a war that he no doubt would see as nothing more than a grand adventure – and she needed help if she were to change his mind.

'Good morning, Mr Armstrong,' she said. 'I need a new clasp for this locket, if you please.'

'It's a pretty thing.' John took it in the palm of his hand and examined it, his fingers delicate on the slender chain. He looked up at her. 'Is it a keepsake?'

Dorothy wondered if he thought it might contain a picture of the Earl. The colour came into her face; she realised that John had noticed the blush and that made her even more irritated.

'It was given to me by my mother,' she said a little stiffly. 'I do not much care for it, but I needed a reason to speak with you.'

'Ah.' Something eased in his manner. Or perhaps she was simply imagining that. He placed the locket on the counter and waited for her to continue.

'You will have heard the news from Scotland.' Dorothy checked that no one else was within earshot before she spoke. Bamburgh had been alive with rumour and feverish speculation about the Jacobite uprising for the last few days, ever since the dramatic end to the dinner party at the castle had sent the redcoats galloping back to their barracks at Berwick.

John nodded. 'I have. The Earl of Mar's forces are marching triumphantly to Aberdeen, whilst General Gordon encourages the clans in the west to rise for the Pretender.'

'Do you think they will support him?' Dorothy asked.

John rubbed a hand around the back of his neck. 'Perhaps. They have a long history of loyalty to the Stuarts. It is not merely Scotland, though.' He met her eyes. 'They say the west country may rise and there is unrest in some of the northern English cities.'

'Are you hearing any rumours of men rallying to the cause in this region?' Dorothy spoke carefully. She did not want to mention Thomas by name. It almost felt that if she did not speak of his treason, she could pretend it was not happening.

'You should know better than I,' John said drily. 'You were at Adderstone Manor last week, as I recall. Did you see any evidence of men gathering in response to your brother's plea for support?'

Dorothy gave a sharp sigh. 'Must you be so blunt?' she complained. 'I was trying to be discreet.'

'Ah.' John smothered a grin. 'That's what you were doing. I'm a simple man so have no truck with subtlety.' He shook his head. 'The entire village – the entire county, in all likelihood – knows that Mr Forster is in hiding at the Hall, stockpiling arms and waiting for men to join him.' He saw the horror reflected in Dorothy's face and added, 'No need for worry, Mistress Forster. No one around here will betray him. Nor will many join Mr Forster's army, mind. They have better things to do with their lives than throw them away on a lost cause.'

'They say that the government intends to offer the land of Jacobite landlords to those tenants who are loyal to King George,'

'You know highwaymen and criminals,' Dorothy said. 'You told me so yourself. And they will have an ear to the ground for the whereabouts of other fugitives and felons such as my brother.'

There was a long, tense silence and then John sighed ruefully. 'Your logic, whilst not particularly complimentary, is impeccable, Mistress Forster,' he said. He picked up the golden locket and held it very gently in his hand, looking at it. 'Supposing I could pass on such a message,' he added, without looking at her, 'what would you have me say to Mr Forster?'

'That a soldier called Lang is on his tail and he is a renowned Jacobite hunter,' Dorothy said, 'but, more importantly, tell him to send Nicholas home. Nick is only a boy and too young to have his life ruined by this.'

For the first time, John looked shocked. 'Your brother *Nicholas* is with the rebels? I had not realised.' His frown was heavy. 'That's damnable. He is – what? Seventeen?'

Dorothy nodded. 'He is eighteen next month. It is not entirely Thomas's fault,' she added, striving to be fair, 'because Nick became involved with the Jacobite cause this past year at Oxford. None of us knew, but, of course, he believes that he is dedicated to a just and righteous ideal.' She rubbed her temples, where her head ached from the heat and the tension. 'I have been pretending this last week that Nick is so engrossed in his studies that he barely ever emerges from his chamber,' she said, 'but that ruse is wearing thin and will not stand up if the house is searched.'

'No indeed,' John said. 'Very few seventeen-year-olds are so studious that they do not emerge even to eat.'

Dorothy managed a faint smile despite her anxiety. 'You can see why I am so desperate to have him home. I am trying to prevent him from being tainted by this. He has his whole future ahead of him.'

John was silent, his expression unreadable. Dorothy felt as though she was holding her breath.

'You ask a lot of me,' he said after a long moment. 'I have a business here to run—' he gestured to the forge '—and people who rely on me. Yet you are asking me to commit treason.'

Dorothy gasped. The colour rushed to her face. Her head swam with the heat and sudden mortification. John spoke quietly, but she could sense his anger. Too late, she realised that in her concern for Nicholas she had given no thought at all to the risk she was asking him to take on her behalf. It must appear that she did not care, did not think his life and livelihood were of any importance. She had sounded like the thoughtless aristocrats whose attitudes she deplored. Her heart lurched and she felt a little sick.

'I am sorry,' she whispered. 'I did not think. I can see that I ask far too much of you—'

'I will do what I can,' John interrupted her as though she had not spoken. 'My nephew Eli is the same age as your brother,' he added roughly. 'I would do all I could to protect him from harm. So I will do it for Nicholas's sake – and for yours. Forster and Derwentwater—' he shook his head '—they must fend for themselves.'

'Thank you,' Dorothy said humbly. 'I am grateful.'

John gave a curt nod. 'I have work to do,' he said. 'Best that you leave now.' A muscle ticked in his cheek. 'Though perhaps you should ask yourself why you turned to me when you needed help, and why you trust me. The real reason, Mistress Forster, not the convenient fiction that I am acquainted with criminals.'

He turned his back on her, reaching for a thick strip of metal. His ignoring of her felt very deliberate.

Dorothy hesitated a moment but he did not look back, so she stepped out into the street. A second later, she heard the smash of hammer on steel.

She realised that she was shaking with shock and emotion. Crossing Front Street, she sat heavily on a bench in the shade of the tall elms and rested her back against the wall of the castle kitchen gardens. She closed her eyes for a moment and waited for her breath to steady and her body to cool down now that she was out in the fresh air.

John had seemed so angry. She had never seen him like that before, but she could scarcely blame him when she had shown so little concern for his welfare. She had had no thought for him at all, in fact, for she had been utterly consumed with getting Nicholas home. Another wave of embarrassment flooded her when she thought that perhaps he might think she could order him about like a servant simply because she was Mistress Forster of Bamburgh Hall. But that was nothing to the shame and upset she felt if John should believe she did not care about what happened to him. Because that was not true. She did care. She cared a great deal.

'*You should ask yourself why you turned to me when you needed help...*' John's angry challenge echoed in her ears. It was true that she had not given the matter much thought beyond knowing that she trusted him. She had run to him almost instinctively and the realisation shocked her.

She suddenly felt very confused, as though she had caught an insight into feelings that she had never imagined existed. But before she could consider what that meant, she heard the clatter of hoofbeats on the road and a man rode into the village on a raking bay horse with a white flash, a soldier in a red coat. He drew rein by the nearest elm tree, jumped down and opened his saddlebag. A pile of placards fluttered in the breeze. One of them, dancing on the edge of the wind, swirled over to where Dorothy sat.

Wanted, she read. *Dead or alive. Thomas Forster, rebel and Jacobite, reward £200.*

She stood up abruptly, feeling sick and light-headed. It was happening, just as she had feared, Thomas now a hunted man and their whole lives upended.

She heard the soldier nail the poster to the tree trunk, then move on to affix another similar one further down the street.

More redcoats were arriving now, swarming the streets, accosting the villagers who had emerged from their shops and cottages to see what the fuss and the noise was all about.

'Have you seen the traitor, Thomas Forster?' Dorothy saw a tall, fair man demanding. 'There is a reward for information leading to his capture.' He turned and looked at her, and Dorothy saw that it was Major Lang. A faint, mocking smile touched his lips as he recognised her. He sketched her a bow. 'Ah, Mistress Forster. Your servant, ma'am.' He gestured towards the poster. 'It is interesting how the worth of a man is calculated, is it not? Only two hundred pounds for an esquire, but were you to reveal to us the whereabouts of Lord Derwentwater, it would be worth a thousand!'

'I fear I cannot help you with either, Major Lang,' Dorothy said. 'You must excuse me.' She turned away, but Lang caught her arm.

'I am not sure I can, Mistress Forster,' he said with no evidence of regret. 'It seems plain to me that at the least you may have some information you could vouchsafe to us—'

'Allow me to escort you back to the Hall, Mistress Forster.' John's voice cut across Lang's contemptuous drawl. 'Take my arm, ma'am. There is not far to walk.'

'Thank you, Mr Armstrong.' Dorothy pulled herself from

Lang's grip and placed her hand on John's arm. She realised that she was shaking again.

John's hand covered hers for a moment and she felt immensely comforted by his strength and presence.

'Have a care, Armstrong.' Major Lang's voice held a sneer. 'You should not taint Mistress Forster with the smell of the forge. Nor should you pin your colours so clearly to the Jacobite mast. You are nothing but a tradesman.'

'I am nothing but a man who has the manners to help a lady in need,' John growled. 'Now stand aside, Major. I cannot believe you wish to cause such a scene here in the street with Lord Crewe's niece.'

There was a moment of simmering tension and then Lang stepped back, a murderous glint in his eyes. Dorothy could feel the anger simmering inside John all the way along the lane and across the road to the Hall, and feel as well Major Lang's gaze drilling into her back. She had known when she met him at Bamburgh Castle that Lang cloaked his ruthlessness in charm and would make a bad enemy. Now he was not making even a pretence at courtesy and his spite had shocked her. Unconsciously, she tightened her grip on John's arm and he glanced down at her. His expression was grim.

'Insolent puppy,' he said. 'Redcoat or not, I should have thrashed him for the way he spoke to you.'

'He would have made you suffer for it,' Dorothy said. 'He is vengeful and dangerous.' The contrast between Lang's self-importance and arrogance and John's steadfastness could not have been greater, she thought. 'Thank you,' she added as they reached the gate to the Hall. 'I had best go in and warn Papa that the major very likely plans to search the house.' She left her hand resting on his arm a second longer to hold John's attention. When he looked down at her, she added, 'I am very sorry for earlier, John. It was wrong of me to ask you to help us.'

John's gaze dropped from hers. 'You were trying to protect your family,' he said. 'I understand.'

Dorothy wanted to say more, to assure him that she did care about him and about his livelihood, but she was afraid she would sound gauche and make matters worse. The moment spun out whilst she hesitated and, finally, she said, 'Pray do not let Major Lang provoke you into a fight, John. He needs no excuse.'

John laughed. 'I have his measure, Mistress Forster. But do not fear...' His amusement faded and his mouth set into the same grim lines again. 'I shall give him no cause to provoke me.' He hesitated. 'I wonder... Would you entrust Garnet to me? Otherwise, it is likely the soldiers will take her when they come to search the Hall, under the guise of requisitioning supplies for the army. I promise I will stable her with my own horses and take the greatest care of her.'

Dorothy looked at the soldiers swarming all over the street. 'Of course I trust you to take care of her, but is it not too late? The soldiers are everywhere and they will be on the doorstep at any moment.'

'They will have to get past Mrs Selden first.' John nodded towards the front steps, where the housekeeper could be seen, sleeves rolled up, somewhat ominously brandishing a rolling pin. 'Quickly, I will go to the stables and you go and prepare your father. Are there any other horses there?'

'No,' Dorothy said. 'Nick took the spare riding horse when—' She stopped, the sick feeling inside her intensifying.

John nodded. 'Very well. I will send word when Garnet is safely stabled. And I will do my utmost to find your brother.' He paused. 'Take care, Dorothy.'

It was the first time he had called her by her name and

Dorothy felt the intimacy of it. With one word, he had breached the social divide between them; for a lady might call a servant by their first name, but a servant would never do the reverse. There was a warmth in his eyes she had never seen before and Dorothy found herself raising her hand to his cheek in a quick, fleeting gesture.

'You too, John,' she whispered. 'Take good care.'

John inclined his head. It struck her then that everything about him was measured and controlled; in a world that seemed suddenly and violently overset, it was a relief to find someone so steady to rely upon. She watched as he strode up the path to exchange a quick word with Mrs Selden, and then she went inside to speak to her father.

It took the soldiers hours to search the Hall. The were looking not only for fugitives, but also for money, weapons, anything that might indicate a connection to the rebellion. They were thorough, and for the most part polite, but they were not tidy or careful. More than once, as she sat beside Sir William in the parlour, the two of them watching the chaos unfold around them, Dorothy heard the sound of breaking china and Mrs Selden exclaim wrathfully as a consequence. The cook had taken it upon herself to oversee the operation and had cunningly bought the soldiers' favour with custard tarts and sweetmeats early on. After that, they were inclined to look on her as a motherly figure and accepted her chiding in good part.

Major Lang had not lowered himself to supervise his men in their task but had ridden up to the castle to see Lord Crewe. For what purpose, Dorothy was not sure. Fortunately, Sir William did not seem particularly disturbed by all the comings and goings, for he was reading a new book that had arrived that morning from Newcastle called *A Geological Survey of the Coastal Rocks of Northumberland*. More than once, on hearing the sound of men thundering overhead and pulling out furniture, he commented on how pleasant it was to have visitors for a change.

Evening was falling by the time the men were finished. They were dirty and empty-handed. Lieutenant Johnstone, who was deputising for the major and looked barely old enough to shave, presented himself to Dorothy and Sir William in the parlour with a stiff bow. He looked as though he was torn between frustration and embarrassment at having found nothing incriminating. 'The search is complete, sir. We will take our leave.'

'You look as though you could do with a drink and a bowl of hot soup to revive you, young man,' Sir William said genially, and Johnstone's nose twitched at the smells of supper emanating from the kitchen.

'There is just one question, ma'am.' He turned to Dorothy. 'Your younger brother – Nicholas, is it? Where is he?'

Dorothy felt her tension ratchet up. She tightened her hand warningly on Sir William's arm; not that he knew what was going on, but he might inadvertently give something away.

'I have no idea,' Dorothy said truthfully. 'He is supposed to be studying but seems to be playing truant today.' She felt grateful that she had had the foresight at least to make Nicholas's chamber look lived in, and smiled at Johnstone. 'You know how it is at that age, Lieutenant. There are so many things more appealing than book learning.'

The lieutenant did not return her smile. Evidently, he did not believe her, and since she knew that Major Lang had his suspicions about Nicholas already, it was no wonder that Johnstone was mistrustful.

'He went fishing,' Sir William said suddenly, displaying the understanding that Dorothy had long suspected him of but which he kept well hidden. 'Lent him my rods this morning,' he added. 'He went off to Ross Sands.'

'Papa, you should have told me!' Dorothy made a great show of gently reproving Sir William, then turned back to Johnstone. 'I am sorry, Lieutenant, I did not realise. I am not sure when Nick will be back – the fishing is often better in at twilight.'

'I told him to be home by nightfall,' Sir William said. 'Besides,' he added simply, 'he will be hungry.'

Dorothy spread her hands and looked at Lieutenant Johnstone. 'There you have it.'

The lieutenant looked unconvinced but gave another short bow. 'You should warn him this is not the time to be wandering about the countryside alone, ma'am,' he said grimly. 'He might fall into bad company.'

'I shall be sure to tell him that,' Dorothy agreed. 'Let me show you out, Lieutenant.'

The soldiers went, clattering down the drive, dusting their uniforms down and complaining about the dirt and the fact that there were only dry rations at their billet up at the castle. The words gave Dorothy an unpleasant jolt, for she had not known that Lord Crewe was allowing Major Lang's troops to use Bamburgh Castle as their base. She wondered whether her uncle offered the castle for government use, or had he been compelled to do it? Was it the price exacted on him to prove his loyalty?

'Good riddance.' Mrs Selden was at her shoulder. 'Supper's ready in the kitchen, pet. You look as though you could do with some of my beef broth.'

'They have left a couple of guards at the front gate,' Dorothy said, wrapping her arms about herself to try to quell her shivering. 'This is just the start, Mrs S. They are garrisoned at the castle now. My uncle is aiding them.'

'Come inside.' Mrs Selden was steering her gently towards the door. 'Don't you fret, Mistress Dorothy. We'll see them off one way or another. You just stay safe and keep away from that slimy Major Lang. He has an eye for you and no mistake.'

Dorothy was startled. 'I don't think so, Mrs Selden. The major dislikes me intensely and suspects me of being a renegade Jacobite.'

'He may suspect you, but that don't mean he doesn't want you,' the housekeeper said stubbornly. She shooed Dorothy inside and shut and bolted the door. 'He's a nasty piece of work.'

Dorothy shuddered, remembering how attentive the major had been when first they had met. She had assumed it was because he was trying to charm information from her, but perhaps there was more to it than that. 'I hope you are mistaken, Mrs S,' she said.

Mrs Selden was busy dishing out bowls of the thick beef and vegetable broth. 'The soldiers took the buggy and one of the farm carts,' she grumbled. 'Requisitioned for use by the military, I heard them say, as though that justifies stealing. And they tried to take some of my stores of pickles and fruit preserves from the cellar until I shamed them by offering up some fresh ham pies in their place.'

'That was generous of you.' Dorothy raised her brows.

'I made them this morning with the special mushrooms,' Mrs Selden said with a conspiratorial smile. 'I doubt they'll be marching anywhere for a day or two after they've eaten those. I hope the latrines at the castle are in good working order.'

'Oh, Mrs Selden!' Dorothy tried to look shocked but could not repress a giggle. 'How could you!'

'Very easily,' Mrs Selden said, dour now. 'Accidents will happen in a kitchen. It's all too easy to mistake one ingredient for another, even with so experienced a cook as I. It will do them no lasting harm.'

She bustled off to fetch Sir William from the parlour and settled the two of them beside the fire.

There was freshly baked bread to accompany the broth and the smell made Dorothy's mouth water. Suddenly, she realised how hungry she was. Anxiety and anger had taken its toll and she was tired and needed to rest. Her head hurt with a dull, persistent ache and she wanted to close her eyes and sleep, but gradually the food and a glass of wine that Mrs Selden coaxed her to take started to make her feel a little better.

Beside her, Sir William applied himself to the food with gusto. Once again, he seemed lost in his own thoughts. Dorothy wanted to ask him if what he had told Lieutenant Johnstone about Nicholas was true or just a figment of his imagination. Perhaps her father did not know. For him, reality and fiction had merged long ago. But it had sounded completely convincing, Sir William lending his younger son his fishing rods and telling him to be back by nightfall... Except that Nicholas had been gone over a fortnight and Dorothy knew in her heart that he was with Thomas...

She dozed a little by the fire, listening to Mrs Selden and the maid Susan chatting softly as they worked. Normally, she would have offered to help, but tonight she simply felt grateful to sit in the warmth and quiet, feeling peaceful for a little while.

Harris came to take Sir William up to his room and help him prepare for bed. The clock in the hall chimed ten and suddenly there was a sharp rap at the door, which Mrs Selden hastened to open.

'There you are at last, Master Nicholas!' Dorothy heard her saying. 'We were starting to think you must have been washed away on that fishing expedition!'

'I found him walking back from Budle Bay,' John Armstrong's voice sounded taut, 'and brought him the rest of the way in my trap. I've explained to the troops guarding the gate. They have sent word up to the castle that Master Forster has returned.'

Dorothy was on her feet, her heart thumping, but before she could hurry out to see John, Nicholas walked into the kitchen. In one hand, he held a couple of fishing rods and in the other he carried a wicker basket.

'Fresh flounder for our dinner tomorrow, Mrs S!' Nicholas was brimming with excitement, his eyes bright, like a naughty child who had pulled off a surprisingly clever trick. 'I showed it to the guards and they were most envious.' He sniffed the air like a hungry dog. 'Is there any of that soup left for me? I could eat a whole vat of it!' Leaning over to kiss Dorothy's cheek, he took the chair opposite her and gave her a huge wink.

Dorothy was torn between utter relief at seeing him and deep irritation at his light-hearted manner. She wanted simultaneously to hug him and shake him.

'You had us worried, Nick,' she managed to say, but he just flashed her another grin.

'Sorry, Dot!' There was no hint of apology in his voice. 'You know what I am like.'

'I do indeed,' Dorothy said with an edge. She glanced towards the door. 'Is Mr Armstrong still without? I must thank him for... bringing you home.'

'He has gone.' Nicholas spoke through a mouthful of bread and broth. 'He said to tell you that he was glad to be of service.'

Dorothy nodded. She was sorry not to have the chance to thank John in person but was deeply grateful to him for his intervention. She wondered where he had found Nicholas and what he had said to him to convince him to return home. Likely she would never know. Nor was she likely to find out how they had pulled off the ruse of the fishing trip, but she would ask John that when next she saw him. It seemed he was a natural conspirator.

Nicholas ate like a starving wolf. A closer look at him made Dorothy realise that he was absolutely filthy and above the scent of the beef broth she could smell sweat and hay on him, as though he had spent the past few weeks living in a stable.

She stood up, intending to head to her bed, but then there came a faint tapping at the window, so light that she thought at first that she had mistaken it. Then it came again.

'What now?' Mrs Selden grumbled. 'It is nigh on eleven!'

The way Nicholas's face lit up gave Dorothy the answer even before Mrs Selden had thrown open the window and she heard her fierce whisper.

'What the devil are you two doing out there? Get inside, now!'

Under other circumstances, Dorothy might have found it amusing to see the Earl of Derwentwater climb through the window to end up in a stone sink full of sprouts and carrots waiting to be scrubbed the next morning. He scrambled out, shook some peelings off his jacket with aplomb and reached out to help Thomas, who was of considerably greater bulk. There was a moment when Dorothy thought her elder brother might get stuck half-in, half-out, but then he was through and he and Derwentwater and Nicholas were standing in the kitchen slapping each other on the back as though they had achieved some splendid escapade, Dorothy thought, rather than putting the entire household at risk.

She exchanged a look with Mrs Selden, who rolled her eyes. Susan was standing, red-faced with her mouth agape, staring at the Earl as though she had seen a vision.

'Are you mad coming here?' Dorothy demanded. 'We are being watched! There are soldiers everywhere.'

'Don't be angry, Dot.' Derwentwater had turned to her with

his easy smile, as though their bitter argument had never taken place. 'There is nowhere safer than a house that has just been searched. Besides, we have been out on Spindlestone Moor for a full week, sheltering in a cave of all places, and we need food—'

'And wine,' Thomas put in.

'And a comfortable bed,' Derwentwater finished.

Dorothy bit down on her fury. 'We may have been searched earlier,' she said sharply, 'but that will not stop them from returning.'

'They won't come back so soon,' Derwentwater said, sounding as though he was explaining to a child. 'They looked like fools earlier when they left empty-handed, and now Lang is at dinner with your uncle up at the castle. He will scarce tear himself away from Lord Crewe's dinner table on another wild goose chase.'

'I wish I had your confidence,' Dorothy said. She thought that Major Lang would probably wade through hell to capture the two of them, let alone sacrifice dinner at the castle.

'Besides,' Derwentwater swept on as though she had not spoken, 'we crept through the churchyard and over the garden wall. No one saw us. It is perfectly safe. Dear Mrs Selden—' he turned to the housekeeper '—is there any of that most delicious-smelling soup left in your pot? I've eaten nothing but berries and roots for so long, I am in danger of turning into a rabbit.'

'Aye, and bring out a bottle of port,' Thomas ordered, assuming the role of host, 'if you please.'

Dorothy realised that Thomas had not bothered to greet her and now his gaze flickered over her and dismissed her objections as unimportant. It made her even more angry than his careless endangering of his family, his rebellion and his arrogant belief that he was a hero of the Jacobite cause. She thought of the threats he had made to her, his distrust and his accusations of disloyalty. He was insufferable.

'This isn't some sort of parlour game where you can drop in for supper, Thomas!' Dorothy seized his arm and shook it. 'Do you understand what is happening? There is a reward on your head, dead or alive—'

'Two hundred pounds,' Nicholas put in. 'I have seen the posters. It's a thousand for you, my lord,' he added to Derwentwater.

'Damned if you're worth five times as much as I am, Derwentwater.' Thomas seemed aggrieved. 'How do these fellows calculate such absurd sums?'

'We'll see how much we are both worth on the battlefield.' The Earl sounded unruffled and Thomas laughed heartily, as though he had made a hilarious joke.

Dorothy put a hand to her aching head. What was the matter with these overgrown children that they laughed about such matters of life and death? Was it to ward off the truth because they did not want to face the fact that they were hunted for treason? She felt exhausted, wanting nothing but to leave them to their own devices. Yet she could not. There was her father's safety to think of, and Nicholas. She was damned if he would be allowed to run off with the fugitives again.

'Nick, sit down,' she snapped. 'Remember that you are supposed to have been out fishing for the day and are having your dinner. And you two...' She spun around on Thomas. 'You will have to leave. I cannot permit you to stay and endanger the rest of us. It's an absurd idea.'

'We could hide down in the cellar,' her brother said. He was laughing, as though her objections were amusing. 'Plenty of bottles down there to keep us company, eh Derwentwater?'

'Or the attics,' Derwentwater suggested. 'If the soldiers return, we can escape out of a window and over the rooftops.'

Dorothy looked at Thomas's considerable bulk and forbore to comment.

'You are two overgrown schoolboys.' Mrs Selden had been busy putting food into a wicker basket and now she thrust it wrathfully at Lord Derwentwater, who was so surprised he took it from her. 'There's bread and butter and ham and cheese and a bottle of port and some fruit cake in there,' she said. 'Take it and begone. I agree with Mistress Dorothy. We cannot shelter you. Go!' She suited actions to words by pushing them towards the door. 'Shoo!' she added, as though herding sheep. 'No bath and no bed for you two fools!'

It said much for the housekeeper's authority, Dorothy thought, that neither her brother nor the Earl of Derwentwater argued with her. In fact, they both seemed silenced by her ferocity and meekly disappeared through the door, followed by Mrs Selden, who could be heard instructing them to go back the way they had come.

'Oh, Mrs S.' Dorothy was torn between laughter and tears. 'The King should put you in charge of his forces! The rebellion would be over in a trice.'

'Silly boys.' The housekeeper was shaking her head. She fixed Nicholas with a stern glare. 'As for you, young man, it's time you were in your bed. Be glad you have a comfortable one.'

From Nicholas's sulky look, it was clear that he would have preferred to be with Thomas and Derwentwater, but he got up without demur and left the room.

Mrs Selden sighed as she heard his door slam. 'Men. Why must they be so much trouble?'

Dorothy bit her lip on another smile. 'I do not know the answer to that question, Mrs S, assuming you require one. I doubt I ever shall.' She helped the housekeeper tidy up the remaining dishes and glasses and carry them over to the big sink.

'Where is Susan?' she added. 'I don't recall seeing her for a while.'

'I have no notion.' A frown snapped down on Mrs Selden's brow. 'She is sweet on one of the soldiers. That I *do* know. I hope she hasn't...' She stopped, but Dorothy knew what she was going to say. *'I hope she has not betrayed us...'*

'Should we search for her, perhaps?' she asked hesitantly. 'It is late for her to be out alone.'

Mrs Selden shook her head. 'You will go nowhere. It's not safe. I shall ask John Armstrong for help later when you are abed. Susan is his cousin, just as she is mine, and I know he has had concerns about her infatuation with the redcoats.'

'I had no idea you and John were related,' Dorothy said.

'We all are,' Mrs Selden replied. 'All us village folk. We look out for one another.'

They finished up quietly and Mrs Selden was damping down the fire for the night when there was a knock at the door.

'Busy tonight, isn't it,' the housekeeper said drily, 'like Sunderland port when the boats come in.' Then, 'There you are, Susan! We were getting worried for you. Evening, John. I see you and I had the same thought.'

'I brought her home from the barracks.' There was a hard edge to John Armstrong's voice. He followed the maid into the kitchen, nodding a greeting to Dorothy as his gaze fell on her. His presence seemed to fill the room in a way that Derwentwater's had not.

Dorothy made a show of folding the kitchen cloths whilst she composed herself.

Susan was ruffled and tear-stained. 'I didn't mean nothing by it, Mrs Selden. I swear it. He was so handsome, and he paid attention to me—'

'And money too,' John added sharply. He gave her a little push towards Mrs Selden. 'Go along now. Get to your own bed this time.'

As Mrs Selden shepherded the chastened maid away, John turned to Dorothy.

'Poor Susan,' Dorothy said, 'seduced by a charmer in uniform.'

'She's not the first, and won't be the last.' The thread of anger was still clear in John's voice. 'That's what happens when a garrison comes to town. I don't know who it was, but when I do find out—'

Dorothy laid a hand on his arm. 'I thought I asked you to keep away from trouble, John Armstrong, not go looking for it?'

To her surprise, he did not smile, but instead caught her hand, his gaze intense and dark. 'That matters to you?'

'Of course it matters,' Dorothy said. 'I would not have said so otherwise.'

His touch sent a shiver along her skin, not unpleasant but definitely unsettling. She found it hard to concentrate all of a sudden.

'I am deep in your debt for all you have done for us this evening,' she murmured. 'How you were able to pull off the trick with the fishing...'

'I'll tell you one day.' She saw the curve of his smile. He seemed very close and his fingers were entangled with hers. She was happy to let it stay that way. 'I was glad to help with Nicholas,' he continued. 'Pray God he sees sense now and remains at home. As for your brother and Lord Derwentwater—' his tone was sardonic '—they were well away before Susan had the chance to raise the alarm.' He finally released Dorothy's hand and stepped back. 'His lordship asked me to give you this, with his compliments.' He patted his pocket and extracted something, which he handed to her with the formality of a lord.

Dorothy looked at it. It was a white rose, wilting and crushed.

John's gaze went from the dead flower to her face. 'Damnation,' he said, his voice changing completely. 'It must have got squashed in my pocket.'

Dorothy let out a peal of laughter. 'Only the Earl of Derwentwater would interrupt an escape from the law to pick a rose from my own garden and ask another man to present it to me.' She took it and tossed it aside as though it were of no great import, which it was not. 'Thank you, John,' she said, reaching up to kiss his cheek. It was rough beneath her lips and he smelled of fresh air. 'I am grateful for all your help and I know Thomas will be grateful too—'

'I didn't do it for your brother,' John said. 'I did it for you.'

He turned on his heel and walked out without a further word and the door closed sharply behind him.

7

AARON – THE PRESENT

The Grace Darling Museum was generally quiet on a Tuesday morning, which gave Aaron plenty of time to chat about the RNLI to those few visitors who did come in. It also meant that his gaze was drawn more than once to Hannah as she made her way around the displays and exhibits, making notes in a neat, leather-bound book and taking pictures on her phone. She worked with concentration and intent. She still tilted her head to one side when she was thinking hard about something; he remembered seeing her do that at sixteen when she had been toiling over her homework on the dining-room table at Bamburgh Hall. It felt odd that their lives had overlapped, separated and now come back together again. He was unsettled by it and something more, something he didn't want to analyse. Instead, he strolled over to her casually.

'Found anything useful?'

It was a weak sort of opening, but she gave him her bright Hannah smile, the one that always bestowed an almost physical warmth on the recipient.

'Yes, actually. It's a great little museum,' she said. 'I love all the detail...' She gestured towards a display showing items from Grace's domestic background. 'It gives so much context to a subject's life when you're writing a biography. It's interesting—' she tilted her head to the side again '—that this one dramatic event – this amazing rescue – is what makes Grace Darling famous and defines the rest of her life, but it's only the tiniest snapshot of the whole.' She turned to him, her eyes shining. 'The bit of her story that I enjoy the most is what happened to her afterwards. Becoming a Victorian celebrity must have been a crazy experience.'

'Sorry to interrupt you, pet.' Judy from the gift shop came over to join them, giving Aaron a quick nod and a fond smile. She was his mum's best friend and something of an unofficial aunt to both him and Alice. This was another thing that some people might find claustrophobic in a village, he thought, the inter-locking lives, the way everyone knew your business. But it could also be reassuring, especially the way everyone pulled together when there was a problem. Judy handed Hannah a note. 'Caro-line's just rang – the curator,' she said. 'One of her kids is ill and she can't make it in today. She's texted you but just wanted to say how sorry she was and that she'll be here tomorrow instead if that works for you. I've jotted down her number in case you want to ring or text her.'

'Oh... That's no problem,' Hannah said, pocketing the note. 'Thanks for letting me know.' The light in her eyes dimmed a little. 'I'm going to be in Bamburgh for longer than I initially thought, so there's no rush.'

Aaron realised that was likely to be because of Diana's illness and he felt a pang of something that was half-regret, half-plea-sure and wholly unwelcome. He waited until Judy was out of earshot before he touched Hannah lightly on the arm. 'I'm very sorry about Diana,' he said. 'I imagine it was a huge shock to you.'

'Yes...' Hannah was chewing her lip, her gaze fixed on a point in the distance. She refocused on Aaron and gave him a paler version of her smile. 'Thank you. It's been a bit of a bombshell. Diana always seemed indestructible, somehow. Or perhaps that's just how I wanted her to be.' Her chin came up. 'I'm sorry that you were put in an awkward position when we met on the beach the other day, knowing about her illness but not wanting to be the one to tell me. That must have been difficult for you.'

Aaron was taken aback by her thoughtfulness. 'I... Uh... It wasn't appropriate for me to be the one to tell you,' he said, hoping that didn't sound too pious. That wasn't why he had been short with her, though, and they both knew it. For a moment, Brandon's name hovered between them, but neither of them spoke it. Then Hannah gave a decisive nod.

'As Caroline isn't coming, I think I'll go and get a sandwich and a coffee.' She checked her watch. 'Would you like to join me?' She paused and a hint of colour came into her cheeks. 'There's something I'd like to ask you.'

Aaron hesitated and, seeing it, Hannah quickly back-pedalled.

'Sorry. I suppose you're on duty here and can't just take off. I should have thought—'

'No, it's okay.' Her vulnerability made him feel protective, which was another huge red flag. With his training, he should be good at avoiding danger signs, but instead he seemed to be rushing head-long towards them and didn't want to stop. He pressed on, wanting to reassure her. 'I can take a break. Let me just grab my stuff.'

Whilst he shrugged off the RNLI jacket and got his rucksack, Hannah disappeared upstairs to the meeting room she was using as a base for her research. Aaron could see Judy's reflection in the shop display cases; she was looking at him meaningfully, eyebrows raised.

'What?' he said, turning to face her. 'I've finished my shift.'

'She's a lovely girl, is Hannah Armstrong,' Judy opined. 'Always was. Best of a bad lot.'

'That's not much of a recommendation,' Aaron pointed out. 'Anyway, I thought you liked Diana?'

'Aye, I do.' Judy polished the already spotless counter. 'But she's not a real Armstrong born and bred. Most of them have been bad to the bone. Proper trouble they've allus been, the Armstrongs, and no wonder, since they're descended from those border reivers.'

Aaron vaguely remembered studying the reivers in his history classes at school. They were the legendary raiders of cattle and sheep, hard-riding men and women who had lived on the lawless English and Scottish borders from the Middle Ages through to the seventeenth century.

'Right up to date as usual, Judy,' he said, and she whisked at him with her duster.

'Go on with you,' she said, 'you know what I mean.'

Aaron did indeed know what she meant and knew she was trying to encourage him and Hannah together. He felt a slight irritation at her matchmaking. Ever since Daisy had moved out, he had had well-meaning people pushing their candidates in his direction. Normally, he was able to shake it off without really caring. Hannah was different.

She came back down the stairs in a bright red coat, flipping her long brown hair over the collar. 'I've left my stuff in the meeting room, Judy,' she called out, 'I hope that's okay? I'll be back later.'

'Course it is, pet,' Judy confirmed, adding, 'Have fun!' as though they were on a date.

Hannah caught Aaron's eye, saw his discomfort and smiled. 'It's okay, Aaron,' she said. 'You're safe with me.' Which only made him feel more awkward. When had he regressed to feeling like a gauche teenager? He wasn't sure, but he didn't like it.

He held open the door of the museum for her and they stepped out into the fresh air. It was a bright day and the sun was warm, but the easterly wind still had its cutting edge and Hannah turned up the collar of her coat and pulled on some leather gloves.

'I was going to get takeout from the deli and sit over by the church,' she said, 'but we'd need to find somewhere sheltered.'

'I know a good spot,' Aaron offered.

They crossed the road by the walled garden and strolled down the main street, past the butchers and the gift shops.

'Things don't change much here, do they?' Hannah said, but she sounded contented rather than critical.

'The butchers make Scotch eggs now,' Aaron smiled. 'That's an innovation.'

They went into the deli and picked up a couple of sandwiches. 'If you'd like a hot kipper in a bun—' Hannah wrinkled up her nose at the smell '—don't let me stand in your way.'

Aaron laughed. 'The crab rolls are actually my favourite, but they're not on the menu today, so I'll settle for local ham and cheese.'

'I'll look like a southerner if I go for brie and cranberry,' Hannah remarked, 'but hey, I suppose I am these days.'

Walking back up the road past Bamburgh Hall, Aaron noticed that the bed and breakfast sign had been taken down. It was another reminder of the change in Diana's situation. He felt a rush of sympathy for Hannah, coming home and being confronted by so much unexpected emotional upheaval.

'I don't suppose Diana has any more guests booked in?' he asked. 'She once told me she loves hosting – she's met so many interesting people.'

Hannah laughed. 'Oh, Diana is a born hostess. She has a way of making people feel at home.' She glanced sideways at him. 'There's one set of guests coming in about ten days. She refused to cancel them – said they had stayed a few times and she'd like to see them again.'

'Oh.' Aaron grinned as the penny dropped. 'I think that must be Lizzie Kingdom.'

He watched Hannah do a rather comical double take, nodding, and then stopping dead when the significance of the name hit her. A couple behind them just avoided walking into her, but Hannah was so dumbstruck she didn't appear to notice.

'Not *the* Lizzie Kingdom?' she spluttered.

'The one and only.' Aaron was enjoying her surprise.

All manner of people had stayed at the Bamburgh Hall guest house over the years and Diana had never treated any of them as though they were in any way special, but Lizzie Kingdom, one-time pop star, TV personality and celebrity turned music school mentor, had definitely caused a stir when she had first rocked up in Bamburgh with her husband and baby. The village hadn't seen that much excitement since Grace Darling's famous rescue.

'Wow.' Hannah recovered and started walking again. 'Diana never said.'

'Diana is the soul of discretion, as you know.' Aaron stood aside so that Hannah could go through the lychgate into the churchyard. 'If we go around the west side, we'll be out of the wind and have a view of Spindlestone Hill,' he added.

There was a bench sheltered by the churchyard wall and overhung with an ancient yew tree. Hannah sat down and unwrapped her sandwich. Clearly, she was still thinking about Diana's guests, because after a moment she said, 'Diana mentioned that they would be on their way back from a wedding somewhere in Scotland. She said there was a group of them...'

'Yeah...' Aaron realised he was enjoying winding her up a bit. 'Finn MacIntyre is getting married. I think he's godfather to Lizzie's eldest. Lizzie and Arthur are going to the wedding along with some other friends – Jack Lovell and his wife Serena. Jack's a writer – maybe you've met him?'

'Jack Lovell the journalist?' Hannah sounded slightly faint and her sandwich drooped, forgotten, in her hand. 'Oh my God, he won the Orwell Prize a year ago, didn't he? And didn't Finn MacIntyre design that amazing urban garden in Manchester that they featured in a documentary recently? No, of course I don't know them!' Her voice had gone up an octave. 'They're celebrities!'

'And you are a biographer whose books have been made into films,' Aaron pointed out. 'No need to get starstruck. Besides, they are all nice people. Diana wouldn't give them the time of day otherwise, let alone have them to stay again.'

'Huh.' Hannah finally remembered her sandwich and took a bite. 'That's true.'

They sat in comfortable silence for a few moments, looking out at Spindlestone Hill. The wind was chasing the clouds overhead, but in the shelter of the wall, it was warm enough and the hill glowed in its green and gorse glory.

'I was almost named Aidan in honour of our local saint,' Aaron said, leaning back against the sun-warmed wood of the bench and taking his water bottle out of his rucksack. 'Mum wanted something biblical that began with A.'

'That's specific,' Hannah commented. He thought she was

trying not to laugh. 'Aidan was very holy, wasn't he? That might have been a lot to live up to.'

'Whereas I seem to remember that Aaron brought the three plagues down on Egypt,' Aaron said, 'which seems considerably less saintly.'

'Nice name, though.' Hannah said it unselfconsciously, biting into the brie and cranberry sandwich. Some cranberry smeared at the corner of her mouth and she raised the napkin to rub it away, only succeeding in spreading it over her chin.

'Erm... Cranberry.' Aaron pointed, wondering why he felt simultaneously so self-conscious and yet so happy to be with her. There was no point in pretending that he didn't; he was enjoying her company. A lot. Too much, probably. 'Do you think Bamburgh has changed much over the years?' he asked, searching for a neutral topic to distract him. 'I know you've been back frequently, but it's sometimes easier to see the differences when you live elsewhere.'

'Not in essence,' Hannah said, smiling. 'There are a few more shops, and it feels busier, but the heart of the place is the same. You've been here all the time though. What do you think is different?'

'Not much,' Aaron said. 'Yes, it's busier for most of the year, but out of season – even now in May – it's still pretty peaceful. The extra business is good for the local economy. And most of the people who come here are respectful of the place, so there's not much trouble with littering or antisocial behaviour.' He smiled. 'It's just a nice place to be and maybe that doesn't sound very exciting to some people, but actually it's pretty good.'

'I used to think that myself,' Hannah said. Her hair had swung forward across her cheek, hiding her face. 'That it was dull here, I mean. That's why I left in the first place, because I wanted broader horizons. But it's always felt like home, and I miss the sea. I'm on the river at Bristol, and it's great, but it's not the same as having this...' She turned and the sweep of her arm encompassed the castle and the wide horizons.

'Do you think you'd ever move back?' Aaron hadn't intended to ask, but the words just came out and now he realised he was holding his breath as he waited for her reply.

A shadow had come down across Hannah's face. 'Maybe,' she said. 'Now's not really the time to decide, though, for lots of reasons.'

'No, of course not.' Aaron cursed himself for being thoughtless. He braced his elbows on his knees, the water bottle dangling from his hand. 'What was it you wanted to ask me?' he added. 'You said back at the museum that there was something.'

'Oh yes...' A shade of pink came into Hannah's cheeks and she looked very endearing.

Aaron found himself wanting to kiss her. The impulse felt very strong. Then his heart did a flip as he realised Hannah's hesitation probably meant that she was going to ask him about his friendship with Brandon. Damn. He hadn't yet decided what he would tell her.

'If it's about—' he started, but she interrupted him, hurrying into speech at last.

'I wondered if you would take me out in your boat,' she said. She gave him a quick look and went on. 'The thing is, I really need to visit the Farne Islands as part of my research into Grace Darling, but as you know, I'm a terrible sailor. I decided it would be better to make a fool of myself in front of someone I know rather than go on a trip from Seahouses with complete strangers and end up throwing up in front of them.' She ran out of breath and shot him another quick glance. 'Although I could be wrong. Do you think it's better to make a fool of yourself in front of someone you know or people you'll never see again, because—'

'Hannah.' Aaron felt ridiculously protective. He laid a gentle hand on her arm and she stopped, biting her lip.

'Sorry,' she said. 'I'm rambling.'

'In my opinion, it's better not to care either way,' Aaron said. 'I'm happy to take you out to the Farnes if you'd like me to and I promise to pass you a bag and look the other way if you're sick.'

Relief broke over her features. 'Thank you so much. I'll pay you the going rate, of course.'

'Mate's rates,' Aaron said.

She turned pink. 'Thanks again.'

'Plus any cleaning fees needed, of course,' Aaron added.

She poked him in the ribs. 'Not funny. You have no idea how vile it is to have seasickness.'

Aaron checked his phone. 'Shall we say Saturday? I've got a day off and it's not my weekend to have Leo, so if the weather's good... Let me have your number,' he added casually, knowing he sounded like a teenager, 'and I'll confirm when the forecast has firmed up.'

Hannah nodded, wiping her fingers and tidying up the crumbs. 'That would be great.' She reeled off a mobile number and he put it into his phone. No wonder he hadn't dated since Daisy left. This was excruciating. At least Hannah didn't seem to have noticed his gaucheness. She simply seemed pleased that he had agreed, which was warming.

'Do you ever hear from your mum?' he asked.

Hannah was watching him and he knew she had read his mind, or at least understood that he was asking because the mention of Leo had inevitably reminded him of how little time he had left with his son.

'Yes,' she said after a moment. 'We reconnected a few years ago. She lives in Singapore at the moment, although I don't think she'll settle there permanently.' She smiled and Aaron thought there was more than a hint of sadness in it. 'The original rolling stone, that's my mum. She loves travel and hates being tied down.'

'You lost touch for quite a few years though, didn't you?' Aaron fixed his gaze on the outline of Spindlestone Hill in the distance. He thought of Leo again and felt the familiar sick sense of regret. He'd do everything in his power and more to make sure that never happened to them.

Hannah touched the back of his hand briefly. 'It's different for you, Aaron,' she said. 'Leo will know you never walked away from him, never chose to leave or put anything or anyone else ahead of him. That gives a child a sense of security even when their life changes.'

She was looking at him earnestly, as though she really wanted him to believe her, and Aaron was shaken, both that she had read him so accurately and also that she trusted he was not the sort of man to abandon his responsibilities.

'It took me a long time to move on because my mum chose herself over Brandon and me,' Hannah continued. 'That was impossible to forgive when I was younger. But I'm glad we got there in the end.' She made a brief, dismissive gesture. 'When you're young, things seem so clear-cut. It's only when you get older that you realise life is a lot more complicated.'

Aaron cleared his throat. 'I'm glad the two of you were able to find a way to move forward. And thank you for what you said about Leo. That means a lot to me.'

Hannah smiled. 'It's a bit weird, isn't it,' she said after a moment, 'to have been a small part of someone's life for a while, to have that shared past, then not to see them for ages and then pick up again.'

It was much the same thought he had had back in the museum. Maybe that was why he was feeling awkward with her –

because he hadn't taken the leap forward to being a thirty-year-old man with her. Somehow, he was stuck as that gangling teen who had had a crush on Brandon's little sister.

It was then, when his defences were down, that she said, 'Would you tell me what happened between you and Brandon? Why did you fall out with him? Did he steal from you as well?'

* * *

Hannah

Aaron looked shocked, although Hannah wasn't sure whether that was because her guess about Brandon stealing from him had been correct or whether she was totally wrong and he was wondering what the hell she was talking about. Up until the last minute, she hadn't even known if she was going to ask him about Brandon, but this was Aaron, so steady and so sure, and she felt she could trust him.

'Stealing? What? No.' He ran a hand over his face and then rubbed the back of his neck for good measure. 'Ah... Hell, Hannah...' He sounded resigned.

She waited, not saying anything, and after a moment, Aaron sighed. She knew then that he was going to tell her. He didn't say that it was all water under the bridge now, or that it didn't matter, so clearly it still did.

'Tell me,' he said after a moment, 'why you thought Brandon had stolen from me.'

Hannah shook her head. She was taken aback at how much she wanted to confide in him the story Diana had told her, but she needed to know this first. 'I'll explain later, I promise. But I need to understand why you quarrelled. Please, Aaron.'

Aaron looked at her silently with that steady, dark gaze for what seemed a very long time. She watched as he thought it through. Then he took a breath.

'Do you remember a boy at school called Richard Arundel?' he asked. 'He was in the same year as Brandon and me.'

This wasn't at all what Hannah had been expecting, but it rang a faint bell for her and after a moment she was able to put a face to the name. 'He was that very studious boy who was good at maths, wasn't he?' she asked. 'Brandon became friends with him halfway through the final year, but then...' She stopped, remembering. 'Oh God, he was the one who ran away, wasn't he?' She shook her head slightly. 'Was it... Did Brandon do something to upset him? Was it his fault?'

Aaron's face had set into grim lines. 'Brandon only befriended him in the first place to see if he could make Richard popular,' he said. 'He boasted to me that he could make the other kids think Richard was cool and he did exactly that.' He met her eyes. 'But then he decided to reverse the process and make Richard unpopular again. Basically, he bullied him and everyone else followed his lead.'

'That's an awful thing to do.' Hannah pulled a disgusted face. 'He did it because he could,' she whispered. She was starting to think that should be Brandon's motto.

'Yeah.' Aaron was watching her. She could see the tension in the lines of his body. 'I didn't really take it seriously enough,' he said. 'I should have done more. I mean, I told Brandon he was an idiot and that he should stop playing around with people's lives, but I don't think any of us realised how serious it was until Richard ran away.' He pushed a hand through his hair. 'I think that's when I finally grew up and saw Brandon for what he was,' he added. 'After that, well...' He shrugged. 'I could never see our friendship in the same light.'

'No,' Hannah said slowly. 'I can imagine.' She looked at him. 'How horrible, Aaron. I'm so sorry.'

'You weren't responsible for Brandon's behaviour,' Aaron said. There was a rough edge to his voice. 'None of us were. It took me a while to realise that, because I was his best friend and I felt... I don't know... contaminated by his behaviour or perhaps that I should have stopped him.' He saw Hannah shake her head and added, 'People cut Brandon a lot of slack because your dad had died and your mum had walked out, and it's true you both went through a load of crap but...' He gave her a faint smile. 'Brandon has to take some responsibility for himself, doesn't he? People tried to help him and he knocked them back. I'm sorry if I sound too harsh...' He stopped.

'No,' Hannah reassured him. 'I don't think you're being unfair. We all indulged Brandon and made excuses for him.' She rubbed her forehead. 'What happened to Richard Arundel? I remember the police coming to school and questioning everyone. Did he turn up?'

'No,' Aaron said quietly. 'I don't think they ever found him... At least I didn't hear that they had.'

Hannah stared out across the hills as she tried to absorb this. It was appalling that Brandon had played around with someone else's life – something of a theme for him, she thought tiredly – but tragic that Richard Arundel had disappeared never to be seen again. Brandon had to take some of the blame for that if he had bullied him as Aaron had said, and she had no reason to disbelieve him. She could understand why Aaron had suddenly seen Brandon in a different way and their friendship had come to an abrupt end.

'I suppose Diana knew,' she said. 'She told me last night that Brandon had got involved in all sorts of trouble at school and that she had tried to help him, but he didn't seem to want to be helped.'

'No,' Aaron said, 'he didn't. People did their best for Brandon; my parents fell over backwards to try to help, but Brandon was always a bit like Loki – he enjoyed causing chaos.'

Hannah gave a snort of laughter. 'I think he'd be flattered by a comparison to the god of mischief. But you're right.' She sighed. 'He had that troublesome, charismatic, manipulative thing going on. Probably still does. No, scrap that,' she added. 'He definitely still does.'

There was a moment of quiet and then Aaron said: 'Why did you think Brandon might have stolen from me? You said "as well". Does that mean he makes a habit of it?'

'He may well do,' Hannah said. She gave Aaron a summary of what Diana had told her the previous night about Brandon's thefts over the years. 'Apparently he justified taking stuff from the house on the basis that it would all be his one day.'

'Entitled idiot.' Aaron sounded disgusted. 'What about Diana? Surely it's her house, not his?' He looked enraged. 'And what about *you*?'

'I don't think other people feature high on Brandon's priority list,' Hannah noted wryly. 'And, to be fair, I feel as though I've been almost as self-absorbed as he is. I had no idea any of this was going on.'

Aaron's gaze was suddenly very direct. 'Trust me, Hannah, you are the least self-absorbed person I know. You spend your life researching and writing about other people. You're the exact reverse of your brother.'

'Thanks.' Hannah dropped her gaze, feeling self-conscious. She was taken aback by Aaron's defence of her. He sounded as though he genuinely cared.

'Does Brandon know that Diana is ill?' Aaron asked. 'Is he

planning on coming back—' his tone became heavily ironic '—to claim his inheritance?'

'Diana doesn't want to see him,' Hannah admitted.

'Which is quite understandable.'

'He did text me to say he had heard I was in Bamburgh and he was planning on stopping by on his way back from Scotland. What is weird is that I don't know who told him I was back. Even stranger, I think I've seen him twice in the last couple of days, but he hasn't been in touch. I've just glimpsed him in the distance and then he's disappeared.'

'That sounds classic Brandon.' Aaron was blunt. 'He's messing with your head. God knows why – because he thinks it's funny, I suppose. Ignore him. He'll come out of the woodwork sooner or later.' He stood up, checking his watch. 'I've got to get back to the boatyard, but I'll ask around, see if anyone has seen Brandon or knows anything.'

'Thanks,' Hannah said. 'I just want to get hold of him so that I can tell him I think he's a complete prat.'

'Fair play,' Aaron said with a grin, 'since he is.'

Hannah got up, smoothing her coat and placing the sandwich wrapper in the bin. 'I'd better get back to my research, I suppose.' She was aware of the wistful note in her voice. It was nice sitting out here in the spring sunshine chatting to Aaron; somehow it had made the huge weight of troubles seem lighter and more bearable. 'I'll walk back via Grace's tomb.'

'I'll come with you,' Aaron said.

Together, they skirted the north side of the church, threading their way between the gravestones until they reached the path that led to the largest and showiest burial vault over by the eastern wall.

'It's very Victorian Gothic,' Hannah sighed, looking at the stone effigy of Grace lying beneath her canopy. 'Poor Grace, she seems such a modest person. I can't imagine her feeling comfortable with this.'

'Her life really was transformed, wasn't it,' Aaron said. He looked at her. 'How are you finding the work? Is it hard to concentrate with so much other stuff going on?'

'It is,' Hannah admitted, 'but I can't really use that as an excuse.' She looked back at Grace's tomb and sighed again. 'I'm not inspired. I think Grace was a remarkable woman and I hope I can do justice to her life story, but I'm more interested in a different historical character at the moment – Dorothy Forster. Have you heard of her?'

Aaron looked blank and she laughed.

'Dorothy was a Jacobite. Her family owned the castle in the seventeenth and early eighteenth century.'

'You need to talk to Judy in the RNLI shop, then,' Aaron said. 'She's an expert on the Jacobite history in this area. And the border reivers,' he added, 'but don't listen to her if she tells you there's bad blood in your family. She means there was five hundred years ago.'

Hannah giggled. 'I know the Armstrongs were a bad lot; they were the most violent and dangerous clan riding the border. Maybe that's where Brandon gets his destructive side.'

'Now you mention that name, I think there's a memorial to Dorothy Forster in the church,' Aaron said thoughtfully. 'You should pop in, unless you feel you'd be playing truant going to see it. I'm sure Grace could spare you for a half-hour.'

'I'm easily persuaded.' Hannah felt her heart skip a beat at the thought of finding out more about Dorothy. 'Thanks, Aaron,' she said, 'and I'll see you on Saturday.'

'If not before.' Aaron smiled at her and strolled away down the path and out onto the street. Hannah realised she was watching him go with a slightly starstruck expression on her face. Thank goodness he hadn't turned around and seen her.

She hurried into the church porch. St Aidan's was full of hush and pale pink light. Hannah had always loved the building for its ineffable sense of peace. It didn't matter how busy the world was outside the doors, in here there was space and time to breathe. She wandered around for a little while simply taking in the atmosphere. There had been a church on the site for a thousand years or more and it felt heavy with a sense of history, although that could have been her imagination investing it with all the scenes it must have witnessed. Baptisms, marriages and funerals, of course, but also all the other events through time – border raids, Vikings, men seeking sanctuary, armies marching, saints preaching, shipwrecks and rescues, kings, queens and, most importantly, the ordinary people who had carried on with their lives in its shadow. Bamburgh Castle had risen and fallen and risen again in the same period of time that the church had stood here. Hannah found that comforting. It didn't make her own problems go away, but it put them into a wider perspective. She was startled to feel as though she belonged in that procession of history.

The original effigy of Grace Darling that had been in the churchyard was to be found in the North Aisle, so Hannah dutifully inspected that first and took some photographs. As always, she was drawn to the tomb of the Bamburgh knight in the chancel. As a child, she had found the stone effigy haunting, so ancient that it was worn smooth, with no clue as to his identity. She had imagined him as a Templar or an English knight of the Hundred Years War brought home for a hero's burial. Now she looked at the tomb more closely, noting the spurs that dated it to the fourteenth century and the carved lion on which the knight rested his feet. Next to the lion, so worn it was almost invisible, was the outline of a rose.

Opposite the tomb, across the chancel was another suit of armour; the helmet, breastplate, sword and gauntlets of Ferdinando Forster, according to the interpretation board. Hannah read with renewed interest that he had been an uncle of Dorothy and Thomas Forster and had died in a street brawl in 1701. Next to it was the memorial that Aaron had mentioned to members of the Forster family, including Claudius, who had been appointed Constable of Bamburgh Castle by James I in 1610, General Thomas Forster, and his sister Dorothy Forster. The Forsters, Hannah noted, were buried in the crypt, which was now accessed from outside the church.

She was about to go to find the crypt when she noticed a small carved motif on the bottom left-hand corner of the memorial frame by Dorothy Forster's name. It was another rose, clearer than the one on the knight's tomb, like the ones in the portrait and on the wine glasses. *The Keepers of the Rose.*

Hannah felt a shiver run down her spine.

After a few more minutes absorbing the peace, Hannah went outside to the small doorway leading down into the crypt. She had read that it had only been discovered in the nineteenth century when some work was being done in the church and the Forster mausoleum had been found. Recently, the crypt itself had been rebuilt to accommodate the ancient bones found during an archaeological excavation in the sand dunes by the castle.

She took a deep breath before she went in – since the episode when she had been trapped in the cave and Aaron had rescued her, she had had struggled with claustrophobia sometimes, but the crypt, though small, was so beautiful and well-lit that she immediately relaxed and enjoyed the play of the light across the floor.

As she was on her way out, she saw another carved stone Jacobite rose on a pillar to the left of the steps, illuminated in rainbow colours from the stained-glass windows. She paused and ran her fingers over it, feeling the outline of the petals against her skin. The sensation triggered some sort of touch memory, much to her surprise. She knew she had done the same thing before, but when and where? She looked at the intricate design and the memory came back to her. She had been a little girl, in one of the rooms at Bamburgh Hall – had it been Brandon's? – discovering a rose carved onto a chimney surround. She could remember her excitement at spotting the flower, as though she had been playing a game of hide-and-seek and had found a clue. And there was a voice – her father – telling her, *'Press the centre of the flower, Hannah, and see what happens...'*

Her small hand had not been strong enough to trigger the switch, so her father had helped her and she had heard the click and slide of a panel moving and there, in front of her, was a hidden compartment and in the secret space had been a birthday present...

She smiled, remembering how she had squealed with excitement to see the wrapped parcel and how she had pulled off the paper and found the box inside. In it had been – what? Some sort of necklace, she thought, small, golden, with a funny pattern on it, like a charm for a bracelet. She had been bit disappointed by it and her father must have realised because he had smiled and said, *'When you're older, I'll tell you all about it, Han. It's very special.'*

Hannah had nodded, but she'd thought it wasn't anywhere near as exciting as the octopus kite she'd also got, which they had tried out on the beach the next day. She'd put the charm away with her other bits of jewellery – the signet ring, the pieces she'd bought with her pocket money over the years – and then she had forgotten about it.

Someone opened the door to the crypt and Hannah jumped, recalled to the present. She stood to one side whilst a small group of visitors came down, then went up the steps and out into the graveyard, cutting back across to the museum.

Judy was busy serving a customer, placing a selection of post-cards and other gifts into a big paper bag. She turned to Hannah with a broad smile when the last of the visitors had gone out.

'Fancy a cuppa, love? Did you have a nice lunch with Aaron?'

'Yes, please and yes, thank you,' Hannah said, grinning. 'Actually, I wondered if you had a moment, Judy? Aaron says you're the expert on Jacobite history around here and I wanted to pick your brains.'

'The Jacobites, is it?' Judy looked thrilled to be referred to as an expert. 'Is there a connection to Grace Darling?'

'Not as far as I know.' Hannah followed her into the little kitchen that led off the shop and leaned against the doorway whilst Judy filled the kettle. 'The Jacobites is a bit of a project of my own. I'm interested in Dorothy Forster and the 1715 rebellion.'

'Ah, Dorothy.' Judy beamed proudly as though Hannah had referred to one of her own children. 'Rode to London to rescue her brother from the Tower, if you believe the stories about her – which I don't. There's not a scrap of evidence I can find to support the tale, sadly.'

'I'm glad you said that,' Hannah remarked, 'because in my admittedly scanty searches online I couldn't find any references in contemporary reports of Dorothy doing any such thing either; nor that she arranged the fake funeral for her brother to throw the authorities off the scent after he escaped.'

The kettle snapped off and Judy stuck a teabag in two mugs and filled them up. 'Funny how these legends evolve,' she said. 'Dorothy Forster was definitely involved in the 1715 uprising, since her brother Thomas was the Jacobite General in England, but I don't think it was quite the way the story tells it. I do agree she was clever, as well as beautiful, and it seems that she did everything she could to save her brother after his arrest, even though he seems to have been a pointless waste of space.'

'That's a bit of a theme in legends about Bamburgh, isn't it.' Hannah took the mug with a word of thanks and added her own milk. 'Brothers saving sisters, sisters saving brothers, evil stepmothers... I don't like that trope,' she added with feeling.

'You're thinking of the story of the Laidley Worm,' Judy said, smiling. 'It's a classic fairy tale.'

'I have a lovely stepmother,' Hannah said. 'It's my brother who's the problem, just like Dorothy's.'

'Aye, well, brothers and sisters.' Judy shrugged. 'It's not always an easy relationship. Is it, pet?'

Hannah sighed. 'I'm reading Walter Besant's book about Dorothy at the moment,' she said. 'It's a great story, but I don't know how historically accurate it is. He makes reference to something called the Rose, which is supposed to be some sort of Jacobite talisman. Have you ever heard of it?'

She was expecting Judy to look blank, but she nodded. 'Oh aye. I know all about that.'

The museum door pinged to indicate a visitor and Judy picked up her mug and headed out into the shop. Hannah followed, waiting whilst Judy issued tickets to the new arrivals. Outside, the wind was picking up even more, whistling around the flag on the church tower opposite and battering the long grass in the graveyard.

'There'll be a downpour before nightfall,' Judy opined, looking at the purple clouds piling up behind Spindlestone Hill. She turned back to Hannah. 'Sorry about that, pet. Where were we?'

'You were going to tell me about the Rose,' Hannah said.

'Oh aye.' Judy moved some plastic figures of knights around on the display shelves and reached for a duster. 'You know the Bamburgh knight, the one in the church?'

'Of course.' Hannah thought of the worn effigy she'd seen earlier. 'The anonymous crusader.'

'Aye, well there's a theory that he was a Forster,' Judy said. 'Sir Bartholomew Forster, to be precise. He fought in the last crusade in 1271 but died in the Holy Land. Some say he was killed when he tried to use the power of the Rose to gain wealth and riches. The Forsters were the Keepers, you see, sworn to protect the talisman rather than profit from it, but he broke the code.'

Hannah felt the hairs rise on the back of her neck. She could hear the family who had just gone into the museum oohing and aahing over the size of the boat Grace Darling had rowed during her rescue of the survivors from the *Forfarshire*, then their foot-steps on the stairs up to the viewing gallery, but it felt as though for a moment she had slipped into a different time. Goose pimples rose on her skin and she shivered.

'That sounds pretty ruthless,' she said.

'The Keepers were always women,' Judy explained. 'Sir Bart transgressed first when he took it from his wife's possession and again when he tried to use it for gain.'

It sounded to Hannah, striving for some historical impartial-ity, to be a typical moral fable in the same way that the legend of the Laidley Worm was a fairy tale. All the same, she thought, you wouldn't want to mess with the Rose.

'But if the Rose was a Jacobite treasure,' she said, 'it can't have been around in the thirteenth century.'

'Oh no,' Judy said, 'it was much older than that.' She whisked the duster over the plastic knights. 'Some sources say Arthurian, although I think that's unlikely. But it could be early Saxon, like the little golden plaque they found in the excavations at the castle back in the seventies.'

'The Bamburgh Beast?' Hannah asked. 'It was an amazing find, wasn't it. The archaeologists think it's an engraving of a dragon, don't they?'

'Inspired by the legend of the Laidley Worm,' Judy confirmed, 'and dating to about the seventh century. The Rose could have been produced at the same time.'

'Wow.' Hannah felt overwhelmed. 'But where is the Rose now?'

'Who knows?' There was a misty look in Judy's eyes, as though she was looking a long way back into the past. Then she became practical again. 'Like the Beast, it was probably lost at some point in history and is waiting to be found.'

'Yet it was in the possession of Dorothy Forster in 1715 if the story is to be believed,' Hannah mused, 'and it was considered to be a talisman with magical powers.'

Judy smiled. 'Aye, well there's a lot of speculation in all these folk tales. That's why proper historians don't give them much credence. One thing I do know, though, is that the portrait of Dorothy Forster your stepmum has was painted in the garden at the Forge Cottage, the place Aaron rents.'

'No!' Hannah was taken aback. 'I thought – I assumed – it was in the gardens at Bamburgh Hall since Dorothy and her brother lived there for a time.'

Judy shook her head. 'They lost the Hall when Thomas Forster was attainted in 1715. Next time you visit Aaron, take a look at the courtyard garden – you'll recognise it from the portrait.'

Hannah repressed a smile that Judy clearly thought she was a regular visitor to Aaron and the Forge already. There was no stopping the matchmakers of Bamburgh.

'I haven't been to Forge Cottage for years,' she said. 'Not since Diana bought it. I wonder why the artist used it as the setting for the picture, though?'

'Dorothy Forster was married to the blacksmith,' Judy explained. 'John Armstrong.' She sniffed. 'Her posh relatives looked down on him, said he was their social inferior, but that was the way of it in those days. I'd rather have a good man than a ne'er-do-well aristocrat, wouldn't you?'

'Hell, yes,' Dorothy agreed, smiling. 'Judy, you're a star! Diana thought there was some connection between the Armstrongs and the Forsters and my Uncle Peter agreed, but you're the only one who's been able to pinpoint it.' She remembered the blank on the family tree where the name of Dorothy's husband should have been. 'I wonder if that's why John Armstrong wasn't mentioned in the genealogy,' she said. 'Because they were ashamed of the connection?'

'Very likely.' Judy gave a snort. 'Bunch of snobs. All the same —' she looked at Hannah thoughtfully '—John Armstrong would have been a strong man. Blacksmiths had to be. And he was descended from the border reivers, so there was plenty of—'

'Bad blood there,' Hannah finished for her, smiling. 'Yes, I've heard all about the dangerous Armstrong clan. Let's hope John was the exception that proved the rule.' She checked her watch. 'I should get back to the Hall and Grace's biography rather than allowing myself to be so distracted by Dorothy,' she said regretfully. 'Thanks so much for all the information you've given me, Judy. You've been amazing.'

'You're welcome, pet.' Judy beamed. 'I'm glad it was helpful. There's those like your brother who say these tales are just so much hogwash, but I know better.'

Hannah stopped halfway to the door. 'Wait, what?' She turned back. '*Brandon* knows about the Rose?'

Judy avoided her eyes, dusting with a concentrated vigour that betrayed her irritation. 'Aye,' she said. 'I told him all about Dorothy and the Rose a couple of years ago when Diana was first given the portrait. I went round to the Hall one day and saw him studying it, you see. He was very dismissive, contemptuous even...' Her voice tailed off and Hannah could see how hurt she still was by Brandon's rudeness.

'So, Brandon knows about the painting,' Hannah said slowly.

Judy looked at her over her spectacles. 'Aye,' she confirmed. Her lips tightened. 'Despite what he said to me, I think he was curious about the painting because Diana told me that he asked her to give it to him. When she refused, he stormed out and I don't think he's been back since.'

8

DOROTHY – OCTOBER 1715

October was a beautiful month that year. The mist hung low beneath the apple trees in the orchard and the sea sparkled like a jewel in the autumn sun. It was almost possible to imagine that the country was at peace, were it not for the endless comings and goings of men and supplies to Bamburgh Castle, and the now-common sight of the redcoats in the village and the king's messengers on the road. The forge, too, was very busy with commissions for the army and when Dorothy had gone to ask John if he might help them with some work at the Hall, she had had the unpleasant shock of seeing Major Lang lounging in the corner whilst John hammered fiercely at a set of stirrups, his face dark and angry. When Dorothy had quickly stammered her request, Lang had sneered, 'Your garden gate will have to wait, I fear, Mistress Forster. Armstrong is engaged in business for His Majesty's forces now.'

Dorothy saw John give him a covert look of loathing. 'I shall call on you and your father as soon as I am able, Mistress Forster,' he said. 'My good wishes to Sir William.'

It was a not-so-subtle reminder to Lang, Dorothy thought,

that whilst Sir William might be an invalid, his connections and influence were not negligible. The major might have Lord Crewe in his pocket, but the Forsters still had some allies. She had heard from Sir Guy in London the previous day and whilst all the news had been bad, it had at least encouraged her that they were not entirely alone. Then there was Sir William's cousin at Warkworth who had offered them shelter if they needed it. It was comforting.

Dorothy was not pleased when Major Lang chose to abandon his post in the smithy and escort her home. John looked as though he might object, but she gave him a slight shake of the head and a reassuring smile. With Nicholas safely back, she felt strong enough to deal with the major.

'You will have heard that the Earl of Mar has been appointed commander of the Jacobite forces by the Pretender James,' Lang said conversationally as they crossed the village green. Dorothy was walking as quickly as she could in order to get home and be rid of his company, but now she paused and turned to face him.

'No, I had not, sir,' she said. 'I pay as little attention as possible to the rumours about the uprising. There is too much to do here to keep the villagers fed and cared for to allow myself to become distracted.'

'Most laudable, Mistress Forster,' Lang drawled. 'Then allow me to inform you of the latest news, as opposed to gossip. The Earl is marching on Stirling Castle. He holds almost all of Scotland now with a force of twenty thousand men, and there is intelligence to suggest that he will be joining up with the English Jacobite army shortly, unless we capture its leaders before then. You may be assured we are searching for them with great determination.'

Dorothy had known he would try to bait her and she looked him straight in the eye. 'I would expect no less of you, Major,' she said. 'You are, after all, a renowned Jacobite hunter.'

Lang's lip curled into a sneer. 'And your brother is far out of his depth. It is only a matter of time until we catch him. As for that popinjay Derwentwater, he is as good as dead already.'

'I will pray that all may be resolved without bloodshed,' Dorothy said. Out of the corner of her eye, she could see that John was standing in the doorway of the forge and was watching them. She felt a rush of comfort and reassurance to see him there. 'You will excuse me, Major. I have a tisane of rosehips and lavender to make for my aunt, Lady Crewe. She finds it sovereign against a chill.'

Lang bowed. 'Then I will see you at the castle soon, Mistress Forster. I believe your uncle will shortly have some news to impart to you as well.' He gave her a smile that suggested he had been deliberately mysterious to irritate her and strolled away down the street, whistling under his breath.

'Insufferable coxcomb,' Dorothy muttered as she pushed open the gate.

Across the green, John had withdrawn into the forge and she could hear the rhythmic beat of the hammer again. She thought of the way that Lang had treated him with such casual disdain and felt a rush of anger at the major's rudeness. It was the behaviour of a man who considered himself far superior to others and it infuriated her. John was worth ten of him.

In the kitchen, she busied herself washing the rosehips and trimming the lavender before steeping them in hot water. The house was quiet; Mrs Selden had gone to the market in North Sunderland, but Susan was moping as she swept the floor, her eyes and nose red from what seemed to be a permanent state of weeping. She did not even brighten when Nicholas appeared, clattering down the stairs and into the kitchen with his usual cheerful smile.

'I'm half-starved, Dot!' he announced. 'Is there any bread and cheese to spare?' He was already raiding the pantry and took a plate out into the gardens, where he joined Sir William, who was reading beneath the apple trees. Watching them, their two dark heads bent together, Dorothy felt a rush of love for them at the same time as a sharp pang of grief, for how could so seemingly ordinary an event as a man sitting peacefully with his youngest son be so poignant? And yet the everyday event hid so much loss and uncertainty.

* * *

Later that afternoon, when the tisane for Lady Crewe was brewing but was not yet ready, Dorothy received the threatened summons from her uncle, although it was couched in terms of an invitation to tea. She was tempted to decline, for she was utterly out of charity with him for his collusion with the military, but the more sensible part of her knew he held the purse strings and there was little to be achieved by opposing him. Accordingly, she dressed in her most becoming blue silk and lace gown as it gave her confidence and borrowed the doctor's carriage so that she could arrive at the castle in style.

The first person she saw on entering Lord Crewe's study was Major Lang, who gave her another of his sardonic bows.

'Two meetings in one day, Mistress Forster! I am blessed.'

Whilst Lord Crewe was seated behind the desk, a vast, shining walnut expanse untroubled by either papers or books, the major was lounging in the window alcove, seemingly very much at home. Dorothy could not read his expression as he was deliberately standing with his back to the light, but her uncle gestured her to a seat in front of his desk, a chair that was considerably lower than his and, she was certain, designed to make her feel small and at a disadvantage.

'I am sure that you know why I have summoned you today, Dorothy,' he began.

Dorothy shook out her skirts and settled herself comfortably. 'On the contrary, sir, I have not the least idea. Although—' she gave him a dazzling smile '—it is always a pleasure to see you and my aunt.'

Lord Crewe was watching her, his lips tight with annoyance at what he no doubt saw as her flippancy. He set his glasses more firmly on his nose and reached for the only item on the desk: a letter with a very fine wax seal that looked freshly broken. 'This is from Viscount Townshend,' Lord Crewe announced. 'He is—'

'Secretary of State for the Northern Department,' Dorothy said. 'I am aware.'

Lord Crewe's frown deepened. 'And are you also aware,' he snapped, 'that after your brother's treasonous alliance with the rebels, Lord Townshend has moved immediately to confiscate Thomas's share of the Bamburgh estate? He gives you two days in which to vacate the Hall.'

Dorothy clenched her fingers together so tightly that the material of her reticule scored her skin. This was the news she had been dreading. It was not at all unexpected, for they had been warned, but that did not make it any easier to accept the loss of their home.

'I had heard that rebels' estates were being sequestered and offered to their tenants,' she admitted, with as much composure as she was able to muster. 'I suppose there was no reason to make an exception in Thomas's case, but it is very sad.'

'To the contrary, there was every reason to treat your brother's case particularly harshly,' Lang interposed, 'since he is one of the ringleaders of this infernal uprising.'

Lord Crewe nodded his agreement. Dorothy could see he was

furious that her brother had brought such shame on the family and, by default, on him as well.

'Very well.' She drew herself up straighter in the chair. 'I will prepare for us all to return to Adderstone Manor. At least that is still my father's and cannot be taken away from him.'

'No,' Lord Crewe said sharply. 'Adderstone is uninhabitable and your father, sadly, too unwell to direct his own household any more. It is simply not possible.'

'Very well,' Dorothy repeated. She knew there was some truth in what Lord Crewe said, for Adderstone was in a parlous state and would take a huge amount of work to be made comfortable again. 'Then I shall speak with Papa's cousin, George Forster of Warkworth,' she said. 'He has already offered us shelter at the Grange—'

'No,' Lord Crewe said again, even more strongly. 'Your aunt and I feel it would be better were you both to come here to the castle. That way, you will also be protected should the rebels invade from Scotland. Nicholas,' he added, 'will return to Oxford. The authorities there are naturally unhappy to have the brother of a traitor in their midst, but I have smoothed the matter over sufficiently for him to be accepted back as long as he renounces his previous rebellious tendencies.'

'What? I... No!' The refusal was out before Dorothy could stop herself. Seeing Lord Crewe's angry, narrowed gaze, she took a breath to try to salvage the situation. 'I am sorry, Uncle,' she said. 'You took me by surprise. I am glad that Nick will be able to resume his studies. As for the offer of a stay here at the castle, it is most generous but...' Her mind was working feverishly, 'I am not sure that Papa would cope well with the move. It would sorely disturb his mind and confuse him to be away from all that is familiar. Even though the castle is close by, he has never lived here—'

Lord Crewe leaned forward, both hands on the shiny desk top. 'Listen to me, Dorothy. Your aunt is prostrate with distress at everything that is happening. Winter is coming and so are troubled times.' He fixed Dorothy with a stern look that brooked no disagreement. 'Your father will benefit from being here under our protection and so will you. Besides, you have no alternative. Lord Townshend requests – nay, orders – that you should turn all of Thomas's financial and estate business over to my agent on behalf of the government. I will send a man over to the Hall tomorrow, and you will give the ledgers to him.'

Dorothy stood, steadying herself with a hand on the back of her chair. Her legs were shaking. 'The government is allocating Thomas's confiscated estates to *you*, my lord?'

'Of course,' Lord Crewe said, as though it were the most natural thing in the world and not a betrayal of his own family. 'I will administer them in the interests of us all, as I already do your aunt's share of the Bamburgh lands.'

'I see,' Dorothy said. She felt her heart sink as she realised how adroitly Lord Crewe had taken control and closed off all alternatives. He had absolute authority. She could not fight him; she had no option other than to do as he ordered.

'It is a generous offer, Mistress Forster,' Major Lang intervened, his tone reproachful. 'Here in the castle, both you and your father will be safe and well cared for. You should thank Lord Crewe for his kindness.'

It is a prison. Dorothy did not say the words aloud, but she was thinking them. Generous it might be on one level, but it was also a neat way of keeping an eye on her, with Sir William as a hostage for her good behaviour. Clearly both Lang and her uncle thought that she was a threat in one way or another and wanted her closely watched. She felt trapped, cornered like a hunted animal.

'As you will, my lord,' she said. 'I trust that I shall still have the freedom to come and go in the village as I am accustomed, in order to help those who need me?'

'Oh...' Lord Crewe avoided her eyes. 'I feel sure that there will be plenty here to occupy you, my dear. Your aunt will be delighted to have you closer by. And there are others in the village who can take up your duties there. Dr Grant's wife for one, and the vicar's wife, of course... You need not worry about that.'

Dorothy could feel the walls of the castle closing about her. It was a luxurious home compared to the Hall, but she already knew how frustrated she would feel standing on the battlements looking down on the shining beach she was no longer permitted to walk on, or over the rooftops to the village. And then there was John. She would not be able to see him or talk to him... She felt suddenly sick with longing for him.

'You must excuse me, Uncle,' she said. 'I need to return...' She was about to say '*home*' but the word stuck in her throat and she thought she might cry. '...To the Hall to prepare for our remove here.'

Lord Crewe looked gratified that she made no further demur. 'Very good, Dorothy. We shall send the carriage for you and Sir William the day after tomorrow. In the meantime, Lang here will despatch a few of his men to transport any books and belongings you wish to bring with you.'

'Delighted, my lord,' Major Lang said promptly.

'You are all generosity, Major,' Dorothy observed bitterly. 'Perhaps we could transport our luggage in the cart your men confiscated when they searched the Hall a few weeks ago.'

She dropped a curtsey to both men and, without further word, she turned and walked out of the room, head held high. By the time she reached the entrance hall, her gaze was obscured by tears, but she nodded regally to Neverson as he held the door for her and walked with the deportment of a duchess across the sweep of grass outside. God forbid that Lord Crewe or the major would look out of the window and see her in a state of distress.

Once she was following the carriage drive down the crag, however, it was a different matter. As the huge encircling wall of the castle rose up to hide her from view, Dorothy started to run, faster and faster down the slope, onto the sand dunes and down towards the sea. The marram grass caught at her skirts, the sand filled her slippers and eventually she was obliged to stop when she had a stitch in her side. Her bonnet had blown off somewhere along the way. Her hair was whipped into a tangle around her head, and the cold tears had dried on her cheeks. Panting, she doubled over to catch her breath before sitting down out of sight in the dunes. Suddenly, she was aware of how cold it was, the wind cutting through her thin silk gown and her shawl little protection against it.

She stared out at the expanse of blue-grey sea stretching to the horizon, and the Farne Islands fading into an autumn mist that was creeping towards the shore. It was a view that was so familiar and yet so dear to her. And now her uncle was taking away the life she knew, curtailing all the small freedoms she had worked so hard to preserve, both for herself and for the benefit of others. She supposed she should not be surprised – for years he had complained about her inappropriate behaviour in running their estates on behalf of her father and brother. Her situation had always been precarious. But now, Thomas's disgrace also meant an end to the life she had known and upheaval for her father as well. Nicholas, she hoped, would at least soon settle in back at Oxford. He had the resilience of youth and now that his brief involvement with the rebellion had been squashed and no one knew of it, he could continue his education. One of them at least had a chance of a future.

Eventually, she struggled to her feet and turned towards the village, because there was no alternative. She needed to go back and explain matters as best she could to her father, chivvy both him and Nicholas into packing their bags and make a thousand and one other arrangements for the handover of the estate books to Lord Crewe's agent.

She also wanted to see John. She needed him. She remembered him telling her to think about why she always turned to him when she was in danger or fear. She knew the answer to that question now. At last, she understood her own feelings, and given the perilous nature of all their futures, she wanted to tell him, before it was too late.

But he could not see her like this. She admitted that she was too vain to wish for that as she smoothed her bedraggled skirt self-consciously. She would return home, get changed, compose herself and then go to the forge.

Bamburgh Hall was strangely quiet when she reached home, as though the house already knew what was to befall it and had withdrawn into itself. There were no voices or sounds from the kitchens. The door of Sir William's study was open, but the room was empty. Dorothy stood at the bottom of the stair, water dripping from her skirts all over the floor. A sense of foreboding grabbed her and she ran up the steps to the first floor and along the corridor to Nicholas's room.

She had obviously caught up with her father and Mrs Selden only a few minutes after they had made the discovery, for they were standing inside the doorway, conferring in low voices. In her hand, Mrs Selden held a sheet of paper which Dorothy could clearly see was addressed to her. When she appeared, the two of them broke off and simply stared at her.

Sir William was looking confused. 'Why, here is Dorothy now!' he exclaimed. 'She has not run away at all!'

Mrs Selden gave him a sad, indulgent look and held out the

letter to Dorothy. 'I'm sorry, pet.' Her voice had a crack in it. 'We've just found this.'

Dorothy took the letter and sank down onto the bed, careless of the cold, damp wrap of her skirts about her legs. She recognised Nicholas's spidery black writing racing across the page in the same way that the thoughts ran through his mind.

I'm sorry, Dot, the note read. *I know you won't like it, but I couldn't sit tamely at home whilst Tom and the others risk all for the rightful cause. Have no fears for me. We will surely triumph and all will be well and I shall see you soon. Your loving brother, Nicholas.*

Dorothy was so tired that for a moment, all she felt was emptiness. Then the misery and frustration washed through her and she crumpled the parchment in her hand and threw it across the room. First Lord Crewe's edicts and now this. In her heart of hearts, she had always feared that Nicholas would run away again to fight alongside his heroes. It was impossible to prevail against such idealism.

'It is his choice,' she said bleakly. 'There is nothing more we can do.'

Mrs Selden looked appalled, as though she had expected Dorothy to have a solution that would conjure Nicholas up immediately.

'Perhaps John Armstrong could help,' the housekeeper offered after a moment. 'He found Master Nicholas the last time and persuaded him to come home—'

'Hush.' Dorothy glanced around. 'Walls have ears these days.'

Sir William, who had been looking from one to the other as he tried to follow the conversation, had clearly lost interest. He drifted across to the desk and picked up one of Nicholas's discarded university textbooks. 'Ah, Vergil!' he said happily. 'Splendid. I shall rediscover the glories of the *Aeneid*.' He tucked it under his arm and wandered away, whistling.

'At least he is spared the worry of all that is going on,' Dorothy sighed. Her father was once again locked away in his mind in a place that protected him from the worst of their troubles. She waited until she heard him go downstairs and the door of the study close behind him. Then she stood up, retrieving Nicholas's note and smoothing it out, rereading the impassioned words, although she already knew them by heart. 'I shall not ask for John's help again,' she said after a moment. 'He has risked enough for us already.'

'Aye, that is fair enough,' Mrs Selden agreed. 'He is too good a man to draw into more danger.' Her gaze sharpened on Dorothy. 'My word, but you are soaked to the skin, pet! We must get you out of those wet clothes before you take a chill.' She shooed Dorothy out of the room and down the corridor into her own chamber, where she bustled over to the clothes press to get her some fresh linen. Dorothy understood. Like her, Mrs Selden always felt better when she had something practical to do and really there was nothing left for them to talk about as far as Nicholas was concerned. He had gone and everything was in the lap of the gods now.

Dorothy grabbed a towel and blotted the water from her hair as best she could. 'I was at the castle just now,' she said. 'I got caught in the rainstorm on the way home.'

'Oh aye?' Mrs Selden eyed her sore red eyes knowingly. 'And you've been crying, Miss Dorothy. What has that divil done now?' She stepped forward to help Dorothy unlace her sodden gown.

'If you refer to Lord Crewe,' Dorothy said, her lips twitching to repress a smile at Mrs Selden's description of her uncle, 'he has decreed that we are all to move into the castle. The government has ordered the confiscation of Bamburgh Hall because of Thomas's treason and Lord Crewe is acting on their behalf in closing it.'

Mrs Selden was silent for a moment. 'Well, we knew it was coming,' she said on a sigh. 'At least it may preserve the place from worse damage if Lord Crewe has the administration of the estate rather than anyone else. He understands the value of money and property.'

Dorothy took the clean and dry petticoat the housekeeper offered with a word of thanks. She reflected on what Major Lang had told her earlier that day, the fact that the Earl of Mar had taken control of almost all of Scotland for the Jacobites and had twenty thousand men in his army. The English forces were well drilled and well equipped. They were professional soldiers. The only advantage that she could see the Jacobites possessed was a passion for their cause.

She thought of Nicholas's message again and his unshakeable belief that what he was doing was right. If the Jacobites were successful in taking the throne back for the Stuarts, Thomas would be lauded with titles, high office and many more estates. For a moment, she permitted herself to consider the possibility and it made her feel slightly dizzy. She should not want her brother to succeed when he was a traitor outside the law, and yet it was a seductive thought that he might win and the tables be turned...

She shook herself out of the daydream. This was not like the revolution thirty years before when the government had invited Dutch William to take the throne. This was an invasion, an uprising against the established order. She was no history scholar, but she knew Thomas was unlikely to prevail. A ruling monarch held all the cards; they had the money, resources, government, the army and the law on their side. And somehow it was worse that Thomas was a member of the parliament and sworn to uphold the very laws that he was now breaking. That was what really stuck in her throat. Yet should not all men – and women – stand up for what they believed in? It felt like an intractable knot, an unsolvable dilemma.

'Your poor father.' Mrs Selden's voice broke into her thoughts. 'He will not enjoy being uprooted to an unfamiliar place, even if it is only down the road. At least you will be with him, Miss Dorothy.'

'We shall pack up all his books,' Dorothy said. 'As long as he has them with him, he will have a refuge. He may remember the castle from the days when he courted my mother. It might not all be completely unfamiliar.'

'You are brave, my love.' Mrs Selden gave her a tight hug. 'I will help you, of course. We shall store everything safely before milord's agent comes sniffing around.'

'Not that we have much of value,' Dorothy said, 'but it is a matter of principle. The government may take the house, but it will not take the items that make it our home. I have been thinking that once we are within the castle, my uncle may believe it better that we neither receive nor send any letters, nor make any visits or calls. Before that happens, I must write to Sir Guy to acquaint him with our situation. Also, Mr Forster in Warkworth, in case we require his help at any time.'

Mrs Selden nodded. 'That sounds wise, Mistress Dorothy.' She was looking troubled. 'It feels as though you and Sir William are being made to pay for your brother's misdeeds, or, at the very least, you are hostages.'

Dorothy squeezed her hand. 'That is exactly what we are. I would ask you to come with us, Mrs Selden, but I know how much you would hate to be subject to Mr Neverson's authority when you have run the household here.'

Mrs Selden gave a snort of laughter. 'Don't you worry about that, pet! For you I would even put up with working in the kitchens for his lordship's fancy French chef! I doubt they will turn down the extra pair of hands, not with all of you staying and the soldiers encamped about the place as well.'

'That is a true sacrifice,' Dorothy said, smiling, 'for I know how much you dislike Monsieur Du Blanc. However, if you would prefer to come with us as my lady's maid, that would give you a higher status in the servant's hall.'

'Aye,' Mrs Selden exclaimed, 'that will be just the thing. Although,' she added despondently, 'that means I shall most likely have to deal more with that wet lettuce, Maria Danson. Hasn't it been pleasant here with her gone to the castle?' She gave a heavy sigh. 'Ah well, we must all make do as best we can. Which dress do you require, Mistress Dorothy?'

'I shall wear the cherry red one,' Dorothy said. She wanted to look cheerful, no matter how she felt inside. 'I have a call to make before dinner.'

* * *

On the short journey to the forge, Dorothy went over and over in her mind what she planned to say to John, with the result that by the time she arrived, she had even less idea of how to begin than when she had set out. Her thoughts were in such turmoil that when she saw John's nephew, Eli, behind the counter, she simply looked at him blankly. It had not occurred to her that anyone else would be there.

'Oh!' She could feel herself stuttering. 'I came... I wanted—'

'To collect your mother's locket.' John spoke smoothly from behind his nephew. He deposited a pile of fresh charcoal on the floor beside the fire and dusted his hands. His gaze appraised her and then he beckoned her through the doorway into the court-yard at the back. 'This way, Mistress Forster.'

If Eli was as surprised as she was, Dorothy thought he was

better at hiding it. Not a flicker of expression crossed the young man's face as he stood aside to allow her to pass by and follow John out into the yard. Before she was even outside, there was the scrape of the shovel on the floor as he resumed his work, piling the fresh charcoal into the forge. John, meanwhile, closed the door behind them and gestured Dorothy to take a seat on a bench set against the courtyard wall. He was rolling down his shirtsleeves as though that made him more appropriately dressed to converse with a lady and for some reason that shot Dorothy through with a sense of regret and fondness and a dozen other emotions that were far stronger than she had anticipated.

It was peaceful here as the evening shadows started to fall. The cobbles were clean and a rose climbed up a trellis on the wall opposite, which bordered John's cottage garden. She had not imagined him to be a man who cultivated flowers, but she realised with a pang of the heart that she knew so little about his life, the real life of a widower and working man. For a moment, that thought stopped her, for how could she pour out her heart to him when she barely knew him? Then he spoke and it felt as though the gaps in her knowledge of him did not matter, because in all ways that were important, she *did* know him and that he understood her.

'What is wrong?' he asked quietly.

Dorothy took a breath that was more of a gulp and realised that she was on the edge of tears. John put one hand over her tightly clasped ones and waited. His touch steadied her, his hand warm and strong.

'Nick has run off again,' Dorothy said. 'I tried to pretend I could persuade him against it, but I always knew deep in my heart that I could not. He is young and full of courage and curiosity and...' She gave a little shrug. 'Perhaps I should be proud of his spirit rather than fearful for his future, yet I find I cannot be hopeful.'

'You raised him since he was a child,' John said. 'It is natural that you fear for him in such a dangerous situation as this.' He sighed. 'It's true, though, that the young seldom listen to their elders. They have to make their own mistakes.'

Dorothy's lips twitched. 'We are not so old ourselves, John Armstrong.'

The intensity in his eyes made her catch her breath. 'That is true.' He seemed to remember all of a sudden that he was still holding her hand and swiftly removed his. 'Do you wish me to see if I can find him again and try to persuade him to return? I cannot promise success, but I can try.'

'No,' Dorothy said. 'I thank you,' she added hastily, lest John think she was ungrateful. 'You have already done so much. I should not have asked it of you...' She stopped as John touched her arm lightly.

'We have spoken of that.' His voice was a little rough. 'There is no need to say more.'

Dorothy struggled with her feelings and with the distance he seemed determined to keep between them. She did not know how to bridge it other than by expressing the emotions she felt, but suddenly she was afraid of how John might react. She could not bear to tell him she loved him, only for him to turn away from her. Perhaps it was better to keep this fragile friendship between them than to risk losing it by asking for more.

'We are to remove to the castle.' She blurted out the other news she had to tell him. 'The government has confiscated Bamburgh Hall because of Thomas's treason, just as we had feared. My uncle's agent is to have the administration of it. Lord Crewe has decreed that Father and I must move into Bamburgh Castle for our own safety.' She met his dark gaze, then looked away. 'It is not so bad,' she added. 'I should not complain, for we might be entirely without a home. But—' She broke off, afraid she was about to cry again, and pressed a hand to her mouth as though to hold back the sobs.

'But you are afraid it will be a prison.' John finished the sentence for her. His voice was angry. 'How dare your uncle try to crush your bright spirit?'

His arms were around her and he pulled her close against his body, and the shock and unfamiliarity of it distracted Dorothy completely. He smelled of cinders and fresh air and something she did not recognise but only knew that she liked. His arms were very strong, as she had known they must be, and so was the chest she was resting her head against, yet she felt safe and protected in a way she had not known since she was young and her father had been fit and well.

'Dorothy,' he whispered, and she raised her face to his and felt the brush of his cheek against hers, rough against the smoothness of her skin, and then he was kissing her, which, she recognised, was all she had ever wanted. She did not know why it had taken her so long to understand it.

Not that she knew *how* to kiss. A number of gentlemen had tried to force their attentions on her over the years, but she had always resisted. Now that it came to *wanting* to do it, she realised she was completely ignorant. Then, with a leap of pleasure, she knew it did not matter. Whatever was happening between them felt utterly right and perfect.

'Oh...' When he released her, she pressed her fingers to her lips again, but this time in surprise and wonder.

John, though, was on his feet, running an agitated hand though his hair. 'Dorothy,' he said. 'Mistress Forster... I apologise—'

Dorothy jumped up too. She knew exactly what he was going

to say; that he was sorry, it had been wrong, he should never have touched her. Under the circumstances, there was only one thing to do. She put both hands on his upper arms, feeling the hard muscle beneath her fingers, and leaned in to kiss him again. He made a startled sound in his throat and she felt him start to draw back, but then his arms encircled her again and he kissed her back. It was different this time, less gentle, more demanding, and she liked it all the more for that. Suddenly, it felt as though a trap-door sprang open in her mind. Emotions and sensations raced through her as the final part of the puzzle fell into place.

'It was you,' she whispered. '*You* were Ross. You were my childhood love. I should have known...'

There was both desire and amusement in John's eyes. 'How did you guess?' he asked.

'I felt it,' Dorothy said. She searched his face, seeing the confirmation there in the love in his eyes. 'I always felt so close to you and I could not understand why. Now I do.' She took a breath. There was a question she had always wanted to ask: 'Why did you abandon me six years ago?' she asked. 'What happened?'

John took a step away from her. She understood that he was deliberately putting distance between them. 'Because you are a gentleman's daughter and I am a working man.' John's jaw set stubbornly. 'I ended it because it could never be. I should have done it sooner, no doubt, but I hoped that you would forget Ross, forget me.' He scrubbed a hand over his face. 'And then, as we grew older, I discovered we no longer had that gift. We could not speak to one another as we used to do and it was better that way.'

Dorothy smiled at him. 'It's true that it feels different now,' she admitted, 'but I still feel the bond between us. I can sense how you feel... I *know* you.'

John smiled. There was something rueful in it. 'Aye, I feel the same,' he said. His eyes held hers for a long moment and then he shook his head. 'I'm a simple man. I could not understand how the connection between us worked and, Lord knows, I tried often enough. All I knew was that you were *mine* and yet I could never have you.'

Dorothy threaded her fingers through his, drawing him back down to sit on the bench. 'You have me now,' she whispered.

The heat flared in John's eyes for a second, then died away. 'I've wanted you since the night of the Midsummer Fair,' he confessed, 'but known, too, that you could never be for me. How could you be? You are Sir William Forster's daughter, heiress to Lord Crewe. Even as a lad I understood that. So I took up my trade and I married Mary and I tried to pretend it wasn't real between us. And then Mary died, and the babe too, and I felt guilt that there was a part of me I had kept from them, a part that had always belonged to you...' He shook his head. 'I cared for her very much—' his voice was rough '—and I loved my son, but when they were taken from me, I allowed myself the smallest hope that you and I might somehow find each other.' His smile was rueful now. 'But then, of course, you thought Ross was that coxcomb, the Earl of Derwentwater.'

'I did not!' Dorothy saw his quizzical look and amended her words. 'Perhaps for a little while I thought so,' she admitted, 'but it never felt right and I soon realised it could not be true, thank goodness.'

John laughed. 'I thought you were sweet on the noble lord.'

'I know you did.' Dorothy blushed a little. 'Everyone was a little sweet on Lord Derwentwater,' she said. 'Even Mrs Selden. It was difficult not to be, but—' she gripped John's hand tighter '—I respect you far more than I ever could him; you are a man who solves problems rather than creates them.'

'Aye, well, I don't have the time or the money to indulge in high-minded principles,' John said with feeling.

'Yet you are still a man of honour,' Dorothy said. 'I know you are.'

John pressed a finger to her lips. 'Don't make me out to be more than I am, Dot,' he warned. 'I'm no gentleman, nor do I have the fine words to woo you.'

Dorothy smiled at his use of the nickname. 'I like you just as you are,' she whispered. 'And we have already had a courtship. We have known each other for years.'

She moved closer to him again and he placed an arm about her, drawing her in. It felt such a luxury to be together like this as though, despite everything, her world had come right, safe and sure on its axis. This one, fundamental thing – loving John and being loved in return – could surely help her conquer anything. She was dizzy with it.

'I would marry you in a heartbeat and ask you to live here with me, Dot, but I cannot,' John said, against her hair. 'Not yet. Your brothers are fighting for the Pretender and your home has been taken from you. To make a runaway match would bring even more trouble down upon you.'

'You are worried that people will disapprove.' Dorothy understood his reservations. 'I do not care,' she added recklessly. 'People may think and say of me what they will. I only wish to be with you.'

'And I love you for that,' John said gruffly, 'but your enemies will use anything they can against you, and we cannot give them that advantage. Your uncle would deplore such a match; very likely he would try to annul it. He would separate you from your father and try to take Adderstone as well as Bamburgh from you.' As Dorothy opened her mouth to protest, he raised her hand to his lips, turned it over and kissed her palm. 'Soon,' he said. 'When this great matter is resolved for good or ill, then we will be together. I swear it.'

Dorothy turned her palm against his chest and pressed it to his heart. 'I know you are right, but I want us to be together now,' she whispered. 'I don't care about my uncle or his opinions—'

John gave a frustrated sigh. 'I want it too, Dot, but I am trying to think clearly here. You may not care for Lord Crewe, but you do care for your father. Suppose that your uncle was to declare him insane and have him incarcerated?'

'He would not dare!' Dorothy was horrified. 'Papa was a member of the parliament and is a knight of the shire—'

'And now he is the father of two renegade traitors, sick in his body and stands upon a knife-edge,' John said bleakly. 'My love, he needs you now, just as you need him.'

Dorothy knew he was right, even as her heart rebelled against the truth of it. For a moment, she was silent, not wanting to acknowledge that John was right and they must wait, but she was not the sort of person to hide from reality no matter how harsh.

'I am writing to Sir Guy Forster, my father's kinsman in London, to acquaint him with our new situation,' she said with a sigh. 'It may be that he can help us in some way, although at present I know not how.'

'I shall take your letter to Sir William's kinsman myself,' John promised, 'and speak for you and your father.' He gave her a quick smile. 'After all, he may soon be my kinsman too.'

'But your work is here...' Dorothy was overwhelmed by the generosity of his offer, 'Surely you cannot leave the forge?' Other doubts closed in on her. 'You should do nothing to invite my uncle's enmity,' she added. 'He could crush you as easily as he could the rest of us and ruin your business. I could not bear to be the cause of that.'

John's chin came up. 'I am not afraid of Lord Crewe and I can take my business elsewhere if I must. A smith will always be in demand.' He helped her to her feet. 'Send Margaret Selden to me with the letter when it is ready,' he urged. 'She is the only one we can still trust.'

Dorothy was suddenly self-conscious about the rumpled red gown and her state of disarray. When Mrs Selden saw her, she would immediately guess what had happened at the smithy.

John was also looking at her thoughtfully and she felt heated to see the expression in his eyes. 'You had best put up your hood to cover your hair,' he said. 'I have undone all the fine work of your lady's maid.'

'You must know I do not have a maid,' Dorothy said, nevertheless tucking her hair beneath the hood of her cloak. 'We cannot afford one.'

John's expression warmed. 'Maybe we are not so different, after all then.'

'Even if we are, it is too late,' Dorothy replied. 'You proposed to me, if you recall. You said you wished to wed me, so we are betrothed.'

John took both her hands in his. 'Aye, that was poorly done. The proposal, I mean,' he added hastily on seeing her reaction. 'Next time, I will do it properly.'

'It was quite proper enough for me,' Dorothy said, 'and I shall hold you to it.'

John laughed. 'What a woman you are, Dorothy Forster!' he said. 'My own, brave one true love.'

He tilted up her chin and kissed her again and Dorothy clung to him, bereft when they finally broke apart. She was acutely aware of the fact that she did not know when she might see him again, yet at the same time she felt lighter inside because of the indissoluble bond between the two of them. *No one can take this away from us now,* she thought.

'When there is a safe place for you and your father to go,'

John said fiercely, echoing her thoughts, 'I shall come for you. Nothing will stop me, Dorothy, I swear it.'

He opened the courtyard gate for her. Out in the lane, the shadows were deep and the air felt chill. Evening had approached whilst they talked. A soldier loitered on the village green, and seeing him, John straightened.

'Godspeed, Mistress Forster,' he said formally. 'I shall hope to see you again before too long.'

As she waited for a cart to rumble past so that she could cross Front Street, Dorothy heard John go back into the forge and Eli say, rather drily, 'That took an unconscionable long time for one small locket.'

'What locket?' John replied blankly, and Dorothy smiled to herself as she crossed the road. Hovering at the back of her mind was the thought that now she had something else, something infinitely precious, to defend along with her father and Nicholas. She would do anything for John, just as he had pledged himself to do anything for her. It was beautiful, but it was another weapon someone might use against her, so it had to be their secret and she hugged it close.

9

HANNAH – THE PRESENT

'There was a break-in at the church yesterday evening.' The kitchen was full of light and the scent of coffee. Bill was reading the local newspaper at the breakfast table. Hannah and Tarka had been out for a run earlier along the beach; it was the day that she was due to go out in Aaron's boat and she was already feeling queasy at the prospect and was keeping busy to stop herself dwelling on it. In the past few days, she'd focused on Grace Darling's biography and had met up with Alice and Sarah for a drink at the Lord Crewe Arms. Life had felt almost normal, except when she looked at Diana and saw the strain beneath her stepmother's determined cheerfulness, or when she thought about Brandon.

'A break-in?' Diana paused, cafetière in hand. 'Was anything stolen?'

'Seems not.' Bill was scanning the article. 'They tried to open the Bamburgh knight's tomb and there was some damage to the Forster monument, which was wrenched off the wall. And they ransacked the crypt as well. Threw the bones all over the place, bloody vandals.'

'How awful.' Diana waved a hand towards to the croissants. 'Would you pass me the butter, Hannah, darling? I seem to have a bit more appetite today.'

Hannah reached for the butter dish and handed it over automatically, thinking about what Bill had said. It could be nothing more than a coincidence that all the vandalism had been done to the monuments and tombs she had been looking at on her last visit there. They were the places where she had found the rose motifs which matched the one on the fireplace in Brandon's room here at the Hall. She'd gone to take a look at it when she had got back from the museum that day, creeping into his bedroom as though she was up to something suspicious.

It had not been as she remembered it from their childhood: a typical teenage boy's room with an unmade bed, trainers discarded on the floor and posters all over the walls. Diana had given it a makeover in the last ten years and it was a beautiful pale green colour with shocking pink accents. Brandon's bunk bed had been replaced by a sumptuous queen-sized one with wooden head and footboard, but one thing was the same – the carved Jacobean overmantel around the fireplace, now highly polished to a deep, rich brown, covered in carvings of roses, sunflowers, butterflies and other plants and animals. Hannah's heart had sunk on seeing it. She had no idea which rose she had pressed as a child all those years ago and she had felt suddenly foolish searching for a latch and a secret panel, but now, hearing the newspaper report, she felt uneasy.

She decided against another coffee and took her cereal bowl and plate over to the dishwasher, pausing for a moment to lean against the worktop and take in the view of Spindlestone Hill and the lighthouse to the west. It was a beautiful day, with light winds and fluffy white clouds, perfect for sailing, as Aaron had said when he had texted earlier that morning. She had no excuses to get out of the trip to the Farnes, but the apprehension churned around in her stomach, along with a new sense of disquiet about the robbery.

When Bill headed off to the farm, kissing Diana on the way as though they had been married for years, Hannah grabbed the discarded newspaper and quickly read the article about the break-in. It had happened in the early evening, there had been no witnesses and as far as the church authorities were aware, nothing had been stolen. The Forster Plaque had been pulled away from the wall and the wood was splintered and broken, requiring conservation. The lid of the tomb of the Bamburgh knight had been moved, although there was no evidence to suggest the tomb itself had been ransacked. Archaeologists would be coming later in the day to assess the damage and also to view the crypt, which was currently closed to visitors. Anyone who had an information should contact the police on the number given...

'Are you all right, darling?' Diana enquired and Hannah met her guileless expression and felt once again that something was slightly out of kilter.

'I'm a bit shocked by what's happened at the church,' she said honestly. 'I was in there earlier in the week for my research.'

'Oh?' Diana took a bite of croissant liberally laced with butter and marmalade. 'Did you find anything interesting in there? There's Grace Darling's original monument, isn't there?'

Hannah nodded. 'Yes. It's rather lovely. I like it much more than the fancy one in the graveyard.' She hesitated, then took the plunge. 'I noticed lots of carved stone roses in the church as well. They reminded me of the roses in Dorothy Forster's portrait.'

Diana moved sharply, spilling some of her coffee. Hannah saw her hand tremble slightly before Diana put the mug down. 'Are there roses on Grace's tomb?' she asked.

Odd question, Hannah thought. 'No,' she said, 'though they are on the column by the Bamburgh knight and the plaque commemorating the Forsters, and in the crypt. But I imagine it's a common enough decoration. Roses are used a lot in Christian symbolism.'

'Of course,' Diana said. 'You seem to be getting on well with the book, darling. I'm so pleased. Which bit of Grace's life are you writing about at the moment?'

Hannah had in fact been surprised at how much progress she had made in the past week. The museum had proved to be a treasure trove of artefacts and information, and she had also had the chance to visit Newcastle Libraries, and make an appointment with the Alnwick Castle archives for the following week. Now, though, it felt as though Diana was asking about Grace to divert her from the subject of Dorothy's portrait.

'I've gone back to Grace's childhood,' she said. 'There's loads of good stuff at the museum.' She moved over to the sink to wash up a few bits and pieces so that Diana wouldn't feel she was watching her. 'Judy's also been telling me a bit about the Jacobite legends as well,' she added casually.

'Oh, really...' Diana sounded suddenly sharp. 'I thought you'd put all those legends out of your mind to concentrate on Grace? After all, you're a *proper* historian, darling. You work on facts, not fantasy.'

Hannah was taken aback by her stepmother's vehemence. 'All of history is interpretation to one degree or another,' she said as mildly as she could, 'and often there is truth at the heart of these myths.'

'Balderdash,' Diana said. She fidgeted with her phone. 'Judy makes stuff up because she's superstitious and she wants it to be true.' Her tone eased a little. 'Sorry if I sound snappy, darling. I'm just so tired all the time at the moment. I think I'll rest for a little bit.' She bent to pat Tarka and drifted out of the kitchen. Hannah heard her footsteps click across the flagstones as she went into the sitting room next door, and then silence. She looked at Tarka, who put her head on one side and stared back at her with her big, dark eyes.

'I wonder what Diana is hiding, Tarka,' Hannah mused. 'I'm going to ask her, but not yet because I think she'll just deny it.'

Diana's iPad pinged with a text message and Hannah realised that her stepmother had left it open on the kitchen table. Pausing only a second to feel a little guilty, Hannah squinted at it.

The sender was Brandon Armstrong and the message said, *Any news?*

* * *

Hannah enjoyed the drive along the coast road from Bamburgh to Seahouses, even though she was still preoccupied thinking about Diana. From both the tone and the brief words of Brandon's text, it felt as though it was part of a bigger conversation. It could have been completely innocent, Hannah thought, with her brother enquiring about Diana's health, for example. But in that case, why had Diana not told her that Brandon had been in touch? Why was she being so secretive?

In the end, she had decided to put the whole issue from her mind until later and try to enjoy her time with Aaron. However, nerves were already gnawing at her stomach and she was aware of a sense of incipient panic. It was impossible not to enjoy the view, though. The sun was out, sparkling on the sea, fluffy white clouds sailing lazily overhead as though to emphasise what a calm day it would be out on the water. On one side of the road were the dunes and, to the west, fields full of sheep with lambs at their side. The view stretched away to the Cheviot Hills, all green and golden and purple in the distance. Hannah had the window down and enjoyed the slight breeze. It also helped to calm the butterflies in her stomach.

She found a space in the car park by the RNLI station on the esplanade, bought her ticket and made her way slowly down to the harbour. Under other circumstances, she might have dropped in to the National Trust shop by the roundabout, which she loved, or some of the other gift shops that were buzzing with visitors out in the fine weather. But her stomach was churning again and she wanted to get the boat trip over with. Tracing the route to Longstone lighthouse, to see where Grace Darling had lived, see where the shipwreck happened and get back to Seahouses as quickly as possible was her only aim. Or perhaps she could cancel altogether; after all, she didn't really need to *experience* Grace's life in order to write about it. Plenty of people wrote about stuff they knew nothing about. She could use her imagination...

'Hannah!' Aaron had materialised out of the crowds on the concrete jetty. 'You made it.'

He looked good, Hannah thought, relaxed but competent, which was reassuring. She realised she was not the only one appreciating Aaron – he was attracting attention from the groups signing up for organised boat trips and National Trust passes to Inner Farne.

'You thought I wouldn't show up, didn't you.' Hannah's lips twitched ruefully that Aaron's thoughts had so closely mirrored her own, and he gave her an apologetic smile.

'Of course not,' he said.

'You were right,' Hannah admitted. 'I was just thinking about cancelling. I'm so nervous, I already feel sick and I'm still on dry land.'

Aaron ran a hand through his hair. 'Look,' he said, 'you don't have to do anything at all other than enjoy the view and take photos, make notes or whatever. We don't even need to go if you would really prefer not to. But it's a lovely day for a sail and I'm sea-testing a boat we've been doing some work on. I've got one of the apprentices with me, so he and I will take care of everything whilst you enjoy the trip.' He made a slight gesture. 'He's even signed a waiver that if you're sick, he'll pretend not to notice. There's nothing to worry about.'

Hannah felt slightly put out. She realised that she had expected – hoped – that it would just be her and Aaron. That was not a good sign. But Aaron was the one giving up a beautiful morning when no doubt he would prefer to be surfing, or making the most of his remaining time with Leo, or a hundred and one other things. The least she could do was be grateful.

'That all sounds fine,' she said untruthfully. 'Thanks.'

Aaron's smile told her that he wasn't fooled, but he appreciated her attitude. 'Here's Jack now,' he said, gesturing to a tall, skinny youth in black overalls and boots. 'We're ready to go.'

'Hi, Hannah.' Jack had a thick shock of fair hair and direct blue eyes. He shook Hannah's hand warmly. 'Good to meet you. Aaron says you're a famous author.'

'Does he?' Hannah shot Aaron a look. 'It's nice to meet you too, Jack. Thank you for coming out with us.'

'The boat's all set,' Jack said to Aaron. 'She's moored over the other side because of the high tide.'

'Great.' Aaron hefted some life jackets from a rack on the jetty. 'You'd better put one of these on, Hannah.' He shot her a smile. 'Not to scare you; we're not going to need it, but it is a legal requirement.'

He steered her through the milling tour groups and over to the southern harbour wall, where a boat, shiny and obviously newly fitted out and painted, was tied up.

Hannah almost tripped over her feet in shock. 'She's... ah...' She cleared her throat. 'She's bigger than I was expecting.'

The *Spindlestone* was clearly a refitted fishing boat with an engine house in the bow, a part-covered deck and seating for about thirty people. No wonder Aaron had needed backup taking her out.

'Recommissioned for Farne Island Tours,' Aaron said, running a hand over the side with evident pride. 'We've done a good job on her.'

Jack leapt nimbly on board and stood waiting to help Hannah embark. 'A bigger boat is steadier than a little one,' he said. 'Sailor's grip,' he added with a grin, closing his hand around her wrist as Hannah stepped onto the gunwale and down onto the deck.

Aaron handed her rucksack over and she took it with a word of thanks, moving across to the port side, taking out her camera and notebook, and trying to ignore the swooping feeling in her stomach as the boat rocked gently.

By the time Jack cast off and Aaron steered them away from the quay, there was quite a crowd watching from shore, which only made Hannah feel more uncomfortable. She focused on the brightly coloured boats bobbing at anchor, the smell of the sea and the coolness of the air on her face. Gradually, her pulse slowed and her breathing eased. Then they passed the lighthouse on the harbour bar with its weathervane catching the sun. The boat started to roll from side to side, and she felt genuinely queasy, not just anxious.

'It helps to keep your gaze fixed on the horizon.' Jack was coiling a rope up nearby. 'This bit is always choppy. Cross-currents.'

'Yeah.' Hannah tried a smile. 'I remember.'

She looked at the island of Inner Farne off their port bow. It was only two miles out but never had two miles seemed so far away. Gradually, though, the smooth rumble of the engine and the rock of the boat started to feel more natural. The slap of the little waves against the side and the call of the seabirds as they glided over the surface, the cool breeze and the warmth of the sun on her face, all transformed into something that felt relaxing.

She heard Aaron and Jack chatting easily at the helm; Aaron handled the boat with a cool competence that Hannah thought was very attractive and she realised she must be feeling much better. She watched him coaching Jack on some element of navigation. She couldn't hear what they were talking about over the sound of the boat, but Jack was listening intently. He nodded a couple of times and asked a few questions, and Hannah found herself smiling at their easy camaraderie. It was interesting to see a different side of Aaron. She could understand why his staff would like him. He was not only very good at what he did, he had an easy but authoritative manner. She'd never particularly regretted being self-employed before, but she could see how fulfilling it might be to be a part of a good team.

A puffin zipped past the boat, its tiny wings beating madly, and Aaron broke off to make sure she had seen it, giving her a thumbs up and a grin. Hannah realised they had almost reached Inner Farne. The lighthouse soared above them on the cliff, dazzling white. The air was thick with the calls of seabirds and also, Hannah noted, the smell of their guano.

As Jack steered them round to the jetty, Aaron came over to her.

'I've got a landing pass for you if you'd like to go ashore,' he said. 'I thought you might like to see Castell's Tower and the chapel whilst you're here, as well as the puffins' nests. Then we can go on to Longstone afterwards.'

Hannah was touched. 'Thank you, that's so kind of you.' She

grabbed her bag. 'I'd love to go ashore. Apart from anything else, I might have a better chance of making some notes on dry land.'

'I'll come with you,' Aaron said. 'Jack can mind the boat.'

They spent a blissful hour wandering around the little island, visiting the bird colonies and chatting to the National Trust wardens about the breeding puffins and other seabirds. Aaron was knowledgeable about both the wildlife and the history and had a high-spec camera with which he got some great shots. They laughed together at the sight of the puffins popping in and out of their burrows.

'It's no wonder they have such a struggle to survive,' Hannah said, 'when you see how small they are compared to the other seabirds. They're amazing. So determined.'

'As well as very cute and comical to look at,' Aaron agreed. He checked his watch. 'I need to keep an eye on the tides... Did you want to see the chapel? The tower isn't open to visitors, but there's a little information centre as well.'

'I'll be five minutes,' Hannah promised.

'There's no rush,' Aaron reassured her. 'A tour boat has just come in, but once everyone has disembarked, Jack can bring *Spindlestone* back to the jetty.'

'Thanks,' Hannah said. She put her hand on her arm. 'I'm having a really nice time, Aaron. Thank you for making it so... comfortable for me.'

Aaron smiled and her heart did a little flip. 'You are very welcome,' he said. 'See you in a bit.'

* * *

The rest of the morning sped by as they cruised past Staple Island, where a colony of seals were lounging on the rocks sunning themselves, and Brownsman Island, with its remains of the old lighthouse and cottage where Grace Darling had grown up. The sea grew choppier and the wind was rising. On the outer edge of the islands, where the Longstone lighthouse towered, it felt a lot wilder and more desolate.

'It's much flatter than the other islands, isn't it?' Hannah had gone over to the wheelhouse to chat to Jack and Aaron, and was leaning against the gunwale, studying the bare rocks. 'Somehow it feels much more isolated. I can only imagine how bleak it would have been when the storms rolled in.' She gave a shiver. 'Kudos to Grace,' she said. 'She was a remarkable young woman. The whole family must have been tough to survive out here without going mad.'

'We need to head back, skip,' Jack said to Aaron, when they'd circumnavigated Longstone. 'The tide's dropping.'

Hannah was astonished to realise that she actually felt disappointed. As the boat speeded up and headed back towards the mainland, she gave herself up to the pleasure of being out on the water, watching the birds skimming the waves and the sparkle of the sun on the sea.

Jack gave a shout. 'Look behind!'

And there, in the wake of the boat, were two dolphins performing the most beautiful leaps and jumps, the water cascading off them in shining streams.

Hannah gave a whoop of excitement as Aaron immediately slowed the boat and the dolphins came alongside, flying through the water like the acrobats they were, before, with a flick of the tail, they were gone as quickly as they had appeared.

'Wow!' Hannah said. Her heart was racing. 'Wow.'

Aaron had the broadest grin on his face and Jack was laughing. 'It doesn't matter how many times you see them,' he said. 'It's always magical.'

Hannah was still buzzing by the time they entered the

harbour twenty minutes later. Jack tied the boat up and then, with a wave to Aaron, disappeared into the crowd. The quay had been busy earlier, but now it was packed.

Aaron helped Hannah ashore. It felt odd to stand on solid land again.

He kept hold of her hand. 'Okay?' he asked softly.

His face was very close to hers. Hannah wanted to throw herself into his arms and kiss him to within an inch of his life. She told herself it was gratitude for the fabulous experience and also for the fact she had forgotten about feeling sick. But then his focus shifted from her and he straightened, stiffening, and let her go.

'I hope you enjoyed the trip,' he said formally.

Hannah was thrown for a moment by his withdrawal. Then she turned to see that Alice was coming towards them, chatting to a blonde woman who had a small boy by the hand.

'Daddy!' the boy yelled, freeing himself from his mother and hurling himself at Aaron, who scooped him up into his arms.

'Hi, Hannah.' Alice was at her shoulder now, signalling apology with her gaze. 'How was it?'

Hannah pasted on her brightest smile. 'It was brilliant, thanks! We saw puffins and dolphins! Who could ask for more?' She thought she sounded like an over-enthusiastic tour guide, but she doubted anyone would notice. Aaron was preoccupied with Leo, and the blonde woman, whom Hannah assumed must be Daisy, looked entirely at home in the happy family group. Suddenly, she knew she had to get away, and quickly. 'Thanks so much, Aaron,' she said loudly. 'That was great. I really appreciate your help with my work. See you around, perhaps.'

Aaron's gaze snapped back to her. 'Hannah, wait—' he started, but Daisy cut across him.

'Hi, Hannah,' she said, smiling without warmth. 'Sorry to

gatecrash your trip, but there was something urgent I needed to talk to Aaron about.'

'Of course.' Hannah's returning smile felt forced. 'We're done, anyway.' She raised a hand. 'Thanks again.'

'I'll come with you,' Alice said. 'We can grab a snack. Sorry about that,' she added, when the others were out of earshot. 'Daisy had been trying to ring Aaron about something and said he wasn't answering. She called me to find out where he was. Apparently, it was an emergency, but...' Alice's shrug said it all. 'What constitutes an emergency to Daisy is usually something that's happened that she doesn't like, rather than a genuine crisis.'

'It's fine,' Hannah lied. 'We had a great trip. It was just what I needed. And I wasn't even sick.'

'Really?' Alice brightened up. 'Well, that is a result. I want to hear all about it.' She stopped next to a cafe. 'Do you want an ice cream? They do amazing flavours here. Salted caramel? Pistachio?'

Out of the corner of her eye, Hannah saw Daisy with her hand through Aaron's arm, hugging him close. He was carrying Leo. They all looked happy. Abruptly, her queasiness caught up with her. What was she doing? Even before Daisy and Leo had shown up, she'd known Aaron wasn't looking for a relationship. There was nothing for her here even if she had wanted to stay.

'I didn't say I felt that good,' she said, giving Alice her best smile, faking it until she felt better. 'I'll settle for a sandwich and a coffee. But don't let me stop you. I know butterscotch is your favourite.'

* * *

Hannah woke suddenly, confused for a moment as to where she was. She reached for her phone. It was one thirty and the darkness in the bedroom was absolute. She'd been dreaming about dolphins arcing through the sea beside the boat, of the sun shining and Aaron turning from the wheel to smile at her.

Aaron. She wasn't sure whether she had said his name aloud or only in her head, but suddenly he felt so close to her that she would not have been surprised if he had been standing outside in the garden.

She slipped from the bed and crossed to the window, pulling back the curtain. There was no one on the path below and no one in the still garden which stood out in stark black and white, moonlight and shadow. Of course Aaron wasn't there. She felt foolish even to have imagined it. Just because her dream was so vivid and she wanted more than a friendship with him, she was starting to believe that the connection between them was real.

Then she saw, out beyond the flashing green and red of the lighthouse, tiny pinpricks of light from a boat travelling north at speed. A moment later and much closer to hand, she saw the blue flashing lights of the emergency services on the road to Budle Bay and heard the distant blare of sirens.

Downstairs, a door closed softly. She heard Diana talking quietly to Tarka and she went out onto the landing and down the stairs.

'I'm so sorry if we woke you.' Diana, wrapped in a most fetching tartan dressing gown, was closing the back door as Hannah went into the kitchen. 'Tarka wanted out, although I think that was more to do with nosiness than anything else.'

'I'm the same,' Hannah confessed, as Tarka bustled over to her for a cuddle. 'I saw the lights on the road and heard sirens in the distance. I wondered if there had been an accident.' Looking round the kitchen, she noticed that there were two empty mugs on the table. Diana had mentioned that she wasn't sleeping well at the moment. Perhaps Bill had been keeping her company in a midnight cup of cocoa.

'There was a mayday call to the coastguard about half an hour ago,' Diana said. 'I don't know the details, but the D Class boat has gone out. Bill was on call.'

Hannah shivered, wondering whether Aaron was part of the crew and what the nature of the emergency might be.

'It's hard, isn't it?' Diana was watching her thoughtfully. 'Caring about someone who deliberately puts themselves in the way of danger to help other people. Sometimes I'm angry with Bill simply for being selfless.'

They looked at one another for a long moment.

'Diana—' Hannah started to say, but Diana had already turned away.

'There's some cocoa on the stove if you fancy it,' she said. 'I'm off back to bed.'

* * *

There was no one on the beach when Tarka and Hannah went for their run. Hannah had only slept fitfully, relaxing a little when she heard Bill come back at some point, but she had found herself wide awake when the grandfather clock in the hall had chimed six-thirty. It was an overcast morning with a sharp wind and choppy little waves, but the pale silver stretch of sand was smooth and welcoming and, gradually, she felt herself start to relax with the rhythmic beat of her footsteps and Tarka running alongside.

After a while, she stopped in the shelter of the dunes, took out her water bottle and tipped some into the foldaway bowl she carried for Tarka. The tide was coming in and Tarka, panting gently, went off to explore along the strand. Hannah sat watching the sea and thinking about the previous night and how she had almost confronted Diana about Brandon, and how her stepmother had known it and had hurried away. She still couldn't believe that her stepmother could be involved in anything illegal and nor could she believe that Diana wanted to hurt her in any way. The awkwardness she could sense between them was precisely because Diana was uncomfortable with whatever was going on...

Tarka barked a couple of times and Hannah looked up to see that Aaron was running along the beach towards her, somewhat hampered by the excited leaping of a happy Labrador retriever. She stood up and called Tarka over to her. Aaron followed. Hannah had texted him a short message the previous afternoon thanking him again for the trip, but she hadn't expected to see him again so soon, especially if he had been out in the night on a rescue.

'Morning,' she said as he approached her. 'You're up early. Or late.'

'Yeah, we had a busy night.' Aaron tilted his water bottle to his lips and gestured to the sand next to her. 'May I?'

'Of course,' Hannah said, 'although it feels a bit chilly to sit too long. I heard Bill come back in the early hours. What happened?'

'There's nothing as romantic as a beach at night,' Aaron said drily, 'until you get trapped by a rising tide. A couple went for a moonlit picnic at Budle Bay and ended up waist deep in the quicksand.'

'Yikes,' Hannah grimaced. 'Were they okay?'

'They were taken to hospital as a precaution,' Aaron said, 'but I think they'll both be fine. They were just very shaken and cold. Fortunately, they hadn't lost their mobile phones in the struggle to get out, or they wouldn't have been able to call for help.'

Hannah shook her head. 'I remember how dangerous those sands can be. And then there's the Lindisfarne causeway. People get trapped on that when they misjudge the tides.'

'You've got to respect the sea.' Aaron was looking out across the grey breakers. 'You're right,' he added. 'It's cold in the wind. Shall we walk to the shack and get a coffee?' He checked his watch. 'They opened at eight.'

Hannah stood up. 'Yes, let's keep moving.'

'I'm sorry we didn't have time for a chat yesterday after the boat trip,' Aaron said as they fell into step along the sand. 'I really didn't want Daisy to interrupt us at that moment.'

Hannah had been about to brush it off, but the set of his jaw suggested it wasn't going to be that easy. 'I know she needed to see you urgently,' she said carefully. 'It's fine – I understand.' She hesitated. 'I hope everything's okay?'

Aaron's lips twitched. The half-smile surprised her. 'Well, that depends on your point of view,' he said. 'Daisy's pretty upset, to be honest. As you know, she was looking forward to the move to New Zealand, but it's been postponed. Ben – her partner – is staying on in the UK for at least another six months. His boss was poached by a competitor, so the company has asked Ben to cover the post for the time being, possibly even permanently. But I'm not getting my hopes up.' He squared his shoulders. 'I'll settle for another six months with Leo and just be grateful, then we'll see what happens.'

Hannah put a hand on his arm. 'I'm very glad for you,' she said honestly. 'I know it's more uncertainty, but you deserve this break, Aaron. You deserve as much time with Leo as you can possibly get. I'll have everything crossed it works out permanently.'

'Thanks.' Aaron's eyes were bright with emotion. He smiled. 'That's very sweet of you, Hannah. Who knows how it will turn out, but for now, it's great.' He gave a rueful laugh. 'Daisy's hopping mad though. She wanted to travel, see the world, do something different and now Ben's talking about putting down permanent roots here and having kids...' He shook his head. 'I shouldn't laugh, I know, but talk about irony.'

'Oh God.' Hannah struggled with various conflicting emotions. 'Poor Daisy. I guess it's hard for her too. She'll have put so much work and planning into the move, preparing Leo and everything. It's no fun to have all of that upended—'

'You are, without a doubt, the kindest person I know,' Aaron commented, 'but don't waste your sympathy. Daisy wanted something to change in her life, but, as always, she wanted someone else to facilitate that for her rather than taking responsibility for it herself.' He saw Hannah's expression and raised his hands in a gesture of surrender. 'Okay, sorry, I know I probably sound harsh, but I've been through the emotional ringer with her not once but twice now. She's addicted to drama and I can do without it.'

'Yes,' Hannah said. 'I understand. I'm sorry it's been that way for you.'

Aaron gave her another of his heart-shaking smiles. 'Things are getting better now... in lots of different ways.'

They followed the path up to the coffee shack. A few early dog walkers were already there, along with a keep-fit group. The smell of bacon was very seductive. Tarka looked hopeful.

'I'll grab us a drink and a bacon butty,' Aaron suggested, 'if you and Tarka want to go and sit at that table.' He nodded to a picnic table around the back, out of the wind, the benches laden with cushions. 'They have blankets if you need them.'

'Thanks,' Hannah said. 'This is really nice.'

'They do a roaring trade here,' Aaron said five minutes later, as he put down the tray with its two steaming mugs of coffee and bacon sandwiches. 'They've even done a sausage for you,' he added to Tarka, 'but you need to let it cool down.'

Tarka looked disappointed but took up station under the table.

'You were great yesterday, you know,' Aaron said to Hannah as he settled himself on the bench. 'For someone who gets seasick and doesn't like boats, you handled it all really well.'

'I forgot I didn't like sailing,' Hannah admitted. 'I had a lovely time, and you and Jack were great – you made it very easy for me.'

'Jack's a good worker,' Aaron said, picking up his sandwich. 'I'm lucky to have him. I've got a great team.'

'You should take some of the credit for that,' Hannah said, smiling as Aaron looked a bit taken aback. 'From what I've seen, you're a good boss.' Then, when he looked as though he was going to demur, 'Take the compliment, Aaron.'

'Okay,' Aaron said after a moment. 'Thanks.'

'I'm only buttering you up because I want to ask your advice on something,' Hannah continued, a twinkle in her eye. 'I'm worried about Diana. I think she's keeping secrets from me.'

'You mean because of her illness?' Aaron was cutting Tarka's sausage up into small pieces for her, which made Hannah like him even more. He looked up at her. 'It's natural, surely, that she won't want to tell you all the horrible details.'

'No, I meant...' She took a breath. 'She's been in touch with Brandon, even though she told me she didn't want to see him or speak to him.' She told him about the text. 'I wasn't snooping,' she protested when she saw Aaron's brows rise, 'but I knew Diana was acting strangely and I thought there was something going on.'

Aaron did not respond immediately. It was one of the things she liked so much about him, the considered way he thought everything through. 'Brandon could simply have been asking after her health,' he said eventually, echoing the thought she had

had the previous day. 'He might have heard she was ill and wanted the latest.'

'I know,' Hannah agreed. 'There's always a seemingly innocuous explanation for most things, isn't there? But I have such a weird feeling that something is wrong. Diana seemed so interested in Dorothy Forster when she showed me her portrait and then, suddenly, she wasn't. She took the painting from the Hall and made up some cock-and-bull story about getting it restored. She's being cross and evasive with me and I'm really worried. And then there was the break-in at the church.'

'I heard about that,' Aaron said, 'but nothing was taken, was it? What's that got to do with Diana?'

'Nothing, as far as I know,' Hannah said, 'but it's strange that all the things I was looking at last week were vandalised: the memorial plaque to the Forsters, the crypt and the knight's tomb. All those memorials had a rose motif on them, just like Dorothy's painting. It feels as though someone was looking for something.'

Aaron burst out laughing. 'You think that Brandon is on the track of some sort of Jacobite treasure, don't you, and that Diana's helping him. She's given him the portrait because it holds a clue and he's searching all the places it might be hidden. Meanwhile, she's trying to put you off the scent so you don't get in the way.'

'No!' Hannah gasped. She turned bright red, realising that this was exactly what she had been thinking but hadn't articulated before.

'Yes, you do,' Aaron countered, the laughter still in his eyes. 'You think they are in cahoots in some Indiana Jones-style mystery.'

'Well.' Hannah gathered her dignity. 'I know it sounds far-fetched when you put it like that and I can't see why Diana would be helping Brandon, but yes, essentially, I think they are up to something shifty. And it's not just paranoia on my part,' she added, warming to her theme. 'Judy told me about a lost treasure called the Rose that was in Dorothy Foster's keeping.' Quickly, she outlined the legend that Judy had recounted. 'Brandon is an antiques dealer and art historian,' she pointed out. 'He knows about art symbolism and he wouldn't be too scrupulous about getting his hands on something valuable like the Rose and selling it privately for a fortune.'

'Do you really believe in the story of the Rose, though? Isn't it just a legend?' Aaron finished his bacon roll and Hannah belatedly realised she was letting hers go cold. She took a bite before she answered.

'I'm not sure,' she admitted. 'The stuff about the talismanic powers sounds like pure myth, but it could well have been some sort of small golden plaque like the Bamburgh Beast, a priceless piece of early Saxon gold. Just think what something like that would be worth to a private collector.'

'It would be unique,' Aaron said slowly.

'Although I'm sure Brandon would come up with a price if he was selling it,' Hannah was dry. 'He'd probably ask for millions of pounds. Judy said that she told Brandon about the symbolism in the portrait years ago,' she added, 'but he squashed her theories.'

Aaron drained his coffee and sat back. 'I'm beginning to see it might be plausible,' he admitted, 'but you do realise you have little to no evidence for your theory?'

'I know,' Hannah said, 'but I feel better telling you because I was worried that I might be paranoid. I'm relieved you seem prepared to at least consider the possibility it might be true.'

'Maybe I'm as paranoid as you are.' Aaron grimaced. 'You need to talk to Diana, and sort this out once and for all.'

'I will,' Hannah promised. 'Thanks for listening,' She finished the roll and wiped her hands on the napkin. 'Wow, that was awesome. Just what I needed before a morning at my desk.'

'Let me walk you both back,' Aaron said. 'I'm heading home to the cottage before I go for lunch with the family later.'

'Sunday again,' Hannah said. 'I've been here over a week.'

'Any plans to stay longer?' Aaron asked as they stacked the tray and took it across to the counter.

'I'm definitely going to be around for several weeks,' Hannah said. 'I've an appointment at Alnwick Castle and some more work to do in the archives. Plus, I promised Diana I'd help with the visitors on Friday. So yeah, I'll be staying for a while.'

'I'm glad,' Aaron spoke simply, and Hannah thought how refreshing it was to be with someone who was so straightforward and didn't play games.

'You're renting the old forge cottage, aren't you?' she asked as they walked back along the Wynding. Tarka was on her lead, sniffing at the valerian and chicory sprouting from the old field wall. 'What's it like?'

'Cosy,' Aaron said. 'Atmospheric. It was the village blacksmith's shop until the early twentieth century. There are loads of period features and it's got a fabulous courtyard garden with climbing roses.'

His words reminded Hannah of what Judy had told her about the forge cottage being the setting for Dorothy's portrait. She hesitated. 'I don't suppose I could come back and see the garden, could I?' she asked. Then, seeing Aaron's look of amused surprise, she added, 'Sorry, I didn't mean that to sound... um... weird. It's just that Judy told me that the portrait we've been talking about was painted with that background and I'd like to see it for myself.'

'Sure,' Aaron said. He looked intrigued. 'Why would anyone paint a portrait of an eighteenth-century lady in the surroundings of a blacksmith's garden? It seems unlikely.'

'I know,' Hannah said. 'But according to Judy, Dorothy and the blacksmith were an item.'

Aaron raised his eyebrows. 'Interesting.'

'And unusual in the eighteenth century,' Hannah agreed. 'I haven't been able to find any corroborating evidence yet – no marriage certificate or other record – but I'm working on it.'

'I expect the garden will have changed a lot in three hundred years,' Aaron warned. 'Just so you manage your expectations.'

But when Hannah saw it, the garden looked very familiar. They entered by a wooden gate in the picket fence and were immediately surrounded by high walls and climbing roses, some pink and yellow buds already starting to open. By the side of the door was a thick cluster of what looked like sunflowers, already starting to show their buds.

'They're the perennial variety,' Aaron confirmed when Hannah asked. 'Most sunflowers are annuals, but these ones have been here a while. You can tell by the way they've formed such a strong clump. I found them underneath a huge pile of bindweed when I tackled the garden over the winter.'

'I hadn't realised you were a gardener.' Hannah was surprised.

'I like being outdoors.' Aaron smiled at her. 'It doesn't matter really whether it's surfing or sailing or gardening – it's all therapeutic.'

'Yes, of course.' Hannah was thinking of the way in which he must have struggled to come to terms with the changes in his personal life and how nature was said to be a great healer. Here in the warmth of the little courtyard, it was entirely possible to believe in its restorative powers.

'Have you seen the sundial?' Aaron had brushed away a spray of white clematis to reveal an old stone column with a metal disc on the top.

'How beautiful,' Hannah said. Then, when she saw the pointer in the middle, 'Oh! That's a figure of Atropos, one of the Fates. This was in the portrait!'

'Are you sure?' Aaron touched the sundial's pointer with one finger. 'It does look very old, but surely it can't have survived all this time.'

'I'm sure it's the same,' Hannah said. She was feeling a little breathless. 'I noticed it in the painting because I recognised Atropos with her shears. She's the Fate who cuts the thread of life, and I thought it was rather a creepy image. That means that Dorothy was standing here...' She whirled around to stand with her back to the courtyard door. 'And there was a butterfly on a rose *here*, with its wings pointing downwards to the base of the column.' She bent down. Moss grew thickly on the stone, but as she ran her fingers over it, she was sure she could feel a design beneath. Scraping it away, she knelt down and peered at the column. 'Oh!' she said. 'It's another rose!'

Aaron brushed away the moss. 'A very stylised rose,' he observed. 'It has the same sort of design as the Bamburgh Beast – a notional rather than a real flower.'

'Yes, it looks Anglo-Saxon,' Hannah agreed. 'I don't know much about art from that period, but high-status women certainly wore gold as a signifier of their position in society and a rose was associated with the female, such as the figure of the Virgin Mary.' She shook her head slightly. 'Why would anyone carve a rose on a sundial and why would the butterfly in the painting be pointing to it, as though it were a clue to something?'

'So many questions.' There was laughter in Aaron's voice. 'You're always so passionate about the things that interest you. It's one of the many things I like about you, Hannah Armstrong.'

Their eyes met. Hannah caught her breath. Suddenly she felt very unsure. 'I... um... Is this the moment when I admit that I like you too?' she said. 'That I always did? And not just because you saved my life when I was fourteen, though that did contribute to the huge crush I had on you.'

The warmth in Aaron's eyes intensified. He leaned a shoulder against the old stone wall. His gaze searched her face. 'I did save your life, didn't I,' he mused. 'I thought you had forgotten about that episode.'

'I pretended to have convenient amnesia,' Hannah admitted. 'I was so embarrassed that I had called out to you for help, even though it was only in my mind, that I couldn't face you. Besides,' she added, 'I never knew whether it was just coincidence that you were walking past the headland at the time I fell into the cave.'

'Hardly.' Aaron expelled his breath on a long sigh. 'I was down on the cricket pitch practising in the nets. Your voice sort of exploded in my head and I dropped the bat and ran. I didn't even think. I just knew I had to get to you.'

'That must have been difficult to explain to the rest of the team,' Hannah said, a bit shakily.

Aaron rubbed a hand across the back of his neck. 'Damn it, I promised myself I wouldn't mention any of this to you, that it was all water under the bridge, but last night...' He stopped and looked across the fields to the Hall. 'When we were out in the lifeboat, it felt as though you were nearby and thinking of me.'

Hannah swallowed hard. 'I *was* thinking about you,' she said. 'I saw the boat and wondered if you were on call and hoped you would be all right.'

Aaron took a step forward and put his hands on her upper arms. His closeness made her head spin, as did the intimate expression in his eyes. She reached up to kiss him, but just as his lips brushed hers, Tarka gave a little yelp and he stepped back, laughing.

'I can't do this with Tarka critiquing my technique,' he said.

'Sorry,' Hannah said. 'I think I stood on her tail.' She felt slightly panicked. 'Mmm, maybe it's for the best that she interrupted us. I mean, I don't want to be a cliché...'

'The "fling with your brother's best friend" cliché?' Aaron enquired. 'Or the "holiday romance" cliché?' He was still holding her gently and there was a teasing light in his eyes.

'I'm not on holiday,' Hannah said. 'I'm working. And you're not Brandon's best friend any more, but—'

'Well, that's okay then,' Aaron said, brushing his lips against hers again. 'Isn't it?'

'I guess so.' Hannah relaxed a little, kissing him back. 'Yes,' she added after a moment. 'Yes, it's definitely okay.'

The warmth and intimacy of the garden, the scent of the flowers, the feel of Aaron's arms about her and his kiss... There was a sense of recognition in her that was both familiar and exciting. Hannah drifted for a moment on what felt like a tide of memory, then Tarka shoved her nose between the two of them, forcing them apart.

'She's jealous,' Hannah laughed. 'She thinks you're *her* special friend, not mine.'

'I like you both very much in different ways, bud.' Aaron had crouched down to cuddle Tarka. He looked up at Hannah over the dog's head. 'Can I see you tomorrow?' he asked. 'For a proper date? We could go to a quiet pub down the coast where they do great seafood.'

'I'd like that.' Hannah felt a rush of happiness. There was no need to overthink this, she told herself. She could leave her plans and her spreadsheets aside at least for a little while and just see what happened.

'Great.' Aaron straightened up. 'I'll text you.'

The church clock struck nine. 'I'd better go and make breakfast for Diana,' Hannah said. 'Maybe if I ingratiate myself with her, she'll tell me the truth about what's going on with Brandon.'

She and Tarka went out of the gate and down the lane to Front Street. When she turned back, she saw that Aaron was still standing there, watching them, and she felt her stomach do a little swoop of excitement, just as it had done when she'd been fourteen and Aaron had smiled at her. Tarka was looking at her as though to emphasise just how starry-eyed she thought Hannah was being.

'We're all entitled to a bit of romance, Tarka,' Hannah said.

When she reached the Hall, it was empty with that odd, echoing quietness that Hannah had sometimes experienced there and which had always made her feel as though the past was just a touch away. She knew Diana was intending to cook a Sunday lunch for the three of them later, but it was still early, so maybe she hadn't woken up yet. Hannah went to fill the kettle for a cup of tea and it was then she saw the note in Bill's scrawl: *Diana's had a turn for the worst. Taking her to hospital. Call me.*

10

DOROTHY – BAMBURGH, NOVEMBER 1715

The first vestiges of a gloomy grey dawn were edging around Dorothy's bed curtains. She had been lying awake for a while, unwilling to move from the warm cocoon of the bed but aware that the longer she lay there, the more unhappy she was likely to feel. The past several weeks at the castle had worn away her spirit, just as she suspected they had been intended to do.

She and her father were virtual prisoners in the stronghold that had once belonged to her family. There was no news from the outside world, for Lord Crewe had forbidden any discussion of the rebellion, maintaining a harsh and forbidding silence on the subject. Lady Crewe and Mrs Danson seemed concerned with nothing beyond their own small world and Maria Danson, Dorothy thought disdainfully, was no more than Lord Crewe's puppet these days. On her very first night in the guest room high in the South West Tower, she had heard the stealthy turn of a key as Mrs Danson locked her in her bedroom.

'It is for your own safety, my dear,' Lord Crewe had said urbanely when she had complained to him the following morning. 'In such troubled times and with such desperate men roaming the countryside, we will sleep easier in our beds knowing that we are all secure. Besides—' he had managed to look suitably sorrowful '—some of the soldiers in the barracks are rough men. That is why you must let me know if ever you venture into the gardens or to the chapel, and I will ensure you have a reliable escort.'

He was as good as his word. When Dorothy expressed a wish to go down to the beach, she was told that it was not safe, but she was permitted to walk on the battlements each day with Mrs Danson and Lieutenant Johnstone in attendance; what the lieutenant thought of being deputed to a chaperone's role was evident from the glacial courtesy with which he performed his duty.

Dorothy would stand high above the sea, watching it in all its moods, which were mainly dark, sullen and stormy now winter was coming. It echoed her own feelings. The rooftops of the village looked so close, within touching distance almost, and she could hear the sounds of carts on the road and hammering from the forge, where Eli was working whilst John was away in London. She felt so near and yet so achingly far away from all that she held dear.

There were no letters and Dorothy knew better than to try to send any. Lord Crewe, she suspected, checked any and every piece of correspondence entering or leaving the castle and would make sure it never reached its destination.

Mrs Selden had grumbled loudly when a letter sent by her daughter had been opened and destroyed for containing 'seditious materials'.

'Treating me and my Jemima like criminals,' the housekeeper had fumed. 'All she did was write that the villagers miss seeing you, Mistress Dorothy, and send you and Sir William their love and best wishes. I heard Lord Crewe telling Maria Danson, and she said it was unbecoming for the ordinary people to express such familiarity towards their betters.'

'Pish tosh,' Dorothy said crossly. 'Please thank Jemina when you may and send my love to them all.'

They both agreed, however, that there appeared to be no way that they could smuggle anything in or out of the castle.

Dorothy was reduced to listening to servants' and soldiers' gossip in order to get news of the rebellion, but all was so confused and uncertain; there were stories that the Earl of Mar and his army would be crossing the border any day, but there were those who contradicted this and said Mar moved too slowly and that the King's army under the Duke of Argyll was massing against him and there would be a battle soon. And the word from London was vastly less encouraging for the rebels; leading Jacobite sympathisers had been arrested in the south-west and in Oxford, and it seemed that all dissent would be crushed.

Dorothy felt torn with despair. She could speak to no one but Mrs Selden of her feelings and then only in snatched whispers of conversation that Mrs Danson would eavesdrop upon. She missed John desperately; his calm good sense, his strength and his support had always been something she relied on, and although she knew he was still working on her behalf, he felt so far away in London. However, she was reassured that he was safe and well; she could sense his presence with her and she held on to that like a lantern in the darkness.

Without a household to run, Dorothy spent her days sewing – which she was frustratingly poor at, painting, at which she was even worse, and reading, which she loved. To her great relief, Sir William had adapted well to the change of scene and was in ecstasies over the castle library which Lord Crewe had put at his disposal. He spent many hours poring over books and making drawings. Dorothy's heart would contract with a mixture of happiness and regret whenever she saw him so engrossed in his studies. Evidently, his mind was still alert, even if he was frailer than ever in body.

A tapping at the bedroom window drew her from her thoughts. It sounded like the rattle of a branch against the pane, but there were no trees here; she was too high up and the rock outside was bare of vegetation. Indeed, she suspected that Lord Crewe had deliberately placed her in the isolated room, like the proverbial princess in the lonely tower. Perhaps one of the glass quarries in the window had come loose, or a curious seagull were outside...

Slipping from the bed, she winced as her bare toes touched the cold stone of the floor. It was still early and she heard the faint chime of the chapel clock striking a quarter past seven.

The tapping came again, more urgent this time.

Opening the shutters, she drew back, smothering a scream. A face peered in at her, a child, grimy and ragged, clinging on to the stone window frame. A second later, she recognised him as Will Bright, the climbing boy who worked with the Bamburgh chimney sweep. A grin split his face as he saw her and he gestured to her to open the window.

Outside, the castle was blanketed in a thick fog that whirled around the crag and hid the village from view. The cold air streamed in and Dorothy felt its damp chill against her face.

'Will Bright—' she started to say, but the child raised a finger to his lips, hanging on with only the other hand. The sight gave Dorothy palpitations until she remembered that the boy had been scouring the cliffs for birds' eggs since he was little more than an infant. No doubt he found the challenge of scaling Bamburgh crag simple in comparison. 'What are you doing here?' she whispered.

'Mister Armstrong sent you this.' The boy unhooked a leather pouch from his waist, passed it to her and dropped out of sight with a cheery wave.

Dorothy grabbed the satchel and pushed it hastily under some books on the table, even as there was a sharp knock at the bedroom door.

'Dorothy?' Mrs Danson's voice carried through the door panels. 'Are you awake, my dear? Selden has brought you tea.'

The key turned and Mrs Danson walked in without any preamble, a huffy-looking Mrs Selden following with the tea tray. Dorothy knew she detested Mrs Danson treating her with such condescension and disliked her even more for her gaoler's role.

'I thought I heard you talking to someone, dear,' Mrs Danson continued, her sharp eyes going from Dorothy to the open window and back again. 'Brrr, it is a cold day for such fresh breezes! Are you quite well or are you running a temperature?'

'I am very well, thank you, Maria,' Dorothy said. With the very slightest tilt of the head, she indicated to Mrs Selden to put the tray down on top of the pile of books.

Mrs Selden hid a grin and complied with a rattle of china.

'Be careful with the Worcester, Selden,' Mrs Danson snapped. 'So clumsy! I knew you should not have been promoted out of the kitchen.'

'Sorry, ma'am.' Mrs Selden edged around the table until she was standing behind it. Maria Danson crossed to the window and peered out. Quick as a flash, Mrs Selden whipped the leather pouch from under the books and hid it in her capacious pockets. She gave Dorothy a wink.

'The guard thought they saw someone scaling the crag this morning,' Mrs Danson continued, her gaze raking the room now. 'Would you have seen anything, Dorothy dear?'

'Indeed not,' Dorothy said, feigning a yawn. 'I have but woken and opened the window so that the fresh air might help clear my head. You are welcome to check behind my bed curtains, however,' she added sweetly, 'if you suspect me of harbouring company.'

Maria Danson reddened. 'Good gracious, Dorothy, what a suggestion! I would not dream of thinking such a thing. I merely wondered...' But her voice petered away as she realised she could not explain what it was she had been wondering.

She whipped the tea tray off the table, scattering the books all over the floor.

'Let us place this somewhere more secure,' she said. 'Selden, you will stay here to help Mistress Forster dress. Breakfast is at nine, my dear.' With a final, suspicious backward glance, she left the room.

'Bless you, dearest Mrs S,' Dorothy whispered, as the housekeeper took the pouch out of her pocket and handed it back to her. 'You have saved me.'

'Interfering old besom,' Mrs Selden whispered back fiercely. 'She'll get her comeuppance.' She looked at the leather pouch and her expression eased a little. 'It worked then. God be thanked. John said it would, said the lad was agile and bright enough to pull it off.'

Dorothy's heart leapt. 'You and John cooked this up together?' she asked, as she opened the little leather wallet and tipped the contents out onto her bed. 'He's back from London, then?'

'He got back yesterday.' Mrs Selden was pouring her tea, splashing and crashing the china loudly in case Maria Danson had her ear pressed to the door. 'I saw him last night. I'm still permitted to run errands to the village, though they search me whenever I return. Me!' She sounded outraged. 'Pulled and pummelled about by those disrespectful soldiers! Fair makes my blood boil.' She dropped her voice. 'That's why we had to get this to you by another means.'

Dorothy was quickly perusing the contents of the bag. There

was no note from John and she felt a little bereft, though she knew it was probably safer that nothing was committed to print between them. There was, however, a letter from Sir Guy Forster and, even more astonishingly, there was a key. Dorothy held it up to Mrs Selden in mute question and the housekeeper grinned, inclining her head towards the door.

'How?' Dorothy's lips formed the question almost silently.

'Bless you,' Mrs Selden whispered back. 'John's a blacksmith, isn't he? He can make anything. And I "borrowed" the key to your chamber a few days ago. I can be very absent-minded sometimes.'

They caught the sound of passing footsteps and Mrs Selden whisked over to the chest and started to take out some of Dorothy's clothes.

'I thought the blue woollen gown for today,' she said loudly. 'It's cold downstairs even with the fires going.'

She rattled about in the chest and kept up a constant chatter that covered the sound of Dorothy opening Sir Guy's letter. It was short and to the point.

Mistress Forster

Thank you for acquainting me with your situation. I stand ready to assist in whatever manner I may. Should it become necessary to travel to London, seek me out in Litchfield Street immediately. Armstrong holds a sum of money I have made available for your use.

God preserve you and my dear Cousin.

Your servant, Sir Guy Forster.

Dorothy felt a rush of relief that John had evidently been able to meet with Sir Guy and explain their predicament. She had hardly expected Sir Guy, at his advanced age, to come galloping to Bamburgh to release them from Lord Crewe's clutches, but she suspected John would have much to tell her about their discussion. If only she could see him... Her eye fell on the key again and she smiled. Perhaps that might be possible soon.

When Dorothy was ready, she found Mrs Danson waiting for her on the landing outside. The companion locked the door firmly behind them and Dorothy suspected that whilst she was at breakfast there would be a search of her bedroom. They would find nothing, of course. Sir Guy's letter had been burned. Mrs Selden had taken the empty leather pouch and the key was hidden in plain sight in the door of the closet, having been substituted for the one that was already there. For, as Mrs Selden had said, Maria Danson might be a spy, but she was not a clever enough one to see what was under her nose.

* * *

By the end of breakfast, the fog had thickened about the castle and the entire building felt as though it was shrouded in gloom. Sir William hastened away to the library and Dorothy was about to follow when the butler's sonorous tread was heard and the door opened.

'Major Lang requests an urgent interview, my lord. He has news of a battle fought in Lancashire these two days past.'

Dorothy had no memory of how she came to be on her feet, but she found herself holding on to the edge of the table whilst the world spun around her.

Lord Crewe threw down his napkin and stood as well. 'You will wait here, Dorothy,' he said, fixing her with a hard stare. 'I will send for you shortly.'

Dorothy sank slowly back into her seat. It was fortunate that Mrs Danson was taking breakfast with Lady Crewe, she thought.

She could not have borne the woman to witness her fear and any grief she might suffer; she would rather bear it on her own.

Unable to keep still for long, she crossed to the window and stared out into the fog, thinking of John, drawing strength from the sense of his love wrapping about her.

'*Courage*,' she thought she heard him whisper.

It seemed an age before the butler returned to fetch her. The corridor outside the dining parlour was full of servants milling around to hear the latest news and Neverson had to disperse them with a few authoritatively barked orders. Dorothy saw Mrs Selden at the back of the crowd, looking worried, and gave her a little nod. Though her legs were shaking, as she entered her uncle's study, she kept her head high.

'Dorothy.' Lord Crewe gestured to her to be seated on the plush golden sofa by the bookcase rather than the tiny chair this time. 'You remember Major Lang, of course.'

The major gave her an ironic bow. 'A pleasure to see you again, Miss Forster. I hope you are enjoying your sojourn here at the castle? I apologise that I have not had the chance to pay my respects sooner, but I have been too busy hunting Jacobites. I am sure you understand.'

Lang's provocation barely registered with Dorothy. She was feeling sick with anxiety.

'I understand that there is news, sir?' she said to her uncle. Dread choked her throat and filled the room, thick and threatening. She saw Lang smile at the wobble in her voice and knew it could not be a good sign.

'There is indeed.' Lord Crewe walked over to the window and gazed out into the dense fog. 'You must prepare yourself I fear, niece.' He turned back to face her, his expression grim. 'There have been two battles on the same day. One was in Scotland, at Sheriffmuir near Stirling. It was a stalemate, although—' he caught Lang's eye '—the Duke of Argyll's forces have stopped the advance of the enemy and Mar has withdrawn to Perth.'

'Mar will be captured soon enough.' Lang's voice was hard. 'The foreign mercenaries are abandoning him and those Highland rebels will slink off back to their glens.' He straightened. 'But enough of those savages. You should tell Miss Forster about Preston, sir, and the fate of her brothers.'

'Preston?' Dorothy's nerves tightened to screaming pitch. 'I beg you, sir...' She heard her voice break. 'Please tell me.'

'A battle took place in Preston two days ago,' Lord Crewe confirmed. 'For some unknown reason—' his voice grew heavy with irony '—the malcontents chose to place your brother Thomas at the head of their army. I am sorry to say that he was not equal to the task.'

Dorothy knitted her shaking fingers together in her lap. Her heart was beating so hard it seemed to be all she could hear.

'Is Thomas dead?' she whispered.

'Sadly, your brother could not even manage to die with honour,' Major Lang interposed. 'He surrendered like the coward he is and was taken captive by General Wills.'

'And Nicholas?' Dorothy was gripping her hands together so tightly she thought the bones might crack. She tried to loosen her grip.

Lord Crewe exchanged a look with Lang, who cleared his throat. 'He took some hurt – a sword slash to his arm – but his life is not in danger.' He continued to speak, but his words were a blur to Dorothy, swept away in the huge rush of relief that swamped her.

'Oh, thank God,' she whispered. 'Nicholas is safe. They are both safe.'

Lord Crewe's dark brows snapped down. 'Did you hear what I said, niece? Your brothers are being taken to London. They will be imprisoned in Newgate Gaol and put on trial for treason. Very likely, Thomas will be executed – if he survives that hellhole of a prison. I hardly feel—' Lord Crewe rocked back on his heels '— that that constitutes grounds for celebration.'

Dorothy felt sick. There was a buzzing in her ears; she thought she might faint. The initial relief she had felt at knowing her brothers were alive had receded, leaving nothing but a swarm of terrifying fears. Nicholas could easily take an infection as a result of his injury. How would he survive the hardships of Newgate Gaol? Thomas had no money to buy the favour of the guards and precious little influence to help procure him a pardon. And as the leader of the Jacobite troops at Preston, no matter how incompetent he had proved to be, he could hardly expect clemency.

'...Hundreds were killed,' Lord Crewe was saying, 'houses burned to the ground, people and their livelihoods destroyed, the town of Preston has taken lasting harm... I hope your brother is proud of his handiwork.' His gaze hardened on Dorothy. 'I warned you that I would disown the family if it came to this,' he said. 'I will not intercede for him. He has shamed us all.'

The bitter taste of misery was in Dorothy's mouth. She remembered her own words to the Earl of Derwentwater all those months ago, back in the spring when this disaster could have been averted. She had warned him then of the price of treason, not the personal cost, but the price paid by innocents who never had a choice. She wanted to weep for them all, but the horror was so great she found her eyes were dry.

She raised a hand to her head as it spun dizzily.

'Thank you for telling me the news, sir,' she said. 'Papa must be told, of course, but I need a little time before I speak to him.'

'Of course.' Lord Crewe looked gratified by her obvious

distress. 'Sir William need be told nothing immediately.' His lip curled. 'Very likely he will not understand anyway.'

'I pray he will not,' Dorothy said. She took a breath. 'You did not mention Lord Derwentwater, sir. Did he survive – and his brother, Charles?'

'Both taken by the King's army,' Lord Crewe said with satisfaction, 'and that other traitor, Widdrington, as well. They will execute Derwentwater for sure.'

There did indeed seem little doubt of that, Dorothy thought bitterly. The Earl had been such a driving force behind the rebellion, such a talisman for those who believed in the cause.

'Oh, poor Anna,' she whispered, thinking of his wife. 'And their children still babies...' She stood up, unable to take any more. 'If you will excuse me, sir...'

'Sit down, Dorothy.' Lord Crewe's voice was sharp. 'There is more to discuss.'

'Sir?' Apprehension replaced Dorothy's misery. What more could there possibly be? Yet Lang had shifted in anticipation now and there was something in his demeanour that she could not name but did not like. He was watching her and his expression was hard and calculating.

'Major Lang has an offer to make,' Lord Crewe said. 'Under certain circumstances, he is prepared to use his influence to ask for clemency for Thomas when his case comes to court.'

'And Nicholas?' Dorothy put in swiftly.

'Of course, of course.' Lord Crewe did not meet her eyes.

Dorothy's heart settled to a low, hard thud. This could only mean one thing. She doubted that even Lang would have the poor taste to proposition her to be his mistress under her uncle's nose, so they must have come to some sort of agreement beneficial to both of them.

'And those circumstances would be...' she asked.

Major Lang gave her one of his ironic bows. 'Our marriage, of course, Mistress Forster,' he said. 'As your husband, I would do all that was within my power to secure your brothers' release.'

'I shall provide your dowry, of course,' Lord Crewe put in. 'And your husband will be my heir.' He looked at Lang. 'It will be my pleasure to know that you are safely wed to a man who possesses a strength and ambition I admire.'

Dorothy saw then what she had missed before. Her uncle was not a young man and his wife was dying slowly by degrees. Despite Maria Danson's not-so-secret hopes, he did not imagine himself marrying again and fathering a child of his own. His nephews had proved unworthy in his eyes. Here was Lang, a younger son of a good family, who very likely reminded him of himself at the same age: ruthless, determined to make his own way in the world, a man who had already proved himself an ally in the most important matter of all, which was burnishing Lord Crewe's good name and status.

It was a devil's bargain and she had no intention of honouring it. Major Lang did not care for her; she knew he admired her looks but hated her character. She suspected that he would take great pleasure in asserting his authority over her and the thought made her skin crawl. He saw her as a means to access Lord Crewe's fortune and influence, and rise in the world. Aristocratic marriages were frequently made on such a basis, but she thought of John, of his honour and his integrity and his courage, and she knew she could never accept the man who was his opposite in every way. She would not do it, even to save her family.

'And if I were to refuse?' she asked.

Lang's brows rose as though he were offended at the very idea. 'You are in no position to do so, my dear,' he drawled. 'However, if you were to be so headstrong, I daresay we could find a prison cell for you as well. You are, after all, a Jacobite sympathiser.' He paused and the silence was heavy with threat. 'Do think clearly, Mistress Forster,' he added with quiet menace. 'You would not like the things that would happen to you in prison. And what about your father? How do you imagine he would take the news of your arrest? Very likely the shock would kill him.'

Dorothy gazed at him with loathing. Clearly Major Lang had dispensed with any pretence of courtesy now and would stop at nothing to achieve his ambitions. The castle, Lord Crewe's fortune... It was all too tempting, a devil's bargain indeed.

There had to be another way. Her thoughts tumbled over themselves in her desperation. If she was clever, she might use a sham betrothal to her advantage, to lull both her uncle and the major into the belief that she was weakly agreeing to their arrangement. She could buy herself some time to plan for her father's safety and then she could run away, for she must get to London and do all she could to help her brothers. She must save Nicholas before it was too late.

Belatedly, she realised that her thought processes were clear from her expression – her appalled revulsion at the proposal of marriage and then her second thoughts. Lang had been watching her with detached amusement. She had never been very good at hiding her feelings. Fortunately, though, he had completely misinterpreted her.

'It would appear that Mistress Forster has worked out the benefits of the match,' he said drily. He took Dorothy's hand and she tried not to flinch. 'Are we to wed then, ma'am?'

She met his eyes and shuddered inwardly. They were a blank grey, no warmth or humanity in them. 'Thank you, Major Lang.' She forced the words out. 'I am happy to accept.'

'I am honoured.' Major Lang kissed her hand. 'We shall wed here at Bamburgh, tomorrow.'

Panic gripped Dorothy. She had not anticipated that. The following day was far too soon.

'I need some time to prepare,' she stammered, 'to choose an appropriate outfit—'

Lord Crewe unexpectedly came to her rescue. 'My dear Lang, tomorrow is impossible! It will take at least a couple of days to send for all the provisions for the wedding breakfast. You would not wish people to think there was anything havey-cavey about the proceedings. More importantly, my bishop's robes are in Durham and I cannot officiate at my niece's wedding without them. You will need a special licence, which I can provide, of course, but a week's grace is needed—'

'Three days,' Major Lang compromised. He turned to Dorothy. 'I am persuaded you would not wish it to be longer. Not when your brothers are even now being taken to London in chains.' Seeing her turn paler, he added, 'I am glad that we have come to an agreement. I suspected that a woman as intelligent as you are would appreciate the benefits of joining forces with me rather than continuing to oppose me.'

'All that I have ever done, sir,' Dorothy said, 'and continue to do, is work for the best interests of my family. You are offering me the one thing that I desire – my brothers' freedom and safety. I will pay any price for that.'

'Then we understand one another very well.' Major Lang leaned closer, his words for her alone. 'And if you cheat me, I shall make you sorry for it.'

'It is not in my interests to cheat you.' Dorothy tried to keep her voice steady, though the feral anger in him chilled her to the core. She stepped back to put some space between them. 'If you will excuse me, sir,' she added, 'I should like to go to my room to compose myself before speaking to my father to give him the bad news of his sons' arrest.'

'And the good news of the wedding,' Lord Crewe chided. 'He will, I am sure, be delighted to give you away.'

Once upstairs, the events of the previous half-hour finally seemed to catch up with her and she felt breathless and dizzy again. She sat down in the chair beside the window and put her head in her hands. Visions of the destruction and bloodshed in the town of Preston crowded her mind; houses on fire, the crack of muskets, the screams and shouts of the populace, rats pouring from burning buildings, women and children fleeing in terror, cut down in cold blood. How could Thomas have unleashed such suffering? How had Nicholas been able to bear witnessing it, yet alone participating in it?

She ran to the anteroom and was violently sick, then, when the world came back into focus, she washed and dried her face slowly and went to lie down on the bed. She needed to think and plan, and she had so very little time. She must get to London, to Sir Guy, and see what could be done to help Thomas and Nicholas. And she most certainly could not wait long, for in three days, Major Lang would make good on his threat to marry her. If she had not already emptied her stomach, the thought would have made her do so again.

Yet running away would leave her father unprotected, a hostage at Lord Crewe's mercy. She had the key that had been smuggled in, thank God, and she had Mrs Selden to help her, but she had no notion how she might get herself and her father safely out of the castle. She needed a plan and she knew she could not falter. Because, if she did, they would all be lost.

* * *

Day and night for the following two days, carts and carriages rumbled back and forth up the hill to Bamburgh Castle with a huge variety of provisions – meat, vegetables, fruits, beer, wine, flowers to decorate the chapel and more for the great hall, gowns for Dorothy to choose from, Lord Crewe's bishop's robes and regalia delivered from his palace in Auckland and the cathedral in Durham, and a whole host of smaller but no less essential items required in a hurry for the wedding of the season. The castle and its battlements rang with the shouts of tradesmen and the barked orders of soldiers. The night before the nuptials was equally busy, with a last-minute flurry after midnight as the servants polished the silver and set the table in the great hall for the following day. The soldiers practised their marches in the courtyard and the chaplain checked anxiously that the chapel was fully prepared for a service led by the most Reverend Prince Bishop of Durham.

The first sign that something was awry occurred at nine on the morning of the wedding when Lady Crewe's bell rang in a most agitated fashion. The maid who ran to answer it reported to Neverson, the butler, that Lady Crewe was disgruntled that Mrs Danson had not brought her the morning tea. The previous night, the companion had been deputed to attend the bride to her bedroom, ensure she was locked in and to sit outside her door all night – just in case. A soldier had been allocated to stand guard at the end of the corridor. Major Lang was taking no chances that his bride might abscond.

There was no immediate sign of either Mrs Danson or the guard when the harassed butler made his way up to the tower to investigate. Panting a little, Neverson checked the solid door of Mistress Forster's chamber and ascertained that the key was missing. There was no sound from within except snoring. Then he realised that there were two sets of snores.

After a great deal of searching, a spare key was found. By this time, Major Lang and Lord Crewe had been alerted that something untoward might have happened. When Neverson opened the door, it was to reveal Mrs Danson and the hapless soldier tied up together on the bed, both still deeply asleep. Of Mistress Forster, there was no sign.

The major threw an ewer of water over the slumbering couple which succeeded in waking Mrs Danson, who promptly had hysterics. The soldier was only roused when he was dragged down to the courtyard and dumped in the horse trough. Mrs Danson remembered settling down in the rocking chair outside the door but nothing else. The soldier claimed to have been over-powered by no fewer than four brawny Jacobite soldiers, rough fellows dressed in plaid, brandishing huge claymores, but as he smelled strongly of drink, no one believed him.

One thing that was indisputable, however, was that Mistress Forster had vanished. A hasty check of the castle revealed that Sir William Forster was gone too, though, in his case, he had simply wandered out of the gate earlier that morning, telling the sentry that he was searching for lyme-grass. As no one had told the sentry that Sir William was to stay *within* the castle bounds, the man had thought nothing of it.

Major Lang organised a series of search parties, but though they rode out all day on the hunt for the fugitives, they found no clue as to their whereabouts. No one had seen nor heard any sign of Dorothy Forster or her father. Not even a reward of five hundred pounds could jog their memory. Lord Crewe retired to his study in a fury, having made it plain to the major that if he could not hold on to his bride, he certainly would not be receiving her dowry of ten thousand pounds, and the major rode to London, spurred on by having been made to look a complete fool. Someone, he promised himself, was going to pay.

* * *

The little boat crept out of the shadow of the cove at Budle Bay, with John Armstrong pulling hard on the oars. The sea was calm and the night had only a flicker of a moon. Out beyond the rocks, a ketch waited, sails dark, slipping between the slight swells. Dorothy watched the pinpricks of light on land fade away, to be swallowed up in the night, and released a sigh. They were on their way now. She had no notion what might befall any of them and could only pray for their safety, just as she prayed hourly for Thomas and Nicholas in gaol in London, and that her father would arrive safely with his cousins at Warkworth Manor. She was tired and strung out with the anxiety of her escape. Each step away from the castle had been haunted by the fear of discovery, the dread of hearing the galloping of hooves behind them and the shout of soldiers.

Earlier the previous evening, Mrs Selden's concoction of blackberry juice and a draught of monkshood had soon seen Maria Danson off to sleep and Harris, Sir William's valet, had proved surprisingly handy at knocking out the guard, who had already been imbibing plenty of rum to see him through the long hours of the night. No one had noticed Dorothy, in a maid's gown, amongst all the other servants scurrying to and fro across the castle courtyard as they prepared for the wedding. In at the main entrance to the chapel, out at the back, down the vicar's steps on the outside of the castle wall, their treads worn smooth by hundreds of years of time passing... And at the bottom, there was John, who caught her up in his arms and held on to her as though he would never let her go.

'I knew you would come for me,' Dorothy had said, and John had laughed and kissed her, and the stars had swung dizzily over-head. For a brief moment, they had simply held each other, and everything had felt right again in the midst of so much that was wrong.

11

HANNAH – THE PRESENT

Hannah stood outside the hospital cubicle, a reusable coffee cup in one hand, watching as Bill sat beside Diana's bed, his head drooping with tiredness. Diana was asleep, her face chalk-white against the pillows. She had a temperature and was drifting in and out of consciousness. Bill was holding one of her hands and it looked small and frail against the tanned strength of his.

'Bless you, pet,' he said, when Hannah went in to give him the coffee. 'That should keep me going for a few more hours.'

'I'll be back later so you can go home and get some rest,' Hannah said. Time had blurred whilst they had been at the hospital and she was shocked to see it was late afternoon. Diana had been diagnosed with a severe chest infection, a complication of her lymphoma, and she wouldn't be allowed home until it had started to respond to the antibiotics. Looking at her stepmother's thin, pale face, Hannah reflected ruefully how cross Diana would be when she was well enough to realise what was going on.

'No need to come back till the morning,' Bill said comfortably. 'You've been here all day, Hannah love. I can bed down easily in this chair and I'll be near my Di and that will be fine.'

Hannah felt the tears prick her eyes at his down-to-earth expression of affection. 'All right,' she allowed, 'but call me if anything changes. I'll be back first thing so you can get a shower and some breakfast.'

'I can take a hint.' Bill gave her his warm smile. 'Take care, pet. Text me when you get home.'

Hannah kissed Diana's cheek, gave Bill a peck as well, and went out to the car. It was a relief to be outside in the afternoon sun; she felt tired but glad to breathe in the fresh air. Hospitals always made her think of her father's death.

She'd had her phone turned off whilst she was with Diana, but now it pinged with a number of messages. Aaron had texted to ask how she was getting on and reassure her that Tarka had already settled in with him at the cottage and was welcome to stay as long as was needed. Hannah smiled to think of Tarka preening herself to have got Aaron's undivided attention. Alice had messaged to ask if there was anything she could do, as had a couple of Diana's friends. There was also a message from Hannah's uncle Peter. *Dorothy Forster of Adderstone married a John Armstrong of Bamburgh in London in December 1715*, it read. *Copy of marriage entry attached. Could that be the connection you're looking for? xx.* Hannah stared at it blankly for a moment before she remembered that she had asked him to look at their family tree to see if there was any link to the Forsters. Here was the confirmation of the story Judy had told her; Dorothy Forster was indeed her ancestor and the likeness Diana had thought she had seen between them was more than mere coincidence.

Hannah sighed, wishing she could feel more excited over the discovery. It all seemed so long ago, before the reality of Diana's fragility had been brought home to her in such a brutal way.

It took her an hour and a quarter to get back to Bamburgh from Newcastle and by the time she did, Hannah was completely

exhausted. A part of her wanted to go and fetch Tarka from
Aaron's cottage – and to see Aaron himself, if she was honest.
However, she knew the sensible thing would be to have a rest first
and call Aaron later.

She made herself a cup of tea and sat down at the kitchen
table but found she couldn't keep still. Although her body was
tired, her mind was running backwards and forwards over so
many different things: Diana, Brandon, Dorothy Forster, the
Rose... It felt as though her brain was trying to tell her something
and had chosen this most unhelpful moment to do so.

The Rose.

She put down her mug of tea so sharply it spilled onto the
wooden table. The painting of Dorothy with all its symbolism
was a secret affirmation that she had been the Keeper of the Rose.
More importantly, it contained the clue to the Rose's appearance;
the stylised rose carving in the stone of the sundial. It also
contained a warning – take the Rose for your own ends and Atropos, the Fate who cut the threads of life, would very likely kill you
as she had killed Sir Bartholomew Forster and possibly others
who had transgressed.

Hannah stood up. She had been so close before when she'd
been in the church crypt and had remembered the necklace her
father had given her as a child. At that stage, of course, she hadn't
spoken to Judy about the theories that the Rose was a piece of
Saxon jewellery – she had imagined something bigger than a thin
piece of gold only a couple of inches long...

She raced up the two flights of stairs to the attic, throwing
open the door of her childhood bedroom under the eaves. And
stopped dead. She had forgotten that Diana had told her there
had been a water leak and she had had to empty the room. The
floor was bare boards, the paper had been stripped from the walls
and all the furniture had gone, including the little white-painted

chest of drawers with the golden knobs where Hannah had kept all her bits and pieces of make-up, jewellery and perfume. She felt her stomach give a sickening lurch at the thought Diana might simply have thrown it all away.

But no. As she went out onto the landing and closed the door behind her, she spotted the chest of drawers in a dark corner. She ran her hand over the smooth painted surface, feeling the gritty rub of dust against her fingers. The top drawer came open with a slight judder; it had always stuck slightly. There was a faint scent of Daisy perfume. It had been Hannah's favourite as a teenager.

The drawer was full of tissue paper, lipsticks, a couple of beanie hats and a pair of round horn-rimmed spectacles that Hannah vaguely remembered had been considered very cool when she was about fourteen. At the back was the pink velvet box she had kept her jewellery in, such as it was. She took it out and turned on the landing light so that she could see more clearly. Some of the contents had gone with her to college and then into her adult life, but here were the bits and pieces she had left behind – broken plastic friendship bracelets, a pair of owl-shaped earrings, feather hair extensions and some shells and sea glass she must have collected from the beach. She brushed it all aside with fingers that were shaking a little, searching through the piles of childhood detritus.

At the bottom of the box was a small padded bag that she remembered making herself when she had been about eight. It had some very uneven flowers embroidered on it in very bright colours. Hannah smiled. Needlework had never been her speciality, but as she tipped the contents onto her palm and saw the light strike off the stylised pattern engraved on the little golden plaque, she thought how appropriate it was that she should have wrapped the Rose in a rose-decorated cloth.

* * *

'I knew I should have set an alarm.' Hannah grabbed her phone off the nightstand and saw that it was almost ten o'clock. She'd slept for four hours when she'd only meant to have a quick nap. The unaccustomed weight of the Rose necklace was lying against her skin, warm and smooth. It had seemed the only safe place to keep it until she decided what to do with it and, oddly, it felt as though it belonged around her neck.

Darkness had closed in whilst she was asleep and now the room was in shades of grey and black with the last vestiges of twilight outside the window. She felt hungry. The sandwich she had gulped down at lunchtime in the hospital cafe felt a long time ago.

The house was too quiet with no one else in it. Hannah tried to ignore the silence whilst she made herself a chicken salad and replied to the latest batch of texts and WhatsApp messages that had come in. She didn't want to bother Aaron as she knew he was on call again that evening, so she texted to ask him if he would be around for an early breakfast before she headed back to the hospital.

On that thought, she decided to put together a few items that Diana would need. If she prepared it all now, she could just pick the bag up in the morning and be on her way. After a four-hour nap, she wasn't feeling sleepy anyway.

Diana's room had the strange chill about it that came from being recently occupied but now empty. It was missing Diana, just as she was. Hannah collected some underwear and a night-dress from the chest of drawers, and filled a toilet bag. She went over to the marble-topped side table beside the bed where her stepmother kept her reading glasses and her puzzle books. Diana would want something to occupy her when she started to feel a bit better. There was a book of codewords and another sudoku one. The drawer was surprisingly cluttered with tissues and lip balm and a tiny bottle of Diana's signature perfume, the scent of which shot Hannah through with nostalgia and regret. She needed to get a grip, she told herself. Diana was nowhere near dead yet.

On impulse, she decided to add one of Diana's cashmere shawls to the pile because her stepmother would want to look stylish even in hospital. She knew Diana kept them in a suitcase under the bed where they were wrapped in special storage bags.

Under the bed were three suitcases – two navy blue ones with Diana's initials monogrammed onto them and a third that looked older and had the CD logo of Christian Dior on it. That, Hannah was sure, was where Diana would keep her best cashmere. Smiling a little, she drew the case out and snapped open the catches. A rainbow pile of scarves and shawls met her gaze and she realised she had no idea which one Diana would prefer, but she decided to take the deep green one that was on the top of the pile; it was soft and incredibly luxurious.

As she took the shawl out of the case, she felt the hard edge of something that was wrapped up in the layers of cashmere below. The fold of a blue stole fell back, and Hannah caught sight of a frame and the corner of a picture that showed the base of a stone column and the figure of a rose.

Hannah sat back on her heels. She didn't feel surprised, but she was confused. She had suspected that Diana had lied to her about taking Dorothy's portrait to be restored, and here was the proof.

There was something else wrapped up in the scarves as well, something slippery. It was so small that Hannah almost missed it and when it tumbled out onto the floor, she stared at it in puzzlement for a moment. It was a plastic bag, the sort used to keep food in, and inside it was a woven leather bracelet with a silver clasp.

Hannah remembered that Brandon had had a bracelet like that, Aaron too. It had been the height of cool in their friendship group in the last year at school. This one looked old and battered, the leather starting to rot and fray. Hannah opened the bag and a smell of sea water and dust wafted out. She tipped the bracelet into her hand and saw that the silver was tarnished, but when she ran her fingers over the clasp, she could feel the engraved letters, B and A. This must have been Brandon's, then, the one she remembered him wearing. But what on earth was it doing here? Why had Diana hidden it away?

She held it up to the light and saw the tracery of letters beneath the black discoloured silver. The A was clear, but was that a B or something else? Now she looked closely, it could be an R...

With a sudden jolt, she remembered Aaron's story about why he and Brandon had fallen out. She had asked him what had happened to Richard Arundel, the boy who had run away when Brandon had bullied him. And, like a whisper, she heard Aaron's voice again: *'I don't think they ever found him.'*

There was the creak of a floorboard behind her and Hannah spun around. Brandon was standing in the doorway, the overhead light shining on his golden hair like a halo. He walked towards her, smiling. She could hear the jingle of keys in his pocket. That answered the question she had forgotten to ask Diana as to whether Brandon had kept his keys to Bamburgh Hall.

'Hi, Hannah,' he said casually. His gaze went from the suitcase, where the tumble of shawls and scarves revealed Dorothy Forster's painting, to the bracelet Hannah still held in her hand. 'So that's where Diana hid them.'

'Brandon,' Hannah said, 'I wondered when you would turn

up.' As casually as possible, she let the leather bracelet slip back into the suitcase, pretending she had no idea of its significance. She stood up, dusting her trousers. She had felt vulnerable sitting on the floor with her brother looming over her, but she didn't feel much better standing up, since Brandon was between her and the door, and she could tell from the look on his face that there was no way that she could pretend this was a simple social call. Not at ten o'clock at night when she was alone, Diana was in hospital and Brandon had a harsh, hungry light in his eyes as they rested on the painting of Dorothy Forster.

He bent down to retrieve the portrait from the case. 'It's beautiful, isn't it,' he said softly. 'There's no intrinsic worth to it, since the artist is unknown and it wouldn't sell for much, but he did a good job, whoever he was.'

'Surely its value is in the fact that it's a stunning painting and Diana loves it,' Hannah said. 'She wouldn't sell it even if it was valuable in the monetary sense.'

Brandon laughed. 'I know you're naïve, Han, but even you're not that stupid. Its value lies in the fact that it shows Dorothy Forster as the keeper of the Rose treasure.' He shot her a look. 'I know you've worked it all out. You don't need to pretend to me. You've researched Dorothy Forster and you've looked at the rose motifs in the church. You've spoken to Judy and you've visited Forge Cottage. I've been watching you. You know everything. So, what is the Rose and where do I find it?'

His intense blue gaze was fixed on her now and it was all Hannah could do to keep her hand from creeping to her throat, where the Rose was hidden beneath the collar of her shirt.

'You're deluded, Brandon,' she said as steadily as she could. 'I don't know what you're talking about. If you've been following me, you'll know I'm here to research Grace Darling, not Dorothy Forster.' She looked at the portrait. 'Yes, I know a bit about

Dorothy and I thought the picture was lovely when Diana first showed it to me, but she told me she'd sent it for restoration, so I'm not sure what it's doing here. I only found it because I was looking for some stuff to take to her in hospital.' She gestured to the bed, where everything from face cream to silk handkerchiefs were lying in a pile. 'I thought it was you I'd seen in the village,' she added. 'All this creeping around and secrecy is paranoid, Brandon. Your weird games were tiresome enough when we were kids, but they're just embarrassing now.'

Brandon bared his teeth in a smile. 'Have it your own way. It doesn't really matter. I'll find the Rose myself.'

'You do that,' Hannah said. She walked over to the wardrobe and took out a holdall. 'If you'll excuse me,' she added, 'I want to get this all sorted so I can get back to the hospital early tomorrow.' She raised her brows. 'I assume that you know Diana is ill? She's in the Royal Victoria in Newcastle if you want to visit.' *And you won't get past Bill if you try*, she thought.

The reminder that there were other people who could help her deal with Brandon steadied her a little. If she could just get rid of him now, with or without Dorothy's portrait, she could alert Bill and Aaron. Aaron was only a few streets away...

But it was too late. She could feel it. She could see it in his face even before he placed Dorothy's painting carefully on the bed and bent down to pick up the leather bracelet she had hoped was concealed in the suitcase.

'You saw this,' he said. For a moment, he held it in the palm of his hand, head bent. 'I don't know why I kept it, really,' he added quietly. 'As a trophy, I suppose.'

Hannah's heart started to beat harder. She instantly understood what Brandon was confessing to, but she didn't want him to know she knew about Richard Arundel's disappearance.

'That's your old leather bracelet, isn't it?' she said, offhand. 'I don't know why you'd want to keep it. It's rank.'

Their eyes met. Hannah kept her face studiously blank. *This is Brandon*, her mind was saying, *my brother*. He looked the same, he sounded the same, and yet she knew him for what he truly was; not the charming boyish mischief-maker whom everyone had indulged, but the destructive man who could be genuinely dangerous. They had been close once, she thought. That was no illusion. But it had been a long time ago and Brandon had always been erratic. Something in him was broken.

Brandon's gaze went to her throat and with an awful swoop of fear, Hannah realised she had betrayed herself. She had been toying with the necklace whilst she was lying to him. She had not even realised that she had done it.

He took a step towards her. Before she knew it, his hands were around her neck. It was so sudden and so shocking that panic welled up in her chest. Brandon ripped the chain from her and looked down at the golden plaque, turning it over to study the engraving. Then he started to laugh.

'It's tiny!' he said. 'I thought it would be some great golden talisman like the Holy Cross or the Holy Grail! This...' He shook his head. 'Wow. What a disappointment.' He was holding the Rose in his hand much as he had held the bracelet a moment earlier. The gold seemed to spark and flash, but Brandon did not appear to notice. He looked up, his eyes brimming with mirth. 'How ridiculous,' he said. 'Oh well.' He slipped his hand into his pocket and the flash of gold vanished. 'I'll take it anyway.' He turned back towards her.

'Don't,' Hannah said. Her voice was shaking. 'Don't take it, Brandon. It isn't yours. I thought you knew the stories? Judy said she'd told you. The Rose protects its own and punishes those who misuse it.'

'Right.' Brandon looked unimpressed. He took in her stricken expression and started to laugh again. 'Don't tell me you believe that claptrap? Jeez, Hannah, who do you think you are, the keeper of the so-called Rose?'

'It's been mine since I was five years old,' Hannah said. 'Our father gave it to me, Brandon. He gave it to *me*, not to you, because even then he knew you weren't to be trusted. You were greedy. You always knew the price of everything but the value of nothing, like some of your Forster forbears. You were the son and heir right enough, but you weren't the keeper of the Rose.'

Fury flamed in Brandon's eyes. 'You little bitch,' he snarled. 'I wish you'd died when you fell into that cave years ago. You could have drowned, and you would have done if it hadn't been for bloody Aaron Salter.'

'Is that what happened to Richard Arundel?' Hannah's voice was shaking. She thought of the old, sand-encrusted leather bracelet with its smell of seaweed and salt. 'Did you kill him in the sea cave, Brandon?'

Brandon looked at her and suddenly it seemed to Hannah that there was no emotion behind his eyes, no expression at all. 'It was an accident,' he said sulkily, sounding like a little boy. 'I didn't mean to do it. We were fighting, and he fell and hit his head on the rock. It wasn't my fault.'

'But you kept his bracelet as a trophy,' Hannah said. She wasn't sure whether she believed him when he said it was an accident, but she knew she had to keep Brandon talking. She didn't have the physical strength to overpower him, nor was there anything obvious in Diana's room she could use as a weapon, but she might be able to get past him and out of the door, especially if Brandon became distracted. She groped surreptitiously in her pocket for her phone, but Brandon saw her.

'Don't,' he said conversationally. 'Don't call anyone. We haven't finished chatting yet.'

He took the Rose plaque from his pocket and studied it again. The light shone on the stylised golden swirls that represented the petals and the leaves, beautiful strokes of engraving that were as bright and clear now as they had been twelve hundred years before when they were made. Hannah watched him, edging a step or two closer to the door. He seemed engrossed. Then he looked up sharply.

'It really is small,' he said and he sounded disappointed. 'Admittedly, it's a very old piece of gold, but I think my buyer will be disappointed.'

'Then give it back to me,' Hannah suggested. Her throat was as dry as paper. Her head had started to ache with the tension.

'Don't tell me that if I hand it back, we'll forget about everything,' Brandon said, derisive again. 'I'm not a fool, Han.'

'Of course not,' Hannah kept her tone calm, 'but I'm sure we can sort something out—'

Brandon's laugh was bitter. 'I had three million riding on this,' he said, closing his fist over the Rose. 'What a nightmare.'

'Don't take it,' Hannah repeated more urgently. She wondered if she was starting to hallucinate. The room suddenly seemed airless and suffocating, and the pounding in her head was as fierce as the beat of the waves on the shore. She could see sparks at the edge of her vision, flames creeping up the curtains and licking along the window frame. 'Brandon!' she yelled.

There was a crack of sound and a dazzling explosion of light. Hannah could feel herself falling. She thought of Dorothy's portrait, of the sundial and of Atropos, the eldest of the three Fates, who cut the thread of life. She thought of Aaron, his name exploding through her mind.

Brandon gave a wild, high cry. Hannah saw his body crumple,

folding in on itself. There was another flash of light even brighter than the first. Hannah closed her eyes against its fierceness, felt the scorch of the flames ever closer, and desperately clung on to consciousness as she crawled towards the door and the last chance of escape.

* * *

Aaron ran. He dodged the late cars making their way down Front Street, practically rebounding off one and shouting an apology as he raced up the road, his footsteps pounding on the tarmac, his panting breaths disturbing the night-time quiet. The pavement was slick with a fine mist blowing in from the sea. It clung to the shops and terraces, cloaking them in an eerie grey shroud.

Aaron knew exactly where he was going and why. As he drew closer to Bamburgh Hall, he could see the unearthly orange glow of fire licking up the first-floor windows. He pulled out his phone and made an emergency call. The front door was locked and bolted and did not yield to his shouts or the hammering of his fists on the wood; he ran around the side of the house. Brandon's Porsche was in the courtyard and the back door was unlocked. Aaron stormed through it and into the kitchen, the acrid scent of smoke already in his throat.

'Hannah!' There was no answer, but he could smell the fire more strongly as he ran into the hall. Unnervingly, he could hear the fire now as well, the roar of it like a jet engine, a terrifying force of nature that could not be checked. He took the stairs three at a time.

Hannah was lying on the first-floor landing. Aaron dropped to his knees beside her. She was unconscious, but she was breathing steadily, and in her hand was clasped a small plaque with a beautiful, stylised design of a rose. Behind her, the door of the bedroom was closed, but smoke was billowing beneath it and Aaron could feel the heat radiating through the thick wall.

He scooped Hannah up and she opened her eyes. They were dazed and unfocused, but she smiled, and Aaron allowed himself one moment to hold her close, as the relief exploded through him. Then he turned away from the flames and carried her carefully down the stairs and out into the cold night air.

'Brandon,' Hannah murmured.

'It's too dangerous to go back in.' Aaron set his jaw. His instinct as someone trained in lifesaving was always to try to help, but he knew that if he opened that door the whole house would be lost. It was probably already too late.

Other people had been alerted by now; the police had already arrived. The fire engine and an ambulance were on their way. Judy, who lived two doors down, brought Aaron a blanket to wrap Hannah in. The woman who ran the deli shop fetched him some coffee. The neighbours had gathered out in the street and everyone jumped as the upstairs windows smashed in a shower of glass. Aaron found he was holding his breath, waiting for the first creak and groan of timber that would indicate the roof giving way.

There was silence. The flames dropped back, became burning embers and died down. The sea fret blew through the empty, dark window space. A shocked whisper ran through the witnesses: '*What's happening? It's burned itself out... That isn't possible...*'

Nobody moved. When the sound of the fire engine's siren split the night a second later, no one could see any flames at all.

12

DOROTHY – LONDON, NOVEMBER 1715

It was snowing by the time they reached London, huge flakes that floated lazily down from a leaden sky, giving the impression of a peaceful world. But there was nothing peaceful about the capital. It was loud, filthy and busy. Dorothy remembered all the reasons why, when she had visited on previous occasions, she had wished herself back in Northumberland, with its clean sweet-scented air and quiet fields and lanes.

They had travelled fast, with little time for rest. John had wanted to ensure that they kept ahead of Major Lang and any search parties he might send out to hunt for them. Luckily, Lang's imagination had proved limited and he had not thought to search out at sea. The herring ketch had made its way south to Gravesend with no trouble, and from there, swift horses had taken them from Kent to London in three days.

Litchfield Street was full of elegant new houses, three storeys high, built of dark brick and contrasting pale stone. They had made the last part of the journey by carriage, John wishing both to provide her with some comfort in the cold weather and also to make them appear as anonymous as possible, just another tradesman and his wife coming up to London for the shops and the excitement of the Jacobite trials.

Dorothy was shivering with cold and nervousness as they drew up at number twenty-three and John handed her down onto the street. Her limbs were stiff and aching from the journey, and she slipped a little on the snow underfoot, feeling John's arm come about her to steady her. She looked up at him and he smiled, rubbing away a snowflake that had landed on her cheek. There was tenderness in his eyes, but he released her at once and strode away to knock on the door. Dorothy sighed, smoothing her gown in a vain attempt to get rid of the travel wrinkles. She looked and felt grubby and dishevelled, which was not at all the state she wished to be in to meet Sir Guy and Lady Forster.

'My dear, you must be cold and exhausted.' An elderly lady emerged from the house to take her arm and hurry her inside. She was short, almost as small as Dorothy herself, with dark auburn hair generously sprinkled with grey, and vivid green eyes in a smiling face. 'I am Rose Forster,' she continued, 'Sir Guy's wife, and you must be Cousin William's daughter Dorothy. We were out of London when you visited last, but I think I would have known you anyway as you have a great look of your mama about you. Let me take you up to your chamber whilst your fiancé —' she threw John a twinkling glance '—sees to matters such as the stabling and luggage.'

With a series of quick orders, she organised hot water, a dish of tea, crumpets and a clean gown for Dorothy and ushered her up a grand, balustraded staircase into a comfortable chamber that had, to Dorothy's great pleasure, a fire burning in the grate.

'We have been in anticipation of your visit ever since Mr Armstrong delivered your letter last month,' Rose Forster was saying. The light died from her eyes. 'My poor girl, what a terrible time you have endured, with your brothers arrested and you and your father practically held prisoner by that dreadful man, Nathaniel Crewe.' She shook her head. 'I always thought he was a most *ungodly* clergyman! But many of these religious fellows are as ambitious and cunning as any man you would meet at court, or woman too. At least he is no philanderer, being devoted to your poor aunt Doll, so that's a blessing. I remember her as a young woman – so beautiful that all the gentlemen were smitten. But...' She stood back and surveyed Dorothy thoughtfully. 'She cannot hold a candle to you, for you have all the life and energy she lacks. And now—' she gave Dorothy a knowing smile '—you have a handsome and devoted husband-to-be into the bargain. Mr Armstrong seems a most *capable* man, if you take my meaning, and those are by far the best sort of man.'

A knock at the door interrupted her flow before she had the chance to comment any further on John's attributes and Dorothy was a little relieved.

'There now, that will be the hot water,' Lady Forster said. 'The maid will attend to you and I shall leave you to enjoy some refreshment, but do join me downstairs when you are ready. We have much to discuss. Sir Guy is at the coffee house at this moment, ascertaining the latest news on your brothers and their situation.' Upon which words, she waved the servants in with water and refreshments and swept out like a miniature whirlwind.

As she lay in the scented water of the bath, Dorothy reflected that Lady Forster must be old, seventy years at least, for she had been sister to the notorious Madam Nell Gwyn, mistress of the late King Charles, who had died many years before. Sir Guy was her second husband and they had had a long and happy marriage, with many children and grandchildren. Yet despite her many years, Lady Forster was still full of energy, as well as charm. Dorothy looked forward to getting to know her better.

There was a strong temptation to stay in the warm water and from there to crawl into the comfortable bed and fall asleep, but Dorothy had heard Sir Guy arrive home a short while ago and was anxious to hear what he had to report. Besides, she wished to see John, and if possible, have some private conversation with him. Lady Forster, she suspected, was the sort of woman who would understand that and, she hoped, be prepared to help her.

Dressing hastily in the gown Lady Forster had laid out for her, Dorothy hurried downstairs, where a liveried footman directed her to the drawing room. Rose Forster was seated on a sofa beside the fire, whilst the two men were standing close together, conversing quietly. The candles were lit and the room looked warm and reassuring, even though the reasons that had brought them there were so grim.

Dorothy took a moment to study John and reflect how comfortable he seemed here in a gentleman's London drawing room with a glass of wine in hand. It was because John was confident in himself; unlike Lang, he did not try to impress or to puff himself up into something he was not. The thought made her smile and he looked across at her in that moment and raised a quizzical eyebrow.

Sir Guy put down his glass and strode across the room to embrace her. Like his wife, he was in his seventies, but an upright, active figure, elegant in a velvet jacket, his hair still dark and his gaze still shrewd and sharp. 'My dear Dorothy, I am glad to welcome you to my home, though it pains me sadly that I should not be greeting your father as well. Armstrong—' he gestured to John '—tells me he is safe and well with our cousins at Warkworth, which is good news. I understand his health has suffered greatly of late.' He moved to the sideboard to pour a glass of wine for her and Lady Forster patted the seat beside hers to indicate to Dorothy to join her.

'It has been a great comfort to my father to receive your letters these months past, sir,' Dorothy said. 'He is sick in body, but his mind is still sharp most of the time.'

'The news of your brothers' capture and imprisonment cannot have helped,' Sir Guy said. He passed the wine to Dorothy and she took a grateful sip, feeling its warmth spread inside her. 'I was at the coffee house just now and heard that Thomas is incarcerated in Newgate Gaol, awaiting trial for treason. The great lords will be tried first, of course, but as the Jacobite general at Preston, Thomas cannot expect clemency when his time comes.'

His gaze was sympathetic as it rested on her, but Dorothy knew and appreciated that he was not trying to soften the blow. It was far better that she should be prepared for the worst. Over the past ten days, she had teetered between resignation and hope, even whilst knowing that it was highly unlikely that Thomas would escape with his life. She realised that she had lost Thomas long before this; his adherence to the cause and stubborn refusal to see any alternative other than rebellion had come between them long ago, but she was able to forgive him almost anything if he kept Nicholas safe.

'Derwentwater is in the Tower of London,' Sir Guy added. 'I fear the authorities are likely to make an example of him too. The gossip is that his family has offered a fortune for his release, but Walpole is adamant he must not be pardoned.'

Dorothy had glanced at John when the Earl's name was mentioned, fearing he might think she still cared for Derwentwater as more than a friend, but he met her eyes and smiled, and she knew he understood. He came over to sit beside her and took her hand in his. It was a gentle, unselfconscious gesture that was immensely comforting.

'My younger brother, Nicholas...' Dorothy said hesitantly. 'Is there any news of him? I was told... That is, Major Lang told me at Bamburgh that Nick had been captured along with Thomas.'

She felt John tense slightly at the mention of Lang's name. She suspected that he was furious he had not had the opportunity for a reckoning with Lang over his treatment of her, but she had managed to impress upon him that it was more important to rescue Nicholas if they could. Any scores could be settled once that had been achieved, for Dorothy was determined to beg the King in person for Nicholas's freedom if she had to. Unlike Derwentwater's family, they did not have a fortune to offer as ransom.

A frown had settled on Sir Guy's brow. He toyed with his wine glass. 'I have not been able to ascertain Nicholas's situation precisely,' he admitted, 'although I am sure he is in Newgate with Thomas. Charles Radclyffe is in the Tower with his brother Lord Derwentwater, so it would seem likely.'

John stirred slightly. 'I will go to Newgate tomorrow,' he said, 'to see for myself.'

'I shall come with you,' Dorothy said firmly.

'Newgate is no place for a lady.' Sir Guy's brows had risen in disapproval, but a smile played about his wife's lips.

'You are a true Forster, Dorothy,' she commended, 'courageous and full of goodness. I admire you for it.' She glanced at her husband. 'We shall give you some coin to bribe the gaoler to let you in. I would not wish you to have to pawn your mother's jewellery.'

Dorothy blushed because that was exactly what she had planned to do.

Sir Guy harrumphed and looked at John. 'What do you think, Armstrong?'

'I think there is little point in objecting, sir,' John said, with a smile for Dorothy, 'for as your lady rightly notes, Dorothy has a

sharp mind, a strong will and a great deal of bravery.' He tightened his fingers about hers. 'I shall ensure she is well-protected,
however, and—' he turned to Rose Forster '—we are grateful for
your generosity.'

Sir Guy still looked as though he wanted to protest, but his
wife merely laughed at him.

'You yourself married an unconventional woman,' she
pointed out. 'You are in no position to criticise.'

'Aye, it's true I did.' Sir Guy sank into a seat opposite her and
favoured her with a rueful smile. 'Nor have I for one moment
regretted it.' He raised his glass to Dorothy and John. 'I wish you a
long and happy life together – once this dreadful matter is
resolved.'

'Amen to that,' Lady Forster agreed, 'and we shall all pray for
the best outcome.'

'Thank you both for all your kindness,' Dorothy said. It was
wonderful that Sir Guy and Lady Forster had accepted John, a
working man, as her betrothed without a word of censure. Like
her father, they could appreciate his good qualities, and unlike
Lord Crewe, they did not have the sense of snobbery that was so
distasteful to her.

'There is one small matter I need to settle before the morrow,'
John began. He placed his wine very carefully on the table and
went down on one knee before Dorothy, who gave a quick excla-
mation of surprise. 'Mistress Forster,' he said very formally, 'I
requested your hand in marriage before, but not with the ceremony appropriate to such a serious matter. So, I ask again, before
witnesses—' he looked up into her eyes and Dorothy realised
with a shock that he was actually nervous '—will you do me the
honour of becoming my wife?'

'With all my heart,' Dorothy said, pulling him to his feet so that she could throw herself into his arms. 'I would wed you this very moment if I could!'

John laughed and kissed her and then Sir Guy and Lady Forster were hugging and congratulating her too.

'Most elegantly done, Mr Armstrong,' Lady Forster said. She drew Dorothy a little aside. 'Forgive us the deception, my dear Dorothy,' she said, shooting John a look brimful with mischief, 'but Mr Armstrong did confide in us when he was here before that he wished to expedite your marriage as soon as could be arranged, so—'

'So that is why there is a clergyman waiting out in the hall,' Sir Guy finished, a twinkle in his eyes.

'I shall be matron of honour and I am sure that Sir Guy will stand groomsman,' Lady Forster said. 'Come, my dear.' She took Sir Guy's arm. 'We have a wedding to witness.'

* * *

Newgate prison was a hellhole. From the outside, its brutal facade and lack of windows proclaimed its purpose as a grim place of punishment. As Dorothy and John were escorted through the long, dark corridor towards the courtyard cells where those of more genteel birth were housed, they were assaulted by the screams and shouts of the poorer prisoners on each side, who lived their lives in perpetual darkness. The smell of decay and sickness almost smothered Dorothy, who held her handkerchief over her nose and pressed closer to John's side.

They had already spent a third of the money Sir Guy had given them simply gaining entrance to the prison. The warders were reluctant to allow visitors and the price had to be right. For the man who had led the Jacobite army in England to such ignominious defeat and surrender, the price was very high indeed.

''Ere he is,' the gaoler said cheerfully, stepping over the filth draining down the open sewer to slam open the door of a cell. 'The chief rebel 'imself.'

John stood back to allow Dorothy to greet her brothers first. Her heart was racing, beating hard and fast. She could not wait to see Nicholas. Thomas she was less inclined to show kindness, since he had got them all into this terrible mess in the first place.

She rushed into the little chamber. There was barely any light or fresh air, other than from a grating high in the wall. Her gaze took in the cell with its bunk and single wooden chair on which sat Thomas, gazing vacantly into space. His clothes were filthy and torn, his hair straggling and he sported a new, unkempt beard. His eyes were bloodshot; an empty bottle rolled on the stone floor beside him, and the room smelled of spirits. Dorothy, who was trying to keep calm and greet him civilly, found her anger almost too much to bear. But it was not that which consumed her. It took only a brief glance about the cell to see that Nicholas was not there.

'Dot!' Thomas's eyes lit up to see her. His gaze drifted over John, clearly dismissing him as her servant, and he did not trouble to greet him. He hauled himself to his feet, wincing, and took a step forward to embrace his sister. 'At last!' he said. 'Have you brought food for me and clean clothes?' His voice changed, became hopeful. 'Do you have money?'

Enveloped in his foul-smelling embrace, Dorothy sought to free herself as quickly as she could. She could see that John was standing just within the doorway and was looking at Thomas with an odd expression on his face. A cold, hard fear formed in her stomach, expanding through her whole body and causing her to shake.

'Nick?' she asked. Her voice was shaking too. 'Where is he?'

Thomas fell back a step. His gaze dropped from hers. There

was an agonising silence. Dorothy knew the answer before he spoke, but her ears did not want to hear it and her mind would not accept it.

'No,' she said. It felt like a scream in her head and yet it came out as a whisper. 'No!'

'He fell at Preston.' Thomas would not meet her eyes. 'He took a bullet in the chest. A soldier called Lang shot him. We buried him in the church there. I thought you knew...' He sounded aggrieved now that he was the one who had had to tell her. 'I thought you knew,' he repeated.

Dorothy felt her world collapse. She heard John swear; a second later, he was by her side, one arm about her to support her. He was speaking to her softly, but Dorothy could not hear him. Her head rang with Thomas's words: '*A soldier called Lang shot him...*' She thought of Nicholas, so full of life and energy, felled by a single bullet from the Jacobite hunter's pistol.

She dropped the basket that Lady Forster had given her for her brothers, with the freshly laundered clothes Nicholas would never now wear, the food, and the iron file that John had fashioned, that was hidden beneath the cheeses and fruit. The money bag tumbled out, scattering the coins all over the floor.

The gaoler came running at the sound, but Thomas was already scrabbling on the stones to gather it all up. It seemed he had already forgotten Nicholas to concentrate on the more important matter of money.

'Forster,' John sounded disgusted. 'For God's sake—'

But Dorothy interrupted. 'Take it,' she said. She did not recognise the sound of her own voice. 'Take it all. If you have the skill and sense to escape, which I doubt, I pray you do so. I never want to see you again. You are dead to me, Thomas. You could have spared us all this loss, spared me, spared our father. Instead, you encouraged a boy to see war and treason as a game and he lost his life as a result.'

She heard the scrape of the coins as she stepped on them, grinding them beneath her feet. The door yawned darkly before her, the gaoler's face gaping at whatever expression he saw in hers. He fell back, allowing her to pass. She knew John was at her side, but she could not look at him because she was afraid that she would break down if she did, and she had to get out of Newgate first. She thought of Major Lang and her uncle, and how they had both known the truth and yet deliberately lied to her and betrayed her. She would kill Lang, she thought, even if she hanged for it. And she would never speak to her uncle again. Her eyes burned fiercely with unshed tears.

Suddenly, she felt the sun on her face and took a gulp of fresh air, and she knew she was out on the street. Her knees buckled – she could not help it – and John caught her and at last she allowed herself to lean on him and cry as though she would never stop.

* * *

The journey back to Northumberland was slow and arduous. Sir Guy and Lady Forster had pressed them to stay awhile, at least until Dorothy felt a little better, but she knew that the only place her soul might start to heal was back at Adderstone, where she and her father could grieve together. Besides, the Christmas season was approaching and Dorothy could not bear to witness the festivities when she felt so empty and sad inside. Nor did she want to be anywhere near Thomas, or hear the news of the other Jacobite prisoners. Home was the only place she could bear to be.

The weather had entered a mild spell and so they rode, both

because it was quicker than a carriage, but also because it gave Dorothy something to think about other than mile after endless mile rolling along dwelling on Nicholas's terrible death. Each night, they stayed at inns along the way, John holding her and comforting her through the night when she cried or was tormented by nightmares. It was a miserable wedding journey for him, Dorothy thought, but she was desperately glad that he was there. She could not have survived without him.

After almost two weeks on the road, they reached Warkworth Manor at dusk, a candle glowing in the window to guide them, and Dorothy slid from the horse, stumbling with a mixture of exhaustion and unhappiness. She saw Sir William's cousins line up to greet her, Mrs Selden, her eyes red from crying, Harris the valet, deep lines etched in his face, but she had no eyes for anyone other than her father. Sir William stood tall and straight and when Dorothy ran into his arms, he held her tightly and she felt his hot tears dampen her hair.

'My boy,' he repeated, over and over. 'My boy.'

Dorothy had thought her heart broken before, but now it broke all over again.

Adderstone, early the following afternoon, was a sad homecoming. The house sat grim and silent in its overgrown garden. Dorothy was so tired and heartsick that she could not care that it was cold and empty. John had wanted to go directly to Bamburgh, but Dorothy shied away from seeing the Hall, and indeed meeting anyone, until she felt stronger. She knew that people would be kind, but her strength felt so fragile, she thought it might snap under that very kindness. Her only concern was to care for Sir William, who, after his initial tears over Nicholas's death, had lapsed into a distant quietness that frightened her.

She set about making at least a small part of the house habitable, cleaning Sir William's chamber and making up a bed for him with fresh linens that she and Mrs Selden had stored away before they had left Bamburgh Hall, serving a cold supper with the food and wine sent over from Warkworth. The following day, Mrs Selden and Harris were to join them; Dorothy thought that the necessity of cleaning and repairing the entire house would give them all a much-needed focus in the dark days.

Early that morning, John had set off for Bamburgh. He had been reluctant to leave her and Sir William on their own, but Dorothy had reassured him that they would manage for a few hours whilst he went to see Eli at the forge and fetch all the tools and supplies that he needed to begin the long process of rebuilding Adderstone Manor. She had seen her father wandering off into the gardens after breakfast and had decided to leave him to his own devices; if anything could start to heal Sir William, it was the chance to spend some time amongst his beloved trees and plants.

Dorothy was on her hands and knees in the parlour, cleaning out the grate so that they could lay a fire later, when she heard the sound of footsteps in the hall.

'Papa?' she called. 'I am in here.'

There was no reply, but the footsteps came on, steady and unhurried.

Alarm gripped Dorothy and she scrambled to her feet. She had not imagined that they could be in any further danger; the rebellion in England was to all intents and purposes over, Thomas locked up and her family as good as destroyed. There was nothing worth stealing at Adderstone. Yet as the shadow of a man fell across the doorway, she felt terror spike within her.

'Major Lang,' she said, taking a deep breath. 'Why did I not anticipate that you might crawl back to cause more trouble?'

'Indeed, my dear,' Lang drawled. He strolled into the room, a pistol in his hand, the pale winter sunlight shining on the blade of the sword at his side. 'It was a serious oversight on your part. You engineered the rest of your little *adventure* so well, did you not, but then you fell at the final hurdle.'

Dorothy's hand crept up to where the Rose hung around her neck. It was hidden by the frilled neck of her gown, but she could feel it, solid and reassuring against her skin. It was odd, she thought, that in this moment she seemed to be able to think of nothing but who would keep the Rose if Lang killed her; there was no heir. There had not been time...

The major smiled at her, but there was no warmth in it, only anger and malice. 'I should arrest you,' he said conversationally, 'for you have thwarted me at every turn, hiding fugitives from the law, assisting Jacobite offenders, conspiring to commit treason... The list of your crimes is long.'

'I beg to differ,' Dorothy said. She could feel anger licking through her blood now, waking her, helping her feel stronger. '*You* are the liar and the cheat, sir – you and my uncle, pretending that my brother Nicholas was alive when you knew full well that he was already dead. That was shameful, to use blackmail to coerce me into marrying you. I thank God that I escaped that fate.'

'Only to be confronted now by a different one.' Lang prowled across the room towards her and Dorothy looked around frantically for something she could use as a weapon. There were no fire irons and the only chair left in the room was a splintered wreck.

'I pray you to keep still,' Lang said politely, watching her. 'It makes it easier for me to shoot you. A moving target is tiresome.'

Dorothy caught her breath on a gasp. 'Major Lang, I believe

you must be mad. You cannot walk in here and murder me in cold blood! You would never get away with it.'

'On the contrary, my dear.' Lang strode across the room. 'I have every intention of getting away with it. By the time your *husband* returns—' disdain dripped from his voice '—you will be dead and I long gone.' He stepped closer. 'You made a fool of me and I do not care for it,' he added. 'I lost the promise of your uncle's vast fortune and now my debts consume me.'

'That is none of my fault.' Dorothy backed away from him step by step as he moved towards her. 'You are the architect of your own downfall, Major, and everyone will know the truth.'

Lang ignored her and Dorothy realised that his gaze was fixed on the hollow of her throat, where the Rose was glowing brightly on its golden chain. He seemed transfixed. When she raised a hand to the talisman, it vibrated, although it felt cold to the touch.

'That's a pretty little piece,' Lang said. 'It might go a small way towards paying off my creditors.'

Dorothy saw a flicker of movement in the doorway behind Lang and her heart leapt with hope, only to crash down as she realised it was not John who had returned but her father who stood in the doorway, leaning heavily on his stick. She knew that once Lang had shot her, it would be the work of seconds to cut Sir William down too... A scream of warning rose in her throat and Lang levelled the pistol.

In that moment, Sir William spoke, as clearly and simply as Dorothy had heard him speak in years. 'The Rose called to me,' he said. Then, as Lang spun around to face him, 'You murdered my son, but you will not take my daughter from me.'

The bullet took Lang in the heart. Dorothy heard the shot and saw him crumple and fall, a look of utter bemusement on his face, the pistol spilling from his hand, the barrel smoking. Dorothy rushed across the room to embrace her father, holding him tightly, feeling his bodily frailty but also the absolute strength of his will.

'Papa,' she whispered, and he stroked her hair as though she were still a child.

John burst through the door a second later. He took in the scene in one glance, going down on his knee beside Lang's prone body. 'He's dead,' he said. Then, as he looked from the pistol to the two of them, 'Which of you...?'

'Neither of us killed him.' Dorothy released Sir William and wiped the tears of relief from her eyes. 'Neither of us were armed. I cannot account for it.'

* * *

'That was a shocking business regarding Lang.' Colonel Lestrange was enjoying a glass of brandy after an expansive dinner with Lord Crewe. The colonel, on his way south from Berwick now that the Scottish Jacobite threat was reducing, was only too glad to be leaving the uncivilised north. 'Between us,' the colonel continued, 'the fellow was always something of a dangerous fanatic. You say his body was found at the base of the cliffs near the Castle, milord? A falling out with smugglers or pirates, I'll wager, fool that he was.'

Lord Crewe grunted in assent.

'He was clearly a bad lot,' Lestrange said, shaking his head. 'I hear he fathered some by-blow on a village girl as well? Maybe more than one. The man was good at making enemies, no doubt about it. Probably had angry husbands and fathers after him as well as criminals, eh?'

'I have given the girl's family some money to raise the child,' Lord Crewe said piously. 'I saw it as my duty as lord of the manor now that Forster has fled abroad.'

'Very good of you, I'm sure.' Lestrange gave him a shrewd look. 'You seemed to take quite a fancy to Lang at one time, didn't you, milord? I heard you planned to make him your heir.'

Lord Crewe shook his head sorrowfully. 'I was most deceived in him,' he said. 'Most deceived.'

Lestrange settled more comfortably in his chair. 'It was not entirely unexpected that Forster escaped,' he observed. 'A bribe to the gaoler to look the other way, an iron file somehow smuggled into his cell to allow him to saw through the bars, a boat to France and, hey presto, he may present himself at the Pretender's court as a loyal subject!'

A sharp frown settled on Lord Crewe's brow. 'It was none of *my* doing.' He snapped. 'I wash my hands of the entire Forster family!'

'Your niece,' Lestrange said. He was starting to enjoy himself. 'The charming Miss Forster. I heard she has married a *blacksmith*?'

'A most inferior fellow.' Lord Crewe's face was a mottled red from the fire, the brandy and sheer annoyance. His temper trumped his discretion. 'When I reproved her for her choice and told her that she had disappointed me, guess what she said to me, Lestrange!' It was a rhetorical question and he continued, 'She told me that it was curious I was disappointed in her, because she was equally disappointed in *me*! Outrageous! She said I had been callous and conniving and had lied to her and betrayed her family.' He stopped, finally realising that in his fury he had become rather carried away, and cleared his throat loudly. 'Well, I wish her joy of her choice!'

'The Armstrongs always were wild—' Lestrange hid his smile

in his brandy glass '—and the Forsters too, your own dear wife excepted, of course. Perhaps they are well matched, those two, descending as they do from the border reivers.'

'Disgraceful conduct.' Lord Crewe reached for the bottle. 'More brandy, Lestrange?'

13

HANNAH – THE PRESENT

'I'm dreadfully sorry, darling.' Diana was sitting up in bed, propped up against her huge pillows, the green cashmere shawl wrapped about her thin shoulders. 'I was only trying to protect you, and I ended up lying to you and making things so much worse. Why, I could have killed you!'

'Don't be daft, Di,' Bill said comfortably from the chair at her side. 'Everything that happened was Brandon's fault, not yours.'

'I agree with Bill,' Hannah said. She was curled up on the end of her stepmother's bed. 'You have made rather a hash of things, Diana, but I don't think you can take the blame for Brandon's crimes.'

It was a week after Aaron had rescued her and, physically, Hannah was feeling much better. She had suffered from shock and smoke inhalation, but there was no permanent damage to her lungs. Psychologically, she knew that it would take much longer to recover from the experience. She and Diana had both cried for Brandon. No doubt they would do so whenever a memory caught them unawares. They cried because of the way Brandon had behaved and they cried because it could all have been so very different. It was going to be a hard road ahead, especially as they were displaced from their home until the repairs to the Hall had been completed. Hannah knew that Bill intended to ask Diana to move in with him when she came out of hospital, but she was less sure what she would do. For now, though, she was staying with Alice. Tarka had also joined them, over the moon to be reunited with Hannah, although, Hannah suspected, still wishing she was living with Aaron, who had clearly spoiled her rotten.

The hospital room was filled with flowers. A particularly gorgeous bunch of roses mixed with sunflowers and oak leaves was from Lizzie Kingdom, with a note that said she hoped Diana would be better soon and that she looked forward to calling in on her way home from the wedding in Scotland. Lizzie had been absolutely charming when Hannah had rung her to tell her what had happened and apologise that the Hall was out of commission. She had been adamant that she wanted to see Diana anyway. Hannah had also told her how sorry she was that the Dorothy Forster portrait had been lost in the fire and Lizzie had sighed.

'It was a beautiful portrait,' she had said, 'but I have the oddest sense that it had accomplished its purpose.'

Hannah, running her fingers over the now-familiar pattern on the Rose, had smiled a little.

'Bill, darling.' Diana was giving him a look of entreaty. 'Do you think you might go and get a coffee? There are a few things I need to say to Hannah in private. Don't hurry back!' she added, as Bill good-naturedly rose to his feet and headed for the door.

When he had gone, Diana stretched out her hand to Hannah, beckoning her to sit beside her. Diana was recovering slowly from the infection, more slowly than she wanted, and Hannah knew it frustrated her. They hadn't had much opportunity to talk alone since the fire and Hannah knew there were things her stepmother wanted to know as well as to tell her.

'You are all right, aren't you, darling?' Diana was frowning as she scanned her face. 'Really? No ill effects?'

'I feel fine,' Hannah reassured her. 'Aaron's keeping an eye on me and I'm taking it easy.'

'Thank God Aaron found you,' Diana said, shuddering. 'And how odd that he should have been the one to discover the fire. That's twice he's rescued you. One might almost think that the two of you have some sort of telepathic connection.'

'That would be very fanciful,' Hannah replied, smiling as she remembered all the things that Aaron had whispered to her about soulmates as he had held her in the ambulance on the way to the hospital. 'Tell me, Di,' she said now, taking her stepmother's hand, 'why were you helping Brandon? I know you had been texting him. And obviously you lied about the painting because I found it hidden under your bed. What on earth were you doing?'

'I got myself in a ridiculous tangle!' Diana shot her an unhappy look from out of the corner of her eye. 'When you first showed an interest in Dorothy's portrait and her history, I was thrilled, because I felt somehow that it was meant to be. But Brandon had already been sniffing around it. He asked to buy it from me a few years ago. I knew he thought there was something in the story of Rose even though he pretended it was all just a nonsensical legend.'

'That was what you quarrelled over, wasn't it,' Hannah said. 'It was nothing to do with the Meissen vase. Brandon wanted the portrait and you refused to sell it to him.'

Diana nodded. 'We had a dreadful row, just like I told you. For a while afterwards, I was afraid that he might try to steal the painting, but then it all went quiet and I started to think I had overreacted. Of course, I realise now that he had photographs and he had gone away to find out more about the provenance and about the Rose, so when he turned up again, I hid it.'

Hannah nodded. 'How did Brandon know I was in Bamburgh?' she asked. 'Did you tell him?'

Diana bit her lip. 'I didn't do it on purpose. I didn't even realise I *had* done it to start with, but I'd sent a text to him that was meant for someone else. It was just a stupid mistake, but the next thing I knew, Brandon was messaging me about my diagnosis, and about you and the picture, and I panicked. I couldn't face any unpleasantness with him, not when I was trying to deal with my illness.'

'You should have told me,' Hannah said. 'Better still, you should have told Bill. He would have seen Brandon off.'

'I know!' Diana was plucking at the sheet. 'But I couldn't bear the thought of a confrontation! I love Bill, but he isn't the subtlest of men, and Brandon needed to be dealt with carefully...' She broke off. 'I know it sounds as though I was still trying to protect Brandon,' she added after a moment. 'Perhaps I was. I never quite gave up on the little boy I first knew.' She coughed, a dry crackle that racked her body, and Hannah quicky reached for the water for her.

'Don't worry about it any more,' she said, tilting the cup to Diana's lips. 'You acted out of the best of intentions and it's all over now.'

'Honestly, Di.' Bill had reappeared in the door with a tray balancing two coffees, a pot of tea and some slices of a rather superior-looking sponge cake. He'd obviously overheard the last part of Diana's confession. 'Why didn't you just *say* something to me? I'd have dealt with that wee shite.'

'That's exactly what I was afraid of,' Diana pointed out, with a touch of the old asperity. 'I didn't want to be visiting you in prison, Bill.'

Bill made a huffing sound. 'Seems to me that the Rose was perfectly capable of seeing Brandon off without human intervention,' he said through a mouthful of sponge cake. 'I know everyone thinks there was some sort of electrical fire at the Hall —' he looked at the two of them '—but we know better, don't we?'

'I know nothing,' Hannah said hastily. 'The fire service said it appeared to have been a fierce but contained fire, that started somehow when Brandon and I were upstairs, talking. I'm just grateful there wasn't more damage.'

She had answered all the police and fire investigators' questions with absolute honesty. She had been putting Diana's hospital bag together when Brandon had arrived. They had been chatting; she had not seen how the fire had started; the first thing she had noticed was that the curtains were in flames, and then there had been an explosion... She had seen Brandon fall but had managed to crawl out onto the landing before she had lost consciousness. The alternative would have been to say, *'He tried to steal an ancient talisman and it killed him,'* and she certainly wasn't going there. No one knew the truth except the three of them and Aaron, and that was how she intended to keep it.

'Have you decided what to do with the Rose, darling?' Diana asked. 'Whether or not one is as superstitious as Bill, it feels safer for such a priceless artefact to be under lock and key.'

'I agree,' Hannah said. 'I think it should be placed in the archaeological museum at Bamburgh Castle alongside the Bamburgh Beast. The two plaques probably came from the same forge and the same craftsman. They would have been made in the castle. It's fitting they should be reunited.'

'That sounds perfect,' Diana said. 'And it can always exert its protection over you from a distance. That's the thing about a magical talisman. It's far more powerful than any of us could ever imagine.'

* * *

Midsummer Eve

'Did you know that they used to hold a fair on the beach at Bamburgh every midsummer in the eighteenth century?' Hannah asked Aaron as they walked up the drive towards the castle. 'There was plenty of wine and dancing and more wine and more merry-making. It would have been a health and safety nightmare for the lifeguards.'

'Yeah, I wouldn't have wanted to be on duty that evening,' Aaron remarked with a grin.

Although it was approaching nine o'clock in the evening, it was still light, with the blue translucent glow of a summer twilight. In the late warmth of the sunshine, the castle gleamed pink and gold and, below them, the sea was an echoing pale blue, calm beyond the silver strand. A tiny crescent moon was rising in the sky. Lanterns flared in the wall sconces, giving something of a medieval feel to the old fortress.

The main door of the castle was open and light spilled across the courtyard. 'Dr Bailey is waiting for us,' Hannah said, waving to the man who was standing by the doorway. She slipped her hand into Aaron's. 'This is so exciting. It's not often I get a private view of a very special archaeology exhibition.'

They did not go into the Great Hall but into the Crewe Museum Room. There, in the middle of the floor, was a brightly lit display case lined with dark blue velvet. Around the walls, a new exhibition detailed the latest archaeological finds at Bamburgh Castle, but it was the treasures that commanded the eye: the Bamburgh sword with its six strands of iron pattern welded into a blade, the Bamburgh Beast with its sinuous coils sparkling golden in the light, and its twin plaque, the Rose, glowing softly, as beautiful as the day it had been created in the castle forge.

The discovery of the Rose had caused something of a minor sensation. There was still a lot of work to be done to find out more about it, especially since Hannah could not give the historians and archaeologists any provenance beyond the fact that her father had given it to her on her fifth birthday. However, as she looked at it glittering against the blue velvet cushion, Hannah suspected that the Rose would keep most of its secrets.

The room was starting to fill up now as the guests gathered, chattered, toasted the exhibition with warm white wine and demolished the canapés.

'It doesn't make any mention here of the Rose's magical powers,' Aaron complained, as he scanned the interpretation panels. 'That's the best bit.'

'That's because it's legend, not history,' Hannah said. 'You know what we historians are like when it comes to attested fact. Speaking of which,' she added, 'I discovered the other day that the tale that Dorothy Forster rode all the way to London to save her brother is only half the story. There are some letters in the Alnwick Castle archives I'm going take a look at. I want to write Dorothy's story after I finish Grace Darling's biography.'

'A least you seem a bit more engaged with Grace's story now,' Aaron observed. 'Is that because you're looking forward to finishing it so that you can move on to Dorothy?'

'No.' Hannah shot him a smile. 'Actually, I have you to thank for helping me to see Grace in a different light. When you took me out to Longstone that day I think I gained a new respect for her. Anyone who can handle a boat at night in those seas and rescue all those people has to be a tough cookie. Bravo for Grace, I say.'

'I'm glad.' Aaron squeezed her arm. 'Does that mean you'd like to go out on the boat again soon?'

'Maybe,' Hannah said cautiously. 'We'll see.'

Diana waved to them from across the room. She was looking supremely elegant in a brightly patterned silk trouser suit.

'Bill scrubs up well,' Aaron murmured. 'I've never seen him look so smart before.'

Hannah giggled. 'He's a man of hidden depths, is Bill. I take it you've heard about the not-so-secret engagement between them?'

'Of course,' Aaron said. 'The entire Seahouses crew is going to be Bill's best man.'

Hannah exchanged a smile with Diana and cast a last look at the Rose. 'This is great,' she said, 'but I'd rather play truant and watch the moon rise from the battlements with you. What do you say?'

They walked down to the lower ward and stood in the lee of the old windmill, looking north towards where the lighthouse flashed its steady beam over the darkening sea. Beyond it, the shape of Lindisfarne Castle slipped into the dusk. They wrapped their arms about each other and Hannah leaned into Aaron's body.

Diana was in partial remission for now. Work was progressing on the Hall and she was hoping to move back in the summer, after the wedding. Hannah had found herself a little cottage where she could finish Grace's biography and stay on for as long as Diana needed her. It wasn't perfect, but she had Tarka and her friends, and she had Aaron now as well.

'It's Midsummer and you're still here,' Aaron said. He smoothed a strand of hair from her cheek. 'How does that feel, Hannah Armstrong?'

'It feels good,' Hannah admitted. 'It feels as though I'm home.'

EPILOGUE

DOROTHY – BAMBURGH, FEBRUARY 1716

The northern lights were the brightest that had been seen in years on the night that the Earl of Derwentwater was finally laid to rest in the family mausoleum. He had been executed on Tower Hill for his part in the Jacobite rebellion and neither the pleas of his family nor the offer of vast sums in fines had been sufficient to buy him clemency.

Dorothy sat with John on the headland above Bamburgh beach watching the green and purple lights ripple across the skies like a veil, and thought of lost souls, and of men who gave their lives for the causes they believed in. She thought of Nicholas, full of idealism, and of a life that should have been at its beginning not at its end. It was still overwhelmingly painful to remember the brother she had lost and she thought that throughout her life there would be moments when the grief would catch her off guard, but she knew she had to look forward now.

John's arm was about her and she was wrapped tightly in a blanket to stave off the cold. Sir William had stayed at Adderstone, but lately Dorothy and John had taken to spending some time at the cottage by the forge. Dorothy knew that John had missed his work through the weeks they had spent making the Manor habitable again. He was a man who had to follow his trade to be happy and there was no more noble trade than that of a smith, nor had there been since the forges of Bamburgh had formed and shaped the Rose.

She reached out a hand and touched John's cheek. 'Thank you,' she said softly, 'for being with me every step of the way through these dark times. I could not have done it without you.'

John turned his mouth against her palm and kissed it. He looked up and their eyes met. 'You are my North Star,' he said roughly. 'My guiding light.' Then, 'I swear I will cherish you with every part of my being, Dorothy, and never give you cause to regret giving yourself to me.'

'I have no regrets now, nor shall I ever,' Dorothy said honestly. She pressed more closely into his side, relishing the steadfast strength of him. 'It is very early to say,' she whispered, 'but I do believe that there will be new life soon, coming out of the sadness of this season. Mrs Selden, who knows these things, tells me that by the Midsummer fair I shall be too great with child to dance, but perhaps the fiddler will play a slow saraband for us.'

John's laughter was full of joy. 'You may certainly ask him,' he said, 'though I think the villagers will give it short shrift. They will want jigs and reels to celebrate the coming of our child, and the faster the dance, the better.'

Then he kissed her there beneath the shifting veils of light, with the winter breeze on their faces and the sound of the sea, and it was a farewell to the past and a promise of the future.

* * *

MORE FROM NICOLA CORNICK

Another book from Nicola Cornick, *The Other Gwyn Girl* is available to order now here:

https://mybook.to/GwynGirlBackAd

HISTORICAL NOTE

As with all my books, *The Secrets of the Rose* was inspired by a real character from the footnotes of history. Dorothy Forster of Bamburgh is known as the Northumbrian Jacobite heroine for her part in the 1715 uprising and I have kept as closely as I could to her story. She and her elder brother Thomas really did live at Bamburgh Hall and the characters of Lord and Lady Crewe, Lord Derwentwater and John Armstrong are also based on real people. I changed the name of Dorothy's father from Thomas to William to distinguish him from his son, and also gave him a knighthood in a bit of historical *lèse-majesté*! You can see Dorothy's portraits and her gown on display at Bamburgh Castle.

There are a number of legends about Dorothy's involvement in the rebellion and that she rode to London to help her brother escape from prison after he was captured at the Battle of Preston. None of the 'official' histories of the rebellion record this although it is correct that Thomas Forster did escape to France in 1716.

The Forsters of Bamburgh and the Forsters of Aldermarston were distantly related, although the relationship between Sir Guy and Sir William in the book is fictitious. You can read Guy and Rose's story in my previous novel, *The Other Gwyn Girl*.

Bamburgh, as well as being stunningly beautiful and very dog-friendly, is one of the most inspiring and historically rich places in England with layers and layers of history, myth and legend to explore. I have been visiting the village since I was a child and it is one of the places that kindled my own love of history. It was a huge pleasure finally to set a book there.

ACKNOWLEDGEMENTS

Thank you so much for reading *The Secrets of the Rose* and I hope that you have enjoyed Hannah and Dorothy's intertwined story. To readers old and new, I would like to say that you are the best and you make it all worthwhile. I love writing about history but I love it even more when people like the books and go off down the rabbit holes of history to find out more.

Thank you to the very special team at Boldwood Books for the energy, vision and professionalism they bring to all aspects of publishing; it is so refreshing and I appreciate it very much. A special thank you to my editor, Sarah Ritherdon, whose work on this book helped to make it so much stronger, to Jade Craddock for her very thoughtful copyedit and Gary Jukes for his exemplary proofreading. I am so grateful to you all!

Love and thanks as ever go to my husband Andrew for being wonderful, and a special shout-out to guide dog puppy Wren, without whom this book would have been finished much more quickly and easily, but who has brought so much joy as well as hard work to our family this year. I also owe an even bigger debt of gratitude to my friends and writing colleagues this year, especially Sarah Morgan, Jane Dunn, Christina Courtenay and the members of our Word Wench blog. Your stalwart support when the book and I were stuck helped me to get through.

Writing acknowledgements is a wonderful way to remind myself of what really matters so I will end as I began with a thank you to everyone who reads, reviews and shares their thoughts on books; it is a generous and vibrant community.

ALSO BY NICOLA CORNICK

The Other Gwyn Girl

The Secrets of the Rose

ABOUT THE AUTHOR

Nicola Cornick is the international bestselling and award-winning historian and author of over 40 novels featuring women from the footnotes of history, and has been translated into 25 languages.

Sign up to Nicola Cornick's mailing list here for news, competitions and updates on future books.

Visit Nicola's website: www.nicolacornick.co.uk

Follow Nicola on social media:

 x.com/NicolaCornick
facebook.com/nicola.cornick
instagram.com/nicolacornick
bookbub.com/authors/nicola-cornick

Letters from
the past

Discover page-turning
historical novels from
your favourite authors
and be transported
back in time

*Join our book club
Facebook group*

https://bit.ly/SixpenceGroup

*Sign up to our
newsletter*

https://bit.ly/LettersFrom
PastNews

Boldwㅇㅇd

Boldwood Books is an award-winning fiction publishing company seeking out the best stories from around the world.

Find out more at www.boldwoodbooks.com

Join our reader community for brilliant books, competitions and offers!

Follow us
@BoldwoodBooks
@TheBoldBookClub

Sign up to our weekly deals newsletter

https://bit.ly/BoldwoodBNewsletter

Printed in Great Britain
by Amazon

57832127R00178